# The Magic of Hawk

Sweet McKenna Book Eight

Christine Young

Published by Rogue Phoenix Press, LLP
Copyright © 2023

ISBN: 978-1-62420-781-5

Credits
Cover: Designs by Ms G
Editor: Sherry Derr-Wille

# Chapter One

1753

"I'm here to see Miss Maisie," Hawk said as he rocked on the heels of his well-shined boots.

He held his hat in his hands, twisting the brim, his nerves rattling around inside his body. If she refused to see him, he wasn't at all certain what he intended. Perhaps an abduction would be in order. He wasn't about to waste more time with silly rules of etiquette. She was his. He was hers. This moment had been three years in the making. The woman was his for now and into eternity. Maisie wasn't going to get away from him. Three years ago, he made a ferocious mistake. One he had to fix before making things right was too late.

Three years he spent running from his feelings for Maisie. Terrified. Annoyed. Frustrated. Confused. Sometimes furious. She refused his sincere offer. When Maisie rejected his request for her to come to Selkirk, Hawk's heart broke, splintering into thousands of tiny, jagged pieces. Repairing his heart turned out to be impossible. The woman was his mate. The devil, what was he supposed to do? Maisie didn't want him then. Why would she change her mind now? When he first met her, she acted so sweet, sincere in her feelings, wide-eyed with her innocence. At least he thought she was earnest as well as guiltless. Turns out everything she did was a lie. Lies didn't matter to him. She was his mate. He would have to figure out a means to keep her from lying to him.

"I'll tell her you're here. Would you like to wait in the foyer?"

The man's snowy white eyebrows arched in speculation. He was tall, thin, his speech perfect Scottish brogue. The servant must be new to Highland Manor. Riley was fixing the home up. It appeared nothing as Hawk remembered. The road to the house was no longer rutted. The shutters were fixed to the windows. He didn't see any more peeling paint on the outside walls nor in the interior.

A maid bustled around the drawing room, dusting the tables and plumping the pillows. He knew from everything Houston, Riley's older brother told him, that Riley and Shawna meant to restore the place to its earlier grander. Riley had the money to do so. Now that he found his mate along with the home of his dreams, Riley would prosper. Hawk was happy for his good friend.

"Hawk, welcome."

Shawna's smile could light up a room. She walked to him. Her arms outstretched for a hug. They kissed each other on the cheek. The welcome was warm. Hawk prayed they would both be on his side when it came to his courting of Maisie. While Hawk had not seen Maisie for three years, Shawna and Riley were frequent visitors to McKenna land. They came often to see Riley's brother, Houston, especially now that she was pregnant with their second child. Mac was adorable. The *wee lad* looked just like his papa.

Ah, he sighed softly, inwardly. Shawna's smile was not the one he coveted. After a quick hug and another gentlemanly kiss to her forehead, he said, "It's nice to see you, Shawna. You're looking well. The pregnancy? It's treating you right. I hope."

Distracted by his thoughts for the woman he was here to visit, he turned to look up the stairs leading to the upper floors. A huge breath of air left his lungs in a heartfelt whisper of air. "She doesn't want to see me, does she?"

He didn't understand. All he wanted was to comprehend the stiff rebuff, along with the nerve-straining silence following his letter in response to her questions. Needed to see if there was some way they could try again.

"I didn't say that, now did I? The pregnancy is fine as Houston assured me just a week ago. Come along. I'll pour you a brandy. Told cook to bring something to eat." Shawna whirled, her skirts lifting slightly off the floor. Looking over her shoulder, "Riley is visiting with some of the crofters. He won't be back until dinner. I'm assuming since you rode this far, you plan to stay the night."

Clearing his throat, his gaze continuing to search the upper floor, "If it's not too inconvenient I'd like to stay until I...well...I need to convince Maisie she would not be amiss to let me court her. I hope and I pray that she will talk to me."

"For one of Riley's friends?" she said as the amber liquid spilled into a glass. "Never an inconvenience. Maisie, she has turned inward since you two were unable to come to some type of agreement. I shouldn't say anything more. You will have to determine for yourself how to proceed with her."

"Will Maisie see me?"

He had to discover if he had a chance. If she wouldn't talk to him, he would kidnap her. Take her to the McKenna cabin. Keep her there until he convinced her to marry him. He would do whatever was necessary to fix this conundrum the two of them wallowed in.

"When she gets her fury with you under control, I believe she might speak with you. Be patient." Shawna sat, smoothed her skirts. "She is curious, you know. She didn't understand anything that happened that summer. After that, until I met Riley, our lives were in turmoil. Mac was born. I was married to the wrong Riley Stuart. It took all our energy to survive, to put food on the table. We had nothing except each other and Mac of course once he was born."

"Fury? What does she have to be angry about?" Hawk was confused. He was the one wronged. She didn't even reply to the second letter he sent. His friends convinced him that he was too terse in the first letter, didn't explain himself. When he wrote the second letter imploring her to come to Selkirk, he made certain to tell her he wanted to marry her. She never answered. He waited. After that he waited some more. When two months passed, he sold his practice then left for the colonies hoping to start a new life. Without Maisie he found emptiness, nothing more.

"Oh?" Shawna watched the brandy she poured herself swirl in the glass she held. After she looked up, a sparkle in her eyes, she told him, "Believe that conversation should be between the two people involved. I only have secondhand knowledge. First, she was broken. Next, the hurt turned to despair then anger. Maisie doesn't get angry often. She doesn't have much of a temper. She is always cool and serene. Your expectations toward her changed that."

Ah, but Hawk was certain his knowledge of the event was true. If what he heard from Maisie during their way to their short courtship, the two young women shared everything. "Can't have that conversation if she won't talk to me."

With his harsh words she flinched. Next, she lifted slim shoulders as if she didn't know what to say to him. "You do understand her personality. At times my sister can be painfully shy, one might also call her timid. For you, she opened up. Too bad the new Maisie only lasted a short time. Now, if anything, she's more withdrawn into herself than she was before. She is open with Mac. She laughs at his antics. Mac is the only male who has won her heart. Other than that...I can't say."

Shawna would defend Maisie. He needed to proceed with caution. If he aggravated Shawna, he would get nowhere with the woman he wanted to woo. "I'm impatient. Admit to that fact. I would get this settled then move on. More than three long years have passed without her by my side." He wished the woman was in his arms now. He was a fool to wallow in his own self-pity for so long.

"Get it settled?" One of her eyebrows slanted upward. "Get it settled? You act as if she is something to be purchased." She snapped her fingers, her gaze boring into him. "Believe this settling business of yours will take more than a second. You need to assure her you're not the cad she thinks you are."

Admitting to himself he didn't understand how to court a young woman, Hawk was willing to take advice. He fumbled the first time. He should never have kissed her. Hawk understood that now. Rushing her would never do. She was so damn beautiful; he hadn't been able to keep either his hands or his lips to himself. This time he would have to do better. He didn't even want to think of putting the 'if' in his thoughts. She would come around. They were meant for each other.

He rubbed his sweating hand along his thighs. Berating himself, he sent an apology Shawna's way. "Sorry, didn't mean that the way it sounded. I'm not real good with words." Riley as well as Houston berated him for the proposal he sent after he left for Selkirk three years ago. If it would do his cause any good, he would apologize as many times as it might take to reassure her he didn't mean the proposal the way it sounded.

"No, don't suppose you did. What are your intentions?" Shawna blurted the question then looked surprised. "We thought...well...no, imagine Maisie should ask these questions. I won't like it if you hurt her again."

"As you just stated, I'd rather speak with Maisie about intentions. Don't want her hurt either. Think I can make this right if she will only speak with me." If she would accept his proposal, he'd marry her tomorrow. He was more than ready for a family. Wanted children. His practice with Houston thrived.

Shawna rose, "Thank you, Lilith. You can set the tray on the table. We will serve ourselves. Would you tell Maisie she can come down anytime." She turned her attention to Hawk, "If you're hungry, you can help yourself. I'm certain the ride was long from McKenna land. It must have taken you two days."

"Yes, I stayed at the Stuart townhouse in the city then came out here first thing this morning. I'm eager to get reacquainted with your sister." He felt as if he was repeating himself. His nerves threatened to unravel while he impatiently waited. He shoved his hands in the pockets of his frock coat.

"You should understand, she is not eager to speak with you. It is only Riley's approval of you that has her wavering. You did hurt her." It seemed she needed to keep reminding him of his past horrendous deeds. He still didn't know how he hurt her. A proposal of marriage should never have her furious with him or hurt anyone's tender sense abilities. He wanted to yell that fact.

That was what Riley told him. He didn't want to cause her pain. All he wanted was to love the woman. "Is that why she has not come down?"

Shawna nodded. "Courage..." Shawna paused as she sucked in a raspy breath of air. "She's afraid."

The devil, he didn't want her to be afraid of him, afraid to even talk to him. What could he do to change that if she wouldn't show herself? How could he convince her he wanted only the best for both of them.

Hawk followed Shawna's gaze. Maisie stood at the top of the

stairs. His heart did a little flip, slid to a stop for seconds on end. She was just as beautiful as he remembered. No, she was more so. While the years aged her very little, they did give her a more mature look. She would be twenty-one now. This was three years waisted. If he'd worded that damn letter right, they would be wed now. Might even have a child. His heart sank.

It didn't happen. He couldn't let the past get the better of him. With slowness that didn't speak of his needs, he stood. He wanted to walk to the steps, to escort her into the drawing room. As if floating on air, she walked down the stairs. Dressed in a light blue muslin gown, her skirt flowed around her legs. The fabric molded lovingly against her breasts that were high and rounded sweetly. Once, he knew they would fit in his large hands with perfection. Now, he didn't dare rush her. Her hair was piled in intricate curls on top of her head.

"Maisie."

He nodded to her. Swallowing hard, he held his breath while she walked into the room. "You're more beautiful than I recall."

She was breathtaking, heart stealing. From the moment their gazes met, she enchanted him. The moment seemed magical.

"Hawk," she acknowledged with a curt nod to her head.

All magic vanished.

Her voice held a decided chill. Yes, he would have his work cut out for him. He didn't believe he could erase that wariness he saw in her eyes with a single apology. Shawna poured her sister a cup of tea.

"I'll leave the two of you to talk," Shawna spoke amidst the strained silence.

"No!" Maisie clutched her teacup as if it was a lifeline, staring at her sister as if she'd gone mad.

Hawk's work would be cut out for him. She would not be easy to reassure.

"If you need anything, I'll be in the library. The two of you need time together."

Without a backward look, Shawna left.

The room was so very quiet, so still. Sunlight flitted in from the window behind Maisie. Her hair caught the golden beams shimmering in splendor that left his hands itching. He wanted to run his fingers through the long, silken strands. Maisie's fingers wound in then out of her skirt, crumpling the fabric. Hawk's mouth was parched. The brandy he sipped didn't ease the dryness.

"Maisie..."

She looked at him, her eyes wide with apprehension. Fear. She spoke so very softly. "I don't want you to hurt me again, Hawk. Last time the pain was nearly unbearable."

Well, he didn't want that either. "I promise you I've no intention of causing you any type of pain."

Just as three years ago, he wanted to marry her. He needed to learn how he hurt her. What he did to set her against him. "The problem is, I don't understand how I hurt you. I've no idea what I did wrong."

Putting the cup of tea on a small corner table, she walked to the window. It didn't seem she had anything to say to him. Strained seconds passed while she stared down the long drive to Highland Manor. Her back was stiff, her waist small, her hips curved sweetly. Hawk wanted more than anything to pull her into his arms then promise her anything she wished for. He needed patience.

After some seconds ticked by, she turned to face him. He saw the mad pounding of her pulse at the base of her neck. He cursed himself knowing he was the cause, understanding the wild beating was triggered by fear, fear of him, not passion. That was perhaps why he stayed away for so long.

With an air of finality, she spoke again. "You only wanted me for your mistress. Unless your feelings have changed, you need to walk out that door and never come back. I won't be any man's play thing." When she pointed toward the door, her finger was shaking. "Never will be any man's mistress."

Her words stunned him. He couldn't help the look of shock that must have crossed his face. "What the hell ever gave you that idea!" Now, he was vibrating, his anger increasing with each beat of his heart.

Her back hit the window pane, her eyes huge wide saucers of confusion. "Y-you d-did." She was shaking her head at him. "You..." She ran her sweet pink tongue between her lips. "You wanted me to live in sin with you. I couldn't do that. Even for you." Her voice quivered as hard as her small body.

After he started forward, her hands came up as if to stop his advance. "I never asked you to be my mistress." He was angry, couldn't keep the harshness from his voice. "Never!"

His teeth gnashed together. His jaw twitched. He would have to get control of his emotions. Yelling at her would never help his cause.

"You did," she said her voice so restrained he could barely hear. "Do you want something different this time? I think you should go home. I don't want to see you again. Your presence here is a travesty."

"Like hell I will!"

He didn't move closer. He was moving his head, a wealth of conflicting emotions rolling inside. To Hawk it was apparent she didn't intend to explain herself. He sucked in a deep draught of air, while his fists clenched then unclenched. "I've been invited to stay. I'm going to do that. Come here and sit down. We need to talk about what happened three years ago. We don't seem to have the same understanding of the events."

"No, if all you plan on doing is yell at me, we've nothing to talk about."

She looked as if she was about to run.

He stepped to the door. She would have to leave by another means. "Sit down, Maisie. You need to start from the beginning. Tell me what happened or what you think I did. I thought, hoped, you would fall in love with me."

Her posturing surprised him. She made a tiny face at him, one that spoke of rage. "No! Go away!"

"Why the devil are you picking this moment to show backbone?"

By the thinning of her lips, he understood he was digging his grave even deeper. He didn't care if she showed strength of character.

"Insults? Is that all you know?" Her words were clipped. "I thought you might want something different. Now I know this is the travesty I thought it was three years ago. You haven't changed."

Drawing in a deep, long breath of air, willing himself to calm, "I never asked you to become my mistress. Tell me why you believe that so we can move on. What gave you that idea?"

The moisture forming in those silvery-mauve eyes had him feeling the size of a pinhead. With a heavy sigh, Maisie began, "The letter you sent me asking me to come to Selkirk." While she said the condemning words, her chin tilted into the air. "I think it's time you let me go back to my room. Since you will not, I don't *ken* what more we need to speak about."

"Never!"

He gritted his teeth, searching his mind for more information. The realization he had his work cut out for him didn't go over his head. His nails scraped the palms of his hands. The explosion in his head wouldn't leave him. After great effort coupled with long deep breaths of air, he said, "Could we possibly start over?"

"I don't see why."

She chose this time to become obstinate. Where did the shy, willing woman of three years ago go? Well, he didn't care if she spouted horns. He would deal as best he could with all the pitfalls, she sent his way.

"Because we are meant to be together."

She was his mate. He could marry no other woman. If he didn't claim her in this lifetime, they would never be together again.

She seemed to be more interested in staring at the blue and gold carpet than speaking with him. He thought he should begin where everything went haywire three years ago.

Placing his hands behind his back then bracing his feet apart, he cleared his throat. If they were going to get anywhere, perhaps he should continue to speak. Should tell the story the way he perceived it to be. "I asked you to come to Selkirk. A week or so later, I received a missive asking some pertinent questions. I answered them. Sent the reply to you. After that letter was sent, all I received in response was silence."

He watched her tilt her head as he must have caught her interest. "I didn't receive any answers to my questions."

That reply stopped him cold. Riley told him what he sent made it sound he wanted her to live with him, not that we wished to court her with the hopes of marriage. Momentarily, he'd forgotten about that. If Maisie didn't receive the answers to her questions, of course she would think all he wanted was sex from her. Once more the thought he rushed her with his questions detonated in his head.

"I see..."

He was beginning to see quite clearly. He didn't think a denial would help his cause. He would have to show her how he felt. Win back her trust. She would have to give in a tiny bit, allow him to court her. Persuading her to try seemed a monumental feat.

"What exactly do you believe you see?"

Her lips thinned again. The brows, he wished he could run his finger gently across knit together.

He wished he dared kiss those lips, tug on the bottom one so it wouldn't be so tightly pressed against the top. He wished he could once more taste her sweetness. He sent those thoughts to the back of his head. "You don't believe me, do you, Maisie?"

"I cannot find the trust I once had for your person. You broke that faith. So, I suppose I would have to agree. I don't believe anything you say."

"You trusted me once. You will trust me again. If you remind me of the questions you asked, I'll answer them."

He expected the answer before she said the words.

"You would lie to me for your personal gain. How do I know you just don't want me in your bed?"

"Lies...no...I'll never lie to you, Maisie. I will be honest." Hawk paused as he thought, taking the time to consider his next words. "I do want you in my bed for the rest of my life. I don't want anyone but you."

He certainly didn't know how to rectify this situation. She was stubborn. He'd give her that. Today, he was seeing new sides to her. He liked every component. Except perhaps her stubbornness, her unwillingness to trust him.

When she jerked in a long breath of air, he watched her bottom lip quiver. She tilted her chin up a notch. "I wouldn't *ken* what to believe, Hawk Frasier. Why did you come back? Riley said you were in North Carolina, or was it Virginia?"

She was feeling something for him, weakening a *wee* smidgeon.

He would take that question as a good sign even though by her tone she sounded as if she wished he would have stayed there. He knelt beside her, taking her cold hand in his. "Both. I came back for you. That's the god's honest truth."

Maisie was tugging on her hands. He didn't want to let them go. Reluctantly, he gave in to her wishes.

"To make me your mistress." The icy chill returned. "I *wouldnae* do that."

Unable to help himself he cursed, hoping she wouldn't hear the damning words. "I haven't had a mistress in three years. You are not mistress material, Maisie. Since I met you, I've had sex with no woman."

His grave grew deeper as he watched her tuck her bottom lip beneath her teeth. "You should go, Hawk. Ride back to town, to your home. I wouldn't be your mistress if you asked, then or now."

"Not going anywhere without you."

Hawk wasn't surprised at the conviction in his voice. He would take her with him kicking and screaming if that was the only way. He would keep her close until she listened and understood.

"Hawk! Good to see you." Riley strode into the room, his smile broad. "I see the two of you are speaking to each other."

Riley was looking from Maisie to him. He stopped, seeming to understand the situation was not exactly conducive to good feelings.

"Papa!" Mac ran past Hawk then straight into his father's arm. "You're home."

A green wave of jealousy swamped Hawk when he watched one of his best friends twirl his little boy after tossing him into the air. He wished for a son or a daughter, a child of Maisie's. He sipped in air.

"Look who is here."

Riley pointed to him. He set the boy down.

"Hawk!"

The boy lifted his arms for more play time with his honorary uncle. Hawk did the same as Riley. When he was done, he kept the boy in his arms.

"I missed you," Mac told him, the boy's hands on his cheeks.

"Yes, dear *laddie,* I've missed you too. What, has it been a week since you visited Carnoch with your mama and papa?"

His gaze swiveled to Maisie who, for the first time since she entered the room smiled.

"Are you staying?" Riley asked.

Hawk set the boy back in his father's arms. "For a week. Your Uncle Houston did give me permission to stay as long as needed. Nonetheless, I've a contract to fulfill. I can't leave Houston with too much work."

"Why did you come visiting?" Mac asked, all smiles coupled with a youngun's curiosity.

Riley ruffled the boys deep red hair. "That's none of your business, Mac."

Well, by the end of the week, all would know. He came looking for a wife, a very reluctant wife. His thoughts shuffled around in his head searching for the right words, words she would believe. If he couldn't think of the right phrases, the words would have to wait. It seemed the Stuarts were descending on his and Maisie's private time. So far, all he managed was to put his foot in his mouth time and again. He didn't think his lot would improve until she opened her mind to him.

"Another brandy?" Riley asked while Maisie took that time to flee. "I interrupted something important."

That was blatantly obvious by the expression painting her lovely face. While he watched her back, he murmured, "Might as well. Another brandy would be nice."

This was not how he hoped his evening would end with her. Perhaps she'd join them for dinner. He could always hope. Though he didn't expect her to suddenly gain the needed courage. Hawk knew he needed alone time with her. There was only one way to get it if she wasn't willing to see him here.

"She is very angry." Riley handed him the refilled glass as he too seemed to stare at the chair Maisie once occupied. "You've got a great deal of explaining to do. Not to me. To Maisie." He shrugged his shoulders while he stared over the rim of his glass. "Whether she'll listen to you is another question. Seems she's had her mind made up for the past three years. Your absence wasn't well done."

"I gathered that. I'm a damn nitwit."

Hell, a week? He'd need a month to thaw the ice in Maisie's veins. She wasn't about to give way to the tenderness she once showed him. Drastic measures would have to be employed.

"You should not have waited three years to return." The advice was sage. "Should have returned here as soon as you sensed trouble."

Sensed trouble. That was a novel idea. His sixth sense cut in after the second week he didn't hear from her. "A coward, that's what I was, a damn coward. Everything you're telling me is right on the mark."

"Why didn't you ever write back to her, answer her questions? Shawna told me over then over again that she never heard a word from you. There were days she sat in her room, sobbing. One day she came out, her back set and told Shawna she wasn't going to ever think of you again. Now, you've turned up rather unexpected. The poor frazzled girl doesn't *ken* what to do or think. This situation is new to her."

Riley set his foot on the hearth, his brandy glass in his hand while he looked to be patiently waiting for an answer.

The queries were always the same, directed to the fact he made no attempt to explain the first letter he sent. "I answered every question. Told her I wanted to marry her. Laid my heart on my sleeve. When I didn't hear back from her, thought she just swore me off. I was in such a turmoil; I didn't know what to do with myself. Remembered Kit and Roby went to America to search for their mates. Thought possibly I'd been wrong about Maisie."

"Were you?"

"No. She is my mate, my very reluctant mate." He looked up the steps wishing he dared go to her.

"Wouldn't do what you're thinking," Riley said, his voice bland.

"Mind reader, are you?"

"In this case, yes. Can read you like a book."

Once again, Hawk looked up the stairway as if she might reappear. Not even a shadow. He turned back to Riley. "Do you think she will join us for dinner?"

He wanted to feast his eyes upon her. Needed to take every possible opportunity to show her he wasn't the cad she thought him to be.

Dinner might be a good start. A walk in the gardens afterward would be even better.

In answer, he saw Riley shaking his head. "Probably not, she requested her dinner to be sent to her room earlier today. Shawna told me. That was when she learned you would arrive before dinner with the intention of staying for the meal."

"She despises me that much?"

His heart lurched. He wanted to throw the glass against the stone fireplace. Needed to hit something. There wasn't a damn thing he could do at this moment to change her mind.

"This will take time."

"I understand. Still..."

"No, she doesn't despise you. Believe she loves you with all her heart. Maisie has no experience with men. You were her first. For the longest time she couldn't talk of anything but you. At least that's what Shawna told me. By your absence you hurt her deeply. By the way you invited her to come to Selkirk, she thought you believed she was like her mother."

"I'm trying to rectify that now. What is this about her mother?" He tossed back the brandy wondering exactly what Riley meant by his words.

"That is for Maisie to tell if she's ever speaking to you. Shawna will try to convince her to come down for dinner, though I'm not certain she will come. Shawna thinks you have her sister's best interest in mind. My wife is wary of your intentions. She was also shocked by your silence. When you first met Maisie, Shawna encouraged her to see you."

"I'm a twit."

Riley tossed his head back then hooted with laughter. "At least you don't have a loss of memory. For the longest time I blocked out the night at the Campbell's. While I never saw her face, I forgot about the lady I met there. Thought she was a virgin whore. Mac was conceived that night." Riley seemed to go back in time, his eyes taking on a faraway look. "Because I couldn't find the lady, I lost the first two years of my son's life."

Lilith retrieved Mac. They disappeared up the stairs.

"You know, the moment I saw you with your son I was jealous. I *ken* if she received that letter from me three years ago, we would most likely have a son now. We'd be happily married. I wouldn't be clawing at my mind for ideas to make her trust me again. She let me kiss her that first day I was with her. Not just a peck on the cheek but a real kiss."

One of Riley's dark red eyebrows shot toward the ceiling.

Hawk understood he shouldn't say anything more. This kissing business was between Maisie and himself.

"Most likely," Riley agreed with a smirk. "You will have to contrive to fix this mess you got yourself into. The sooner the better by my way of thinking. Take her somewhere private. A place where family won't interrupt. Where you can have the needed time to talk about what is bothering her."

With very little effort, Hawk recalled the sweetness of her lips, the soft way she responded to him. He taught her how to kiss with her mouth open. Taught her how to give back. He thought of other parts of her that she might open for him to explore. He groaned low in the back of his throat. When he heard his friends soft chuckle, Hawk understood that Riley once more knew what he was craving.

"I've considered your suggestion. Thought to take her to the McKenna cabin. Before I left Carnoch, I got permission from the head of the family. I do need time with her she doesn't want to give me. Maisie doesn't trust me. She believes I will lie to her, hurt her. I won't do that to my life partner."

"Her heart is hardened to you," Riley seemed to agree with his assessment of himself. "Go in the morning. I won't stand in your way. Take her with or without her permission."

If he took her now, she wouldn't be a willing participant. Short of hogtieing her he wouldn't get her there. He didn't know what to do. "Didn't mean to fail her or hurt her. Suppose she had expectations as did I. What she doesn't understand is that her refusal to come to me changed me. In the process I was also hurt. Now, I'm here to set everything right if she will allow me to do so. It's a damn annoying situation. One I don't, at the present, see a way out of."

"Perhaps Shawna and I should go to the city. We've things to purchase for the renovation. We can leave the two of you alone, unchaperoned. Imagine if you seduced her, she wouldn't have a choice except to see things your way."

"No, if you left here, she would remain in her room. Locked, I'm guessing. I would have no recourse to do anything except kidnap her if she doesn't come around in the next day or two. I've that thought stuck in my head. So, I should stay until I feel as if I reached a quagmire. When that happens, I'll take her where I will have her all to myself. Someplace where she cannot hide from me. I must speak my peace soon. My patience is at a low point."

"You will not hurt her."

Hawk stared open mouthed at his friend. How could Riley possibly believe he might hurt his mate, the woman he loved, the woman who would bear his children.

"I apologize," Riley told Hawk, "I've become quite fond of Maisie. She is my wife's sister."

~ * ~

Maisie sat on the big comfortable chair in front of her fireplace watching the flames leap and dance in the grate. All of her was shaking, her entire body. His appearance wasn't a total surprise. Shawna found out he would arrive just after the noon hour then passed on the information.

He was even more handsome than she remembered. When his silver-blue eyes focused on her, she nearly swooned. Her heart did a little dance. She recalled every conversation, his kiss, the way his fingers felt when they caressed her. Maisie wanted to feel all that and more. Her courage though was at a low ebb.

Why did he come back?

How dare Hawk return as if nothing happened between them? He told her he sent answers to her questions. Liar. More than anything she wished she could believe him. She didn't think he had reason to lie to her. He did. The man wanted her for his mistress, not his wife.

*I can't just forgive the man.*

*You love him. If you don't want to chase him away do as he asks.*

*Talk to him. Listen to him. You can start over again. Say the word.*

*I want to.*

*You're a coward, Maisie. A big coward. You understand the letter could have been lost in delivery. If that is the case, he isn't lying to you.*

*Yes, I am. He needs to prove himself to me. I'm not going to give in to his wishes without an apology or without good reason. The man needs to prove to me he is sincere.*

She knew she could argue with herself until dooms day. Debating wouldn't solve the problems that separated them. Listening to him might help. Saying her piece would make her feel better. The fact of the matter was that she was in love with him. In return, she wanted him to love her. She didn't know how he felt about her.

*I'm not mistress material. What the devil did that mean?*

*Well, of course, you aren't. That was your mother's role. Your mother didn't want to be any man's mistress. It just happened.*

"I'm not going to follow in her footsteps.*

She immediately took offense at his words. Why, she didn't know. Being a man's mistress, even Hawk's, was not acceptable. His wife was the only suitable label for her. Demeaning herself wasn't in the way she would live her life. She watched her mother struggle for so many years to keep her head held high. Her mother would wait with breath held for her father to visit. He would come when he could get away. Sometimes once a week, sometimes a little more. Sometimes even less.

When she first saw Hawk, sitting in the drawing room, her heart flipped over several times. Her breath caught in her throat. She wanted to fling herself in his arms. Her finger touched on her lip as she recalled their first kiss. His mouth was so sweet. His tongue touched upon hers. His hands rose to cup a breast. She remembered all the strange feelings, the sensations that centered between her thighs in parts of her she never noticed before.

They needed time alone. She should give him a chance to explain why he wanted her to travel to Selkirk, to answer all her questions.

"Oh, my..." she whispered at the leaping flames. "I vowed not to give in to his easy manner, sweet talking words as well as that Fraser charm that exuded from him. He could melt her socks off if she gave him the chance.

When the knock on her door came, she stiffened. "No..."

She wasn't ready for another confrontation with Hawk, especially a private one. Her mind still vibrated from the last encounter. Coming to terms with her own desires needed to happen before she could give him the consideration he wanted. The pressure she felt in those few minutes she was with him were far too intense. That was what he would do. He would pressure her until she would say yes to whatever he wanted. It would not be difficult, she had to admit to herself.

Shawna would never allow him in her bedroom.

"It's me," Shawna poked her head into the room. "Want to talk?"

"More than you can guess. You must have been reading my mind. I'm so confused. I'm even talking to myself." She didn't want to give in to easy seduction. The first time they were together she allowed him to sweet talk her until she was mindless.

Shawna sat down beside her. She held two wine glasses in one hand, an open bottle of wine in the other. Without speaking she poured them each a generous amount. "A little predinner spirits to relax. I'm sure the men are having something to drink. Now, tell me how you are feeling? Were you excited to see Hawk? Do you want to spend time with him? You can be honest with me. I'd never give your true feelings away."

Maisie drank. The wine was delicious. "I want to believe him." Those words were true. "I can't." As were the next ones. "Yes, I was excited to see him. He's just as handsome as I remember, just as compelling. His eyes hold me. I'm afraid to be with him. Terrified I'll give in to whatever he wishes, give in to whatever he asks of me. Don't know how to be strong where that man is concerned."

"Hawk says he sent you answers to your questions. You don't believe the man? I doubt if he would lie about that."

Shawna seemed to study her sister over the rim of her glass, tapping the crystal with the tip of her finger.

"Where is the letter? What happened to it?" Maisie felt her back stiffen. "He can tell me over and over that he sent me the answers I needed. He can give me the reasons he wanted me to live with him. None of that matters now. The question remains, why didn't I get that letter?

18

Also, why did he wait so long to come here, to talk, to see what happened to me. It's been three years. I'm having a difficult time forgiving him."

"I don't know any answers. Anything could have happened to stop the letter from arriving. It was three years ago. In this current time, does it really matter?"

"That is my point," Maisie spoke with soft longing, looking wistfully into the embers. "He stayed away for three years leading me to believe what I thought we had together was never real. Now he is back expecting me to fall, without a single question, into his arms."

"Why don't you allow him to answer now? It couldn't hurt to listen. You might be pleased with the outcome. If you still love him, do you want to run from him without hearing him out? That would be the height of stupidity."

"I was thinking along the same lines." She let a bit of air whoosh from her lungs. "He's so very charming and handsome. When he talks about the past, he looks remorseful. Is that look just another lie? How will I ever know the truth?"

"He looks desperate to me," Shawna said with dry amusement. "Like a man who *kens* he made a huge mistake and now he doesn't know how to rectify the error. Not that it matters what I think, but I want you to understand I believe him."

"Desperate?" Maisie questioned wondering about that. "He should be desperate."

She wanted to hate the man. She couldn't summon those feelings any more than she could vanquish the love in her heart.

Shawna held her hand for a moment. "A man wouldn't travel all this way to convince a woman he wants to marry her if he doesn't. What do you think? Come to dinner? Give him a chance? You won't regret the action."

"He hasn't said anything about marriage. That word has never entered any conversation we've ever had. Though we haven't had many...conversations," Maisie said, censure in her voice. "All we've spoken about are the questions along with the missing letter. I hardly know the man."

"You understand that you love him. You comprehend the fact you missed him. That his absence hurt you. Let him give you the answers you both seek to understand. After that you can figure out if he's telling the truth. Otherwise, how do you feel about him?"

"You are right. I still love the man. I thought all he wanted from me was my body. You've always told me how beautiful I am. Men seem to gawk when they see me. You're more beautiful. Your backbone as well as spirit shows in your face as well as in the way you carry yourself. All I know about Hawk is that he is a doctor."

"You know how gentle he is."

"There is that. Unless his gentleness was also a lie." Maisie just didn't know what to believe.

Maisie was feeling both confused as well as desperately afraid. She wanted Hawk. Needed him to be in her life. Giving him, them, a chance was important. If she refused this time with him, she would regret it forever.

Reaching out again, Shawna covered her hand with her own. "You should come to dinner. You will have company so you won't have to carry the conversation. Hawk is one of Riley's best friends. He's a doctor because of Houston's influence. I'm certain there are tales that can be told about their life as children. Things that will give you some insight into who the man is."

Shaking her head, she heaved in a huge breath of air. "I don't know. Nothing has changed between us. I'm still terrified of my feelings for him as well as what I don't know about his feelings for me."

Maisie understood it was past time for her to grow up. She couldn't run from herself forever. She had to face her fears. If she wanted to find true happiness, she needed to face Hawk as a woman.

Shawna stood. She smiled. "Think about it. Dinner with the family would be good for both you and Hawk. He cannot try to sway you to his way while we are all gathered around the dinner table. He cannot seduce and charm. Any sweettalking would be wasted on the unwanted company."

"I will think about it."

Shawna was wrong. Hawk could seduce her with his charming smile. Could sweettalk her with the silver shimmer of his eyes when they seemed to caress her. She swallowed down the lump in her throat. She did want him to kiss her again. Telling him so could wait.

"Good. I hope to see you in an hour."

Sitting back and closing her eyes, she let her body relax, felt the heat of the fire warm her body and soul. Her mind refused to relax. The agile brain in her head kept spinning and fabricating different scenarios with Hawk. No, Maisie couldn't stop thinking about the blasted man. Couldn't stop wishing what he told her was true. She drank more of the wine Shawna left on the table.

Mac ran into the room, startling her from her wandering thoughts.

He climbed into her lap, his hair still damp from his bath. "Kiss Maisie goodnight?"

His fingers were on her cheeks, lips puckering in anticipation. His grin so endearing, Maisie knew when he was grown, he'd be a real charmer. The ladies wouldn't have a chance if he set his sights on them. Just like Riley and Hawk. She didn't have a chance.

The lad was incorrigible. Briefly, she wondered if Hawk was so sweet when he was a child, perhaps filled with little boy mischief. "Yes, little man, a goodnight kiss is fine as you well know. Then off to bed."

Mac's lips met hers. When he finished the kiss, he stared at her with the silver-blue eyes all the McKenna men had as well as the Fraser men, "Are you going to marry my Uncle Hawk? I want you to. He will make you happy."

Unable to help herself, she laughed softly. She wanted to tell him Hawk wasn't his uncle. Needed to figure out the answer to his question before she could tell the boy how she felt. "Mr. Frasier hasn't asked me to marry him. If he does, I would have to give it a great deal of thought. One doesn't marry just anyone. A body must be in love." She tapped him on the nose. "You remember that."

"Hawk will ask. Just wait and see. Mama says he loves you like Papa loves her. I want him to be my real uncle. So, you have to say yes."

She did, did she? Maisie wondered why her sister didn't tell her those words of encouragement. How would Shawna know that Hawk loved her when she didn't know. He'd said nothing of the sort to her.

"Yes, I heard Mama and Papa talking." Mac nodded his head; his grin so wide Maisie thought the lad might burst.

Mac left the door open on his mad dash to see his aunt. Lilith now stood in the doorway, her arms crossed beneath her rather large bosom, her graying hair poked out from beneath the white cap she wore. She looked as if stampeding horses ran her over. "Come along, Mac. It's time for bed."

"Aunt Maisie is going to marry Uncle Hawk," Mac said while he climbed down off her lap.

"Is she?" Lilith looked surprised by the little boy's announcement.

Maisie found herself shaking her head. "No, no I haven't been asked. If he does, I don't know what I would say. He would have to love me."

"Good night, Aunt Maisie." Mac was waving his hand a grin so endearing on his little face the sight caused Maisie to groan.

"Good night, Mac. Sleep well. I'll see you in the morning."

The boy wore her out just watching him. He was filled with such energy, even at the end of the day.

Mac stopped at the door to wave then blow her a goodnight kiss.

Marrying without love was not a proposition she could ever consider. While he lived, her mother had been her father's mistress. Her father was wed to Shawna's mother. Nonetheless, the man didn't love either woman. At least that was the conclusion she and her half-sister came to one day when they were lying on their backs in the shade eating apples. If he loved Shawna's mother, he would have never taken hers as his mistress. Of course, he might have loved her mother. A divorce would have been unheard of.

A loveless marriage was not for her. She didn't know if Hawk did love her or how she could ever learn the fact. The situation returned full circle to trust as well as faith. For Hawk. she held neither. She wanted that to change.

Deciding she wasn't going to hide any longer, she dressed for dinner. Shawna was right, in hiding she would never figure out the truth. The gown she wore was a light lavender which highlighted the mauve coloring of her silver-violet eyes. The corsage was modest yet showed the rounded tops of her breasts. Shawna picked it out for her. Once, Hawk told her he loved her eyes, the color, the shimmer when he kissed her, how they darkened with her passion. She wasn't certain exactly what his words meant. She found herself touching her lips, wanting another kiss, perhaps another one after that. She shook her head forcing her mind back to the reality of her situation. Until she comprehended for certain what Hawk wanted, she wasn't about to allow kisses.

*No kisses!*

When she entered the dining room a few minutes later, he looked up seemingly surprised at her appearance, yet pleased too. When he smiled at her, his dimple showed. With easy fluid motion that reminded her of a cat, he stood, escorting her to the empty seat across from his place. His hand on her elbow warmed her, sent shivers of pleasure rushing through her. His simple touch did that to her three years ago. That was when she thought she melted when he touched her, kissed her.

Where Hawk was concerned, she needed to stay resolute against his innate charm. Granting him intimacies despite the fact she longed for him to hold her in his arms would not suit her purpose. Maisie was going to have to learn how to tell Hawk no.

Sitting across from the man, she would have to look at him during the meal. When she did, he smiled at her then winked. He had audacity. Was daring and bold. She looked at her plate, wondering if she dared meet his gaze. Catching her bottom lip beneath her teeth, she looked up. He nodded as if he tried to tell her something.

"You decided to join us." When he spoke softly to her, his murmur was husky and rough, his silver blue eyes darkening to molten steel. "I'm *verra* pleased, *lass*. Thought I wouldn't be seeing you until tomorrow. After dinner will you walk with me?"

He didn't waste time.

"Well, I'm glad Maisie decided to join us for the meal. Won't do the two of you a bit of good if she hides in her room." That bit of information came from Riley. "However, there is to be nothing said here at the table that will ruin the meal. No arguments. No discussions meant for just the two of you."

An agreement with her brother-in-law was necessary. "What Hawk wants to talk to me about is private. Not meant to be shared, even with family. Perhaps we should walk when the meal is finished. The weather is nice."

With that said, she wasn't at all certain she could eat. She worried about what he would say as well as what he would do. Would he try to take liberties? Could she tell him no if he did try? The wine she drank earlier seemed to roll around in her stomach.

"Good," Shawna smiled at her before passing the potatoes. "A walk for the two of you might clear the air. We are about to start on the curtains for Riley's office." She turned to Riley. "What color would you like?"

"You *ken* I favor blue. Nonetheless, I will trust in your judgement on that matter."

He was grinning at his wife and her attempt to keep the conversation bland. She was doing exceptionally well.

That was mundane. The chatter for the rest of the meal revolved around the renovations that now had been three months in the making. They worked on the roof first. Needed to finish it before winter arrived.

"What did you do in the colonies?" Riley asked changing the topic to Hawk. "I recall Roby and Kit had some exciting times with the natives there. Did you end up running the gauntlet?"

"Yes, what's it like there?" Maisie asked more interested in that part of the conversation than the house renovations. She was curious, found she wanted to learn as much about this man as she could.

"Wild, free, much of the land is untamed. For the most part though, I stuck to the cities. Spent time in Raleigh then headed north to New York. The Boston whalers were fascinating just as were the large plantations growing tobacco in Virginia. The colonies are all so unique. Thought to make it to Florida. Never did though. Felt a driving need to return home." Hawk spoke between bites of food using his fork to give emphasis to certain things. "There is unrest there. The colonials are not pleased with the strong British presence. They feel they are taxed unfairly."

"Much like here in Scotland," Riley said using a bland tone while he helped himself to another biscuit. "Seems the Scots don't care for Sassenach interference either."

One of the servants brought desert, slices of almond cake smothered in a caramel icing. All the food was delicious. Hawk ate everything while she found her stomach wasn't up to the food. She was just too nervous.

The men retired to Riley's office to drink a glass of brandy. She and Shawna found themselves in the drawing room doing the same, only their drink of choice was sherry. She wondered about the upcoming walk. What would he say to her? Would he try to kiss her again? Her mind wouldn't stray from the kissing. She needed to learn about what happened three years ago.

"What do you think they are talking about?" Maisie asked turning her head in the direction of the office. "I hope it's not me."

"I'm glad you came down for dinner. You showed him you are not afraid," Shawna said. "He seemed pleased to see you. Ask him what is important to you. After that, listen to what he has to say."

"I'm terrified. I feel as if all my body is about to snap," Maisie murmured as she walked around the room her nerves shattering. "He is going to try to see me tonight. I decided I must talk with him. If I don't listen to his excuses, I might regret it for the rest of my life. Oh, Shawna. I want him to love me. How can he when he barely knows me?"

"Yes, and you will listen to him also. If you can trust him, perhaps the two of you can find a means to begin anew."

"I need to learn to trust, to have faith. I'm not going to let him seduce me. I won't be easy this time around. Don't want him to think he can have his way anytime he wishes without some type of commitment."

She felt his presence. When Maisie looked up, he stood framed in the doorway, a determined look on his well chiseled face. His body tense, straining. For an instant, her heart forgot to beat. She sipped a miniscule bit of air. He was so handsome. Did he hear what she said?

Hawk held out his hand to her. "Walk with me?"

His voice was so very quiet so soft. Gentle.

She rose, extending her hand until he wrapped her fingers within the strength of his hand. "Alright."

Just as at dinner he looked both surprised as well as pleased with her compliance. "You won't regret this. I promise."

His deep husky voice thrummed though her body. Her breath wavered when she tried to breathe while her knees shook.

He squeezed her hand then brought her fingers to the crook of his arm. Maisie closed her eyes for a brief instant, inhaled the spicy scent of him. Memories rushed back to her. Again, the breath she inhaled was shaky, barely there. She didn't know if she could walk without support.

When they reached the porch, he turned her so she looked into his eyes. "Is there a good place to stroll? I would not have you tripping. I know that the grounds have probably not been renovated yet."

She nodded in the direction of the stable. "We can walk that way."

On her way out, she picked up her scarf from the coat stand by the door. He helped her adjust the material around her shoulders. His fingers brushed against the rounded tops of her breasts when he fastened the covering. She gasped at the contact, her lashes flying upward.

He didn't seem to notice. Once more, placing her hand near his elbow they walked toward the stable. Maisie didn't know what to say. Had so many questions, she didn't know where to start.

She pointed. "We can sit. There is a bench under that big oak tree."

Maisie nodded in the direction she wanted him to go, thinking her knees were going to give out any minute.

"I'd like that," Hawk's voice was rich and dark.

His hand dropped to her waist. His fingers were long, bronzed. She felt them at the curve of her hip. Was he taking liberties? She didn't know. Before when they walked together, he didn't touch her waist or her hip. *Of course he didn't, you ninny. You were hardly with him.*

When they stopped, he turned her, one finger under her chin. With slow, gentle precision, he lifted. There was enough moonlight she could see his eyes. They were very dark silver. She ran her tongue along her lips, terrified of the moment of this kiss. "I don't want you to kiss me."

She didn't understand why she blurted those words. Did she expect him to kiss her?

His soft, chuckled words surprised her. "What if I wish to kiss you, Maisie. You know I do." With a heavy sigh, he dropped his hand. "All through dinner I imagined my lips caressing yours, recalled the way you taste, the sweet scent of you. Even now I catch the trace of lavender floating around you. Seems you are partial to that flower. Did you know if you keep a plant in your bedroom the aroma will help you sleep?"

Maisie smiled staring up at his handsome face. She was curious at his knowledge, wondered what else he might tell her. "No, no I didn't know that. Is that something you learn by being a doctor?"

"I learned a lot about herbs before I bought Houston's practice in Selkirk. Many of the people I doctored didn't live near cities or even villages. The people I saw didn't have money to buy medicines. They passed on the healing knowledge from one generation to the next. Leah, Houston's wife, teaches both of us even more. She's very knowledgeable."

"Do you like helping people?"

Still standing, she arranged her skirts, smoothed the fabric with her damp palms. She needed something to do with her hands.

He touched her hands with his, stopping the movement. "You don't need to be nervous. Yes. What I do is rewarding. Would you like to work for me?" He paused at hearing her sudden gasp. "If we marry, would you do what Leah does for her husband?"

"I don't know exactly what she does?" She supposed she could help with some things. "I don't know anything about healing."

"Well, Leah has this way with animals. Before Houston took her away from the mountain where she lived, she used to heal sick and wounded animals. She would keep them at a place she called her sanctuary. Now she pretty much keeps the shelves supplied and well-ordered with medicines. In emergencies, she lends a hand."

"I could do that for you."

She was rushing things, making him believe she would marry him. As of this moment, he hadn't asked. He implied though.

"Shall we sit?"

"Yes..."

For a few seconds nothing more was said. She understood initiating further conversation would be up to her. She needed to begin. "You say you wrote me. So, do you recall the questions I had for you?"

Clearing his throat, he began to speak. "Not all of them. Seems the most prevalent one was why did I want you to live in Selkirk." He touched her chin again, making sure she looked at him. "Because I wanted to court you in the proper manner. Knew we were meant to be together the first time I saw you. I didn't realize I insulted you until it was explained to me by Shawna in an addition to the sweet letter you wrote."

"Why didn't you tell me you wanted to marry me before you left?"

This all would have been so simple if he'd done so.

"I was afraid you'd tell me no. You are so shy, almost timid. I didn't want to have you run the other way if I asked too soon. As it was, I was shocked when you let me kiss you."

He smoothed his finger along her eyebrows.

Maisie was trying to mull over his words in her mind. Yes, she was shy. Her back straightened with determination. With this man she needed more backbone. "I don't wish to be labeled timid. Though I am shy. Was shy in the ways of men. As you well know, you're the only man who has kissed me."

"You're an innocent, Maisie. I had no business kissing you."

He picked up her hand, brought her fingers to his lips. After turning it over, he kissed the heart of her palm. She shivered. "I want to kiss you now, feel you, taste your sweet honey. Though I'm not going to give into my base desires. You deserve better from me."

She shivered with the sensations he orchestrated. While she didn't want him to kiss her, she wanted to be the one to tell him no.

"Not as much as I was three years ago."

Her disappointment in his words flourished. *Base desires?*

"Where were you going to have me stay...if I had come to your village? Seems as if people would have condemned me if I lived in your office. The good people who were your clients would have labeled me your whore."

He flinched at her harsh words. "I would never do that to you, to the woman I treasure more than my life. Mrs. MacKay, she along with her husband, own a small cottage behind her home. I negotiated for you to live there for as long as it took me to convince you marriage to me would be a splendid idea. I hoped that within the month you would agree."

"Alright. That was perhaps a good idea. Why didn't you tell me that to begin with? What was the town like? You say Leah lived there?" She wasn't at all certain how to proceed now. "How were you going to court me?"

"You ask a lot of questions?" He smiled at her, his hand on her shoulder massaging, creating vibrations in her.

"Yes. Most of which were in my letter to you. Some I just thought of."

"Leah lived up the mountain in a shack with her stepfather, a man who never legally adopted her. Because of that fact, she lost the only place where she could live. Ah, but Houston and Leah can share that story." His knuckles grazed her cheek. "I'm certain you've heard some of the tale."

She moved back. Her voice unsteady, "No, won't be doin' that. I don't want to...well..."

He dropped his hand then settled the palm on her thigh. "How would I court you? That's a good question. I'm not certain. Though I would like to spend as much time with you as possible. Maisie, I want to court you now if you'll have me. We can go to the McKenna cabin in the highlands. I do have permission from Connal, the McKenna laird, to stay there. We could have time alone to get to know each other."

"There would be no chaperone. I *cannae* be doin' that. You *ken*?"

Panic set in. She fidgeted with her dress before she could meet his gaze.

"No, you're right about that. The last person I want is a chaperone." He was shaking his head. "No one to watch us or keep us apart. I want you all to myself. My intention when we return is for you to be my wife."

"I would be compromised."

"True. I have Shawna's approval as well as Riley's. Believe they both think that after three long years it's about time I compromised you."

Unable to help herself she sucked in a deep breath of air. "I won't be lettin' you make love to me or use my body for your own purposes. This be lust not love."

She meant to tell him no forcibly if necessary, understanding full well if he set his sights on taking her innocence, he would win.

"We shall see."

~ * ~

"They've gone," Shawna said. "I had no idea he would have so little trouble convincing her to leave with him. Thought we would hear screaming, outrage. This morning there was only silence for their departure."

She was settled in Riley's arms, his hand stroking her back. They made love a few minutes before. Now they were speaking of her sister.

"That surprised me too. Maybe the situation was not as it seems," he murmured, touching the tip of his tongue to her ear before biting gently on the tip. "Ah, but did he persuade her or abduct her? We may never know the answer to that little question."

"He has no idea just how determined she is to withstand his Fraser charm. This will take longer than expected to reassure her he is the one for her. The man is one of the good guys. Though he will have to advance on his best behavior. Hawk is used to taking what he wants."

"She has no idea how easily it will be for Hawk to sweettalk her to his way. The man could charm the socks off any woman he chose. Appears he has chosen your half-sister. The cabin in the hills will be a romantic adventure for the two of them. We haven't been in a long time. I'd like to sit on the porch, drink wine, kiss you, caress those certain places that make you moan those soft and so very sweet feminine noises until you cry out your pleasure. Would you like that?" His questing nimble fingers found another tender spot then another. He was exploring, arousing her. He intoxicated her. She never failed to melt in his embrace.

Instead of melting, Shawna punched him on the arm to stop his ardent advances. She needed to talk. Point out his inaccuracies. "We've never been to the cabin. Is it someone else you took to the cabin to romance? Someone else who screamed your name. Arrogant beast. Big headed man." She smoothed her hand along his chest then lower to his belly, enjoying the quick sucking in of his breath. He would pay for his superciliousness. "Perhaps after their wedding we can take a small honeymoon. You can show me just how romantic the place can be." Her fingers closed around him.

"The devil, I can't concentrate on the conversation. You need to stop that now!"

"Poor baby. Do you say you wanted me to stop? Imagine I didn't hear you...or didn't listen."

"Don't you dare. Who would take care of Mac?"

His ploy was ridiculous. He knew it too. He ran his knuckles down her cheek then along her neck until they grazed the hardened tip of one breast. He flicked the tip with a finger before attending more thoroughly to the hardened peak. Imagined he wanted her to beg.

Her hips arched. She would be ready for him. If she allowed him to do so, he would make love again and again. In this he was insatiable. "I'm certain your mother and father would be delighted to have him for a few days."

She sighed with pleasure when his fingers pressed against her belly then cupped her mound. He found the most sensitive spot on her body. A broken sound escaped her lips then a soft purr, a little mewl of pleasure following. Resisting her husband was impossible.

"You are rounding nicely. His fingers spread from hipbone to hipbone. Soon you will be huge with the life of our child. I want to feel our babe kick. Want to be there when he is born. Missed all that with Mac."

"What you want is to tease me about not being able to get up when I'm sitting. With Mac, I waddled the last month. Could not get out of a chair without assistance. Maisie sometimes would have to help me stand." She would never forget those fearful days. The loneliness she felt from the moment she learned she conceived. For so many weeks she denied the possibilities. When she finally had to face the truth, she broke down in wracking sobs. Maisie held her, soothed her fears. She told her all would be fine. Neither sister believed those words.

"Did you now? I would enjoy helping you in every way possible." He stroked her belly, massaged with gentle fingers. He would feel the tremors ripping through her. His long fingers searched through the swollen folds for that very special knub.

"Too bad you couldn't have the morning sickness for me," she said dryly. "For that matter, give birth. The pain should be yours."

His fingers dipped between her legs, touched her, stroked her. She parted them wider, inviting him inside. Two of his fingers slipped into her core, stretching, heating, preparing his way.

"You like this. Do you want your woman's pleasure again? You are greedy. If you keep this up, I'll be exhausted, come morning."

Not only would she be tired, she'd be sated and sweaty. He would want a bath together. "We will have work to do come morning, a son to take care of. Undoubtedly, he will be in this room wanting to play the game with us. You *ken* he cannot."

"We can do both."

"Only with you, Riley Stuart, only with you."

# Chapter Two

Hawk stood over her, gazing down at her beautiful face, her long glorious hair. Beneath her lashes her eyes were an amazing silver mauve. She would be angry if he carried through with his plans. He didn't have a choice. Not if he wanted to marry her before the end of the month. Last night she refused to go to the cabin with him, refused to kiss him, refused even a simple touch. Every time he attempted to charm her, she flinched away. She did mention she was open to a bit of courting. To Hawk it appeared she lied or she didn't understand the details of courting. How could he get to know her better if she refused to spend time with him?

On the matter of courting, their thoughts were far from the same. How long would she continue to tell him no? A day? A week. He couldn't bear it if she still refused his advances at the end of the month. Private time with Maisie was imperative.

He knelt beside her, stroked her long hair away from her face. She opened her eyes, stared at him as if confused. She was only just waking up from what appeared to be a deep sleep. There was no anger or surprise on her lovely face. She blinked a few times. "Hawk? I'm in bed. What are you doing here?"

Sudden optimism for their future filled his soul. He murmured to reassure. "Hush, sweetheart. I'm going to take you with me. You have no choice. Our lives for the rest of eternity are in jeopardy if this doesn't happen."

He ran the soft fabric through his hands wishing he didn't have to resort to the tactic. He was terribly afraid she would fight him. Before she could protest, the gag was firmly in place. She made tiny noises in protest. Hefting her over his shoulder, he picked up the valise Shawna had packed for her. "Now, don't struggle. I don't want you to hurt yourself. Don't want to tie you further. Will if I must. Remember, fighting me will do nothing but harm you. We'll be in the coach soon. When we're on our way, I'll take the gag off. You'll be fine. You can dress once we are on our way."

She attempted to protest his last words. Regretted saying something that needed more of an explanation. No matter, it was done, another step backward. In the ensuing days, he would have to make a point of moving forward more often than in the other direction. Keeping his hand firm on her back he set off. He fought the desire to place his hand on her amazing rump, small but rounded as well as delightfully soft. A few minutes later, he gently placed her in the carriage setting her with smooth finesse on one of the seats. He tapped the roof. The coach began to move down the long drive to the road.

"I'm pleased you came along with little protest. In a few minutes, once we are away from the manor, I'll remove the gag. I'll be obliged to let you tell me all your thoughts. If you like, you can blast me with both cannons."

The problem was Hawk never saw her temper rise, never watched Maisie blast anyone with her anger. He wanted her to do that with him. After a few minutes, he unfastened the gag before drawing out a blanket to set over her lap. "Don't want you to get cold. When you feel ready to dress, I'll leave the cab."

Her glare was more than frosty. The way her eyes sizzled he felt certain he was experiencing an artic chill. He hoped the freeze wouldn't last too much longer. Maybe this was as close as she would ever come to showing her true feelings. He hoped as well as prayed he could tap into her passion. When he did, they would share the most amazing life.

"Hawk."

"Yes?" One dark red eyebrow arched upward. He wanted to encourage her to express her opinions. "Would you like to vent your spleen at my atrocious behavior. Go ahead. I'm waiting. Wouldn't be acting so barbaric if I saw another way." He stretched out his legs, thinking he'd much rather ride his stallion than remain in the closed carriage that made him nauseous.

Crossing her arms beneath the blanket she'd pulled up to her chest, she remained silent for the longest time. He needed to hear her anger. Once she told him how she felt about his deed, she would begin to come around, would begin to accept that she was meant to become a part of his life, one they would share. According to Shawna, she wanted him as much as he did her.

His woman was too shy. He would have to change that. Throughout their life together he hoped she would always share her hopes as well as her dreams. Needed to sample her passion as well as give her a taste of a woman's pleasure.

She looked away, staring out the window. Her back was stiff. He didn't have one clue as to what she was thinking. *Tell me, Maisie, tell me what is rolling around in your beautiful head.* He decided he would give her time to adjust to her circumstances. Just as she did, he stared outside, watched the road, the scenery. The sun was beginning to rise above the crags. Soft colors lay placidly on the horizon. This was the beginning of a new day, their new life together. He would make the best of this situation.

Smiling, he turned to her. "You don't want to yell at me? You should. You know that don't you?" he asked, bending forward to adjust the blanket around her. "Are you warm enough? I've another blanket if you are not."

She nodded still refusing to speak. He wondered how long the silent treatment would continue. Her lips were thinned, her eyes shimmering with fury directed at him. "We will stop whenever you ask. If you need to relieve yourself or stretch, just let me know." She blanched at his words, obviously embarrassed. "All you need do is ask. I don't want you to be uncomfortable. It will take two full days of travel to reach the cabin."

He was rambling not knowing what to say but needing to talk. The silence grated on every nerve he possessed. Nonetheless, for the first time in three years he felt as if he was taking charge of his life. He now had hope where before he'd felt despair. As to abducting his soon to be wife, he had no regrets. She should have trusted him in the first place to see to her living arrangements in Selkirk. He wasn't exactly flattered by her lack of confidence in his abilities or intentions. In this case, though, he did mean to take advantage of the situation he was orchestrating.

The vehicle hit a nasty bump. She flew into his arms. He felt her soft breast, unfettered, pressing against his chest. Perhaps he should ride his horse that was tied on behind the coach. If he did, his absence would give her a chance to don real clothing. Another encounter with her soft body would not bode well for her chastity. With her touch, lightning bolts seared straight to his groin. He coughed to clear his throat before uttering his next words.

"I would like to dress," she told him with prim determination then looked around the small enclosed space. Her brows drew together. "Hawk...?"

He heard little to no emotion in her softly spoken words. "In a *wee* bit."

Putting enough distance between them and Highland Manor was first on this new agenda of his. "Last night while we were out for that *verra* short walk of ours, Shawna packed a valise for you. Clothing for you to wear." He stumbled over his words. "I hope she chose well. Soon, I'll ride Windwalker. You'll have this space to yourself until we reach the inn where I would like to have our luncheon."

Her dark honeyed lashes lowered over her eyes, hiding her emotions. With a little gasp along with narrowed eyes, she seemed to notice the valise, realized that her sister was giving Hawk permission to do whatever he wanted with her. When she looked back to him, her eyes seemed to cross with both concern coupled with confusion.

"I'm not going to hurt you. The best for both of us is my intention," he told her reaching out to lightly touch her fingers before withdrawing his hand. "We will get to know each other, walk the hills and crags, wade in the creek near the house. Perhaps picnic. What do you think? Would you like to be with me?" An affirmative to his question would certainly be nice.

He wasn't going to get it.

With no hesitation, she lowered her lashes. Maisie meant to hide from him. He sighed with resignation realizing she might not speak to him for two days...or longer Stubborn *lass*. What would it take? Before yesterday, he didn't know she had an immovable streak. Her chin was up now, shoulders squared. This was a good sign. Hawk didn't want to run roughshod over his woman. If she didn't show backbone when he displeased her, he would control all aspects of her life. That was a frightening thought. He would just have to figure out how to sweettalk her until she wanted to talk to him.

"I don't want to go with you. I won't be your mistress."

His smile he kept inside. This appeared to be the first step in many. Maisie didn't listen to him. She too stubborn on the topic of becoming his next mistress. Never heard how he wished to marry her. "Ah, you can talk. I understand that fact, sweetheart. Though you will have to come to the realization that I don't have forever nor do I want to wait forever to hold you in my arms to show you how much you mean to me. We are meant to be together. Our lives blend into one. I also don't want to call you my mistress." He did lean back to watch her more closely, crossed his arms over his chest. He wondered when he should tell her that he was a shifter. She was aware of shifters. Knew they had a mate that would follow them through eternity. At least he thought Shawna must have told her. Mac was a little boy. A parent could never keep their children from experimenting. Mac was a precocious child. Maisie must have seen him shift.

"Take me home." Her voice was so determined the tilt of her chin stubborn. "I won't stay with you a second longer than I have to. You won't seduce me. I'm not going to allow it."

He couldn't do as she asked. "No."

The answer simplistic in the extreme but the one word summed up all his feelings.

Distraught, she rubbed her face with her hands. Hawk wished they wanted the same things. In time, they would see eye-to-eye. All that was needed here was a patient man. Previously, he'd been known for his patience. Where Maisie's obstinance was involved, that commodity seemed to be running thin.

Maisie took her hands away from her face, her scowl spoke just as strongly as her words. "Arrogant bastard!" she snapped out, her fury with him obvious.

That response didn't bode well for the moment. It was possible, when one considered his actions this morning that was exactly what he was. Nonetheless, this was too damn important to let fate shape the outcome or the whim of his mate. Because of his careless actions concerning her over the past three years to be exacerbated by the last twenty-four hours, he deserved her ire. He knocked on the coach roof. The time had come for him to leave her to her silence as well as her thoughts. She would need time to sort through the events of her life since meeting him. A decision needed to reached.

With him absent from the scene, she could dress as well as think without fear of repercussions.

"You won't try to run, Maisie. Be forewarned if you do, I will catch you. That's your first lesson."

Where speed was concerned there would be no contest. He was bigger as well as stronger. She wouldn't attempt to mount the second horse. Maisie was afraid of the animal. He learned that startling piece of information from Shawna. The fact gave him an advantage she wouldn't know about.

"First?"

For a tepid response, she blinked at him. Maisie was an intelligent woman. Even if she wanted to flee, she would understand there was nowhere for her to go. She had limited resources as well as less money.

"I'll be outside on Windwalker. Let me know if you want to talk about anything. Poke your pretty head out the window if you do."

He stepped outside feeling the crisp fall air hit his face. The sun sat low on the horizon waiting for the day to begin and see what would happen. The day might be unseasonably warm. The mist along the road evaporated as soon as the sun hit the vapor.

Again, she didn't reply to his comment. A 'go to the devil' might have been a pleasant rejoinder. He understood he wouldn't hear 'thank you for kidnapping me.' How long would she remain mute to his questions? It didn't bode well for the next two days. After the luncheon he planned at the Green Valley Inn, he would sit with her in the carriage for the rest of that day's trip.

Maybe she would be more conducive to talk when her belly was full.

Maybe not.

How long could a woman remain silent? Interesting thought for a man who'd never had a long-lasting relationship with any woman. That wasn't something a shifter would have until he met his mate. So far, his and Maisie's relationship was anything but long-term. The relationship was short filled with obstacles.

For the following miles, he enjoyed the ride. He let the sun warm all his fears, giving him hope. The slight breeze made the day more pleasant than he thought it could be. When he rode by the window of the carriage, he would peek inside thinking to view Maisie. He hoped she was doing fine. A closed in carriage made some people sick including himself. Stopping often along with a walk coupled with a bit of stretching might help.

They stopped at the inn for lunch. He paid for a private room where they could eat. The food was delicious. She was beautiful, even sporting the frown he was afraid he would see for the next two days. He picked up her hand. She tugged but this time he didn't let go.

"You've a beautiful hand, Maisie. Your fingers are long and slim, the nails neatly manicured. I'd like to nibble on each finger a couple of times." He rubbed his thumb along the underside of her wrist, teasing the sensitive nerves. Felt both her surprise along with the small shudder he knew was desire. "What would you have me say? I'm not the least bit sorry. What is happening here is the way it must be until you come along with more enthusiasm."

Before she could turn her face away from him, he spotted the moisture in her beautiful eyes. "Go away, Hawk."

Though her voice was thin, barely there he heard her annoyance not fury. She didn't like being manipulated. Even though she led a sheltered life, she never did anything she didn't plan on doing. During her time with Shawna, she controlled every aspect of her young life.

She was still angry with him. He thought the emotion might be changing. Anger, in his mind, was better than despair or the feeling she was being used. Fury could turn to passion. He wasn't about to use her, just charm her into understanding they were meant to be together.

"You will feel better if you rant and rave. Yell at me. Tell me how this is all unfair. Scream at me. You can call me an ass again or a bastard or anything else that comes to mind. Doing so will make you feel better."

He imagined she thought she had done so. She did call him an arrogant bastard before he slipped out of the carriage to let her dress. For the remainder of the trip, he was going to ride with her. Needed to tell her who he was. She had a right to understand the changes she would have to go through when they married.

Her nose tilted into the air. Her obvious annoyance with his person could not be denied. Sarcasm was the order of the moment. "Why? You won't listen to me. I want you to take me home." Her words were gritted out between clenched teeth, her brows drawn tight together.

He didn't dare allow her to see his smile. "Just because I don't agree doesn't mean I'm not listening."

He helped her back into the carriage before following behind her. Unable to resist, Hawk used the sweet curve of her bottom to help her step into the vehicle.

She hissed in a breath of air at the contact. "Curse you, Hawk. You take liberties. I don't want you to ride with me. Ride that big stallion of yours. Let me wallow in my self-pity."

"Wouldn't want you to become bored. I'll stay until the rocking gets the better of my innards. There are a few important details I need to tell you about me. Things you should understand before we can wed." After he joined her, he placed his arms across the backseat of the carriage. His legs stretched at a diagonal between the seats.

"Go to the devil, Hawk. I don't want to learn anything more about you. I've learned all that I want to know." She crossed her arms beneath her bosom delightfully pushing her sweet breasts upward.

"I think you do. Last night..."

"Before you kidnapped me. Yes, I was interested. Thought with time I might find a way to trust you. Now...now...don't believe that will ever happen. You broke faith with me, Hawk. You have no right to come into my bedroom. No right to take me away without my permission. What kind of man are you? I thought you were different."

Now that she was warming up, she would let loose with all her cannons in a few minutes.

"A very frustrated man. One who made a grave mistake three

years ago. Don't want to pay for that error any longer, especially not the rest of my life. One who needs to rectify the wrongs my blunder created. I was a stupid man, with no thought other than for myself. Didn't see past the end of my nose where you are concerned." Once more he picked up her hands. Held them within the warmth of his. "Maisie, we should be wed now. Should have been wed years ago. What happened was a travesty of miscommunication. The devil must have been watching and hooting with laughter at the scene enfolding. We should have a child Mac's age. They could be playmates. We should be expecting another *bairn*. I want children very much. Do you?"

He brought both her hands to his lips, kissed her knuckles, slid his tongue between her fingers.

"D—don't." She stared at their hands pressed so tightly together they appeared as one. Didn't try to pull them away. "Hawk, please don't. If you want me to come around, give me the time I need."

"No, Maisie, we don't have the resources to draw this out weeks maybe months. It's already been too long. Perhaps at one time we could have squandered the hours in the day with simpering smiles and subtle foreplay. Now, we don't. I've a practice to get back to. We've a life together that needs to be lived. I need to tell you about myself."

"What?" The one word sounded defensive. "Once, three years ago I was eager to know everything, what you liked to eat as well as how you enjoyed spending your time. Your hobbies if you had any. The reasons you became a doctor. I no longer want to know more than I already do. I don't care."

"Little liar." The tenderness Hawk felt for Maisie amazed him. "You're just saying those words to protect yourself. You still wish to see where a relationship with me will take you. You're afraid as I am." He bit gently on her knuckles, was pleased to hear the tiny gasp that he hoped was pleasure. When she tugged this time, he let her hands go free. She sat on them.

He kept the crack of laughter to himself. She wouldn't appreciate the fact he understood exactly what she was doing. He wanted to kiss her thinned lips, draw on them until they were just slightly plump as well as swollen from his avid attention.

Soon.

"You do understand that Riley as well as all the Stuarts, including little Mac are shifters." With close regard, Hawk watched her face for a reaction. The knowledge showed clearly in her eyes. Her head bobbed. If he didn't miss his guess, she'd seen Mac shift. Had heard the explanation that Riley also shifted. What she probably didn't *ken* was his abilities paralleled theirs.

She didn't disappoint. Her eyes widened as if she might understand what he was about to disclose. The guess seemed to be on the tip of her tongue as she regarded him from the top of his head to the tips of his toes. "Yes," her single word was hesitant. "Yes, they told me when the little man was so fascinated with what he could do. Riley thought it best I understand. He explained all the dangers. Shawna didn't want me shocked if the little one decided to shift before bath time which is his habit."

Cutting to the chase, understanding he had the absolute right to explain his position in this. "I am too, as are all my siblings, shifters. If we have children, they might all be shifters or not. That will remain to be seen. I hope they are. If they are not..." He lifted his shoulders. "If they are not, I will love them."

"Cameron as well as Harris?" she asked showing interest in the Fraser family. This curiosity pleased him. "They are also?"

At the question, she seemed more interested. "Yes, as I said, all of us. Mother cannot shift though. She is what one might call normal. Still, she is unique. When she was a young girl, she was abused by a man who fathered her daughter. My father adored her the moment he set eyes upon her. Knew at that instant she was his mate. Just as I comprehend you are mine. All shifters possess a sixth sense which let them see beyond the usual five senses."

"You believe I'm your mate? That I am yours in all the ways of the Clan Chattan?" Her questions erupted from her lips. Her eyes filled with inquisitiveness and something he was trying to define. His instincts were not helping him at this moment. He had no idea what ideas were tumbling around in her head.

What he finally realized was that he tasted fear coupled with apprehension emanating from her. She wasn't terrified of the prospects of his abilities, just anxious. Felt in his gut that she didn't fear him but what he was. She was trying to come to grips with the fact he fascinated her. He could read that much of her thoughts. To Hawk it was obvious, he would have to find a means to say the words so she understood she had nothing to fear. Just as Shawna didn't fear the prospects that would rise in her future, she shouldn't either. "You are my mate. I thought that three years ago but wasn't one hundred percent certain. I'd searched and wondered for so very long. Now, I know that you are for a fact, my woman. Perhaps I came on too strong way back then. Pursued you so diligently you needed to take more time to come to terms with your feelings. Even though I *kenned* you didn't understand anything, I proceeded as if you did. Didn't know if I could tell you exactly who I was as well as what I could do. Thought you might run in the opposite direction if you learned the truth. There was also the off chance you would tell the Sassenach. Until I understood your mind, I couldn't speak all my truths."

"Shawna hasn't told me much except that the clan ceremony was different than anything she'd ever known before. That she would never forget what happened. Everything she saw during that time opened her eyes to the life she was meant to have with Riley. Would it be the same for me?"

Good, her curiosity was helping her open her mind just as he prayed. Maisie would ask more questions. "Yes, the clan ceremony is unique as is the experience of every woman who is not a shifter. I won't speak of that now, not yet, not until you've agreed to marry me. You will. You know that. Don't you? When you accept what I am, I'll explain as well as answer whatever you ask. Will tell you everything."

"I'm supposed to trust as well as believe all that you say. I can't, Hawk. Not yet. The tales are all so strange. Before Riley, I thought shifters were talked about because of old wife's tales. I'm not even certain I have faith in all that Shawna has said." She paused for several seconds before she spoke again with indignation. "You kidnapped me out of my bed. That was horrible. Unfair. Outrageous. I can continue with the adjectives."

"True on all counts. I've no regrets. Maisie, I'm able to change into a black panther just as Riley and Mac can do. I don't want to frighten you. Nonetheless, I'm certain you've seen the lad change form. There is a difference, though, when a grown man becomes a black panther. I won't' resemble a small kitten. I won't be adorable. I might terrify you though I pray that I won't. You can still pet me. I still purr."

"He has permission at bath time. One can hear the giggling down the hall to my room. Riley is always with him teaching him about the things he can and cannot do as well as when. Yes, I saw him once. Shawna didn't want me to be frightened if Mac lost control one day and disobeyed his parents." She paused then her eyes nearly crossing, she reached out to him, then quickly drew her hand back, "You can change to a cat?"

"As I just said, I would not be little. Mac is just a kitten. I'm a very large black panther. When I show you my cat you need to be prepared. Don't wish for you to be frightened."

Catching her lip between her teeth, she stared hard at him. "I can't imagine you as a cat. Would you be dangerous?"

"I'd show you but I would have to take all my clothing off. Not too certain but you're probably not quite ready to see a naked man. I would never be dangerous to you. To someone who might choose to hurt you, very dangerous." At the thought he found himself laughing behind his teeth. She was so adorable when she looked at him with her eyes so wide open the violet color so vivid. When her eyes centered on his groin, he nearly groaned aloud. His desire for her swamped him.

"No, don't suppose I am." There were several seconds separating that sentence from the next. Hawk needed to concentrate hard to hear and understand her. "I'd like to see you naked."

When her eyes widened with her words, once again, he was hard pressed to hold his laughter back. He was pleased Maisie wished to see him in his natural form without a stitch. She wouldn't appreciate the humor. He needed to move on to a new subject, one that wouldn't leave him steel hard. "A shifter must claim his woman in each lifetime. It is told that if a man doesn't, he will never see his mate again. That cannot happen to us Maisie. I couldn't let that happen. I want to hold you through all eternity and beyond. Want to love you in our next life as well as the one after that." His feelings on this subject would never change.

"You believe that nonsense?"

It was obvious Maisie didn't credit his words, his very soul hinged on her decision as did hers. Bringing this woman of his over to his way of thinking would be difficult. From the very beginning he understood the task was not an easy one. The consequences were just too dire to ignore or put off what she needed to learn.

"Yes, I would never risk losing you. You see, since you are not too cooperative, I've no choice but to act this way. If you won't agree to wed me, I'll claim you. Without benefit of Father Damian, I'll orchestrate the clan ceremony. The permission is written in the law of our kind if a suitable priest cannot do the service. It is our way to assure out continued existence."

"No, I won't marry you, Hawk. I can't. Don't you see? This...this...is not what I want from a marriage. Forcing me would only serve to put more distance between us."

Outraged, he exploded. "Why on earth not? I *ken* you like me, care about me. Lusting for me, you melt in my arms."

He wanted to shake her until she agreed with him. There were other things he just explained that he could do. He would have to overpower her. That act would be simple. It wasn't the right way. If it was the only way... What choice would he have? He would never risk their future because she was acting impossible.

"You don't love me," she said, moisture clouding her eyes, dimming them. What little spark of curiosity he saw earlier vanished. "I vowed, after what happened to my mother, I would only marry for love. Except for me, mother's life was lonely. I don't want to discover that one day you are visiting another woman."

"What the devil has that got to do with anything? I doubt if you love me. You've never mentioned the word love."

He stashed both of his hands through his hair before knocking on the roof. With the slowness of a turtle, the lumbering vehicle drew to a stop. He leapt out. He needed to shift, to run with the wind. Expending energy was his purpose here. Thinking was impossible now. Once he was exhausted beyond feeling, he might be able to understand her words. With shifters there was always love. How did a man explain that simple fact to a disbeliever?

Riding his stallion to the next inn would be more productive than arguing with this woman who wasn't listening to a word he said. To no avail he could explain until he had no more breath. Before he closed the door, he said, "You should try listening." He watched her bristle with outrage.

One more step in the wrong direction. He wasn't known to have a temper. No, quite the contrary. There were others in the clan who had outrageous tempers. Not Hawk Fraser. No, he was the façade of calm and tranquility. He approached situations rationally never allowing for his emotions to get in the way. That was true until his mate denied him.

"I listen," she countered sticking her small chin into the air before squaring her shoulders.

When she realigned her shoulders, her bosom rose then swayed with enticing beauty. He liked the way her eyes darkened with the passion of her statement.

"It's just that I don't agree with you, Hawk. You're not right for me. You terrify me. If what you say is true about yourself, I don't believe I can live with you. I need a small man, one who doesn't challenge me on any level. Not a man who is bigger than the crags. All I want is to live in peace."

Both furious with himself as well as annoyed with her inflexibility, he slammed the door then leapt onto his horse. Before he took off, he spoke to the driver unwilling to give her the freedom from him she seemed to crave.

"We are almost at the inn. Don't stop for anything. I'll meet you there. If she pleads with you to turn around, remember who pays you."

What did she want? A man who would give in to her every whim? Well, the devil. That man wasn't him. He was the only man she could have. Somehow, he would find a way to coax her from the shell she built around herself. Show her that she need not fear him. Overtime, they could both come to love one another. Right now, he wasn't certain what love was or how the emotion felt inside. All he understood was that Maisie was his and he'd never let her go. He needed her as he needed to breathe as he needed his heart to beat.

Uncompromising, his temper soaring, he pushed Windwalker to run hard. The wind in his face, the scents of heather along with the feel of fall surrounded him. He galloped for several miles before slowing to a walk. Just because he was furious, he wasn't about to abuse his horse. From the moment he decided on this plan, he understood she would not be easy to convince. She would protest, perhaps fight. He expected that to happen. So why was he so at odds with everything? Shawna told him as much. He just didn't believe it would be this damn hard.

His abandonment hurt her. Maisie wasn't about to allow those feeling she held for him to easily surface. Those were Shawna's words of warning. Well, she hurt him with her refusal to join him. She should have known he wasn't going to ravish her. Would treat her right. What occurred three years ago was in the past, should be forgotten. They needed to move on.

That was then not now. He wasn't going to ravish her, but he did intend to seduce her, charm her until she couldn't tell him no. Wanted to feel the fire and heat escalate from her small lithe body. If he had his way in this, she would melt in his arms. He was going to marry her. At this instant, she would never say the words that would bind them together in this lifetime. His brain was muddled. His spirit in tatters. The inn where they would spend their first night was in front of him. He called out for the groomsman to take care of his horse.

Once inside, he ordered a bath for himself then one for Maisie when the carriage arrived. He would be outside to meet her. The rooms he rented had adjoining doors. Once the water was delivered to the room, he bathed then dressed. Tonight, he wouldn't sleep with her. However, he would keep her door bolted from the outside. She would not sneak past him. Maisie was not as submissive as he once thought. He liked her transformation. The driver would not return her to Highland Manor house for all the gold in Scotland. Maisie had no money. Windwalker would never allow her to mount him unless he was with her. The mare he brought along was almost as feisty. She would never try to ride that horse. At least he prayed she wouldn't. Maisie would never have the courage.

After the heated water helped sooth his fears along with his tense muscles, Hawk felt better, more confident with his plans. Ultimately, they would fall into place. Felt as if he could take on his stubborn woman again on a bit more than equal footing. He was so terrified of hurting or frightening her, he backed off at times he knew he shouldn't. The arguments would be the same. He understood a few words would never change her opinions or decisions. If she would do so, they could agree to disagree. Her change in the decision would come with trust in him. He alone held the key to success.

Possibly, tonight he should show her his cat. No, he was shaking his head against the notion. He needed the privacy as well as protection of the cabin to do so. In his opinion, if Maisie saw him naked, most likely aroused before he shifted, she would be terrified. If that happened, he would be stepping backward again. In his mind, he needed to think carefully as to all he said and did around his woman. Hawk had to continue to remind himself she was innocent, a virgin with so little experience with men it was nonexistent.

The thought he would be her first as well as her only man terrified him as well as pleased him. Just because a woman would come to a shifter as his mate, did not always mean she would have never known another male. His mother had been the victim of more men than she could count, yet she was still his father's mate. His father understood, never held the fact against her. How could he? What occurred was never her fault. Heather was a victim of men's lust. She never asked to be raped by multiple men. What his father cursed was that he never found her first. He'd been in the area. Just as all shifters felt that stirring, Elliott Fraser did. He searched near her home. Could have been there for Heather. If he'd found her, could have prevented the pain as well as the shame she endured. If he had, maybe Wynnie would have never been born. If that happened, Connal the head of the McKenna clan would still be searching for his mate.

Fate...

...crazy irreversible component of life.

Hawk supposed everything happens for a reason. Sometimes that reason was just too elusive to comprehend. In this instance, he said a small prayer to fate.

~ * ~

When Maisie first woke to see Hawk's frowning face, his silver blue eyes filled with fear along with concern, she wanted to reassure him. Reached out to touch the frown lines around his eyes before she withdrew thinking herself too bold. Ultimately, she understood she would concede to his wishes since they were also hers. Since that first day she met the man, she wished to become part of his life. She didn't know why he was so very concerned. Why everything was so immediate. He was in such haste. As she came awake, she realized he was in her bedroom fully dressed. She was clothed in her nightgown. Moving backward on the bed she intended to put some distance between them.

The stark realization hit her hard. This was wrong, all wrong. Hawk should not be in her bedroom. As if this was a dream, she closed her eyes. The darkness didn't dispel reality. This scenario was just as it seemed. After she opened them again, even as she prayed, nothing changed. He was speaking to her, apologizing for what he was about to do. Yes, she would fight him if he tried to take her away. As far as she could see, there was no rush. He could spend more time here where she had family, chaperones. Maisie wanted their protection as well as their advice. If she had questions, she wanted to be able to ask Shawna. If he stole her away, there would be no one there for her to ask for advice. She would be alone and in his hands.

Where the devil was he going? What was he doing? Slowly, it seemed he explained himself. Told her he would take her to the McKenna retreat far into the highlands. She couldn't. She wouldn't. While she was shaking her head no, he gaged her with a soft cloth before hefting her over his shoulder. In this he was giving her no choice. When he tried to speak with her in the carriage, she was too enraged to do so. He could have asked her if she would go with him.

He must have understood she would tell him no. Last night she did that very thing. Maisie imagined part of this was her fault. The last part was all his. More than anything she wished she could understand how she felt about a life with him.

Maisie knew she loved the blasted man.

After he began to speak of shifters, she knew he was also one. Given his close relationship with the Stuarts as well as the McKenna's this knowledge didn't surprise her. When she first saw Mac change his form the little boy was so delighted, she needed to feel the same, enjoyment. She didn't. The sight petrified her. Next, when she thought of a grown man being able to do the same, she was even more terrified. Unable to come to terms with the fact that Hawk was also a shifter, she withdrew into herself. The notion was too foreign to her. She didn't understand how her sister so easily accepted the reality of shifters. Shawna was different from her in every way. Courageous where she was meek. Stubborn when she gave into Hawk. Maisie needed to be more like Shawna.

Sleeping in the adjoining room that first night, he abducted her. She weighed the pros along with the cons of her situation. Understanding she was his now for as long as he decided she would be, she decided she would try to listen with more sincerity instead of reacting to the bizarre information. The difficulties lie in the fact he kept infuriating her to such a degree her mind reacted before she could calm herself enough to listen. He would tell her things that to a man were not outlandish but to a woman, they were terribly arrogant.

She wasn't his.

He didn't own her.

Just because he was stronger than she, didn't give him the right to force any type of behavior on her. That was precisely what he was doing. He played at the little boy who would have his way no matter the consequences. He took all that he could. Her largest problem was that she wanted to give him all he asked for.

When he touched her, even after three years coupled with the decision she wanted to see what would come between them, she would never allow him close enough to hurt her. Years ago, he somehow found a way into her heart. In the present, he believed she would try to escape him. How could he? He knew for a fact she was terrified of horses. By the time they reached the cabin in the crags, they were so far from civilization she could never walk home. He knew she would never ride.

She was his for whatever duration he wished to hold her.

While they'd been traveling, he'd always given her a room to herself. He'd been solicitous when it came to bathing, always seeing to her needs first never teasing her with threats of watching her in the tub. He'd been a true gentleman. Never did he take advantage of her.

As soon as they were in the cabin, he dropped her valise inside the master chamber. For a few brief seconds, she believed he would take another room. After he began hanging his clothing in the armoire, she understood that was not his intention. When she moved to leave the room, he stepped in her way, a grim expression on his face.

"I explained to you that we are one now. You are mine as I am yours. There will be no turning back in this. We are both staying in this room, Maisie," he told her as he brushed a stray lock of hair behind her ear. "Our time together begins now. There will be no running away. I'm going to hold you through the night. Sleep with you for the rest of our lives. You are not to fear me. I will never hurt you. You'll get used to me."

The clearing of a throat behind Maisie startled her. "Is all suitable? I'm Mrs. Jenkins. Here to serve the two of you." Mrs. Jenkins poked her head through the open door. The woman was spry with an infectious smile. Her eyes twinkled as if she knew secrets. "I didn't know you wed, Mr. Fraser. Congratulations, your wife is a beautiful *lass*. If there is anything you need, just let me know. I'll make certain your dinner is ready within the hour. I'll be by in the morning to prepare your breakfast." She curtsied several times as she backed from the door.

Maisie was shocked when she saw rose color his face. He nodded, "Thank you. Wed just a few days ago. This is our honeymoon, our retreat. We mean to have fun together."

He grinned; his smile broad no longer under the guise of embarrassment. Now, he seemed to enjoy himself.

The blasted man slanted her a pointed look before winking at her. Bristling with indignation, she turned her attention to the broad backside of Mrs. Jenkins as she hurried down the steps her skirts swishing with each step. She didn't have to ask to understand Hawk protected her from gossip. Gossip could travel faster than a wildfire if the words were allowed to flame. So, Maisie bit back the retort that was on her lips. Though she slanted him a look she hoped sent him to perdition.

She wasn't about to forgive him with the snap of her fingers. He still seemed to be teasing her in ways she didn't understand. As for him chasing the idea that she would climb into that bed with him tonight, well, she would give him other ideas about that. While he neatly folded and hung his clothing, she strode to the window. Even though she knew the drop was too far for her to try to go out the window, she wanted Hawk to believe she might try. If she was lucky and landed with no harm done to her, what would she do then?

A breath of air filtered from her lips as he stepped forward. The man knew her well enough to realize she would never take a horse. Without a horse, she could go nowhere. The driver would have orders from Hawk to keep her here. She was well and truly his prisoner for as long as he wished. When she looked again, the ground seemed a long way away. The air she gulped inside her lungs caught. She coughed.

"Hawk," she spoke with a whisper understanding the wistfulness in her voice couldn't be ignored. "Where are you going with this? I would understand. I'm not your wife. You can't pretend forever. I won't share this bed with you."

"Never said you had to share with me. Be that it may, I don't intend to sleep on the floor. What you will share is the room. Seems just as you don't trust me, I don't trust you. Maisie, you are far too intuitive. You can plead and beg until some unlucky fellow will do as you ask."

"You're wrong. If you let me sleep in another room, I'll figure something out."

"You know, Maisie," he folded one of his shirts then set it in its spot, "would you like me to take care of your clothing? There is plenty of room in the armoire."

It seemed he ignored her previous question. "No. I can take care of myself, but I'm not going to do so."

Removing her things from her valise would not happen. Doing so would put a stamp of permanence to this situation. They would stay put inside her valise until a rescuer would come along. She pointed a trembling finger in the direction of the big bed. "You need to take me home. I'm not lying in that bed with you."

"It will either be the bed or the floor. Rest assured the floor is not comfortable. Even if I gift you with blankets and pillows."

No, it wouldn't be. She didn't see what other choice she had. "I'll take the floor."

He could at least pretend to be a gentleman, perhaps every other night with her.

He continued as if he didn't hear her choice. "When we're wed, we will go to my home. My house is a three-story building near my office and Houston's. The structure has plenty of room for our children along with a few servants. When the children are old enough, they will have a nanny if you wish. The upper floor will have room for whatever help we decide to employ. They will have to come from McKenna land, loyal to the laird. Caln Chattan can never afford to take in outsiders."

"You've the thickest skull of anyone I've ever encountered. I can't believe... Hawk do you never compromise?"

She paced the room, once again staring out the window to the ground. She stared for the longest time. If there was anywhere she could go, she would go out the window just to make a point.

Carelessly, with loose limbed strides, Hawk made his way to the window. Peered downward for a few seconds. After he stepped back, he stroked his beard stubbled jaw. "What is it that has you so fascinated with this drop to the ground? You would hurt yourself if you tried to leave me that way. A broken leg, an arm, perhaps even worse. You're not a stupid woman, certainly not a twit who would make stupid decisions. I wouldn't expect you to take such an extreme measure to flee the man who you will soon come to love."

She turned, her back to the open window, leaning against the sill. Understanding the truth of what he was telling her. "No, Hawk, You're right. I'm not stupid nor am I a twit as you so sweetly put the label. I don't intend to tumble through that window though the overhang would slow the fall somewhat. I've no death wish. Nor would I enjoy the breaking of a bone or two."

"There aren't enough sheets for you to tie together to climb down," he added eyeing the bed thoughtfully. "Possibly I should check the other closets. I'm certain you will need nothing other than my warm body to keep you heated comfortably through the night."

Maisie didn't think his comment worthy of a retort. She moved away from the window, with the intention of making him understand she had no intention of jumping. Her sleeve caught on a protruding nail. She cried out as she tumbled backward through the window.

"Hawk!"

Her fingers wrapped around the sill. She kicked her legs trying to gain a foothold on the overhang. She couldn't. Her hands were slipping. She couldn't hold on much longer. "Hawk, please! Do something!"

Maisie tried to pull herself upward. The strength in her arms was not enough, her weight too great. Her breath heaved as her heart fought furiously to keep blood pumping through her. She heard the pounding of his boots along with the muffled cruses. He was angry, furiously so. This wasn't her fault. Whoever left the protruding nail caused this.

"Maisie! Hold on." His voice sounded way too calm. Emotionless. "Just don't let go of the wood. I'll have you safe in a moment."

With her toes she pushed against the overhang. A bit more support helped her keep her balance, keep her fingers gripped around the rough wood that was stopping her from falling. His strong fingers wrapped around her wrists, just as the tips of her fingers lost their grip. She was falling. All she felt was air along with Hawk's hands. She didn't want to die. Her eyes closed while she felt herself moving.

"I've got you! You're safe. I'll never let anything happen to you," Hawk cried out as he began to bring her upward.

The sill scraped against her chest then her stomach, after that her hips and thighs. Gasping, Maisie was held close within his massive arms. She'd been so very frightened. Beneath her ribs, her heart thundered. Her breath caught in a terrified moan. He pressed her head against his chest. He was warm and strong. She never wanted to move. Maisie wrapped her arms around him. Clung to him.

Her body was shaking against his. Tears slid from her eyes, sliding down her cheeks to be caught by the collar of his shirt. His big hands held her so very close, touched upon her back, soothing, so comforting.

"Take deep breaths. You'll be fine. Don't panic now when it's all over."

He must have heard the shattering sounds that echoed from her lungs.

Trying to do as he said, she gulped air that didn't seem to wish to cooperate. She might have fallen to her death. She forgot her fears where he was concerned. Knew only the tenderness of the man. Against her, she felt his trembling along with the heat of his strong body. His arms around her tightened. She closed her eyes, allowing herself to absorb the warmth he offered, listening to her ragged breaths rip into then out of her lungs.

He was running his hand along her head then down her back, over then over again. Calming. Consoling. Touching her as if he might never feel her against him again.

His lips moved lightly upon the top of her head. "You little fool," he murmured, his voice so close to her ear she felt the shiver of his breath ripple across her neck. She heard the intake of a long deep breath before he spoke. "I was afraid I lost you before I ever truly knew you. Don't ever do anything so reckless again." His big hand stroked her hair. "Promise me. I can't live without you. If you passed on, I would have to find another way to follow you, use the Kinnel Stones perhaps to search for you in another time. As in Kit's and Aila's case they might take me to you."

She didn't understand what he was telling her about Kinnel Stones and following her. What she did know was that she never wanted him to let her go. Wished to remain in his arms forever. When she distanced herself slightly, "I didn't mean to fall out the window. You know that. I...you cannot possibly think...my sleeve...a nail. The point caught my dress and pulled me back." She held out her arm to show her the ripped sleeve.

Once more, he kissed the top of her head, his chin settling there. Several seconds passed while all the sounds of the earth surrounded them, "Good, I would hope you would never risk your life to free yourself of me. I couldn't bear something such as that. Deep down, I believe you will come to love me. Know in my heart you aren't truly afraid of me, the person I am, the man you know me to be. What you fear is yourself along with how you feel."

"I don't know if what you say is true. This moment, though...you are my rock. You saved my life. I will always be indebted to you."

"Want your love, sweet one, not indebtedness. Want to know you more intimately than anyone has ever known you. Wish for you to have my children."

Setting her cheek against his chest, she absorbed the sound of his heartbeat until hers seemed to beat with his. Could that happen? Could two hearts beat with the same time? Beat as one?

She felt the need to explain what happened. "My sleeve caught on something when I was walking away. It pulled me back. I lost my balance. The force sent me careening out the window. When my legs hit the sill, I lost all control. I didn't have the strength to pull myself inside. I needed you."

She was surprised she was able to say as much. Startled, suddenly, she was in his arms again. He strode toward the chairs sitting in front of the fireplace. She'd had no idea what he'd think or if he would believe her.

After he sat down, she was on his lap, still nestled against him. She set her hand on his chest, feeling the gentle rise then fall with each breath of air he inhaled, his larger fingers closed over hers. The realization she trusted this man, had trusted him since the first time she saw him, settled into her soul. He would protect her with his life though she prayed nothing in their lives would cause that need.

She thought of the abduction, the arrogance he must feel to behave in such a manner. The blasted man presumed too much, accepted more than he should. Could have asked. Instead, he blundered through as if he had the right to influence her simply because it was what he wanted because he could. Because he had a plan for their lives. Possibly everything he believed was for the best. Though she felt certain she did have a say. Didn't what she needed and wanted count for anything?

With gentleness that belied the size of the man, he stroked her cheek, then his knuckles traveled along the length of her neck. She was reminded of a different time. A period when she would have fallen into his arms with very little provocation. Now, the need to resist still lingered in her head. She needed for him to understand her feelings counted as much as his. His arrogance was something she was having trouble ignoring. He needed to understand her feelings.

There was distance between them that needed a bridge to pass over. By his careless words he constructed that bridge. She didn't know if she held his callous words against him. He was just a man. He made mistakes. They should be forgiven since he didn't mean to imply what he did. Maybe that was her role as a woman, to forgive the mistakes a foolish man made during his quest to find the perfect mate.

This stunt of his would not close the gap immediately. He would have to do a *wee dram* of finagling. A few apologies would be nice, coupled with groveling or begging. Though she had to admit she was falling under his charms far too quickly. Although she loved the way he held her, the feeling of protective strength emanating from him, she was still as determined as ever to hold back her feelings. To give into this man too soon would set the course for the rest of their lives together. He should understand she wasn't a weak ninny who would say yes to his every whim.

When the fear seemed to ease from her body, she stared at him, her mind open to almost anything he wanted. His eyes simmered silver fire before darkening just as they did that time, he kissed her so many years ago. With seeming reverence, he bent close to her, touched his lips upon the corners of her mouth. Hesitating, she touched his mouth with her tongue. Heard the small sound he made at the contact. Heat shimmered through her with the titillating caress. A soft sound of pleasure slipped from the back of her throat. He stopped the caress as suddenly as it began. What she saw now, was a tender look, one of careful regard. With his calloused fingertip, he touched the tip of her nose.

His smile was gentle, concerned. He looked as if he wanted to lecture but held back. "You need to take better care of yourself, little one. If you fell from that window, I would not have been beneath the window to catch you. Your sweet response to my caress tells me you are not as angry or as immune to me as I thought you were. Tell me I'm right. Tell me you will forgive my rash actions in bringing you here without your permission."

It seemed he was fighting for her. Trying to make amends with no apology in sight.

Maisie shook her head feeling a moment of power when before she'd had none. For a short time, she wished to hold onto this feeling of unusual strength. Hawk was never vulnerable. In this time and place, he needed to learn to give as well as take. Although she couldn't fault the giving of the tender kiss, of the gentle care he took with her. If she allowed him to do so, he would take her virginity tonight. Part of her wanted to give herself over to his skills of seduction. She wanted to stop fighting her attraction to him. For her personal needs, she could not deliver herself to him so without more discussion.

To Maisie it seemed everything in Hawk's life had been handed to him on a silver platter. She was not a morsel on his plate to be lapped up without a thought.

She tried not to appear impervious to his gentle persuasion. She was not. "I won't give in to your every demand. I'm an independent person. In case you haven't noticed, I've done some changing over the years you've been gone. Shawna taught me a lot about strength in a woman. She was pregnant with no man to help her survive. For the first two years of his life, she had to raise Mac by herself. I understand what could happen if I allowed you the use of my body. I'm not that person despite my feelings for you. I was the lucky one that day so many years ago. This evening, while the kiss was nice, it does not mean I intend to wed you or fall into your bed or even give over to whatever plan you've concocted. I've still of the opinion marriage tomorrow, this week or even this month is too soon, much too soon. I like you Hawk. Like is not enough for marriage which is supposed to last a lifetime."

"Eternity," he corrected with a soft kiss to her lips then one to each cheek.

They were chaste kisses. Nonetheless, they garnered emotions in her she didn't wish to acknowledge. "We have already been wed many times in the past. What is one more time when it is the way it is supposed to happen? We will come to love each other, Maisie. You will come to love me."

*I do love you, Hawk. I'm just waiting on you to love me in return.*

*I don't know if my love is enough to carry for two.*

"Dinner is ready," Mrs. Jenkins called up from below. "You two don't dally too long. Don't want all my work to grow cold. You need to eat. Keep up your strength so you can..."

Maisie heard her footsteps on the stairs. Pushing away from him, "We don't want her to see us like this. Me sprawled in your arms, my hair a mess. She'll think I've been..."

"May I remind you, Mrs. Jenkins believes we are married. Besides there is little to see. If I wished, your lips could be kiss swollen your hair in a tangle of waves around your head, not just a few misplaced tendrils. Your sweetly curved bosom would heave with the air you would be trying to grasp into your lungs."

His hands on her waist, he lifted her from his lap, setting her gently on the plush rug beneath their feet. Unstable from the encounter, she swayed. He held out his hand. His eyes narrowed on her lips. "Shall we see what is for dinner. She told me earlier since she wasn't at all certain when we would arrive dinner would be simple."

"I am hungry."

To make her words sound more the truth, her stomach growled. At least he wouldn't believe she was hungry for him. That was something he taught her when they spent their first day together, when they went for lunch. That day she recalled that she was only hungry for his touch. Food had not seemed important.

He hooted. For the first time today, he felt able to laugh at something she said. When she looked at him, the only word he could use to describe her expression was a glower. Not allowing her time, he took her arm in his then led the way to the kitchen table that had been set for two. While they walked, he hummed a tune she'd heard Riley singing. The ditty wasn't at all proper yet she didn't understand the meaning of any of the words. Wanting to ask, she decided on the side of prudence. Maisie kept the question to herself.

The aromas emanating from the table top were amazing. She drank in a deep breath of air, wondering what fine meal was hidden beneath the domes keeping the food warm. Her stomach rumbled again as if it couldn't wait to savor the delicacies.

"Mr. Jenkins was able to snare two partridges. I've roasted them. There are mashed potatoes along with some turnips, greens of some sort on the side. There are shortbread cookies for desert if you're still inclined to eat. I'll be here at six o'clock sharp tomorrow morning to fix a splendid breakfast for the newlyweds. I'll keep the food warm so the both of you can stay in bed if you wish. Though I'm certain you two lovebirds will be down by then." She chuckled as if she said something funny.

"Thank you, Mrs. Jenkins. The mister as well for making sure the cabin is taken care of. I see there is enough fire wood for the winter. A ham is cured in the smoke house. There are wheels of cheese and I noticed there are several loaves of bread ready for our use. We all appreciate the care you take for our home away from home."

"Of course, I forgot. I took a fresh loaf from the oven about fifteen minutes ago. There is honey from the hives we maintain along with peach jam I made when the peaches were ready. The almond butter turned out extra creamy this time. Should be delicious. If there is something special you'd like me to make for you, let me know. If we don't have it, I'll send Timothy into the next village to purchase it from the store. Want you two newlyweds to be happy here."

Maisie thought for certain she'd gone to heaven. The food simply looked divine while she tried to remember the last time they ate. This morning was the last good meal. Between the inn where they stopped and here, there was nothing except the basket Hawk purchased. She watched as Hawk opened a bottle of wine. There was a rack on the far wall holding at least fifty bottles. The clan must keep this place well stocked. As if he read her mind again, "We all contribute to the goods in the cabin. I brought along flour and sugar this time as well as a case of brandy. If you'd like we could have some before we retire for the evening.

"Oh."

There was nothing more to say. With the notion to retire for the night with Hawk, a heated chill swept through her. She crossed her arms around her body watching him. She studied his huge form, the way he held himself. He was smiling as if thinking of something pleasant. She hoped she wasn't what he was thinking about.

Though, she knew she was at the center of his attention. Knew the sooner she allowed him to make love to her the more pleased he would be.

With deft movements, he poured them each a glass of the sweet Bordeaux the wine racks were stocked with. He held his into the air as a salute encouraging her to do the same. "Here is to learning as much about each other as we possibly can."

For a few tense seconds she looked to her feet unwilling to meet his gaze. True, she wanted to learn about the man. Wished to know more about the way he thought the things that altered as well as molded his life. After she finally found the courage to look at him, she said, her voice soft, "I understand what you really mean, Hawk. I will toast to what you said. Perhaps, time will give me the necessary knowledge to accept your plans for us. Maybe I can become your mate."

As time passed, she hoped it would not be too much longer before they both had everything they wanted.

They clicked glasses then drank gazing into each other's eyes. "That's all a man can wish for. Here's to our happiness, Maisie."

After that, he pulled out a chair for her. They ate dinner in companionable silence. Both seemed to be hungry for the delicious fare Mrs. Jenkins made for them.

Maisie understood she was experiencing the same feelings for the blasted man that she had three years ago. Nothing changed between them. It was far too easy for him to sweettalk her, charm her with his devastating smile. How did a girl stay strong against such unfightable odds. He didn't even have to seduce her. She was melting in a puddle at his feet every time he smiled at her. His charming grin sent bolts of lightning through her. When he held her less than an hour ago, she wanted more from him. Maisie imagined she wanted everything, not just a part of him. When he brushed kisses on her the lips, almost chastely, she needed to feel his lips enclose hers. She longed to deepen the kiss, enjoy his tongue against hers. If she'd done so, all would be lost. He would have responded with heat and fire. There would have been no turning back. She needed to remind herself just how potent his masculine charm was. How easily he seduced and charmed her to his way.

What the devil was he doing? Sweettalking then backing off?

Making her want him then leaving her wondering?

This isn't the way she wanted to proceed this second time around with the man. Unfortunately, she didn't think she had a ghost of a chance to bend him to her will. He would do what he wanted when he wanted. In a logical very rational order, Hawke's plans were laid out in his head. He would continue without asking her how she felt. She would continue to deny his plans for them...until she couldn't.

At times she wondered if it wouldn't just be easier if she accepted what he wanted as inevitable. If she did so, they would make love tonight. She would no longer be innocent. He said he would claim her as soon as possible. She imagined claiming was about the same as making love. He never told her what this act he talked about entailed. Although she wasn't as feisty or as self-assured as her half-sister, she still had a mind of her own, wants along with cravings for what her future could hold. Over the last few years, she learned how to stand up for herself.

He seemed to be staring at her empty plate. "Are you finished?" His husky voice broke her away from her day dreaming. "If you are, we can get more comfortable. Would you like to change into something less constricting. You could get rid of your corset. Don't like the damn things, twisting a woman's body in shapes it's not supposed to have."

She looked at him surprised that she was so out of tune with her surroundings that she didn't notice the sudden lack of activity, surprised he was speaking of comforts along with corsets. She reminded herself he was a doctor and would have knowledge about everything female. Heat rushed to her face.

He was several steps ahead of her. Looking at her plate she realized she'd eaten everything. There was nothing save a bit of gravy left as a reminder as to the delicious meal. "Yes, yes, I imagine I am finished. What now?" She shouldn't have asked that question. He'd already explained several courses of action available to them.

"Shall we take this to the porch." He held up a bottle of wine, seeming to ignore his previous statements. "To sit on the swing so we can finish while we enjoy the beautiful night. The sun is about to set. We can watch and experience all the magnificent colors of a highland sunset. I want to hold you in my arms while we appreciate the sights. Want to kiss you when the sun dips behind the craigs. Will *ye* allow me to steal a *wee* kiss, *lass*?"

Perhaps he will try to steal a kiss. Twit, he just told you he wanted a kiss. She hoped he would do so. After that thought she immediately felt guilt swamp her. His kisses would lead to other things which would eventually lead to the uniting of their bodies. From all he told her the last few days that would happen whether there was a marriage ceremony or not. She needed to say her vows in front of a man of the cloth. If nothing else, she would hold out for that small concession. As if Mrs. Jenkins didn't believe the validity of their marriage, Maisie heard her speak of a father in the nearby village.

"I'd like that," she told him knowing her words for the truth. "Sunsets are nice." *Kisses nicer.*

"Better than nice."

Starting out the door in front of him, he placed his hand at her waist. His thumb moved with evocative slowness on her back. Casual. Indifferent. As if Hawk didn't know what he did. Maisie comprehended the fact he was purposefully seducing. She fought back. Gritted her teeth against the sensations. After that his hand curved around to settle on the curve of her hip. At that moment, she thought she would give him anything, anything at all. The mercuric heat he generated ripped through her. They weren't even outside and he was using all his talents to bend her to his will. Her stiffened resolve did nothing to help ease the tempestuous flames created by this man's hand. With each new stroke of his nimble fingers, the inferno inside increased, butterflies dancing deep, very low beneath her belly.

Maisie didn't want to stop the trend he set for the evening with his spur-of-the-moment manipulation. On the porch he was setting up a romantic liaison. She wanted to learn what he would do next along with all the heat that would suffuse her when he did compose such bewitching tactics. Before they reached the door, he pulled two blankets from a chest.

With a sultry half smile that left her knees weak, he told her with a whiskey smooth voice, "Need to keep you warm tonight. Don't want you to catch a chill. Would like to stay outside as long as possible," he murmured, his mouth next to her ear his animated breath rushing past her flesh. "After we see the sun lower itself perhaps the moon will rise to shine its silver light upon the countryside. The sight will almost be as beautiful as you."

Her shudder seemed to please him, appeared to tell him she was open to more of his premeditated advances. His tongue touched the tip of her earlobe. He nipped then pulled away grinning, his eyes dancing with pleasure. She leaned into him wishing for more of his tantalizing attentions. The blasted man knew what he was doing to her untried innocence. He stopped while he arranged the paraphernalia he brought with him.

Hawk set the bottle along with their glasses on the table before spreading one of the blankets on the back of the swing. He arranged pillows on either side of the blankets. "Sit then I'll wrap the coverings around us. Use the pillows as you like to get more comfortable. We'll be warm as if this was a hot summer night. Our body heat will keep us toasty."

When he did so they would be cocooned within the blankets. He would be able to touch as well as explore anywhere he wished without the chance of anyone seeing them. The tips of her breasts hardened. At the thought of his hands roaming, her heart leapt, skipping a beat or two before reaching a point of excitement she never felt before. She gasped in a tiny bit of air, staring at him wide eyed. Without hesitation, as if she couldn't stop herself, she reached through an opening to touch the day's growth of stubble on his chin. His jaw rough, enticing. She felt entranced by all of him. With a quick breath of determination, she drew her hand back. She was making this far too easy for the blasted man.

She was a ninny. A silly twit. There was no one within miles to see him doing anything whether they were covered by blankets or not. No, that wasn't true. There were the groomsmen along with the Jenkins's. The missus told them she would be back in the morning. Without a doubt, the groomsmen would be asleep in his quarters. They were virtually alone.

"There could be unexpected visitors," he said as if reading her mind while he shook out the second blanket. "I wouldn't want any man, woman or child to see where my hands are sightseeing." Teasing, he ran a calloused fingertip down the column of her throat.

*His hands sightseeing? Charming. Enchanting. Bringing her to a place of no return? She knew his doing so was quite possible. His hands worked magic. Heated her. Turned her to liquid fire.*

The thought of him visiting different parts of her body left her brain in a pile of sawdust and the rest of her coiling, aching with need only he could appease. She didn't understand what he was trying to tell her. If his hand ended up somewhere that was not appropriate, he could remove it before anyone would know what he was doing. Several seconds passed while she thought on the course of events since the morning he abducted her.

Once, she ran across Shawna and Riley. He had the hem of her dress around her hips, Shawna's legs were clearly exposed as well as the tip of one breast. With a swift move, Riley covered her. Shawna turned red. Riley grinned at her as if he did nothing to mortify his wife before kissing her on the nose.

"Hawk!"

Her reaction clearly bordered on hysteria. His name in the silence of the night held a wealth of alarm. She pushed at unmovable hands.

"Yes."

He sat down beside her enfolding them in the blankets then handed her the wine he poured for her. "Drink up. The wine will taste good as well as relax you. Why, you are as stiff as a board. This small dalliance we are having should not alarm you. Would you like a massage. That would certainly ease whatever distress you might be feeling. I could loosen your corset. I did mention that we should get more comfortable."

"You're going to...you're not going to...are you?"

She ran her tongue along her parched lips while she thought what should be wicked thoughts. Her hand still rested on his chest. Touched upon hard muscle and sinew, dark red hair that spread across his chest. Sometime between walking from the dinner table and sitting down beside her, he unfastened his shirt. The hair she felt was crips as well as soft. When she started to draw away, he covered her hand with his. Her thoughts were wicked because she hoped she would dare what she was thinking along with everything she wasn't, simply because she had no experience.

"Don't move your fingers. I like them exactly where they are. Now, to the comment. The question boggles my mind while the answer eludes me. What the devil are you asking? You'll have to be more explicit if you expect an answer. What exactly is it that I am or I am not going to do. Be specific."

He smirked at her, his even white teeth showing handsomely against his bronzed face.

She wanted to hit him, to tell him to stop teasing her so. "I can't." She stared at the bottle of wine for too many seconds. "I can't be explicit. It's too...too...shameful. Plus...I'm not at all certain what it is I want. Don't know how to say the words."

"Or don't want to do so. Step out of your comfort area, Maisie" he added beaming down upon her with shimmering silver eyes. Close your eyes so you can imagine what you want."

"Yes...no."

"If you don't wish to ask, that is fine by me. I can always make a guessing game out of your question, or was it a statement?" He lifted his shoulders seeming pleased with his response. "The night is beautiful. Don't you think?"

He pointed to a hawk hovering on the wind about a half-mile from them. The bird floated as if there were no cares in the world to concern him. The wind currents seemed to keep the bird afloat. She wished there was some type of current that would keep her aloft or even one step ahead of this brazen man. When all was said where Hawk was concerned, she was mired in quicksand and sinking fast.

Beneath the blanket his fingers played with the sleeves of her gown. They were tiny sleeves, barely their sleeves. With leisure in his moves, he brough the fabric downward to lightly touch her flesh before bringing the material back to where it was supposed to be. He ran his knuckles across her collarbone then lower until they traveled atop the fullness of her breasts, hinting at more carnal pleasures. She held her breath, expecting him to explore further, hoping he would do so. With the hand that had been investigating, he picked up his wine glass, drank deeply ignoring her for the moment.

When he finished, he said, "Drink your wine, Little One. It's very good. Tomorrow, I'm planning a busy day."

His finger swept up then down her neck. He kissed her lightly on the lips just as he did earlier.

"Oh!"

She nearly jumped out of her skin when his hand rested on her upper thigh. Her body was a jumble of constricted nerves. His fingers traveled the length then back higher still to rest on her belly. His long finger spreading across it from hipbone to hipbone.

"What is wrong?"

His question was bland, his eyes shining with silver highlights. He brought his hand to rest beneath her breast, his thumb rubbing lightly across the undersides. She quivered then choked on the wine she tried to swallow. She sputtered. A few drops spewed from her mouth.

He acted as if touching her was perfectly normal. Maybe for him and other ladies, the way he traveled her body with his hand was normal. For her his advances weren't. She'd never done anything like this before with him or anyone. Before she could voice words to his question his fingers left her. She felt bereft with longing. Again, he tasted his wine then encouraged her to do the same.

As the evening passed, he pointed out various animals as well as birds that flitted across the front yard or flew to the trees. Somewhere nearby a frog croaked. In a tree near the stable an owl hooted. A family of skunks took refuge beneath the stable.

"That owl will be after some unsuspecting mouse or rabbit this night. Entrapment, the bigger animal will catch the smaller one." He paused as if in thought. "I will have to ask Mr. Jenkins to find some way to urge the skunk family to a new destination without stinking up the countryside."

The baby skunks were adorable. Somewhere they found a few tiny tomatoes. They were playing with them, tossing, or rolling them to each other. She didn't think she'd seen anything more endearing than the sweet babies.

"They will grow up. Remember that fact," Hawk laughed while he watched her smile at their antics. "If you get too close or frighten any one of them, you do understand what will happen." Hawk continued laughing when he finished speaking.

When he referred to the unsuspecting moues or rabbit, Maisie understood he was speaking of them. He was the bigger animal. He would catch her ensnare her to his will. After the first deductions he didn't tease her further or take more liberties. She expected him to seduce her. Expected at least one heated kiss. She found she was thoroughly disappointed when all he did was hold her.

Darkness fell upon the land. She imagined the time was coming for bed. What to expect she had no idea. All that was left was to walk upstairs to the room they would share. He told her they were sleeping in the same room, the same bed.

*Naked.*

She'd never been naked with a man. What did that entail? You're a twit, Maisie. It entails not wearing clothing. He would have to make an exception. She wasn't about to climb into bed with any man, even Hawk not wearing a stitch.

He topped off their glasses leaving the empty bottle of wine on the nearby table. Once again, he lifted his glass in a salute. "Here is to the night, Maisie. I for one will enjoy your company. As I hope you will take pleasure in mine."

She gulped air. Her eyes wide with anxiety. Unable to stop herself she did the same, downed the remainder of wine in her glass. Hawk set the glasses on the table before scooping her into his arms blankets and all. As they made their way up the long staircase the blankets slowly fell away from her. Once inside, he kicked the door closed. With tenderness that belied the size of the man, Hawk set her on the bed then stepped back to look at her.

Her hair was a mess. He'd played and toyed with the strands until they fell around her face in disarray. She inhaled a minute bit of air.

"I'll give you five minutes to ready yourself. You are to wear nothing, nothing at all." He left.

Maisie sat on the bed wondering what he meant, ready herself. Well, she imagined he meant take all her clothes off. She couldn't bring herself to do such a thing. It would not take her five minutes to disrobe.

She just couldn't.

*Five minutes?*

*What did he expect?*

*Naked?*

She looked at the old clock sitting on the mantel. Five minutes, she had five minutes to get into bed. For too many seconds she stared at the hands, watching the second hand move around the clock. She should make a pile of blankets on the floor, a soft, little nest just for her. He would only move them to the bed. She washed then brushed her teeth. A bath would have been nice was a fleeting thought before four of the five minutes passed.

In the armoire, she rummaged, searching for her nightdress. She pulled out all kinds of underclothing, petticoats, pantalettes, stockings, along with garters. There were no nightdresses. The cad, he got rid of her night clothes. Told her she would sleep naked with him the rest of their lives. She supposed this was the beginning, the first night of the rest of their lives. Damn, she needed to be in the bed before he came into the room. With newfound haste, Maisie rid herself of all her clothing except her chemise. If he wished her naked, he would have to take the meager swath of material off her himself. For now, the chemise would serve as her armor, her shield.

Before she heard his booted feet, before the door opened then closed with a creak and was latched, Maisie was buried beneath the quilts on his big bed. When she squinted at him through her lowered lashes, she wished she'd opted for a place on the floor. She could have created a layer of blankets and pillows that might have kept her comfortable. Not that it would have done her any good to do so.

Trying not to look, she watched as he disrobed, folding each piece of clothing before setting them on the chair closest to the bed. His boots rested beneath the chair. Good Lord, he was magnificent from the back. Perfection. When he turned, as she saw all of him from the front, air hissed into her lungs. He was more perfect from the front. She witnessed what made him so very different from her.

*What did she have to compare?*

*No matter. No one could equal him.*

"Didn't think you were asleep," he murmured his voice holding a hint of humor. "Let me guess. When I crawl beneath the covers to pull you into my arms, you will still be wearing your chemise...or more. What should we do about that? I mean to begin as we should continue."

He stood beside the bed, staring down at her. His eyes twinkled with merriment. "Maisie, no you don't have to answer that. I *ken* the truth. Would expect nothing else." He pulled back the covers.

She felt the bed dip slightly as he slid in beside her. "What should we do now?" His fingers toyed with the blue satin ribbons holding her chemise together.

*What should we do now?*

*Go to sleep!*

Why was he asking her? She didn't have one good idea. Nor could she change whatever he planned. She worried her bottom lip with her teeth.

"Hmm...I could divest you of your armor, now, couldn't I? Did you truly think a cotton chemise would stop a determined man? It won't. One ribbon after another slowly slid from the eyelet where it was fastened. Leisurely, he slid the straps down her arms until the garment pooled at her waist. He pushed it off then down her legs to end up tossing the chemise onto the floor.

No, she didn't but she understood the chemise would give her a few extra seconds, perhaps even minutes. Now the tiniest of barriers was gone. She was naked, vulnerable. Her body shook.

With one graceful movement, she was in his arms, her head against his chest. "I'm not going to ravish you tonight. Go to sleep, Maisie. Dream wonderful dreams of me, of us and all we can be together."

He ran his hand along the ladder of her ribs across her hips. He splayed his fingers across her belly. Did nothing else. She was a tight bundle of nerves until she heard the even cadence of his breathing then the soft snoring that told her he slept.

There was nothing about this she understood. She wore nothing against his naked flesh. Nonetheless, he didn't seduce. He didn't make love to her. Her body was a jumble of quivering nerves seeking what he was denying her.

What the devil was he doing to her? This was not at all what she expected. The clock on the mantel ticked then chimed twelve times. The day had been long, the carriage ride jolting. She needed to sleep.

He acted somewhat the gentleman. That wasn't something she expected. What was she supposed to do? When she woke the first time, her hand rested on his chest. His dark hair was soft. She ran her fingers through the short strands exploring, investigating. He was asleep so he would never know. With her curiosity rampant, she investigated lower, followed the trail of dark hair to the most fascinating part of him.

He wasn't as she thought he would be. She gasped as he began to change form with her touch. Before her eyes he was growing, taking on a new size. Was this what happened when he shifted? She could only guess.

His hand covered hers. "Unless you would like me to make love to you here and now you should let your hands roam somewhere else a little less delightful."

"Hawk, I thought you were asleep."

"So, you could take wicked advantage of me?"

# Chapter Three

If Maisie took wicked advantage of him, he would believe he died and traveled to heaven. Last night he thought he would expire. Naked, she lay so very close to him, her body pressed against his. Not to make love with his mate was the most difficult night he'd ever spent. He didn't know how many more days he could hold himself back. When he woke, she was sprawled across him as if he was her personal pillow.

He'd be her pillow any time.

Wishing he could make love to her then sighing because he couldn't, Hawk removed her arms and legs from his body, astonished he didn't wake her. She was on her back, her long white legs sprawled open. He could see most all of her. Her beauty...well...he didn't have words to describe. She was pink as well as sumptuous in all the right places, the rest of her was white and creamy. During the night her long silken strands of honey-colored hair wrapped around him, burned across his chest. He spent most of the evening wishing he dared taste all of her, touch every silken part. Just in these few days he spent with her, she'd become such an intricate part of him.

Before going to bed last night, Hawk held the distinct impression she wished for him to kiss her other than the chaste pecks on her forehead, the tip of her nose as well as her cheeks. When he took their sexual relationship to a higher level, he wanted to make certain she wanted him as much as he did her. He hoped to be certain she wanted marriage. No matter the length of time despite what he told her, he would wait her out. He would see just how far he could tempt her, tease her until she took the initiative or asked him to make love to her. Maisie seducing him would be the highlight of their trip to the cabin.

A lot was planned for this day. Watching Maisie sip small breaths of air, he left her to sleep so he could make arrangements with Mrs.

Jenkins for the rest of the morning then on into the afternoon. Hawk wanted to take her to one of his favorite places. The mossy glen was near the house in case they needed a hasty retreat. A small creek with a pool tumbled down the crags. If one was lucky, he could catch a trout or two. When he peered outside there were clouds on the horizon. They didn't appear threatening. Understandably, it was still the *wee* hours just after dawn. One could not predict the weather from a few clouds dotting the highland sky. The morning colors created from the rising of the sun were just dissipating.

"Mrs. Jenkins, how was your night?"

He quickly gave her a quick kiss on the cheek, greeting her as he was thrilled to be starting a new day with his soon to be wife. The wooing was going considerably well. He felt certain it would continue in the same vein. From the way she acted the evening beforehand, he knew she wasn't averse to his attentions. She still craved his kisses, hoped he would deepen the caress. His job now was to make her the instigator.

The housekeeper shook her finger at him, a smile on her plump lips. She was a lively woman well into her forties. Most of her was well-rounded, her cheeks always held a rosy blush. "Your sweet-talking ways will get you just about anything you would like, you handsome devil. Now, tell me true that beautiful woman upstairs is not your wife. You're a bad boy for taking such wicked advantage of the *lass*. You need to rectify this situation as soon as possible. The mister and I will do everything we can to help."

Yes, he was but he couldn't think of any other way to bring her around. "You're right, of course. In a few days, I'm hoping you along with your husband will stand witness to our marriage. I've sent word to father Damian to be along as soon as he can get away from his duties. Keep all your fingers along with your toes crossed that is all the time it will take for me to win her over. Three years ago, when we parted, the separation was not well done by either of us. There was a great deal of miscommunication. Maisie needs to learn to trust me."

"With your looks I'm sore surprised it has taken this long, however long that might be. Three years! If you treat her right, Maisie will come around. You mark my words." She winked at him. "You're *no* be treating her right. I saw that you've got her in your bed. You're not meaning to get her with child so she will have no choice. That is not right or proper."

No, Hawk would not breed with her until they were wed. That wasn't his way. They would not be making love until she initiated the action. If that accidentally happened, he would take the necessary precautions. "That I do not intend."

With the tips of his fingers, he reached into the hot pan to retrieve a perfectly cooked piece of bacon. Chewing as he contemplated the next few nights, "However, if the bedding precedes the wedding, I'll have no regrets. Neither will my bride because it will be of her doing."

Mrs. Jenkins rapped him on the back of his hand with her wooden spoon before scowling at him. "All I can say is that I'm hopin' Father Damian gets here soon. You're a lusty young man. If you've decided the *lass* is your mate, she is in a welter of trouble if she means to remain chaste for the wedding night."

What Hawk couldn't tell Mrs. Jenkins was that at this point in her life Maisie didn't want a wedding night, at least not with him. He didn't force women. He might cajole and charm but he would never force himself upon her. Though last night she seemed to soak up his warmth. Seemed to enjoy everywhere he touched her. She didn't complain once when he slipped her chemise from her lovely body so they could lie together as man and wife. This morning was a new day. He needed to proceed with grave caution every step he took. At this point the evenings were his. The days would be hers. That didn't mean he wouldn't make suggestions.

"After breakfast I'd like to take her to Glen Cove for the day."

In his imagination, he conjured the soft green moss lining the forest floor. The trees that provided shelter from the sun. He could hear the brook rushing between the rocks to lay dormant for a few short seconds in the pond before tumbling to the sea.

"Ah, a *bonny* good place for a little of this along with a little of that. We've *no* had Sassenach sited around here for a few months. The troops withdrew from the nearby fort. The only reason they remained this last year was in hopes of catching a shifter. Not a good enough reason to keep fighting men in one place. Doesn't mean you don't be needin' to be takin' precautions though."

She was shaking her head as if he knew she was saying 'there'd be no shiftin' for him even to impress his little gal. She stopped frying the potatoes long enough to shake the spatula at him. "Don't be thinkin' that you can be havin' your way with your *wee lassie* out in the open. There are other unsavory men about. My husband sighted old Joplin out there the other day. Tetched in the head some say. After Culloden he was never the same. Hid away he did, for over two years just to keep from prison. You and I both know that's not the case. That man is as spry and as smart as any I know. He just pretends so the Sassenach will leave him be."

"Joplin's a friend of the family. Thanks for the warning though. Will you pack a lunch with some of that warm fresh bread you bake. If you've got fried chicken, we'd like some of that and I'll see what I can do about bringing home some fish."

"My mouth is waterin' already. Some haggis coupled with shepherd's pie for this evening's meal if you don't catch trout. Got a feelin' your mind is going to be off somewhere else for the duration. Don't let it wander too far afield. As I said, there's still danger out there and you don't have anyone to stand guard in case you get a *wee* bit amorous."

"No harm will come to Maisie. I promise you that even if I do get a *wee* bit amorous," Hawk laughed.

"You be takin' a warm jacket for both of you. The skies are clear but my mister told me he smelled a storm a brewin.' Wouldn't do your plans a bit of good if'n the two of you got caught up in a rain that's blowin' sideways. If she takes a chill, you won't be havin' that wedding until she recovers."

"I'll heed your advice. Don't be too alarmed when you see we're riding Windwalker. Maisie is afraid of horses. Don't want to take the time today to change that. Want to do a bit of gentle courting."

Hawk was thinking about the lush curves of her warm body pressed against him for the ride to the glen. The thought was indeed a fine one. A small groan ruffled from the back of his throat. He spent the night hard as steel. Because of his decisions, he assumed there would be more nights along with days he would spend in that same condition.

"Seems, riding double might hasten the process along with your *lass* all cuddled up close to you. Why I remember..." Mrs. Jenkins shook her head. "Sure, and I be tellin' you any notions that you might be thinkin' about puttin' into play. Just because me and my mister did certain things 'afore, we wed doesn't mean they were right and proper for a man such as yourself. You're most likely just like those cousins of yours. Randy boys all of you."

Hawk yowled with the pent-up laughter. This housekeeper of the McKennas was delightful. She didn't hold back on her thoughts. Mrs. Jenkins seemed to be encouraging him to seduce Maisie. He didn't need encouragement. Today was not the day. Just as he told his housekeeper gentle wooing was all he had in mind until she was taking the lead. Hawk hoped that wouldn't be too much longer.

He did have a plan up his sleeve.

"Hawk?"

Maisie stood at the door dressed in a pale-yellow muslin day dress. Blond lace trimmed the corsage as well as the bottom of the skirt and sleeves. The corsage was more daring than most of her gowns yet the dress was still modest. She brushed her long, sunny-colored locks but didn't put them into a bun. He liked her hair lose, ready for his fingers to wind through the silken length. That would have to wait until he was able to set up the romantic scene at Glen Cove. With Mrs. Jenkins help, he had all the necessary paraphernalia.

"I didn't expect you up so soon."

The pink color spewing across her cheeks delighted him. He hoped she rose because she missed him missed the warmth of his body next to hers. Quick strides brought him to her. He pulled her into his arms for a hug then a kiss to her forehead. With his hand around her neck, he smoothed his thumb across her lower lip, once then twice. Her moist tongue touched upon his flesh. Wide-eyed she gazed at him the silver-mauve color darkening with the passion he hoped she felt. Stepping back, she looked from the housekeeper to him as if either one of them could give her the answers she desired.

"I...Mrs. Jenkins...I was curious what was going to happen today.

Hawk never actually told me. Just said I would enjoy the adventure." She breathed in deeply. "Oh, my, the food smells heavenly."

Her stomach obligingly rumbled. Her hands formed over her belly as if she could keep the sound away from his ears. When she looked up at him, she appeared embarrassed, no, mortified.

"Mr. Fraser tells me you're going fishing. 'Twill be a fun outing for the two of you. Me and my mister love to go fishing."

She winked at Maisie, a broad grin on her chubby cheeks. The housekeeper started to go on about the rest of what he said was planned but fell silent at the blank look as well as lack of coloring on Maisie's face.

"F-fishing? Whatever for?" She held onto the back of a chair as if she might fall. Hawk raced to her side. "Fishing...?"

"You don't enjoy the taste of fish?"

Hawk laughed as he watched her, concerned as well as attempting to lighten the mood somewhat before she fell on her head either that or her knees gave way. Before a second could pass, he stood beside her, his hands on her tiny waist steadying her. "Here, let me help you sit down. We don't have to fish. Just thought we could contribute something to dinner this evening. By the look on your face, I take it fishing isn't one of your favorite pastimes." He eased her way to sit in the chair she'd been leaning on. Her forearms rested on the table.

She inhaled once then twice before it seemed she could speak. "Fishing...as in kill a fish to eat? I don't think I can murder anything."

He walked around the table to see into her eyes while he heaped a plate of food for her. The plate contained several slices of bacon along with eggs and potatoes. Except for the potatoes, something was killed for this food to find its place at the breakfast table.

"Tell me again what the mere mention of fishing has you thinking?" After the last comment he held a pretty good idea in his head what was bothering her. It didn't surprise him. Nonetheless he wanted to hear the words once more just to be certain.

"I..." She ran her tongue along her lips. "I..." She swallowed hard, her color slowly beginning to return. "I do like the taste of fish. Cannot clean them. Do not want to be the means to its end." She held up her hands as if she needed to defend herself. "I *ken* what you are thinking. You are right. That is, however, how I feel."

Hawk needed to laugh, didn't think this would be an appropriate time to do so. Even through the lean years, he assumed Shawna did the fishing. Most likely she killed the chickens they ate. "You won't have to do anything that disturbs you. Sorry, Mrs. Jenkins tonight there won't be fish on the menu."

"Oh, no, you can certainly fish if you wish." Maisie was quick to point out as she studied the food on her plate. "Wouldn't want to keep you from something you wish to do. If you are lucky enough to catch some fish, just don't let me see it...or them."

*As in making love with my mate?* "Whatever fish we catch, I'll clean and I'll be certain to put them some place where your tender sensibilities won't be disturbed." He waved his hands in the air as if anticipating her next statement. "You won't have to cook them either nor catch them if you don't want to be responsible for their demise."

This new side of Maisie he was seeing didn't surprise him. She was such a tender heart, a sweet person. Cooing over babies, anyone's babies, would probably be part of her character. She seemed to love flowers along with small animals.

"Oh, no dearie, my goodness, I do all the cooking in these parts. You are here just to enjoy yourself with your new man. Now, I'll have your luncheon ready in less than the time it takes for the man to...well perhaps those are not the right words. The luncheon will be in a basket in a few minutes."

"We're not eating breakfast?" She stared longingly at the plate Hawk heaped with food her belly protesting anew.

"Eat as much as you wish. There is no hurry. The entire day stretches in front of us. We have all the time in the world to enjoy everything that comes our way."

He made a plate for himself sitting next to her when he finished dishing up a serving.

On purpose, he let his leg touch hers. Saw the little start of surprise, the subtle flush of color. He set his hand on her thigh while he ate, never moving it, just letting the heat warm her. Letting her wonder what he would do next. He hoped his little expedition with his hand wouldn't deter her from eating her fill. When she began to push her food around on her plate, he left his seat to rinse his plate. She needed to eat. He wasn't going to make her so nervous she couldn't do so.

"Take your time, Little One. I'll get Windwalker ready. You finish eating. I'm certain we won't go hungry during the day. Mrs. Jenkins will have more than enough staples along with an array of delicious treats for our enjoyment."

Hawk scraped his plate before setting it on the counter. Whistling, he stepped through the kitchen door then down the steps.

Cavil, the groomsmen had Windwalker ready to go except for the saddle. Hawk fed him apples then stroked his nose. The horse was a dark bay color with a splash of white on his nose. He stood sixteen hands high. The little mare Hawk brought to teach Maisie how to ride was about fourteen hands and a soft gray color. She wore a few splotches of black shapes on her torso and was gentle, the perfect mount for Maisie. Maybe tomorrow he would begin the lessons.

She would balk. He understood from a few conversations with Shawna that Maisie was afraid of the big animals. He would have to figure out a way around that huge problem. With this little mare the task shouldn't be too difficult.

Hawk wasn't at all certain if she'd agree to ride pillion with him. If she was going to be part of his life, he wanted her to learn. He loved riding along the wild heather covered hills, loved listening to the wind, swimming in the lochs. Deep in his soul, he loved to be in the country with his thoughts, now hopefully with his wife. His instincts told him Maisie was the opposite. There needed to be some way for the both of them to meet in the middle.

Did she know how to swim?

If not, that was something else he could teach her. She would be an apt pupil. He was a good instructor in most everything.

He sensed her before he even heard her. She stood in the open doorway of the barn, Mrs. Jenkins beside her leading the way. Her hands were folded in front of her. She looked about as eager to ride as she would if she were walking to the hangman's noose.

"Hawk." His house keeper was waving her hand in the air, beckoning to him. Her grin nearly reached from one ear to the other. "Maisie is ready. At least she tells me she is. All that means though is she finished with her breakfast." As they approached, his housekeeper kept up the chatter. "I found a rain coat that Mrs. McKenna left here about a month ago. Maisie can wear that if a storm catches the two of you off guard."

Which Mrs. McKenna, he wondered for a moment. Not that it mattered. That was one piece of Mrs. Jenkins advice he forgot, rain gear. "Thanks." He packed it in the saddle bags then tied the luncheon onto the saddle before starting out.

"Now, you certain you have everything you need?"

Mrs. Jenkins hands were on her well-rounded hips. She was tapping one toe as if she expected him to ask for something else.

"I'm not taking a pack horse a few miles. Everything we will be needin' can be attached to my saddle." Hawk figured it would take close to an hour to get to Glenn Cove. He wouldn't frighten Maisie by ridding too fast. They could look at the countryside. He could point out animals along with landmarks. She would be at ease on Windwalker.

"No and I *dinnae* think you were."

Mrs. Jenkins' hands settled on her broad hips. She shot him a glare he felt certain she practiced on the mister, one that was meant to have him shrinking in his boots. "You be getting this little gal back before the sun sets," she told him nodding toward Maisie.

"What if we wish to seen the sun go down behind the crags? Hmm...want a tiny bit of romance today." He extended his hand for Maisie. "I'll be getting my *wee lassie* back all safe and sound when she wants to return and not a moment sooner. If the sight is anything like last night, we'll be riding home as the night begins to grow dark." Hawk held up his hands as he saw Mrs. Jenkins begin to sputter a protest. "Now you be knowin' I know this land with my eyes closed. You've nothing to be worried about as far as Maisie returning safe and sound is concerned."

"Hawk." She held him by the arm, her fingers tightening around his muscles. Her breasts pressed close against his arm. "Let's go. I don't want to argue. Mrs. Jenkins just has my best interest in mind."

"As do I," he snarled with a low voice feeling as if this day was about to get out of hand. After that he smiled at her to encourage as well as show her his anger wasn't at her. "You ready?" he asked, his hands around her waist. "Here we go." He lifted her onto Windwalker's saddle. The stallion sidestepped at the unsuspected weight. Maisie screamed. Hawk held onto her. "Easy now." He was speaking with both the horse as well as Maisie. "Nothing is going to happen." He leapt on behind her, taking the reins in his hands.

As they left the barn, Maisie waved at Mrs. Jenkins. "I'll be just fine," she called out in a thin voice as they moved into the open.

Hawk wasn't at all certain Maisie meant what she said. He kept the pace at an easy walk for the first mile. Maisie's fingernails dug into his forearms. He held the reins with one hand while he wrapped his free arm around her waist, holding her close. Her little butt fit nicely cradled between his legs. He loved the feel of her softness against the angled muscles of his body. If he could make it so, this would be a day made in heaven. Her woman's scent drifted around him. After a time, she seemed to relax. Her back was no longer quite so stiff.

"Are you comfortable?" he asked as he pressed her closer. As far as Hawk was concerned, she couldn't be close enough.

"I don't like horses," was her mumbled reply.

"Do you like me?" his was a loaded question one he waited for the answer, his impatience growing. "Just trust me. I won't let anything happen to you."

For her to fall into his arms, was his greatest wish.

She nodded. He assumed her yes was to all three statements. When she leaned her head against his chest, he imagined part of the battles he was fighting he was now winning. With time, he let the arm that was wrapped around her waist move higher. After he felt the roundness of her breasts against him, he stopped. When she sighed then moved even closer as if she wished she could get nearer, he was pleased. She responded to him just as he would wish.

"Would you like to go a *wee* bit faster? I'll hang on to you. The wind will wash across your face, the exhilaration will have you breathing hard. At any time, you say the word, I'll stop." He told her as she appeared to be settling into this slow pace.

"How much faster?"

There was weariness in her tone. When she turned to look at him, he read the same in the widening of her eyes. "I've never ridden with anyone before. Shawna always asked."

"You always declined," he finished the statement for her. "What will it be, Maisie? Faster or the same pace. Promise if you ask, I'll slow Windwalker. I think you'll like the way it will feel."

"Faster."

"Good answer."

Hawk urged his big stallion to an easy canter. Moving with him, she still clung to his arm. Now her breasts moved delightfully on his forearm, swaying from side to side then bouncing against him. As if unaware of her actions she brought the hand that had been clinging to him to her breasts. She tried to stop the bouncing, swaying movement.

Bending close to her ear he whispered so that his breath would flutter across her cheek. "I can do that for you, hold them. Only if you like though."

Her head popped up banging against his chin. His teeth caught his tongue. She turned to look at him. Her lips were a breath away from his. He grinned at her. "Truly, let me help you out. I would love to hold your beautiful breasts for you. That way you can still hang onto my arm."

Maisie looked as if she didn't know what to say. He brushed his lips across hers once then a second time. Next without waiting for a reply he spread his hands across her breasts holding them still. He guided his horse with his knees, the reins still in one of his hands. He did nothing except hold them so they no longer moved so delightfully. For Hawk this was much more delicious. Her nipples pressed against his palms as they tightened.

"H-Hawk..." she hesitated. "...You shouldn't be doing that." Her voice was paper thin almost nonexistent. He nipped her earlobe then soothed the small mark with his tongue. Against him, even if she wished to do so, she couldn't hide the sweet response she felt with his attentions. He pushed her breasts together. Wished he could taste as well as savor their softness, the turgid tips.

"Why not?" He tried for patience.

"It...it isn't proper."

His soft chuckle was meant for his ears only, nonetheless she heard and stiffened. "Do you feel better when I hold your beautiful breasts? Are you more relaxed perhaps snug? Of course, I don't yet know if they are beautiful. Last night, I didn't have a chance to take a good look. Nonetheless, I would wager that they are. Plump, so very white, tipped with hard pink buds made for my mouth to suckle."

She nodded.

"Was that to answer that you feel better when they are cupped safely in my hands or that they are beautiful and made for me to take into my mouth?"

She didn't answer him. He would have to make do with that. The next step was his. After that he would let her lead the way to seducing him. Heaven knew it didn't take much. He was hard as steel with very little provocation. Maisie did that to him. All he had to do was look at her...or think about her.

After some time, she whispered to him, "You know what I meant. Teasing me...well...I *dinna* like that."

"No, sweetheart, unless you tell me, I can only guess. That wasn't teasing. What I told you was the truth as I see it."

He brushed a few wayward tendrils of hair from her neck, bit gently in several places. The tiny moan she let him hear, enchanted him, cast magic into his heart. He would have to wait for more. Seducing without her realizing what was happening was his goal.

While he held her in his hands, he circled her nipples with his thumbs. He didn't touch, didn't need to. She was arching against him, moving in ways that told him how very much she wanted more from him. Ah, but this afternoon would prove interesting. Perhaps he would garner a sweet taste of her.

When he could see Glen Cove, he kissed her neck again, swept his tongue across the spot, sucked for a few seconds. He pointed. See all that green in the distance. That is where we are headed."

Her head moved up and down. He'd wager a week's income that between her legs in her most private parts she was hot and wet, her honey raining down to center between her thighs. He wanted to feel her, touch her there. For that to happen it was way too soon. He had days to accomplish his task.

Beneath the shadow of the trees, the air was vibrant, cool, refreshing. A soft breeze wafted across the stream. He dismounted then helped her from Windwalker. Holding her close, her feet off the ground, he felt the length of her pressed so very close to him. Felt the softness of her breasts pushed against his chest. He knew she felt his member hard against her belly. Whether she understood the significance, he wasn't aware of the fact. To keep her against him, he cupped her deliciously tiny butt in his hands. He wanted her to wrap her legs around him. She would never think of doing so on her own.

"We are here. Will you kiss me? I did keep you safe as well as comfortable?" he asked his voice husky with the desire that grew over the last hour on their ride to the first romantic spot they would visit.

Over the next week, he had others in his mind.

The deep mauve of her eyes darkened with building passion. She passed her darling sweet tongue between her lips staring at him her expression mirroring the confusion she appeared to be feeling. While she closed her eyes, she seemed to wait for him. The tempo of her breaths changed from slow and even to fast and ragged. Her heart did the same. Still, she waited while he continued to hold her against him. In this position, it would be so easy to see if she was hot and wet.

Without warning, she opened her eyes. There were questions in their depths. To one side she tilted her head for a moment. "I thought, well, I..."

"I asked you to kiss me. We are eye level. Nonetheless, I might grow tired and need to set you upon your feet."

She was so featherlight it would take a long time for her to be too heavy for him to hold her.

"Me, kiss you?" She looked as if she'd just seen a ghost. "I...me kiss you? I can do that?"

"Yes."

He was trying for patience attempting to hide his smile. Doing so was devilishly hard.

"What do I do?" It seemed she was warming to the idea. "I'd like to kiss you since you suggested it."

"The process is very simple, Little One. To begin the sweet process, press your lips on mine."

Inside he was grinning. Just what she would do was beyond him. He'd kissed her before, touched his tongue to hers. She should remember he opened her lips for his entry. Perhaps she would do the same with him.

"Alright."

She leaned forward, her closed lips on his. She moved them slightly, straining to figure out what to do next.

To Hawk's surprise, she ran her tongue between his lips, pushed with some hesitation inside his mouth. She did remember. He wasn't going to make this hard for her. He opened far enough so she could slide that warm pink tongue of hers inside his mouth. His groan stopped her exploration for a moment. "Go on," he managed to say.

She slid her tongue to the back of his mouth then the sides as if she wanted to investigate every spot. At one point, she ran it along his teeth. He could hold back no longer. He sucked on her tongue, played then dueled with hers. He allowed her to take the initiative once she understood what it was, she wanted. When he retreated from the contact, she slid down the length of his body. The tiny sounds he heard, delighted him, pleased him more than he could ever admit. Sooner than she would admit to herself, she would be his.

"Hawk?"

Within his embrace, she wobbled. With his hands on her hips, he steadied her. "Yes," he said, smiling at her, understanding his nimble plotting caused her shakiness.

"Was that right? Did I kiss you right?"

She blinked a few times before staring at her feet as if embarrassed by her behavior.

The devil if it had been any righter he would have perished. The only reason he was still standing was experience. "Look at me." He lifted her chin so they had eye contact. "Perfect, Little One. You can kiss me anytime you wish. All you have to do is ask or not ask. You can always suit yourself. I'll never refuse a kiss." He didn't dare let go of her yet.

Picking her up, he carried her to a boulder where he set her down. "You wait here. I'll get our little adventure playground ready for the two of us."

"Adventure playground?" she whispered in such a soft tone he could barely hear.

He smirked understanding she wouldn't understand what he spoke of. Today they would have adventures, play with each other until neither could walk. "Well, I'm going to spread the blankets that are rolled behind the saddle. Next, I will set the fishing poles so we don't have to hold them. If we catch a fish, wonderful. If not, there will always be another time. After that I will set the basket with the food in it on the blankets so it will be ready when we wish to eat."

"Ready...ready for what?" she questioned, her eyes wide huge saucers as if the passion that heated her from the shared kiss was still seething within.

"For us, silly. For whatever we wish, for whenever we are hungry. I would like to take a short walk. There is a path that follows the creek. If you wish and if the water is not too cold, we can splash around in the pond. Do you know how to swim?"

If she didn't, she would by the end of next summer. It was too late in the season now to spend any amount of time in the loch or any of the rivers. They would both expire from the cold. He would have a delightful time with the teaching. Even the warming if they got too wet.

Her back went up after his question, obviously peeved. She snorted a noise very unlike Maisie. "I can paddle around."

He grinned. "Paddling is not swimming. I would like to have confidence when you are in the water that you will not go under then not come back up. Precisely what you can or cannot do in the water today makes no difference to me. Shall we walk? Explore the countryside. See what we can see?"

*Feel what we can feel?*

She seemed both apprehensive as well as eager. Her eyes were shining with what appeared to be excitement. "Yes, yes, we can walk. How far?"

"As far as you want. We can walk until you tell me to stop. Or... until you ask me to kiss you again." The experiment he planned was working out quite the way he wished it to.

She started off down the trail, her hips swinging. He caught sweet flashes of trim ankles as she strode along the narrow path. While he gawked, she was walking away from him.

"Wait, not without me."

Striding toward her, he caught up to her. Hawk wrapped his arm around her shoulder, his hand hanging down, his finger touching upon the bare skin above her bodice. She sucked in air. He trailed the finger along the top of the fabric, wishing he dared go lower. If she didn't push him away, perhaps he would tease the tender flesh beneath the fabric.

~ * ~

Maisie no longer understood her feelings toward Hawk. He was so much a man. He enchanted as well as mesmerized her. Hawk was so confident in every part of his life. He'd seen as well as done so very much while she remained isolated. As much as she wanted to wait, to make certain, he understood how he hurt her, she also wanted to give into him. Just as the first time he kissed her, her body possessed a mind of its own. She responded to him even though she tried desperately to feel nothing.

Other issues along with memories began to surface. Her mother was the crux of the problems that came to the forefront of her head every time he became close to her. Perhaps those same memories played an integral part of her reasoning when she decided not to go to Selkirk.

Now while his finger trailed along the top of her lace, she wished he would kiss her again, wished he would dip a bit lower. She recalled more sensual pleasure when she thought of her mother in bed with her father. Those were good memories. There were others after her father passed. The money coming from her father was very little and far between. Her mother had to support herself.

Oh, she sighed to herself when Hawk grew bolder. Along the top of the fabric his hand passed across the hardened tip of her breast while he pointed to a bird soaring high above them with his free hand then a fox that disappeared in a thicket of a berry bush. He didn't seem to notice that he was touching her in so many places that were far from suitable.

What he was trying to do she had no idea. His fingers wandered everywhere, touched, caressed her side to her hip. Still, he seemed oblivious. He stopped, pressed her against a tree trunk, while he smoothed her hair behind her ears. His eyes alight with mischief, he ran his thumb across her lower lip. She couldn't help but follow the path with her tongue.

"It's beautiful here but not as lovely as you."

His lips touched upon her forehead, then the tip of her nose. He brushed hair from the side of her face where he nipped her ear. Unable to help herself she purred softly; a fragmented sound left her lips. He smiled. "Do you like that, *lass*? I needed to get a taste of you. Would you like to taste me? Ask and I will open for you."

She tried to swallow. Her throat was so dry she couldn't speak. Instead, she nodded closing her eyes to stare at the hard muscles of his chest. She did like everything he did. Thinking of her mother again, this charming seduction must have been the way her father seduced her mother. After that, her memory settled on the man who kept her for two years after the passing of her father. He made her mother do things she didn't like. When he left, she would be in her room sobbing. Maisie didn't want any part of that type of relationship. While Maisie understood she was not supposed to watch, she couldn't help herself. Her mother's whimpers coupled with the pleading, always brought her to the door to her room which she cracked open so she could see. Maisie wanted to help but there was nothing she could do.

"Can't speak?"

He moistened his finger before running the tip along her bottom lip, tugging it slightly so she was open to him. With tender caresses, he placed his finger inside her mouth, touched, ignited heat. She squirmed. Her body coiled with need.

"Hawk, will you..."

She closed out the images of her mother's last protector. Focused on Hawk.

"Kiss you? No, but you can kiss me if you like. His hand cupped her breast, lightly stroking the veiled nipple. The thumb passed over the hard bud then over it again, while he waited for her to give him an answer.

She rested her hands on his muscled chest, so flat, so very hard. She reveled in the differences. Through the fabric of his white shirt, she could feel the hard tips of his nipples. They were so small. "You...you are so different from me. Does it feel the same when I touch you here?" she stroked, the palms of her hands across his nipples.

"I don't know," his voice husky so deep she barely recognized the sound. "What do you feel when I touch you here?" He mimicked her exploration as if he hadn't been caressing her first.

"I like the way it makes me feel."

"That's all, good *lass* but what you say doesn't tell me much. How does my touch upon the hardened peak of your breast make you feel?"

She felt the blush from his words heat her from the inside. Blood rushed to her face. "Hot, aching deep below my belly. Your touch makes me feel as if I need something more that I'm not getting. Something you won't give me."

She was feeling sorry for herself, frustrated that he could take this so lightly. He seemed to find this situation amusing even though it was obvious to her he was keeping his laughter in check.

"Me too," he told her his voice husky. "I want more but at this moment in time if I were to take what we both want, you would regret my actions. When it comes to the relationship between the two of us, I don't wish for you to harbor regrets. You will have to lead the way."

He was so close she felt each mint-scented breath. With his teeth, he tugged on her lower lip, opening her mouth for his exploration. He did nothing else. She thought then that now the kiss was up to her. She swept her tongue across his lips thinking it was hers she was moistening. He teased her, taunted her. His hand rested on her hips before sliding down her legs.

"Can I feel you?" he asked her. "Can I stroke what is beneath your gown? You would like the way my hand makes you feel."

"Feel me?" she countered, confused by his question, thinking of her mother lying beneath her father, the soft sounds she made when he stroked her. For the moment, she blocked the other man from her mind. "Isn't that what you are doing now?"

"Not the way I'd like. Just for a second you understand." His feet pushed hers apart. "There is something I need to know."

She looked at him sideways, confused yet interested in what he tried to do. She was intrigued, fascinated. Wished she understood his purpose. His knee came between her legs, pressed against her, higher then higher. Was that where he wanted to touch her? She stifled a shudder that swept from her head to the tips of her toes.

"Hawk? What is it? Why do you want to feel me?"

Her mind raced to the time she inadvertently watched Shawna with Riley. She was enjoying the way his hands moved on her.

"Want to get rid of these. Would like to rid you of the damn corset too."

Before she understood his intention, her petticoat was in his pocket, a bit of lace dangling free. Today she only wore one. Beneath her skirt she was naked. Cool air brushed across her legs. His hands explored the length of her leg up then down after that he turned his attention to her other leg. Her body quivered with wanting. She felt hot and swollen. Her hands wrapped around his back. He covered her naked belly with his hand. She whimpered, sighed, cried out when his fingers cupped her. She arched against him feeling that part of him hard against her. Her body throbbed, pulsed with yearning him.

"That's it, sweetheart. Tell me if you don't like what I'm going to do."

His voice was gentle, tender. He sounded as if he wanted her to guide him. She wanted to understand. "Touch my hand."

"Wh-which one?"

The one beneath your dress. The one pressed against the round softness of your belly," he murmured a hint of amusement in his voice.

"All right." She knew many seconds passed before she got the nerve to place her hand on his. He flipped his hand over so hers was beneath his. Hawk brought her fingers between her thighs where she was the hottest, the wettest.

She gulped a lungful of air that didn't seem to do anything for her. She was feeling herself. Felt the heat where he pressed her hand.

"What do you feel?"

His lips pressed against her neck, laved, and sucked. He nipped then brought more pressure against the same spot. She arched, pushing against him.

She looked at him with widened eyes. "I don't understand. What do you want me to do? I thought you were going to touch me."

"I intend to. Are you wet for me?" He moved her hand so she caressed herself finding a spot that seemed to chase a tempest of heat throbbing where her fingers rested. "May I touch you here? Where your fingers are? Do I have your permission?"

She nodded wanting that more than anything she could think of at this moment. His fingers slipped between her. With his feet he spread her feet farther apart giving him more room to explore. She gasped, startled when one then two of his fingers slipped inside her.

"Your sweet nectar is pouring down on me, sweetheart." He slipped his finger from her then brought them to touch her cheek. "I love your scent. This is your body getting ready for mine." He pushed her dress back into place smoothed the fabric. "That's all for now. We should walk back. Have something to eat. Maybe take a little nap. Splash in the pond. See if we've caught a fish or two."

"I don't want to go back," she said, licking her lips, her body swaying as she felt certain her knees would crumble.

Maisie didn't think she could walk even one step.

"We need to return. I might ravish you right here against this sturdy oak tree if we stay. I'm hard as steel, ready for the sweetness of you. You would lose your innocence if we don't stop now. Do you want that?"

She did and she didn't. She recalled her mother kneeling in front of her protector. His hand was on her head, holding her so she couldn't move away from him. He would tell her to suck harder. When she didn't respond he would thrash her. To the day she died she wore scars on her back from her protector's handywork. Hawk wasn't like that. "No, I want you to love me first," she stated flatly with a sudden rush getting her senses back.

He didn't need to stop seducing her. She was the one who wanted the kiss. He never asked her for anything except to touch her. At the thought of where his fingers were, her face flamed.

Hawk didn't respond with the words she longed to hear. Her heart sank while fury coupled with frustration grew. The blasted man knew exactly what he was about. He would let her give her heart to him. "Come along," he offered his arm with so much calm she knew he wasn't affected in the least by what they did here while leaning against the oak tree.

Petulant as well as pouty, she wanted to ignore the overture. She stumbled on a rock, falling into him. He kept her upright, otherwise she would have been on hands and knees. With every passing second, she was becoming more dependent on him.

*Just like her mother.*

"Don't let your pique get the better of your judgment," he told her once more extending his arm. When she didn't accept his overture, he wrapped his arm around her shoulder as he'd done when they first walked along the path. This time instead of teasing, he cupped her breast in his large hand, playing with the hardened bud, twisting the tip until she wanted to yowl with the pleasure he gave her. She thought she might indeed swoon. Instead, to keep her feet moving she leaned into him reveling in the warmth of the man she adored. To keep up with him, Maisie wrapped her arm around his waist.

"I," she told him once they stopped at the adventure playground he set up before their brief walk, "Hawk, I'd like my petticoat back."

"No."

She bristled not understanding his reasons for keeping them from her. "Why?" This made no sense to her. She felt naked without them, air caressing her most intimately just as his fingers did as hers did. Knew he could toss her skirts then do as he pleased. At this point in their fledgling relationship, he seemed more interested in teasing than acting.

He could if he wanted despite the absence of her underwear.

His grin left her speechless. "Because," he said ever so slowly while his eyes seemed to see into her, touching her emotions just as his fingers caressed her intimately, "just as I wish to sleep with you naked, I also wish to be with you when you wear nothing beneath your dress. The notion fascinates me. Believe from this point on that is the way you will dress. If I find that you have donned multiple petticoats or even one, I will remove whatever is beneath your gown. Promise me you won't wear a corset." He tapped a finger on his chin as if dreaming up some new devilish ideas. "When we return, I'll either burn your underclothing or place them where you will not be able to find them."

Arms akimbo, Maisie stared at him as if he'd gone crazy. "You can't be serious. You would burn my clothing?"

"Never more in my life have I been so serious. Yes, if you insist on wearing your underthings, I would burn them." Appearing pleased with himself, he continued, "Have some wine."

He uncorked the bottle then rummaged through the basket of food for the glasses she was certain Mrs. Jenkins must have packed. After he poured the wine, he placed bread and cheese on plates. "Should we go down to the pond? See if we've caught a fish or two?"

Unable to stop herself, she drank the glass then handed it to him for more. If anything, she needed fortification. She was naked beneath her gown. Vulnerable. She felt the heat pooling between her thighs. He was unconcerned about this condition which she was positive he created purposefully. She tried to ignore the tempest along with the dancing and flitting butterflies.

She could not.

"Come sit." He patted the place near the fishing poles.

The plate of food was in easy reach. She didn't want to sit anywhere near him. He would touch her again. She would ask for more caresses by the purring sounds she made just for him.

"It's my great misfortune but we haven't caught anything."

He popped a piece of bread topped with cheese in his mouth. She watched him chew then drink his wine as if he didn't have a concern in the world, small sips not like her gigantic gulps that emptied her glass. With nerves unraveling as well as stretching she sat down on the opposite side of the cheese plate. Smiling at her, he filled her glass. Studying him over the rim of hers, she saw the enjoyment in his silver eyes. The outdoors was his passion. That was so opposite from herself. Having lived in the city for the first part of her life she never took to the forest and the crags despite Shawna's efforts.

"Don't want to catch anything," she told him a petulant tone to her voice.

She'd already been caught in a web of Hawk's design. He maneuvered his way into her life. Now, she understood, he wasn't leaving. He would take her with him despite any protest she might make. For her part there was no protest to be had. She couldn't think nor did she want to do anything except kiss and touch him. She wished she could run her hands beneath his shirt, could feel the hard length of him that pressed against her stomach. At the very notion, heat flooded her face again. She'd become a raging bundle of nerves. Beneath her fingers, how would he feel? Her mother had been forced to stroke, to lick, to swallow her last protector's member into her mouth.

Force was different than desire. She understood a woman could desire a man. Could also loathe the very sight of a different man. She wanted Hawk in every elemental way she knew about.

She'd seen Hawk naked. He was splendid. She imagined, at least to her, he was the most beautiful man in the world. Her imagination, working with very little effort fantasized his member hard and erect. Her body quivered. Keeping her wine steady, she wrapped her arms around her body, rocking back and forth as she mulled all the wicked thoughts around in her brain. She wondered how he would taste. If she would enjoy him that way.

"Something wrong?" Hawk asked as he touched beneath her chin, lifting her face high enough she couldn't hide from him. "There is something you're not telling me. I would never judge you, Maisie. Need to know as well as understand everything about you. Tell me what you've been thinking about." His grin widened as if he knew or guessed, "You were thinking about me. Weren't you?"

"The wine went down the wrong way." She lied to him, unwilling to tell him her thoughts or the last years of her mother's life.

The degradation her mother suffered just to put food on the table along with clothing on their backs, a roof over her head. She didn't intend to end up that way. Unless she held back from her passionate desire for this man, she would become her mother. She would be his mistress. Maisie shuddered, stiffening her resolve to remain aloof from this man who stole her breath every time she looked at him. For the first time in all her short life, she understood why her father was able to seduce her mother.

"Uh—huh... I didn't notice. You're lying to me, Maisie. This time I'll let it go. Don't want you to make a habit of telling falsehoods." He leaned back his forearms on the mossy ground as he looked her over. "If we tuck your hem into the waistband of your dress, we can wade in the water without getting you too wet. Don't need to have you take a chill. What do you say? A little more adventurous play before we take a nap?"

*More play? Adventure? Nap?*

Was that what he called what they'd been doing? "I don't think so." She couldn't help but remember she wore nothing beneath her dress. If he tucked it up, he might be able to see... She gulped for oxygen.

He would touch her again. She would dissolve. Liquify. Her mind was mush. What was she thinking?

The devil, she wanted him to do so. She wasn't going to beg for his attention. Hawk wanted her to beg. He'd said as much. With every word as well as gesture, he implied he wanted more of her. Maisie found herself weakening. It wasn't just the words coupled with her wild imagination. It was that devilish smile he flashed her. It was the Fraser charm as Mrs. Jenkins said.

"Thought you had more courage."

"You do realize I'm not a shy mouse." She tossed that out appreciating the fact she was no longer the least bit shy or a mouse.

It was just that she wasn't as bold as Shawna. She always shrank in her half-sister's presence. Always became her shadow. Deciding at that moment she would meet his dare, would play with him in the shallow pond. Whatever came of her brazen behavior, she would deal with.

"Prove it," Hawk challenged her, his grin flashing against the tan of his face. His silver-blue eyes darkened to pewter anticipation keen in his expression. "Prove to me how bold and daring you are. Finish your wine then I'll fix your skirt. Our toes will freeze but I promise you when we're done, I'll warm them."

"I can do it... Warm my toes? How?"

Curiosity took over her common sense. Deep down she understood the answer to this question would send heat swamping her, turn her stomach upside down.

"Not as well as I can. As to the other, you will just have to wait and see. A man has many ways to warm toes. My ways will be delightful. I believe your toes will be deliciously waiting for my consideration. For now, the answer is to remain a secret."

The challenge was there, presented to her on a silver platter. This time she sipped on the wine, prolonging the event. Thinking of how he would go about warming her feet. The fishing line nearest him jerked then jerked again.

He sat up. "We've got one!" Setting his glass on a flat place he reached for the pole, grinning, his boyish delight evident. "Before we leave, we'll have to try for one more."

This would take some skill for him to bring the fish in. She didn't want to see the poor thing and know it would grace their dinner table. "I'll take a short walk." She left him to deal with the fish she didn't want to eat.

"Coward." She heard his words along with his laughter as she wandered away from the small area he set up as theirs to play in. When she reached Windwalker, she stroked his nose, whispering nothingness to the big stallion. This animal was a darling. She knew though that he was strong, not a horse she would be able to handle. Could she handle Windwalker's master who was also strong as well as determined to live life his way? That remained to be seen. She would do her best. She would not be shy or submissive. She would show him just how bold she could be.

Her life was changing too fast for her to understand. Maisie understood it would continue to revolve around this wonderful man. Hawk was at the center of the conversion in her mind. He wanted to teach her to swim, to ride, most likely to fish. Hawk wanted her by his side in his escapades as well as to work with him in his practice. She could do everything he asked. Could she marry him? He didn't love her. Love was what she bargained for. This was all happening at a blinding speed. He abducted her a mere three days ago. Before that she'd known him two days before he vanished from her life. He returned ready to resume the fledgling relationship they began so long ago. Resuming that relationship as if three years as well as their history never happened was impossible for her.

"Got it in a bucket," she heard him call out to her. "You can come back now. You won't have to see the fish if you don't wish to do so."

She shouldn't have left. By Hawk's standards she was a coward. Proving her mettle became important to her. With some hesitation, she walked back. The fish was in a bucket of water to keep it fresh. She wasn't going to look at it nor think about eating the ill-fated thing. Though she would do so. She liked the taste of fried fish.

"Time to play," Hawk said as he reached out bringing her to him as if she was the fish on his line.

He kissed her hard, his tongue playing havoc with hers then he wasn't kissing her, he was pulling up her skirt and tucking it into the waistband of her skirt as he'd said he would do. The fabric rose high around her. The length of her legs showed in many places. He didn't have to bring it so high. The act was on purpose.

"My knees show! My legs! What are you doing?" She shoved at his hands. Her face heated.

He pushed her fingers aside holding them behind her back as he kissed her again.

"I see as well as feel more than your knees and thighs last night when we slept. Want to see them now while we frolic in the water, while the sun is till shining, while I can admire them. You look different in the sunlight. Besides this is all part of our journey, our adventure."

He wasn't taking a particular interest in her legs, just proceeding with measured precision to keep her skirts from getting wet.

"What about you?"

"What about me?" he asked as his britches were rolled to above his knees, as far as they would go. "I could take them off," he suggested with a flirtatious wink that sent her heart skittering to an abrupt halt. "Is that what you would like, Maisie. You want to see me naked. If I disrobed, I would expect the same from my beautiful partner."

"Oh." He was a miserable bounder taunting her. Nonetheless. if she was to prove anything to him, she should shock him. "Yes, take them off. I want to see your legs just as you are seeing mine."

He stepped forward, his hands relaxed at his sides, waiting. "You can do the honors."

Perhaps that was too much to ask. She should never be so bold or say something she couldn't do. "That's all right. If you want to get your pants wet that's fine by me." She turned her back on him, wishing to escape his perusal for a few seconds while her cheeks flamed.

He hooted with laughter. She didn't pass the first test of her courage where sensual play was concerned. She wasn't passing the second either. If she wanted to prove she wasn't shy, she would have to be different. At this time that was fine by her. They played, splashing water on each other. She kicked with her feet, watching the droplets hover in the air until they fell to the pond. He would splash her way. There were times when she kicked, she felt certain he could see all of her.

Maisie found she didn't care. She laughed. Giggled. Enjoyed Hawk's robust laughter

As he told her he held her naked at night. Tonight, he would do so again. To Maisie's surprise, she was terribly cold. A crisp wind seemed to pick up blowing down from the north. Wrapping her arms around herself, she shivered.

"You're cold."

In an instant, he was beside her, enfolding her in his arms to heat her body.

"Yes."

Hawk cradled her, striding to the blankets set out on the ground.

Before she could think of anything to say, she was draped in a quilt. "Mrs. Jenkins made this when the McKenna married Wynnie, my mother's daughter. Are you warmer?" He blew his warm breath on her hands. "Should have stopped sooner. Were you having fun?"

"Warm, yes, except for my feet. Perhaps I should put my shoes and stockings on. Yes, your escapade was fun. I've never done anything so decadent before now." She was wondering if he would warm them as he suggested earlier.

"No stockings just yet. If you recall, I told you I would create the needed heat." Hawk was looking at her his gaze tender.

They were growing colder by the minute, just as the clouds seemed to be darkening on the northern horizon. He reached for her, her feet in his hands. He set them on his lap, clasping them, rubbing gentle circles, pushing her knees up so he could bend forward and reach her toes. She found her legs separated. He must be able to see all the way to her naval. He was now blowing his warm breath on her toes. She was open to him. Once again, he didn't seem to notice how vulnerable she was.

"Oh my!"

His mouth closed over her toes. He nipped and laved just as he did on other parts of her body when he wanted to charm as well as seduce. The tempest she was growing more and more familiar with flashed through her. He spent minutes upon more minutes giving her toes his ardent attention. Her skirts rose higher on her legs. The fabric gathered around her hips. She was leaning her back against the large boulder where he set her earlier while he was erecting his adventure playground.

He was staring at her, his gaze upon the most private part of her. "You are so beautiful, all pink and swollen. If I touched you, I would feel your sweet nectar showering down upon my fingers. Would you like that?"

He set her feet down. Not hesitating, Maisie covered herself. It seemed he wasn't finished. Taking her stockings in hand, he put one then the other on her legs, tying her garters, touching sensitive flesh whenever he could. When he finally looked up, "Are you warmer?"

Tongue tied, she couldn't say a word. All she could manage was to nod her head. He laughed appearing pleased with himself.

"Let's watch the sunset before we go home. I'm going to toss that fish back in the pond since we don't have a second fish. Perhaps we will be luckier next time."

He wrapped the blanket around her then poured two glasses of wine. They walked to a hill that looked onto the western horizon. Colors were beginning to form. She shivered. It seemed her dress got wet after all.

"You still cold?" he asked so much concern in his voice the sound surprised her.

"I'll be fine. It's just that my gown got a bit wet during our play time. Even with the blanket, I cannot seem to warm up."

After they sat down, he wrapped them in the second blanket,

holding her close. She sat in front of him, his legs separated to cradle her between his thighs. She leaned her head on his chest as she watched the beautiful colors; mauves, pinks, oranges and so many more. The heat from his body warming her, she sipped her wine. One of his hands was around her waist. He held her close. This was a moment she would remember forever. He wasn't seducing her. Hawk was just holding her. A feeling of warmth stole through her.

Once the sun was down, the night would end. She came closer to some conclusions of her own today. While she wasn't going to give into him with no complaints, she understood with time if he continued to be his charming self, she would say yes. They packed up. When he set her atop Windwalker, she wasn't nearly as frightened as she'd been earlier in the day.

They rode home in silence as she was absorbed in thoughts about the man who wooed her so gently.

~ * ~

Where is your little lassie?" Mrs. Jenkins asked the next morning. She was busy preparing breakfast of fried trout. "Mister Jenkins caught some fish yesterday. Figured the two of you would be too involved doing other things to spend time with the fishing poles."

He laughed then kissed her pink cheek. "We did catch one. I tossed it back. Seems she doesn't mind eating fish, just doesn't like all the things that come before."

"You didn't get her cold now did you? The wind picked up last night to something fierce. She isn't sick? Seems she must be sleeping the day away," Mrs. Jenkins said in an accusatory tone as if he purposely kept her out too late. She was shaking her spatula at him to make her point.

"No, she's not sick. After we returned around eight o'clock, we sat on the porch and talked for an hour or so. By the way, the sunset was beautiful. Tonight, I'm going to take her to the bonfire Houston built out here since he liked the one at home so well. The heat from the flames will keep us both warm all the way to our toes."

He thought of her toes, delicate little pink toes that tasted delightful. The view when he kissed each one to warm them would tempt a saint. He was no saint.

"You *ken* it's no real bonfire." Mrs. Jenkins tossed the pieces of fish in flower, listening to the butter in the pan sizzle, heating. "What you plan on doing there? Some more seducing and sweet talking your way into her skirts?" Again, she waved the spatula in the air using it to make her point. "You best wed that girl before she carries another little shifter in her belly."

He took care of the extra skirts along with the hated corset yesterday, hoping she would heed his wishes. He enjoyed thinking of her bare bottom beneath her gown. "Father Damian was delayed. He'll be here by the end of the week with the intention of seeing the two of us married. The bonfire is meant to charm her. We'll stay warm there even after the sun goes down. Can your boy make sure there is a ready supply of firewood for us? As you suggested, wouldn't want her to take a chill."

"You must not have the same Fraser charm your papa was known for. Seems when he decided on wedding Heather, there was no dilly dallying around. They were wed and nine months later you were born. Seems if I'm remembering correctly, Houston only beat you by a day or two. If you two keep carrying on in this way, she'll have the *bairn* before nine months has passed. You mark my words, you scoundrel. Best you wed this little gal as soon as possible."

He picked up a fried slice of potato, "You're right. He's two days the eldest. The old man found his mate sooner than me. Nonetheless, now that I've my woman in my bedroom, we won't be needing much more time. Last night she almost told me yes."

"What did I almost say yes to?" Maisie stood in the open doorway her hands placed on her slender hips as if she meant to stand her ground. That pleased him. "You shouldn't be talking about me."

The devil, she was beautiful. Today she was dressed in pale pink that set the stunning blush on her cheeks to a simmering glow. "To marrying me. Mayhap tonight you'll answer in the affirmative. What do you think? Will you say yes to this man who adores you?"

Hawk swept her into his arms, twirling her around without allowing her feet to touch down. "You almost agreed. Now, deny that and

I'll *ken* you're not telling the truth." He understood he was taking a chance here. There was a moment though when she might have said yes to anything he asked.

She punched him on his shoulder. "No, last night you never asked. Maybe you should try asking before you start telling untruths. I'm not going to be tellin' the likes of you yes tonight."

"You would have agreed if I popped the question? I'm waiting until I stand a ghost of a chance." He grinned at her understanding she would not commit to marriage in front of another person.

"You'll never know," she sidestepped his question quite handedly. "What are we doing today? I'm certain you've something planned."

"I do."

"Another adventure?" she queried her eyes widening as if she was thinking of all the wicked things they did together.

"Father Damian will be here at the end of the week to marry us." He put the statement to her to watch for a reaction. It wasn't what he wanted to see. The beautiful rosy glow from earlier vanished, turning to a death shade.

"Hawk, we need to talk. I've got to tell you something." Her hands were formed prayer fashion next to her lips.

Her tone more than her words frightened him. Maisie's eyes were dimmed. "Tonight, you can tell me what is on your mind. As for the rest of the day, I've some things to see to. Don't mean to ignore you but there are some necessities that must be taken care of. Need to ride to the fort to make certain the Sassenach as rumored have indeed left the territory. Also intend to check on a few of the elderly residing nearby. Make certain they have any medicines they might need."

"Why is the fort so important? I understand about your patients. Would ask to go with you, but..."

"Even if you weren't afraid of horses, I've a lot of territory to cover before this evening. You would never keep up. If you did manage, you wouldn't be able to move once you tried to stand on two feet."

Reminding her he was unique to most people in this world, wasn't on the tip of his tongue. He needed to be honest with her. She might not understand there was a bounty on shifters. All he'd told her was that he was one. Tonight, if possible, he wanted to show her his cat. If there were still English soldiers in the area, he could not do so, at least not at the bonfire. To shift in the privacy of their bedroom would be the only place he could show her who he was.

"You *ken* I'm a shifter."

She nodded. "Sometime I'd like to see you in your other form. Is that why you're traveling to the fort? Once, I heard Riley talking about a bounty on shifters. He didn't use that word because he was talking to Mac. I understood though. It's awful."

Once again Mrs. Jenkins interjected her thoughts, waving her kitchen utensil in the air to give more credence to her thoughts. "You need to be showin' your woman everything about you. It's all important. You don't want her to be frightened if she catches site of you unexpectedly. A big man makes a bigger cat. You also need to make certain she understands the ceremonies that go with the wedding of a shifter. You don't want her too frightened. At least she's not a virgin. One less thing to fear.

The devil, he thought, Maisie had been white before. Now she appeared covered in arctic frost.

"Ceremonies?" Her voice quivered.

"Yes, there is the claiming of the bride as well as the Clan Chattan wedding ceremony which is in addition to the first marriage. The Chattan ceremony is only witnessed by relatives. In our case, Father Damian will be the only person there."

Clutching the table, she sat down on a chair. He knew she'd just been blindsided by the McKenna's housekeeper's foolish prattle. If there were certain things she needed to tell him about herself tonight...well...Mrs. Jenkins just put more fuel on the fire to keep her from saying yes. If he read her expression correctly, she was now terrified.

"Perhaps you should leave the rest of the story to me, Mrs. Jenkins," he spoke with a soft voice hiding his fury with the good woman who meant no harm. She didn't understand the tenuous position he was in with Maisie. Didn't understand though, Maisie, slept in his bed she was still innocent in most every way. She didn't have a mother in her later years to explain the differences between men and women or what would happen on a wedding night. With this conversation that didn't come from him, he took several huge strides backward in the wooing of his soon to be bride.

# Chapter Four

Hawk met Maisie at dinner. Mrs. Jenkins seemed to have understood her *faux pas* this morning. She remained silent keeping her thoughts to herself. The dinner rivaled any she'd ever fixed for him or his cousins. There were three types of vegetables, haggis along with bangers and mash. The ale was delicious as was the wine she procured from the McKenna cellars. He watched as Maisie ate sparingly seemingly still disturbed by the hasty words of the morning.

With still food on the table, he sat back, his hands on his belly, replete. Even if he wanted, he couldn't eat any more of the delicious fare Mrs. Jenkins laid out for them. He grinned at her, "Don't think I could eat another bite. Not even certain I can get up from the table. How about you? You ready to sit in front of a fire and watch the flames vanish into the darkened sky?"

He imagined the wood smoke, coupled with the flames. To hold her while watching the twinkling stars in the velvet blackness of the night would be heaven. In the village, the sky was never so black, the darkness seemed to reach into eternity. The clouds were few. He felt certain the moon would shine in all its splendor.

"I have eaten too much. Nonetheless, I suppose all I will have to do is sit on the horse while he takes me wherever you want to go."

With her fork, she was playing with a few pieces of sausage left on her plate. She looked at him wistfully. This morning she'd told him there were things they needed to discuss.

He wanted that also. The air between them needed to be cleansed of all uncertainties if they were to move forward.

"The bonfire is not far from the house. We will walk off some of this blessedly delicious meal. What do you say? Should we take a bottle of wine and some glasses?" Carefully watching her, he searched her expression. He was beginning to read her moods quite well. His intuition kicked in. She was afraid of what she intended to tell him. He didn't like that. Didn't she understand she could tell her mate anything? No, of course not, she didn't believe she was his mate, that they traveled though time to be together.

The moment for her to vanquish whatever was bothering her wasn't now. There would be plenty of time to talk while they watched the flames. She looked so adorable while she stared at her plate. His senses told him she was mulling over the words she would share with him.

He had life issues to share too.

"We should bring some blankets with us. I've been a *wee* bit chilled all day. Earlier my head ached but I napped."

Her voice was soft when she spoke, her eyes not as brilliantly beautiful as usual.

Alarm for her health gripped him. He reached across the table to feel her forehead. Her temperature was normal. His thumb on her wrist, her pulse was a *wee* bit fast. Perhaps because he was touching her. As far as her health went, nothing seemed off beat. His instincts told him something different.

Maisie just wasn't the same.

"Maybe we should stay home in front of the fireplace in the drawing room. There we can watch the sparks with the amber-gold flames," Hawk was quick to say, unwilling to take chances.

Maisie was a small woman, fragile in stature. Though he knew she possessed inner strength.

"No, I want to look at the stars with you. I feel fine now. Truly. The headache is gone. Shouldn't have said anything. Didn't think you would change your plans because I told you my head hurt this morning."

She shot him a precocious smile that stopped his breath for an instant.

With too many reservations to count, he asked her again. "You're certain you feel up to a walk."

As a doctor, he looked her over from head to toe. Her cheeks were a bit too pink. That could be attributed to many different scenarios. Her forehead was cool to the touch. Her pulse was normal, strong.

She nodded. "You should believe the patient."

No, many patients lied because they were afraid. He hoped she wasn't one of them. He agreed, "Very well, we'll take our warmest coats. You must promise though," he paused thinking about their life ahead of them, "if you feel at all sick, you will tell me. If your headache returns, you will let me know. If for any reason, you are chilled or hot—"

She set her finger against his lips. "Promise," her voice held a fondness he never heard before.

Perhaps she was softening toward him.

He didn't know if Shawna packed her a warm coat. If not, perhaps a sweater of his could be worn over her gown. For the first time today, he was apprehensive about this excursion. Rather than feeling eager he was concerned. He was ready to call a halt to the journey. The yearning in her expression stopped him. She left to dress warmer. He packed the supplies he needed to take. A few minutes later, he watched her skipping down the steps, a smile brightening her features.

She glowed.

Was that good or bad? All his medical instincts kicked in again. His question was probably boring her. "Are you certain you feel fine?"

"Certain as the stars will be twinkling above us and the moon will send a silver glow onto the land."

Her hands on his shoulders she stood on her tiptoes to place a chaste kiss to his cheek. She'd never done anything like that before. His heart lurched; anticipation heady.

"Very well."

He gave in to her happiness, both confused by his concerns as well as delighted with this new persona she showed him. She must be fine. His imagination was working overtime in this scenario. He seemed to be inventing problems where there were none.

Hand in hand they walked the short distance to the top of the hill where the bonfire was constructed. From here, looking to the east, he could see the cabin and stable. A ring of smoke rose from the chimney. In the other directions only forests along with heather covered hills could be seen. To Hawk this land held paradise. When he moved to Selkirk years ago, he gave up his roaming. Now that he joined with Houston, he did the same once again. He set to work on the fire. Mrs. Jenkins' boy did a fine job gathering the needed fire wood. A huge stack waited for their use including a sizable amount of kindling. He brought along a special treat for Maisie. Something he and his brothers along with the McKennas and Stuarts loved when they spent time at the bonfire. By the time the fire blazed the sun had set.

This was an evening made of dreams. Snuggled into the blankets, they each held a glass of wine. He set his down having need of both hands. Unable to stop the impulse, he kissed the side of her neck, slipped his hands beneath the sweater she wore over her dress. While he savored the moment, he undid the fasteners of her gown then the laces of her chemise. She didn't wear a corset. She gasped when his cold hands touched the heat of her body.

"Hawk, your hands are freezing!"

To no avail she pushed at them to dislodge them.

His breath feathered across her. "Will you warm them for me? As I did your toes?" He laughed beneath his breath when he felt the slight shiver of her body then the nod of her head. She would be a willing participant to all his carefully laid plans this evening.

Within moments he cupped her breasts in his hands, toyed with the tender tips that seemed sensitized to his every caress. "What was it you wanted to talk to me about?"

She leaned against him; her head tilted up giving him easy access to her neck. He took full advantage with his teeth and tongue. Somehow, he realized if he continued in this way, they would not have that needed discussion for some time nor would they have the delightful treat he brought along with him. Tonight, he hoped to savor every moment between them. He wished to further his cause, which of course, was marriage.

"You first, don't believe I can manage to think let alone talk," she sighed mewled, appearing to enjoy the way his mouth traveled down her neck and his hands played with the full pink jewels he adored.

Keeping his hands to himself was so very impossible. Without conscious effort she tantalized and intrigued him.

"No, I've other plans for the moment. Leave your gown just the way it is. Don't you dare fasten anything." He reached for two green sticks that had sharpened ends. "One for you and one for me." He chuckled at her confused look. The way her eyes sparkled in the brilliant firelight created mercuric sensation that raced to his loins. He needed for his body to behave until the time was right for the sensual activity he planned.

"What are these for?" She held the blanket over her bared breasts with one hand, in the other she held the stick.

"To cook marshmallows. What did you think?" He handed her two of the white confections then placed two on his stick. "Like this." He waved the stick in the air. "I'm going to roast them. They are delicious."

Hawk leaned toward the flames extending his stick so the marshmallow was in the coals. "If you want to burn them, put them straight into the flames. If you want them toasted to perfection, you can find some coals. Like this."

He kept eyes on both his sugary treat as well as her. He wanted to watch her maneuver the blankets along with the marshmallows hoping to get a glimpse of tender white flesh, perhaps also a ripe pink bud.

Much to his chagrin, she did a splendid job of keeping herself concealed from his inquisitive eyes as well as roasting the treat. The quilt only slipped once. He caught sight of one rounded globe before she pulled the fabric back into place. For the time it took to cook them, they sat in silence. His were done first. He slipped one off the stick, placing it on her lips.

"See if you like this." He rubbed the marshmallow across her mouth.

Giggling, Maisie opened for him taking a small bite. Bits of white clung to her lips while she chewed. "How did you dream up this?"

"It was an accident," Hawk laughed delighted when she allowed him to feed her another piece. "Does this mean I get yours?"

With light brushes of his lips against hers he caught the leftovers with his tongue.

"Only if I can feed them to you," Maisie told him as she held one to his lips. Her fingers became part of the bite. She gasped as he sucked. "You cheat."

"You taste better than the marshmallow," he explained himself.

Minutes ticked by as they continued roasting then feeding each other. "I'm sticky," Maisie finally said as she licked one of her fingers.

"Allow me." Hawk pulled her back in front of him. With his lips and tongue, he collected the bits left behind from her fingers. She was sweet, so very tasty. He handed her wine. He sipped his then set it back on the flat surface. "Suppose we should have that discussion now."

His hands once again roamed beneath the blanket. With his fingers exploring soft curves, he was more interested in her delicious body than he was in talking though now was the time to put some of their concerns to rest.

Hawk didn't think he'd ever felt quite so relaxed or pleased. Maisie was in his arms. The stars twinkled above and the fire blazed in front of them. All he needed now was to discover what she was anxious to tell him.

"You were going to tell me about the fort and why you spent the day traveling the hills," she said. "I imagine, I've a few guesses. I did listen to Riley several times when he spoke to Mac about shifting. They had to be cautious all the time. Mac, however, is a two-year-old. One can only say so much."

He found her tender flesh still unfettered beneath the blanket, fondled the softness he discovered waiting for him. "The fort, ah yes...there are only a handful of soldiers there. Nonetheless, the English are still a strong presence in the highlands. I'll not be showin' you my cat tonight if that is what you are getting at. Perhaps when we return to our bedroom, I could give you a glimpse of the different me. Would you like that?"

He needed to see her reaction to the change. Thought of teasing her in his other form. Chasing her might be entertaining. She would not be able to get away from him. Though he didn't need to be in his cat to catch her.

"Now, sweet one, did you do as I asked?"

"What are you talking about?"

He reached beneath her skirt hoping she followed his directive from the night before. He wished to find no fabric barring him from his heavenly goal. "Naughty girl." He nipped her neck once then twice. "You're wearing far too many petticoats that I must struggle with to touch you. I can't allow that. What should we do? Hmm... seems I told you I would burn all your underclothing if you thought to put them on. You disobeyed."

Before she could react to his words, they were off. He tossed the snowy white fabric into the fire. The fabric caught the flames, sizzling to nothing. She had no time to protest. "Hawk! What do you think you are you doing?"

"Umm..." Hawk settled his mouth on a small red mark at the base of her neck, sucking and nipping while she arched against him seeming to have forgotten her earlier distress. Moving back, he stopped, appearing to study his handiwork. "I told you what would happen. Didn't you believe me? Now you know better."

She grunted, holding on to one of his hands that fondled her breast, tweaking the tender tight bud until she could only make incoherent sounds in the back of her throat. Finally, she was able to speak when he quit kissing her. "N...no...didn't...well...no I didn't think you would do as you said. Why would you do something so absurd? You threw them in the fire. They burned."

I don't lie, sweetheart. If I tell you I will do something, you should always believe me. For me it's not absurd or crazy. I like thinking about you naked beneath your gown, one thin layer of fabric between you and me. If you wish to keep your petticoats or corsets, you will not wear them any longer." He stroked her, touched as well as teased her.

She nodded as if she understood now. Once again, she was naked beneath the fabric of her dress. They could continue from here. Her protests seemed to have stopped. She enjoyed his attentiveness.

"What else would you like to know about my day?"

He understood her questions would have to come first. She would need to get used to him, his hands wherever he wanted to investigate. If he had his way this evening, he would make certain she learned about a woman's pleasure. He hoped to see her expression when she spiraled into another dimension, into the delightful ecstasy he would provide.

"Let me see. Saw old Sadie. Seems to me the woman has always looked the same from one year into the next. She doesn't age. Either that or she aged in the first part of her life. Now she builds little statues made from peat. They are ingenious. It is fortunate for her she comes from a wealthy family. Her brother provides for her needs. She is a bit touched in the head. Years ago, when she was a child, she fell from her horse. Hit her head and hasn't been the same since. Sadie is harmless."

"Sadie? Does she have a last name? You said her brother provided?" Maisie queried while his fingers explored lower.

Her gown was hiked up her crossed legs. She was open to him. His fingers were touching her, roaming along her ribcage, sashaying across her breasts, massaging her belly. She twisted within his arms reaching for more pleasure. Hawk enjoyed her soft sighs of pleasure.

"Not that I know of. She's always been ol'Sadie to all of us. Houston checks on her occasionally whenever he's out this way. She collects peat for her fires along with her statues. Has an old dog she keeps with her for protection as well as company. "She was doing fine. She offered me lunch. We ate together then I saw Colton."

"...and he was..."

"Again, just fine except he hurt his leg in a trap. You see he shifted to run free. It's a dangerous past time in the crags. The Sassenach set traps to catch shifters. He managed to change back to a human so he could rid himself of the steel jaws that could have ended his life. Unfortunately, he had to walk back to his cabin naked. I gave him some salve to stop the infection that might settle in."

"You shift naked?" she asked sounding surprised.

"Yes, don't wish to ruin clothing. Now it's your turn...how did you spend your day?" he inquired understanding that while she didn't need to speak of her day doing so might be an easy stepping stone into what was bothering her.

"No," she placed her hand on his, pushing against his strength. "Stop...Hawk don't. You don't know...can't understand."

He fondled her nipple tugging, "I want to understand though. You don't expect me to stop, sweet one. Do you?"

He withdrew his hand that had found the tiny pearl that would give her the ecstasy she deserved. He sensed her fear. The terror didn't come from their intimacy. The anxiety he read in her was caused by something else. He imagined they would have to get past her apprehension. He kept his hand where it was even though he stopped in his quest. Listened to her breathing as she tried to tug air into her parched lungs.

"No, but I'm afraid that once I tell you...tell...well...you might not want anything to do with me. You might be horrified."

Her tiny hand was wrapped around his wrist. No longer was she pushing him away but urging him closer. He pressed against her telling her in the only way he knew that he wasn't going anywhere.

"Should I give you pleasure first then we can speak of your fears, the anxiety that has you turning away from me when you should be doing the opposite. You are not afraid of me. Are you, Maisie? It's something else that holds fear in your heart to such an extent you are terrified of being with a man. What have you seen that you shouldn't have?"

Hawk didn't believe her fear came from anything that happened to her. She was too willing to allow his explorations. Too curious by far as to what he would do next. Seemed to revel in the intimacy between them. What Maisie saw happened to a second party, most likely her mother before Maisie was brought to Highland Manor. From what Shawna told him, her grandfather never acknowledged her. That wouldn't create the fears she felt with him.

"Yes," she told him, breathless, panting with her need.

"If you talk to me, you'll feel better."

When he entered her with his fingers, she was so small, so tight and hot. Hawk moved his fingers in then out, again and again while he massaged the sensitive nubbin with his thumb. She was spiraling higher. Unable to help herself she arched against him. He sucked on her neck; bit, laved in that same spot while he intensified his assault on her breast along with the sweetest vagina he'd ever been inside. He moved at a slow pace, easing her way, bringing her to that peak she would want to know again then again. If she allowed him, next time his member would be inside her. She would understand pain then pleasure. They would proceed with all the clan ceremonies then they would be united through life. It was his greatest wish.

When her sheathe began to pulse against his fingers, he understood she would climax soon. "Let it go, Little One. I've got you. Relax and let all the feelings swamp you. They will rush over you, take all of you for the moment. The pleasure will vibrate deep inside the heat of you." Her breath rushed out in a fragmented sound. She purred. Sighed softly. Cried out when the climax overtook her body. She continued to writhe against him, her body responding sweetly to him.

"Hawk!"

She gripped his wrist tighter as if it was her lifeline. Moments passed while she eased to normalcy. He stayed inside her wishing his penis were where his fingers were. Soon. He felt her maidenhead. Knew there would be pain on their wedding night. There was nothing he could do to relieve what would happen. She would also feel his claws when he claimed her as his own.

*Well, hell!*

Why? He saw no reason, no reason at all that a woman would have pain before she could explore the pleasure at the hands of a man, her mate.

Time passed while they didn't speak, didn't move except to breathe. She was calming now, her breaths coming much easier. He felt the slow relaxation of her muscles then with lingering regret pulled his fingers from inside her. Felt her flinch as they moved in her tiny sheathe.

After several moments passed, she spoke, "That was not fair of you..." she sighed again.

He could see her breath in the frosty night air. At least encompassed by the quilts and surround by their body heat, they were warm.

"Not fair?" he asked as he settled his hands on her belly, measured the width, hoping children would be in their future.

She would bear her *bairns* with ease. Her hips were wide. "That I don't want you to wear all your petticoats and stays or that I gave you immense pleasure?" he spoke, watching her, studying her.

"Neither, at least I wasn't thinking about that until you suggested it."

"Not fair?" he asked again wishing to know her unfettered thoughts.

He sensed what she was about to say but needed to hear the words.

"That you can manipulate me without trying very hard. That I turn to liquid mush when you touch me. I did not intend to give into your charming self."

He knew she closed her eyes.

"That is some of what I need to talk to you about."

He felt the shiver, felt her indrawn breath as she seemed far too relaxed. He thought that perhaps they should head for home. The sky was dark, endlessly black except for the glimmering stars and the slipper of the silver moon that sat high on the horizon. Several minutes ticked by while he held her and thought about all that was still between them, separating them, keeping them from uniting as a couple. For her to come to his way of thinking he would have to do far more than seduce. He would have to understand her past then find a way to make her believe his feelings for her wouldn't change.

"We should head back." Hawk's mind reeled. He had a bad feeling. The night no longer seemed glorious. To ignore his instincts twice in a matter of a few hours would never be prudent or wise.

She sat up pulling her dress closer despite the presence of his hand. Staring into his eyes she spoke feeling uncertain as to how to proceed. "It was my mother, the second party," she blurted as her voice wavered.

Her hand on his chest, she'd turned to look at him. Her eyes were closed but she swayed. Maisie gripped the fabric of his shirt as if it was a lifeline. "I don't want to be so dependent on a man that I have no choices. I am though. If I stay with you, I'll have no identity. If I don't, I'll have to live with Shawana and Riley for the rest of my life. I would be underfoot, in their way constantly. Would never have a child of my own."

The shaking he now felt was not coming from the end of her climax. There was something else causing the shivers. "You will always be you. If you marry me, you will become part of me just as I will be part of you. One could say we would both lose our independence. To my mind that is not a bad thing. What did you see of your mother?"

Her fingers gripped the cloth of his shirt so tight the material pulled across his back. "Before she died, she had a protector. Unlike my father, he was not a nice man. He made her do things to him she didn't want to do. She had no choices. Without the income from this man, we would have been lost on the streets, starving. I suppose if I had not been born, she might have risked her life. With me in tow, she could not."

"What?" His brows drew together.

Her words shocked him though he understood they should not. The sooner he got to the crux of the problem the better. The directions of his thoughts were horrific. No woman should be made to perform sexually. "What did he make her do?"

For several seconds she looked away. When she returned her attention. "He couldn't...I heard him...he couldn't get hard. He made her kneel in front of him. She had to take him into her mouth until he could penetrate her. I heard him use those words. They are like a nightmare in my head."

"Oh god...Maisie, I'm sorry. You were so young. Didn't your mother keep you..." He was beginning to comprehend more than he wanted.

"Mama tried. She would tell me to go to bed and not open the door no matter what I heard. I know now from what I remember, she wanted me to be in my bedroom. He insisted that they start in the main room. My bedroom door opened to that room."

"The man knew you would look. He wanted you to see them together to see what he was doing to your mother."

The thoughts Hawk had now about what went on were way too clear. "Maisie, that man wanted you. Doubted if he cared that much about your mother. He liked little girls. If your mother hadn't passed on and if Shawna hadn't found you before he could get his hands on you, you would be under that man's protection. Your life would have been very different." He pulled her close, cradled her head with his hand against his chest. Silent prayers he sent heavenward as well as to Shawna for reading the letter that was directed to her grandfather.

Rocking her, he tried to ease the nearly silent sobs. She was so precious, so adorable. Her mother had been placed in an indefensible position and did all that she could to shield Maisie. Her efforts were not good enough. The fire began to die down. They needed to get home. It didn't seem she wanted to move. He began to think she might have fallen asleep in his arms. If she did, they could stay until she woke. Something wasn't quite right. The sleep wasn't an easy peaceful one.

With the back of his knuckles, he lightly stroked her cheek. "Maisie?" Alarmed, Hawk touched his hand to her forehead. Held it there for several seconds absorbing the implications of what he felt as well as attempting to deny the heat. She was burning. He had to cool her. Sometime since leaving for this place that was meant to set the stage for their marriage a fever set into her body. She was sick, very sick.

"I don't feel so well," she moaned, her hand on her stomach. "I'm dizzy. The ground seems to be turning." She laughed, the sound thin then grimaced when she looked at him, her fingers on his chin. "There are two of you."

He didn't care about the supplies he brought to the bonfire or that it had begun to rain. The rain slicker he brought with him he swathed around her. Before he could begin to run, rain fell in torrents to the earth. Sideways rain beat against them. He cursed. Had not seen the tempest coming. With Maisie cradled in his arms, Hawk set off at a swift pace toward the cabin. She was shivering, moaning. Her teeth chattered. He felt certain her lips would be blue by the time he got her home. He should kick himself. Ignoring his instincts always got him into trouble. This time was no different.

His heart racing, Hawk two stepped the front porch stairs, hollering for his housekeeper. Brought up short by the sight of Mrs. Jenkins standing in the doorway to the kitchen drying her hands on a towel, he said another silent prayer. The heavens answered with a bolt of lightning then the roar of thunder.

"You two are back sooner than expected. Why, I thought half the night would be gone before I saw the two of..." She broke off seeming to realize something was dreadfully wrong. "What happened? Is she hurt?"

"What are you doing here?" Hawk asked noting that his voice wasn't exactly amenable. He ignored her questions, his thoughts centered on Maisie.

She bristled, indignation taking the forefront. She started to flap the dishtowel at him then with abruptness changed her mind. "Thought the two of you young people might need some warming when you returned. That's what I be doin' here. You're all wet, goodness gracious that can't be good for either of you." It was then she seemed to notice that the slicker was wrapped around Maisie and that water dripped from him pooling on the floor by his feet. "I've heated water. Have it waiting for the two you. You take her upstairs. I'll be there in a minute."

Hawk garnered a small measure of control. He would need her to help tonight, then tomorrow depending on the intensity of the fever. Using all the control he could muster to absolve the fear penetrating his mind, he spoke. After all, he was a doctor. For a few minutes because the patient was Maisie, he panicked. "Maisie had a fever now. She's chilled in every part of her. Got to warm her up then put her to bed. While she is freezing now all that will change. In a few hours she will most likely be burning up. I will have to be with her the entire night. You understand she is very sick."

Mrs. Jenkins straightened her back seeming to comprehend the situation now that he got around to explaining it to her. "Got water heating on the stove. If you take the little one up to your room, I'll see to her. There's enough water for both of you to bathe and warm yourselves."

"I'll see to her," Hawk gritted out through clenched teeth. He wasn't about to leave Maisie alone. She needed his expertise.

"Yes, you will, as soon as you've seen to yourself. What good is it to be a doctor when you haven't the good sense to make sure you don't catch what your patient has. When you can't figure out that you need to take care of yourself before you can do her any good, how will you help her?"

In her usual fashion, having tucked the dishtowel into her apron strings, she was shaking her finger at him. "Soon as you warm up you come figure out what is wrong with Miss Maisie. I'll get her into the tub with hot water."

Arguing with her would take too much time as well as effort since she was right. He was pigheaded. Stubborn pride would do no good here. He took a hot bath in the scullery behind the kitchen then dressed in the dry warm clothing Mrs. Jenkins brought downstairs. Terrified of what he might find, he headed up the steps.

By the time he reached his bedroom, Maisie was lying on the bed in a pink flannel nightdress. The covers were pulled to her chin. Sweat beaded on her forehead. She moaned then whimpered, trying to push the covers from herself. She was too weak.

Beneath his breath, he swore, cursed in several languages. It seemed Maisie was warm now. Sitting on the chair Mrs. Jenkins placed next to the bed, he felt her forehead. She was hot, much too hot. Her face was red. The bath must have heated her more than necessary. Now she needed to be cooled. The flannel gown would have to vanish.

"Is she going to be alright?" Mrs. Jenkins asked. Now, she was wringing her hands, her eyes filled with moisture. "Got her bath too hot. Didn't I?"

"We'll see. I'm certain all will turn out just perfect. None of this is your fault. That's just the way a fever goes until it has run its course."

He was terrified. Her fever was spiking. He didn't want to argue with the housekeeper but he needed to cool her off. Needed to get her out of the flannel clothing so he could run a cool damp cloth over her body. He held up his hands to ward off the comments that would undoubtedly come his way. "Remember, I'm the doctor here."

He pulled the covers from her. The buttons on her nightdress drew his attention next. After that he pulled her to a sitting position to rid her of the gown.

"Never questioned that you are a doctor. What I do know is that...never mind. The little one has been in your bed. I'm certain the two of you have been intimate," she said indignantly a slight hmmf...in her tone. "What can I do now?"

"Nothing. Maisie was chilled bone deep when we arrived here. This instant, she is boiling hot. Now that I've got her out of the dressing gown, I'm going to need cool water. She might have to go back into the tub when it's cold." His urgency was something he never felt before while dealing with his patients. Maisie wasn't just any patient.

"I'll help." Mrs. Jenkins tested the water left in the tub. "It's tepid. Is that good enough?"

"No, to both questions, go home, Mrs. Jenkins. Before you do that, bring me some cool water along with a soft cloth. Once you are home, have the mister and your son put out the bonfire then bring in the supplies I left there. Get a good night's rest then come early tomorrow morning. I might need sleep by then. I'll tend to her the rest of the night. If necessary, we will take turns seeing to her needs."

Hawk wanted to believe he could stay awake until she recovered. He knew better. He would lie down beside her. Hold her tight when she was chilled, cool her when she was burning. That way he would be in tune with her changing temperature. Maisie was very sick. He didn't know what it was she had but the fever was intense. She would feel as if she was burning up from the inside out. Restlessly, she moved on the bed turning over only to turn over another time.

She groaned then whimpered, hugging her arms around herself when she was cold, spread eagled on the bed when fever burned.

Since he managed to take the nightgown off, she was naked in his bed just as he wanted, almost as he wanted. Against the despair swamping him, he closed his eyes for a few seconds reliving those moments at the bonfire before her temperature shot to the sky. He pushed hair that fell into his eyes away from his face. Maisie liked to do that for him, move that piece of hair that always managed to fall into his eyes away so it was where it was supposed to be.

Throughout the night he cooled her with the damp cloth then held her in his arms to warm her. She tossed around on the bed, shoving on him when he ran the wetness across her, moaned when the flames inside her slender body grew too intense. By morning he could barely keep his eyes open. Presently, she was covered with a thin sheet. Hawk had just taken her from the cold bath then dried her before placing her on the bed.

Mrs. Jenkins was a welcome sight. She busied herself in the kitchen bringing up chicken soup for Maisie. He prayed she would be able to swallow most of the broth. He sat behind her, holding her up while Mrs. Jenkins fed her. More soup dribbled down her chin than found its way into her stomach.

Fear gripped Hawk. Terror filled his veins, pulsing hard and deep. He was afraid she might not live. He had to marry her soon, somehow claim her so he could join her in another life.

He had no choice.

She would argue if she could but she had no choice.

~ * ~

Maisie sighed softly staring into the darkness of the night. So far, the night progressed wonderfully. She felt comfortable as well as relaxed in his arms. Tension tonight didn't plague her. The flames flickered into the sky, sparks shooting out to land on the ground. She understood she was falling under his spell. The cooked marshmallows were a delicious as well as unexpected treat. She laughed with him when the roasted marshmallows stuck to them. When he tossed her petticoats into the fire she sputtered with heartfelt indignation. He would do what he wished. She supposed she didn't care. It was enticing to know she was naked beneath her gown and that he wanted her that way. The feeling excited her in ways she didn't comprehend. Perhaps he would know that.

He touched her and she yearned to be caressed again. When Hawk spoke of the Sassenach, she understood his fears. After she told him about her mother, she was surprised by his reaction. She'd never thought the man might have expected her to do the same things to him that he insisted of her mother.

She never thought beyond the horror her mother endured for her. She imagined mothers were like that, placing their children before them.

While she wasn't afraid of sex with Hawk, she had misgivings. Most of the misgivings revolved around her parent's relationship then the ones after that when she was expected to participate.

There was the fact he was so perfect, so very handsome. She didn't believe she could live up to expectations such as those. When she began to feel hot, she thought it was because of him coupled with the way he touched her body. When he brought her to a pinnacle so high and so demanding she lost control, he became cemented in her heart. She understood then she could never give the man a negative answer. If he wanted to make love to her, she would always say yes.

Oh...she couldn't stop thinking. He tossed her underclothing into the fire! She should be furious with the man. She wasn't. He would do the same if he discovered her wearing them again. She wouldn't have any left. Shawna only packed a few. Why would she need more?

Now she felt as if she was burning from the inside out. All the heat wasn't sparked from his attentions. She closed her eyes. When she began to sob, he placed her head against his chest. She heard the soothing beat of his heart. The fluid intake then outtake of his breaths. It was a good feeling. Her crying began after she told her story then changed to sobs of anguish from the heat simmering inside her body.

"Maisie?" he queried as he talked to her. Coupled with more comments or questions.

She didn't understand what he was saying or what he was asking her. She heard herself groan. Wanted to tell him how hot she was but she couldn't speak the words, or did she? She didn't know what was her imagination or what was real.

When he suddenly picked her up and wrapped his rain slicker around her, she was surprised she knew what he did. To her astonishment, Hawk started running. It had to be toward the house. During his race to the cabin, she was in and out of consciousness. When he confronted Mrs. Jenkins, she heard his voice. Didn't remember what they said to each other. The world around her turned black. She floated in a blissful dream that turned to a horrific nightmare. When the strange dream began, snow and ice encompassed her. She shivered, her teeth chattering as she gasped for each stunted breath of air.

Now the sun beat down upon her, heating her. She wanted to find shade, searched for the snow and ice knowing that was all that could soothe the heat flaming inside. With her knuckles in her mouth, she stifled the moan. Didn't want Hawk to worry about her. Hawk wasn't with her. It was Mrs. Jenkins who stripped her putting her in the tub. The water was too hot. She burned, desperate to remove herself, her arms and legs didn't work. Tears slid down her cheeks. Helplessness swamped her drowning her in burning fire.

She tried to tell the housekeeper. The words wouldn't form. Unexpectedly, she found herself hauled from the bath then scrubbed dry. After that she was dressed in flannel then thrust beneath the covers. Maisie couldn't get out from under the terrible heat. Moaning, she closed her eyes falling into another wretched nightmare where she floundered in flames that surrounded her. She tried to fight. Found that she was helpless.

Cool air swept across her. The gown vanished. She was lying naked in the bed, her eyes open to see Hawk. He wiped her down with a cool cloth. The inferno still burned inside but the heat was not as bad. The cycle of heat and cold continued. She didn't know how long.

Hawk tried to feed her. She wasn't hungry.

It was no good. Nothing he did helped. She thought she would die without ever knowing Hawk. He'd been good to her. Would they ever meet in another lifetime if she died now? As her mind wandered in then out of the daze, she found herself living within herself. She questioned all that she'd done, all that she wanted to be.

"Father Damian, thank you for coming." Hawk was speaking.

To her muddled brain, he sounded distant.

The priest arrived. Was it to give her last rights?

"There was no choice now was there? I'm here to help in every way possible. I don't wish this on any of the clan. Do you think she will live?"

No, she didn't want to die. She also didn't want to hear Hawk's answer to that question. As she opened her eyes, the room spun then shifted. The floor turned to the ceiling. Maisie closed them again, straining to listen to the two men.

"There is no way to know. If the fever doesn't break soon..." Hawk spoke so softly, fear in his voice rang out loudly.

*Live or die?*

He didn't commit one way or the other. She found she wanted to live. She also remembered that Hawk threatened to bring Father Damian her to marry them. Perhaps this wasn't last rites.

"This is dire..."

The men left the room. She heard the door shut behind them as their booted feet made their way down the steps. She was left to wonder about her life. Sleep captured her. For how long, she couldn't have any idea.

When she woke, Hawk sat beside her, brushing her hair from her face, listening to her chest, testing her pulse at her wrist. He spoke, his voice sounding so far away, as if she wasn't there with him. "I'm going to marry you now. Mrs. Jenkins dressed you in a flannel nightgown. It's not the best wedding dress for a woman who deserves the world. It's not what I would have hoped for our wedding day. Nonetheless, it is what it is. It is what must be."

The kiss to her forehead was nice. She wrapped her arms around herself shivering. She didn't know if she'd rather be hot than cold. The extremes were all so horrible. Hawk held her hand in his large one. She was going to marry him today.

"You can begin," Hawk must have spoken to Father Damian.

The words of the ceremony droned on through her head for what seemed an eternity. She knew somewhere during the ceremony she slept. His knuckles ran across her cheek. He kissed her, brushed her lips with his.

"Say I do, sweetheart." He was holding her against his back. Just like that night when he touched her in so many ways. He supported her again. She would be his if she could say the words.

"I do," she murmured softly. "I do." At least she thought she said the right words. Must not have.

"Maisie," he shook her just slightly. "Say I do then I'll let you sleep for a few minutes. You will have to sign the papers."

She recalled looking at him. His silver blue eyes so very concerned there was fear shimmering in the depth. "I do." This time she must have said the words they wanted to hear. He seemed pleased with her. Maisie watched him smile. She wanted to touch that smile.

"Sleep now, I'll be back in about an hour."

He laid her gently on the bed.

Once more she heard bits and pieces of the discussion concerning her.

"I brought the white cape." It was a woman's voice. She didn't recognize the voice.

"Thank you, mother. Don't know if she would survive the Clan Chattan ceremony," he said the tone so very soft yet worried. She heard that in his voice. Worry. Fear. Concern.

His mother was here. Who else? She heard two male voices, a

father along with his brother. She heard his sister too, teasing him in a gentle way, then encouraging him to tell him she was strong, a fighter. She would live though the simple ceremony. It was nothing to fear.

"She cannot stand," Hawk said. "She is weak and vulnerable."

"Well...then...you will lie with her, side by side throughout the journey through time. Your strength will enter her." That voice must be his brother's. "You must take care, Hawk. We all understand the concerns surrounding this situation. All this excitement might worsen the illness. The two of you cannot give this up. It must be finished today."

"I will not claim her while she is ill," Hawk told his father.

"I understand, nor would I if it was Heather who was in grave danger of dying. The ceremony will be done. Here is the cloak. We will all return in a few minutes to witness this uniting of two spirits."

Once more she heard the footsteps leaving the room then the door closing. She felt the dip of the bed when he sat down beside her. Felt his hand caress her shoulder.

His voice so solemn when he spoke surprised her. "We are going to undress, both of us. I will help you. The cloak will cover you so that none of the witnesses to the ritual will see you naked. This is an important ceremony for us, Maisie, for my clan. If it wasn't, I would wait until you were able to participate more completely."

While he talked to her, he undressed her. Soon, she was naked in front of him. Maisie heard nothing for a few seconds then he wrapped them both in a cloak. He lay down beside her. His naked body was pressed against hers. She felt his warmth along with his power and strength. Some of that power seemed to enter her. They would not do this now except he feared she wouldn't live.

"During the time that Father Damian chants to us, you will see me and you in our previous lives. Don't be frightened. No one will hurt you." He was stroking her back, reassuring, always reassuring and encouraging.

She was locked in his arms. Her eyes closed, she listened to the nonsensical words, the humming, the vibrating of the air. Father Damian droned on and on. She passed into the light of a different world. Her body seemed disconnected floating above them on a cushion of air. She saw them with clear eyes; Hawk, Father Damian then his family.

Fire enclosed her. This time she didn't burn from the inside out. Heat encompassed her body. The warmth was almost pleasant. She saw a huge black panther sitting on a craig. He stared at her as if he meant to force her to his will. An eerie silence encircled her. The big cat told her she would survive if she had the will to do so. The power was hers and hers alone. She should not give up. The panther was joined by a woman. The lady rested her hand on his head then ran from him laughing. The cat darted after her. Soon the animal was in his human form twirling her in great circles until they tumbled breathless to the mossy ground beneath their feet.

More scenes shifted through her head. She began to understand more completely what the McKenna clan stood for. They were the Clan Chattan. Hawk ran with her through the mossy glen where he took her that first day. They splashed in the water. He kissed her. With infinite care, he undressed her. The intimacy so strange when she watched him make love to her in a different time.

The fire slowed, the flames dying to change to water. Liquid drops of rainwater fell upon her, cooling her, dousing the earlier flames. In its brilliance, Maisie saw the sun shine, saw that they were meant to live together forever into eternity. The wind dried her. She came to him naked. He shifted into his cat. As she saw him the first time, she placed her hand on his head. He purred, rubbing himself along her leg. Maisie sipped in a huge piece of air as if she felt his soft fur against her.

The dreams stopped. The wind died to nothing. She was awake now, pressed against his length. She felt his member hard against her belly. They were wed now in almost every way. He would consummate the marriage. Now he would make love to her. She wanted that but she was so tired, too exhausted to do so.

"Hawk?" Maisie saw him clearly, witnessed the worry in his beautiful eyes. Saw the love shining through.

He never told her he loved her. She saw the emotion though, noticeable in the way he looked at her. Then, so very drained, she closed her eyes. Maisie slept. The sleep was peaceful.

When she woke, Hawk was next to her. His head was pillowed on the bed while he sat in a chair next to the bed. She set her hand on his head, just as she'd done to him while he was in his cat form. The memory of the dream was so very sharp in her mind. She looked at him with new eyes, enlightened eyes.

When he lifted his head, Maisie saw dark circles rimming his silver-blue eyes. Beard stubble grew on his chin. "You don't look very good," she whispered, her voice scratchy her throat parched. "Water?"

"Maisie? You're awake!" Hawk reached for the glass of water, held it to her mouth. She drank while the clear refreshing liquid dribbled down her chin. She put her hand on his wrist. "Enough," he said.

She wanted more. She nodded to him, accepting the fact he didn't want to give her more liquid. "Why do you look as if you haven't slept in weeks?"

Hesitant, she touched him, ran her hand along his broad shoulders. She wasn't embraced in the cold or the heat. Nothing in the room spun. She inhaled a long deep breath of air feeling as if her world was no longer topsy-turvy.

"Ten days..." he told her. "It's been ten days since your fever started. Ten days since I slept more than a few minutes at a time. Mrs. Jenkins has been here to help. I couldn't leave you. Was too afraid."

Maisie recalled the fever, the terrible burning, after that the freezing cold. "I was very sick then?"

She needed answers to her questions. Remembered saying I do...twice. Recalled signing her name to papers. After that the chanting ceremony came to her mind, the scenes with this man in another place and time. She saw him as an amazing cat.

"You're well now." Hawk flashed her a beautiful smile then strode to the door. "Mrs. Jenkins, she is awake." He turned back to her. "Are you hungry."

"No, I don't think so." To belie the point, Maisie's stomach seemed to have a different opinion as it rumbled making a loud, obnoxious noise.

He was still at the door. "Bring some of that chicken broth. We'll see if it sits well in her stomach. If it does, she can have something more to eat."

"I've been sick for ten days. Did you marry me? Without my

permission?" she blurted the question wondering why she would think that yet knowing they did wed. "Your family was here. Weren't they? I was naked lying in this bed with you." She was confused, embarrassed to her core. What she told him sounded so strange, so unbelievable. She would swear it all happened.

"Yes, to all questions."

She was silent for a few seconds as she tried to absorb the truth. "I was willing? How? I signed papers? We are man and wife?" The very idea left her reeling. She recalled bits and pieces of that day. Nothing solid, nothing that she could grab hold of. She understood it all happened.

"You seemed to be willing. There was no coercion on my part, just desperation coupled with the fear you might not survive the fever. We were left with no choice expect to cement our relationship before it might be too late for us now as well into the future. Father Damian agreed what we chose to do was the only way."

"I saw your cat several times. Saw myself laughing and running with you," she told him as Mrs. Jenkins walked through the door with a bowl of steaming soup.

No longer did she want to think of death. Now she needed to live in the present, to adapt to Hawk. She was his wife just as he wanted three years ago. "We are meant to be together." She mulled over the statement realizing the complete truth of the notion.

"Yes." He drew in a long deep breath she suspected was one of relief. "You will tell me more about what you saw during the clan ritual."

It wasn't a question but a statement. The knowledge was something he needed. She understood that.

With the soup bowl in hand, he sat beside her, feeding her the broth. He dabbed at a drip on her chin. He laughed. The sound was carefree. It seemed a weight had been lifted off his broad shoulders.

"I'm certain I can feed myself."

She felt a bit put out that he treated her as a child, but when she tried to hold the bowl, she was too weak. She lifted her shoulders, slanted him a look, accepting that she would not be able to do some things for a time. She would grow stronger. She absolutely hated this. Disliked intensely the idea that she had to be waited on, spoon fed. It wasn't to be.

When she finished with the soup several minutes later, he sat back on the bedside chair crossing his arms in front of him. She was confused by the expression on his face coupled with the silence between them. She waited for him to act the doctor or the husband by telling her how life would be.

"What now? I would eat more." Once more her stomach rumbled convincingly that she was hungry still.

"Do you feel any nausea? Sick to your stomach?" Hawk asked as his look of indifference disappeared from his well-chiseled features. "If not, what would you like to eat? Solid foods we'll take one tiny bit at a time."

"Warm bread covered with butter and honey," Maisie told him with a contented little sigh on her lips. She felt fatigued though she'd only been awake a short time. She would eat then nap. That would please the good doctor. He told her earlier she needed to rest.

"I'll get it for you. Considering you have eaten next to nothing for ten days; your stomach won't be able to hold much at any one time. I will make sure there is something nearby for you to eat when the mood hits."

After he left the room, she leaned back on the headboard. She lost ten days of her life. Had been so ill, Hawk feared for life. To bring Father Damian here and to wed her when she was barely conscious was a move of a desperate and worried man. She felt in limbo now, a person caught between two worlds. Eventually, she would have agreed to the marriage. This change was happening way too fast.

When he appeared at the door, he was grinning as if pleased with himself. I've brought bread just as you ordered." He set the tray on top her lap. "Don't overeat," he warned her. "Just until you feel satisfied. No more."

It looked and smelled delicious. Her mouth watered. "Right now, I feel as if I could eat everything you just put in front of me."

She paused for a moment to regard the wonderful scent of the bread. Exhausted from the short conversation, she rested her head on the backboard.

She was mistaken about eating all the food. Maisie found she could eat only half of a very large slice before she didn't want more. "Will you leave the bread here? I know that in a few minutes I'll want to eat the other half."

"Whatever you like. All you need do is pull the cord. Someone will be here with whatever you need."

He sat on the bed beside her his long legs stretched out in front and crossed at his ankles. He was the picture of a very sated and relaxed man. When she woke from the illness, he appeared the opposite.

"We'll take this one day at a time. As soon as you are up to travel, we'll go home. I've been away from my practice longer than I expected. Houston sent word that everything was going fine. While I'm certain what he says is true, I'm also positive he is overworked."

"Home, a home I've never seen."

Even in her excitement that she was alive as well as wed to the man she loved, she couldn't keep her eyes from closing. Sleep seemed to take over all her wishes to remain awake. Before she completely fell asleep, she heard his soft chuckle, felt his hand touch her forehead, testing, always testing.

When she opened her eyes again, the room was nearly dark. Hawk had left a candle burning on the windowsill. He also left a bell cord on the bed for her to ring for him when she woke. Before she did, she took a moment to take in all the scents as well as sounds rejoicing in the fact she was alive.

After she pulled it, he arrived all grins, his white teeth flashing in the dim light of the room. "I've fresh bread along with a few slices of ham and cheese." Chuckling with delight, he set the tray on her lap. He sat in the chair beside the bed to wait for her. She ate more this time. When she was finished, he moved the food aside.

"You look too serious. You shaved."

Maisie wanted to run her hands along the now smooth lines of his face then into his hair. He had soft hair, silken to her fingers. She thought on the night of the bonfire and the way his fingers touched her. Heat rose to her cheeks. She'd been so wanton, even brazen. She didn't care at the time. Now, she wondered if he would do similar things to her when they slept together.

"Yes, and yes. I want you to get up and walk. Just around the room. I'll stay by your side. You might find yourself a bit unsteady on your feet. Don't want you to fall."

"Why?"

Maisie decided she was curious about his words. It would be nice to walk. She found she needed to relieve herself too.

"Because you need to be able to get back and forth from the water closet on your own if I'm not around to help. Also..." Hawk touched the tip of her nose. "Some doctors believe exercise helps the patient heal. I'm one of those. Don't want you to do a lot to begin. When you are finished, you should sleep."

"I'm not at all sleepy." She set her hand on her mouth to hide the yawn. "Seems all I've done is sleep, ten days of sleep. I want to be awake. Don't want anything to pass me by."

He hooted with laughter. "Liar. Your eyes are drooping. My best guess is that you'll finish a few more bites of the food on that tray. Walk with me. After that once you're in bed again, you'll be asleep in an instant." He snapped his fingers still chuckling.

It turned out he was right. By the time he put her to bed, she fell asleep what appeared to be the instant her head settled on her pillow. This time when she woke sun shone through the window. The morning passed without her knowing. Before she could pull the cord, he was in the room, a lunch tray in hand.

"Walk first then eat."

Despite her embarrassment, Hawk took her to the water closet then waited for her. She toddled down the corridor outside her room then back to the bedroom. Only when she finished would he allow her to eat. This same routine continued for another week. Each day she walked farther and ate more. She grew stronger.

~ * ~

He set his hand on her forehead. Looking for her temperature was something he felt compelled to do every day as well as listen to her breathing along with the sound of her heart. He examined her carefully. Didn't want to see a recurrence of the fever that might have stolen her life. "By my estimation you are ready to travel if we take the journey slow. There are inns along the way where we can rest each day. The carriage you rode in to get here will do just fine as long as you promise to tell me when you need to stop. Whether the reason is to stretch or walk or to relieve yourself, you must say the words."

She smiled at him, appearing pleased with the announcement. "Good, while this sojourn has been nice, I imagine I'm ready to begin my new life. I want to be your wife in every way, Hawk." She set her hand on his arm, her eyes so crystal clear the beauty took his breath.

"My sentiments too."

"Yes, as Mrs. Fraser. I do like the sound of that."

At her words his body hardened with the need she so easily orchestrated with her smile; her dancing eyes coupled with the suggestion of wifely duties. "Now, do you need help dressing? Mrs. Jenkins has packed us a lunch. Do believe she is eager for her life to return to normalcy. We did give her quite the whirl you know. She was frightened for you also. Whenever I couldn't keep my eyes open, she spent a great deal of time watching over you."

"She is pleased we are married," Maisie said her laughing eyes giving away thoughts she wasn't spilling forth. "She did not like the thought of you sleeping with me without the vows."

"Believe the hard woman enjoyed giving me a bad time about our sleeping arrangements. You are right. She didn't appreciate me sleeping with you before the vows were said." He lifted her chin to look more closely at her. "You are well. Are you not?" He continued to ask since the thought of her not living terrified him for far too long.

"I am well. However, before I dress for the journey, I'd like a quick bath, if that is not too much to ask? I would feel much more refreshed as well as relaxed if could soak for a few minutes. It would help me endure the long carriage ride. The hours with nothing to do."

"Anything to make the travel easier on you."

Hawk pulled the cord. Mrs. Jenkins appeared within minutes. "My wife would like a bath before we leave you in peace. Hope you have a bit of respite before your next visitors."

"The water is already heating." She shook her finger at him. "You *ken* I like to be of help. I'm just heartened we didn't lose the poor little thing."

Hawk laid out comfortable clothing for her omitting the hated petticoats and stays. "As soon as you finish, meet me downstairs. Unless you would like to share the bath."

Shaking her head at him, Maisie graced him with a soft smile. A flush of rose color blossomed on her face. "Will you ride with me in the carriage?"

"If you would like, though all the swaying and bouncing does tend to make a strong man nauseous. Let's just say, I'll begin there then see how long I last. Mrs. Jenkins will pack for you while you bathe."

He had ideas, big plans for the carriage. It would be so easy to seduce her when they were alone for miles upon miles.

"I would enjoy the conversation."

He would enjoy holding her, caressing her. Her passion needed to be aroused to such a degree, she would beg him. Perhaps tonight when they stopped for the evening, he could make love to her. His father told him a marriage feast would be prepared upon their arrival. He suspected all the traditions would be enacted. They would spend the night in one of the tower rooms at the McKenna keep. The women would prepare Maisie while he waited for the signal from his mother that all was ready for him upstairs.

At one of the two stops he should make love to her. If he did so, he would not steal her virginity on the same night he claimed her. In the eyes of God as well as man, they were wed. He didn't need to wait for all the traditions to be fulfilled.

Perhaps what those traditions entailed could be part of the conversation during the long expedition today. He wished she could ride with him. Because of her illness he never got around to teaching her. Riding lessons would be part of their future. The sooner the better. He knew of a lot of places he wished to show her. Although riding pillion with her left no room for complaints.

Hawk left the room, pacing downstairs while he waited for Maisie. This journey to the highlands did result in his marriage. Nonetheless, that same marriage needed to be consummated. He wondered what he should as well as what he should not tell his bride of a week. The pain she would feel upon their union was not a fact he wished to dwell on. As transpired all too often, he wondered what she knew as well as what she did not. Wanted to tell her what would happen to her. Her mother died before she could explain. His only hope was that Shawna might have said something.

In this he was a coward.

When she glided down the stairs, his heart leapt as it always did when he saw her. "Lovely," he murmured. She was graceful, beautiful in every way, so very calm as well as reserved. Seeing her feathers ruffled a *wee* bit was always enjoyable. He never met a woman he wished to seduce who was just as wonderful inside as she was out.

She held out her hand to him. Hawk pulled her to him, kissed her lightly, touching her. Maisie's gasp of pleasure was all he needed to encourage more exploration. He wanted to investigate all the places he missed for the last weeks. His hand cupped her butt as he wondered if she found multiple petticoats to wear. If she did, he'd remove them as soon as he could. Spending the morning in the carriage with her took on new ideas. Needing no more encouragement, his member became steel hard. Blood rushed to all his parts.

Close to her ear, delighting in the feel of her breasts pressing against his chest, he whispered, "Are you wearing your underclothing?"

He laughed at the heated blush that swept across her face. Though he wasn't certain what her blush meant. First hand, he would find out soon enough. If she wore anything they would be tossed out the window. "Come, my dear. The sooner we begin the sooner we will get there." While dawdling here and seeing the rose color paint her cheeks was nice, he was looking forward to the next stage of the journey home.

As it turned out, she recalled what he'd done that night at the bonfire. To his immense delight, Maisie wore nothing under her dress. The trip home was long as well as difficult for her. After they would eat in the evening, she would fall asleep within minutes. There were times Hawk believed he should have stayed at the cabin for another week rather than start out for home as soon as she gained strength. He did not make love to her in the carriage or otherwise, not to say he didn't think about her naked as well as in his arms nearly every waking moment. Didn't think about the way her body ignited when she was near her climax.

Her illness took a great deal from her. She was not recovering as fast as he hoped. Now as they pulled up in front of his home, he was ready to begin their life together in earnest. The time was late afternoon. She would have an hour to rest before the celebration. He would see Houston, check in with his patients.

# Chapter Five

At the last inn where they stayed the night, Hawk sent a message ahead as to when they would arrive home the next day. Before he could help Maisie from the carriage, his father was beside him giving orders. So exhausted from the two days of travel, Hawk carried Maisie into his home, setting her on the big wing chair in front of the fireplace. He hovered over her, asking her what she needed or wanted. He would give her anything.

"How is your bride?" His mother carried a tray holding a pot of tea and a few treats for them. "Did you push her too hard?"

The words were condemning. Hawk knew a moment of guilt.

Hawk didn't think he pushed hard. Maisie never complained. For the greater part of the excursion, she remained calm as well as quiet. The trip here did not occur as he hoped.

Maisie sat up, obviously disturbed by his mother's question. Her eyes flashed while she arranged her skirt around her legs. She was showing a bit of sass, a good sign he hoped. "Why don't you ask me? I would certainly know better than my husband how I'm feeling. Although he does enjoy assuming the role of all-knowing. Since he is a doctor, he believes he knows better than the patient. I'm certain at times this is the truth. As matters are at this time, however, he couldn't possibly be able to speak for me."

"Maisie dear, Mother didn't mean..."

He'd been standing near the fireplace. Now, he strode toward her intent on soothing feelings that might find themselves a bit ruffled.

"She's right. I had no business speaking behind her back though my dear son is a doctor and can shed different light on your health," Heather was contrite as she set the tray on the nearby table. "Refreshments?" she directed the question to Maisie. "If you are hungry, please help yourself. Dinner will not be served for some time." There was an edge to her voice Hawk didn't hear earlier.

"Of course, I would like some. Thank you." Maisie reached out to pour a cup of tea for herself. "It was thoughtful of you to think of us."

Heather stopped her with one hand held high. "I would play hostess this afternoon as I would like to get to know my new daughter-in-law. Tell me how are you feeling? There are events planned for the newlyweds tonight. You might need a bit of rest. I will not query the good doctor, my son. I'm asking you."

Hawk sat back his arms crossed in front of him, waiting to hear just how dandy his wife felt. If he guessed correctly, she was ready for a nap. She was also brimming with indignation at his mother's highhanded question. The thought she was up to presenting herself as an individual pleased him.

"Tired. Both nights when we reached our destination all I could do was crawl into bed. I ate first. My dearest husband wouldn't allow me to do otherwise. Told me I needed my strength for the next day of travel. He thought he was right. All I did during the day was sit and watch the scenery go by. Why would I be tired?" She lifted her shoulders in a delicate shrug.

Because the silly goose had been severely ill for ten days. She needed sleep to heal. He didn't want her to have a relapse. Hawk wasn't about to voice his medical advice.

"Now, you're home. You'll have a wealth of things to accomplish. Busy tasks so you can put your home to order. It is a bachelor's quarter. Will need a woman's touch. Has Hawk asked you to work with him?" Heather asked looking expectantly from one to the other.

Hawk knew his mother guessed they'd not consummated the marriage. Because of that she would know he'd not claimed her. Tonight, there would be expectations he couldn't ignore or make excuses for.

"If you are tired you should rest, take a nap after your midafternoon snack. We've planned your wedding feast. It is to begin tonight at seven o'clock sharp. We will not part from traditions that have been in the family for hundreds of years just because your marriage occurred in an unorthodox way," Heather told her in her no nonsense way.

Confusion in her beautiful mauve eyes, Maisie looked at him, seemed to search his face for confirmation. He nodded.

"I suspected as much. As mother mentions, the wedding feast is a tradition among the Clan Chattan. We will spend the night in one of the tower rooms at the McKenna keep. There will be a feast that I'm certain mother along with Wynnie have been orchestrating since Father Damian's return."

"...and..."

It seemed Maisie wanted to know more. Over the rim of her tea cup, she gazed at him, her smile barely there. He wished this conversation to hell and back. Perhaps that was why he ignored it for days. Despite his earlier urgent need to consummate their relationship he now seemed to drag his feet.

"We will be married in every way by the end of the evening."

He wasn't at all certain what was going on in her head. Over the passing weeks, he thought himself adept at reading her ever changing mind. Now, his muddled brain was blank parchment.

"The wedding feast?" Maisie blinked a few times still questioning, still needing answers he wasn't in a blazing hurry to give.

"We can talk after your nap."

He wanted to put this off. For some reason he assumed now he'd been putting the wedding night to the back of his head. He was a coward, a dastardly coward. In order to move forward, she needed knowledge.

"If your parents leave, we can talk now, nap later." She suddenly became abrupt with him. "I've the right to know everything that will be expected of me. It's not right you refuse to explain your family traditions. It frightens me."

That was the truth. He kept telling himself her change in character was good. It became her. Now that he didn't want to talk, he wished she would revert to some of her previous shyness. The fact that he wasn't telling her what was going to happen was frightening her, didn't sit well on his shoulders either.

"We will see you at the feast. Don't be late," his father said as he watched the pair with curiosity brimming in his eyes.

"We won't be tardy."

He held Maisie's hand in his going over what he would explain, elaborate on, so she would understand. All the truth, part of it, or none. He realized she had every reason to be frightened. Knowledge, the exactness of the night might send her running in the opposite direction. There was nowhere to run. In every way, except the consummation along with the claiming they were wed.

His mother bent to brush a light kiss to his cheek. As if she guessed his indecision, she whispered to him. "Take care. Answer her questions. All of them. If you don't, in the end the fact will come back to haunt you. She will blame you for things that were not your doing."

A prediction he didn't like, Maisie would have heard the blatant statement. She would question him fully. Not listening to his mother's sage advice, he would evade the questions the best he could. Perhaps before the feast he should at least make love to her. Part of what bothered him would be taken care of if he did so. There would be no time before the wedding celebration. He blew his chances the last two nights when he had the opportunity.

The devil, he cursed the fact that when he had the chance, he didn't capitalize on her willingness. She would have allowed him more than the few kisses in the carriage then in their room at night before he left her to fall asleep by herself. This entire journey home was not something to be proud of. He didn't act in her best interest. He considered only his gutless fears. Even when his body ached with the need to hold her, to thrust inside her, he refused to initiate her into the carnal side of marriage.

The clock on his mantle ticked ominously, counting down the seconds until the decision would be made for them, taken out of his hands. The door shut behind his parents minutes ago. Silence reigned. Hawk heard each long, drawn-out breath he inhaled. Felt the thud of his heart against his chest.

*I'm a spineless fool, a half-wit.*

"Well..." she began, a lemon pastry perched on her lips, a soft coating of powdered sugar adorning her soft flesh. "Are you going to tell me or leave me at a loss. Everyone should know a few facts. Don't you think? Everyone here, except me, understands the Clan Chattan traditions.

You have not even made love to me. After I recovered from the illness, I believed you were overly concerned for my health. Now, I'm not so certain. Something else is bothering you. I would know before tonight, before it's too late."

Clearing his throat, he thought he would tell her all she asked then nothing more. "Where would you like me to begin?"

Hawk was resigned to a miserable afternoon of questions and answers. The truth, if he told there would be pain in their bedding, she would have nothing to look forward to. Fearing the night was not something he wanted for Maisie. She did comprehend there would be pleasure.

"At the beginning is usually considered a good start. Would you *ken* where that is?"

Her tone was sarcastic. Obvious to him, she didn't expect him to explain anything.

Maisie baited him. Hawk liked her this way as he never wished to tiptoe around tender sensibilities. She needed to speak her mind. Her doing so now put him in an awkward position of speaking about things a mother should tell her daughter. This was out of order. The sequence absurd. It was not the man's prerogative to explain the wedding night to his bride.

"Ah, the wedding feast. The celebration usually happens right after all the wedding ceremonies are completed. Our cook fixes everyone's favorite foods. We eat, dance then the mother of the bride or the groom along with all the female cousins go upstairs to prepare the bride for the night's adventures."

Hawk ate something that had been placed on the tray. Chewing as he mulled over his next words to Maisie, he decided this beginning was good, the facts sound. He was doing a fine job. Now, if they could just leave off here.

"I see...go on."

With slow precise rhythm, Maisie tapped her fingers on the side of the tea cup before setting the thin China in the saucer.

Going on was not something he wished for. He thought he was finished. "Could you ask a question or two to help me out. If you think hard, you must have a guess that might need clarification."

He felt as if he was treading water. A life line was what he needed. He was sinking fast. She wasn't going to toss him one.

Without blinking an eye, she did ask, "How do they prepare me, your mother, the other women? Why would I allow them to do so?" Maisie's back was stiff as the metal poker sitting by the fireplace. "You said they take me upstairs to one of the rooms to prepare me. Why?"

Letting up didn't seem to be part of her plans.

"You do *ken* the male of the species is never privy to what goes on between the women once they leave the celebration. I have no idea what is said or done. Perhaps they bathe then perfume the bride. Maybe they tell tales of their wedding night."

Since he was sidestepping her question, he expected her to reach out further. She wasn't stupid.

"People talk. You must know something. Just speak to what you know."

She tilted her chin slightly. Her determination seemed to grow with leaps and bounds.

They weren't going to get anywhere. "Aren't you tired? A nap might well be in order now. I for one could use some shuteye before the big event."

"Not anymore. Seems everyone else thinks I should be fatigued. Appears this afternoon is full of surprises. What do you know? Hawk, it's not like you to skirt around the corners without going for the center. All you're managing to do is frighten me."

As if searching for another way to evade her, he stood. Pacing the room, Hawk thought on what he could tell her. Thought to say only that which was necessary. What he said was true. He didn't know what happened in that room with the women. With his back against the windowsill, he began with what he did know.

"The women will take you to the room. I will wait downstairs until mother signals that you are ready for me. At that point the men will hoist me above their shoulders carrying me to the room. When they set me down, they will disrobe me until I wear only my kilt. You will be gowned in a beautifully sheer negligée. I will be jealous because no one but me should ever see you robed in that fashion."

"I can refuse to go to the feast. This doesn't sound like much fun to me."

Her once stiff shoulders were now shaking.

"You can choose that path. It would not bode well for the rest of our lives together if you would do so."

He understood better now the significance of all the traditions. No one looked at the woman, the bride. Never when he'd been involved had he stared or gaped. All the men involved were family. The bride would be there as would the groom. Everyone would leave them to enjoy the night. He realized then that once the pain was at an end the night could be magical, could be filled with mercuric passion along with raw hunger, so much pleasure it could leave a grown man to weep.

"You want to go through with this?"

Her question surprised him. She was staring at him, her hands clasped in her lap.

"You want to attend this feast then meet me already prepared for you in the tower room. After that you will make love to me as well as claim me."

He was ready for an argument as to why they should continue the traditions. "Yes." There was no other possible answer for them. "I would be disappointed if you chose to remain here. If we turned our noses up at the traditions that mark the way of the clan, we will come to regret our actions for the rest of our lives."

"I suppose so." Maisie looked to the clock then to him. "It's six. We've only an hour. Is there anything else you would like to tell me? I would know why your mother wanted you to share everything. I never took you for a coward, Hawk Fraser. It seems to me that is the way you are now acting. What has you quivering in your boots?"

Before he could catch himself, he was nodding his head. He didn't want to acknowledge how she pictured him as well as how true her words were. "There is, though I've put the telling off because it disturbs me."

"Is it something I will do?"

Maisie was guessing now, grasping at straws. Her body swayed. He felt certain she was fatigued. The trip had not been easy for her. Her illness drained her of energy that she was now just gaining back.

"No, you are simply a participant. In order to be joined through eternity I will have to claim you. The process, I've been told is painful for the woman. There is blood where my claws will mark you. I don't like thinking about hurting you. That's what has me so tied up in knots."

No emotion crossed her lovely face. It was as if she accepted her fate. She was the picture of calm serenity. "As is the breaching of my maidenhead. Shawna told me of both. I've known something of what will happen since before you kidnapped me. I take it tonight is the night. Do not deceive yourself, Hawk. I'm strong. I'll endure whatever pain is necessary for me to be with you."

Her words didn't surprise him. Maisie did possess inner strength. "It is. When all is done, I promise you I'll never hurt you again." With all his heart he meant to keep that promise through the end of their days on earth together.

"Shall we dress for the evening. Is there anything special I should wear?" She spoke calmly as if she wasn't terrified.

Hawk thought she was far too composed considering all he just told her. Nevertheless, he saw both fear as well as concern in her beautiful eyes. She didn't want to disappoint him or anyone else. Only a few days ago she told him she wanted to be his wife in every way.

Mother told me she laid out one of your dresses she thought would be suitable as well as a sash made from the Frasier tartan. You should wear that. It will signify your acceptance into my clan.

When they entered the main hall of the keep, bagpipes were playing lovely Scottish tunes. Servants milled around the family tables serving ale along with wine. The newlywed's table was set on a dais in the back of the room. The wooden planks were set with trays of all types of foods. Enough to fill them until they were sated.

Hawk grabbed two goblets of wine from a tray as a serving lad passed by him. He handed one to Maisie. "Here's to my beautiful bride." He held the glass high. To make the most of this evening was in the forefront of all his thoughts. He wanted to pleasure her so much she would forget about the pain

It seemed his friends and family saw the gesture as they roared with delight. Watching her carefully he sipped his wine then encouraged her to do so. All he wanted now was to ease her way to the wedding night. Taking her elbow in one hand he guided her to their table.

"We shall sit for a while, watch the festivities. What do you think? Would you like to dance once we've eaten our fill? I'm quite certain my father will want to dance with the new family member."

He placed his hand on her thigh, held it very still while she looked at him, her eyes wide. Taking care to not startle Maisie, Hawk moved his hand higher until he cupped her mound, he hoped only the fabric of the gown was keeping him from his goal. He bent low to her once again his whispered words glided across her cheek. "Do you wear your petticoats and stays? Don't want so much fabric to keep your heat from my hands."

She gulped as he pressed his fingers against her. It seemed she couldn't help but answer with the truth. After she nodded, he understood his first order of business would be to remove them. When he did, he wasn't at all certain what he should do with the frilly underwear. Perhaps leave the petticoats beneath the table for some servant to come across in the morning. He couldn't undo the hated corset with so many people present. Maybe, he would fly them from one of the posts holding up the platform for all the clan to see. Except for the fact she'd be embarrassed to the tips of her delicate pink toes, he appreciated that idea.

In this she disobeyed him. Ah, she was not taking all her marriage vows seriously even though she had not been cognizant at the time to truly appreciate them. When she said 'I do' she did vow to obey him. The slight was small. He didn't care. He would quite enjoy eliminating their presence. Tonight, he would move heaven and earth to ease her way through all the pain that would be inflicted. He would give her pleasure first. Before that, he meant to remove one of the hindrances to his plans.

"You understood what would happen, did you not?" he asked, one eyebrow lifting in question even though he felt certain she *kenned* the answer.

Previously, he had

burned a petticoat. Her stays had also been worn. He didn't believe a woman should wear a corset, tighten it to make her smaller to restrict all the organs in her body. A woman was built a certain way for a reason.

"You wouldn't. Not here where there is no privacy. Everyone would know or see what you were about." Her voice shook with the words she now must understand by the light in his eyes that he would relish doing that very thing.

"We are very private here. Did you not notice the cloth lining the table falls nearly to the floor. No one can see what goes on beneath the table unless your eyes give you away. Believe the women of this clan have been in this situation before you. It is their job to see to the bride's interest, protect her privacy from over-eager bride grooms."

Maisie, seemingly floored by his answer, ran her sweet pink tongue across her tender mouth, provoking all his male senses. "P-private? You mean...y...you want me to take them off. Here? Now?"

"Yes, and no that is what I intend to do. Disconnect the damn petticoats from your person so you will be naked beneath the beautiful gown with my clan tartan adorning your slim waist as well as your white shoulders."

He loved the way her eyes began to cross when he confirmed her fears. He delighted in the feel of her calf muscle beneath his fingers as he moved upward so he could reach his goal. His enjoyment increased when he managed to tug her underclothing off her bottom then down her legs. Just as he thought earlier, he allowed them to stay on the floor. He kicked them to the end of the table. His fingers now rested with no obstruction on her hot, damp flesh.

"I..." Maisie swallowed hard her eyes wide as saucers as his hand pressed against her, touching her so very intimately. "Didn't think...oh...oh..."

"Do you remember the bonfire? Your pleasure? How my nimble fingers made you feel, moan, cry out. I love the tiny sounds you make just for me. Just because I'm a man who knows what he is about."

She nodded. He wondered what exactly she recalled. Her legs were pressed tightly together. He hoped her memory included the amazing pleasure she felt at his hands. "Yes...it was when I got the fever."

"You experienced a different fever before you were sick. You're going to experience that steel melting inferno again. Right here in front of all our family and friends. They won't know though because you'll be concealed beneath the huge table cloth my mother had the wits to cover the table with. I'm the only person who will understand what your eyes are telling me."

With one foot tucked behind and next to one of her feet he pushed her legs apart. He slid his finger into her folds. She was so wet, more than damp. Hot. He'd barely touched her. Her body poured her desire on to his fingers.

"Not here. Everyone is watching."

Sounding mortified, she tried to push her legs closed against his quest.

He wouldn't allow her to gain the advantage. As he found the small hidden jewel that would send her to a place of oblivion, her breath caught in the back of her throat. "Hawk," she sighed softly, a tiny mewl of pleasure slipped from her lungs in sweet ribbons as her hips bucked, arched toward him, begging for what he offered. It seemed prudent to slow the seduction.

"Have some more wine, some nourishment." He lifted her goblet to her mouth. She drank while he continued to work his magic.

He wanted to touch her breasts, to lick as well as nibble at their sensitive peaks, to blow softly across them so he could see them quiver with the deliciousness of his attentions. Something he would have to wait until later to sample.

The grapes that were set on the table, he fed her one at a time. He smiled at the musicians, nodded at his cousins as well as his mother and father while his hand remained placed upon her bared, damp flesh. He sampled the delicacies cook spent two days baking. Sharing each one with his bride, he was able to kiss her, taste the wine she drank, dip his tongue deep into her to sample the lingering tastes of their small meal. Beneath the table he slowed the seduction of Maisie, not wishing to send her to that place of ecstasy too soon. No, he desired to prolong the pleasure.

"Are you happy, Maisie?" he asked as he slipped one then two fingers into the heat of her, into the dampness.

Her honey flowed swiftly, as if a summer storm filled her sheathe. Even though her eyes were closed, her face pressed against his chest, she nodded. "Are you?" He felt the whisper of her words against his flesh.

Hawk didn't expect the question. The thought she cared pleased him. "Ecstatic. Hush now, don't whimper, don't cry out my name as you did the night of the bonfire. This is our secret pleasure. Your arousal is for no one to know except me. No one except you and me will know what we do here."

He deepened his caress watched the movement of her small body. Something she couldn't control. Nor did he want her to do so. He needed to direct what was happening to her body.

His thumb worked the small jewel of her greatest pleasure while his fingers slowly moved in then out of her again and again. He felt the pressure grow, felt her body throbbing and pulsing asking him for more about to shatter around him. Instead of sending her to the climax she begged for, he fed her more food, bade her drink more wine. Kissed her again and again, tasting as well as exploring.

Hawk saw the people begin to finish eating. His family danced to the songs played by the pipers. He needed to end this before it would be their turn to dance. With no more thought, he finished what he began. Her body fragmented into a thousand pieces as she fought not to whimper or moan. Her eyes were closed, her fists tight around his forearm as she clung to him. She turned her head into the hollow of his shoulder. He felt the convulsions of her pleasure ripping through her slender body.

Seconds later she slowly began to calm. Knowing pure pleasure at her response, he slipped his fingers from inside her, bringing them to her cheek, touching her so she would understand how willing she'd been.

"This is you," he murmured softly to her.

He left some of the dampness on her cheek. He kissed her damp forehead, her cheeks her nose then kissed her hard, her lips opening for his entrance. After he removed his tongue from inside her sultry heat, he pressed it back inside deepening his kiss bringing his hand to cup one breast, to flick across a distended nipple.

"You are wicked, Hawk Frasier," she whispered her voice cracking on a note of bewilderment. "Oh...I cannot move."

"You must. We are expected to dance. This is our wedding, after all."

He stood, holding out his hand to her. She looked at him, her eyes wild and dark still from the raging passion she experienced moments earlier.

"You expect too much."

She tucked in a deep breath of air as if that would give her the needed strength to stand. It seemed she could not.

He lifted her then, steadying her with his arm around her waist. Guiding her onto the dance floor, he thought of her beautiful face in the throes of her passion. Tonight would not be filled only with pain. He would find a way to make the marriage bed one she would look forward to. "We will dance, cut cake then the women will take you from me."

Twirling her around the room, he realized she recovered rather quicky. He saw the white lace of her petticoats poking out from beneath the table cloth at their table. His grin widened. People would know something went on during the feast. The fact was true, none of the eager grooms who came before him could ever keep their enthusiastic hands to themselves before the women departed with their bride. Seemed to be a rite of passage.

He wasn't the first to seduce his wife in this situation.

Nor would he be the last.

This evening, the pain coupled with the pleasure still waited for both of them. She wore no underclothing. He wondered if she would have to explain herself to the women. That he would like to see. If he knew his mother, she wouldn't mention the fact. No, Heather would understand. He caught his parents many times dallying in various places in their home as well as the garden. They would be eager for their first grandchild. There would be no complaints from his mother or father.

With her hand clasped in his, he brought her to the dance floor. Tucked into his arms, he whirled her around the room, thinking about her naked body beneath the gown. Thinking about the speed with which she reacted to his ardent seduction. They danced to a secluded spot, the balcony overlooking the gardens. He heard stories about those gardens, secret trysts, dalliances even during the wedding feast. He wanted to have a secret tryst there with his wife. Tonight would be enjoyable. He understood that wouldn't happen.

Backing her against a pillar, he held her head in his hands. "I need to kiss you, sweetheart."

He didn't give her a chance to respond. His lips closed over hers, his tongue plunging as well as probing into the dark, humid recesses of her mouth. Her fingers rose to his shoulders then into his hair. She purred for him. Touched her tongue to his.

He heard the clearing of the throat coupled with a chuckle. Heard his father behind him. "Believe this is my dance. You will have to give her up for a few seconds. After all you will have her for the entire night, all to yourself."

Reluctantly, Hawk handed Maisie over to his father, understanding it would not be long now before the women would guide her upstairs. What they would tell her about the evening he didn't know. He found he no longer cared. This was his job now as she was his wife. He would do what was necessary.

It was not much longer before the cake was cut and she was whisked away. She looked over her shoulder at him as if hoping he would stop whatever it was that was going to happen. Even if he wanted to do so, he could not.

With a large glass of ale in hand he wandered around the room, spoke to the well-wishers. Came to an abrupt stop when he saw his sister with an English soldier. Harris was with the Sassenach who was in charge of the fort near the cabin, Ashton Walcott. Hawk believed the man had a 'third' attached to his name.

No Sassenach should be in the keep on a day such as this. Hawk felt rage building. He didn't understand what his sister was doing with this man nor why this Englishman was celebrating a Clan Chattan tradition. He didn't belong. If he told of the wearing of the kilts all involved could be imprisoned.

Furious strides brought him to his sister's side. "What are you doing here?" He pointed a finger at Ashton's chest. "You *ken* you don't belong."

"I was invited. Gained permission from your father, Elliott Fraser. Do you remember him?" His smile was directed to Harris.

Harris shoved him. "He is with me. If you don't want to begin a fight that will end badly for all of us, I suggest you save your questions for another time."

Houston was beside him, his hand on his shoulder. "Harris is right. Ashton is an invited guest. Seems he has connections to this part of the highlands we never knew about. Best you forget about anything except your bride."

"He's with me," Harris repeated, a small voice amidst the male ones. "I invited him. Ashton is leaving in a week to go back to London. He's going to be reassigned. He won't be at the fort in the highlands any longer."

She didn't seem to be pleased by the comment. While she stared at him heatedly, he grinned lazily. Hawk didn't like the look the Englishman slanted his sister. The man's intentions were bold as well as far too easy to read.

"No, sweet one, I'm selling my commission. I'm done with the army. I will be back," his words sounded like a promise to Hawk.

He would be back for his sister.

What the devil was going on?

Connal McKenna's daughter wed a Sassenach. Hawk didn't like the idea of his sister following the same path. His sister was far from being wed to this man. He should let everything sort itself out. This was none of his business. This was up to his father to put a stop to. Ashton must have had to get down on his knees and beg for Elliott to allow him entry into this feast. All the clan members wore their kilts. Kilts had been banned from Scotland ever since Culloden. He was witness to something illegal.

Hawk allowed Houston to lead him away. "Need my partner as soon as possible. Now, I'm not saying you would lose in a fair fight but the man is huge, even larger than you. You *dinnae* want to be fightin' a fight you might lose on your wedding night. Don't want to come to your bride with a split lip or a black eye."

"You're right. Don't want to fight on my wedding night."

"Glad to see you don't need convincing. As I said, your wife would not be pleased to see her groom with a black eye or a busted rib or a bloody lip. Of course, the injuries could be limited to a swollen lip," Houston hooted his amusement. "Would have trouble with the mouth contact if that were to be the case."

The silence of the room startled Hawk, caught his attention. He turned to see his mother at the bottom of the steps. She was smiling, grinning from one ear to the next. When she nodded, he understood it was time for him to meet his bride. The wedding night was about to commence.

After that he found himself surrounded by the McKenna's, Stuarts, and the Fraser brothers. They hefted him to their shoulders. Laying prone on their massive bodies, they carried him up the steps then down the long corridor to the tower room where he and Maisie would spend the night.

Once inside, they placed him on his feet. Just as he described to Maisie earlier in the day, the men disrobed him down to his kilt. She was lovely, so beautiful he thought his breath caught. He could see all her sweet curves, her breasts, the sweet rosy pinnacles of her breasts, her hips, the shape of her thighs. It was just as he told her. As soon as the men set him on his feet they departed with ribald gests. No one spent time gawking. Except for his younger brother, they all had their own very lovely wives to see to.

His mother poured him a glass of wine. Maisie held one in her hand. Heather nodded to the table where there were dishes of food along with more wine to be enjoyed throughout the evening.

He wanted to know what was in her head now. What the women told her about tonight.

"Maisie?"

Hawk held out his hand to her. Her eyes wide spheres, hesitating with each step, she walked to him. The silver mauve of her eyes turned dark purple.

"Hawk. I don't want you to worry about me. I would get all this nastiness over with then we can enjoy what is left of the night."

She wasn't smiling. Her expression was indeed grim.

"I would not like to think of love making as nastiness."

He visibly flinched as he spoke his thoughts muddling around in his brain in hope of figuring out how to change her mind. It seemed impossible for him to see this from her point of view.

~ * ~

Maisie understood. She had all explained to her by his mother. The gentle soul that he is, Hawk was a coward. "You understood what I meant, Hawk. We need to..." She moistened her lips. "I know you will give me pleasure. I've felt it twice. Once that happens, there will be the pain." She lifted her shoulders in a casual shrug. "I want to stop being afraid. Need to have this part of the ceremony done...over." She waved her hand in the air giving emphasis to her words. "Need to move on to more pleasant diversions."

She came to him, lifted herself to the tips of her toes then kissed him, opened her mouth to him, encouraging and enticing. The kiss was long and hot, melting her to her core. He cupped her face with his hands sending his tongue deep inside her mouth touching her, surveying. She felt the first stirring of her reaction to his warmth, to the heat of him. She found herself wrapped within his magic, protected as well as shielded from anything in the outside world that might hurt her.

His hands moved along her back, up then down, resting on her buttocks then around to settle on the curve of her hip. He moved again, pushing her feet apart, his thigh between them touching her intimately. He moved again so she was now cradled between his thighs, both his hands on her bottom, pulling her to him. She felt the evidence of his arousal against her belly. Understood he would push his member inside her and that this would cause her pain as well as pleasure.

She wished he would move faster. Her quiet moan of enjoyment brought a low, husky groan from him. She knew he wanted to be deep inside her. His mother told her as much. The conversation seemed strange coming from the woman who sired him. Did all mothers know these things? She supposed they did. Would have to understand or they wouldn't be mothers.

He tugged the sheer outer covering from her. She felt the silken fabric of her dressing gown slide down her arms. Knew the material pooled on the floor around her feet. She ran her hands along his chest, enjoyed the crispness of his dark hair that fanned across his muscles. Just a few minutes ago, when she saw him standing in front of her, almost naked, she thought he was the most handsome man alive.

People always told her how beautiful she was. She wasn't anywhere near as beautiful as Hawk. With ease, he swung her into his arms. When they came down upon the bed, his heaviness was above her, pressing against her blanketing as well as heating her. Before when he pleasured her, he never was on top of her. She never felt the heat of his body against her. Maisie liked the way he covered her.

Braced on his forearms, he stared into her eyes then brushed her long hair from her face. He nibbled on her ear then blew on flyaway strands creating a heavenly dance of heat within her. His breath ruffled across her cheek. "Do you know how beautiful you are?"

"You are the beautiful one," she murmured, caught up in all that he did, all that he was.

They were wed and after all this time he was going to consummate the marriage. She was both eager and frightened of the prospect. When this first time was over, there would be no more pain, only ecstasy she was told.

With his teeth, he tugged on the delicate ribbons that were tied on her shoulders. With an ease so slow she quivered, fabric slipped from her. For a few seconds, he gazed upon her breasts. She felt them harden, the tips tightening with the cool air as well as the flame of his eyes that caressed them. He cupped one breast in his hand. His lips closed over the nipple. He sucked then laved, pulling her deep within the sultry warmth of his mouth.

Heat flowed through her, the inferno building with each movement of his tongue and teeth upon the tight bud he caressed with so much tender care. Her hips arched begging for him, demanding, more thorough.

"Hawk...please...I need you. I want you inside me."

She understood what she needed. All of her was both hot and melting. She writhed beneath his tempestuous onslaught. Her fingers dug into his shoulders. Mercuric magic guided her hands. He turned his attention to her other breast. While he kneaded the free one with his fingers.

"This evening I wasn't able to touch your breasts or give them the attention they cried out for. Now..."

His gaze focused on her breasts then her eyes. "Now I can do whatever I want."

He came between her legs, spreading them wide with his then kissed his way down her belly. With his hands beneath her, he lifted her spread legs. His mouth found her, caressed intimately. Maisie gasped at the startling contact.

So aroused she thrashed against him, her insides shattering as she tried not to detonate from the attention, he gave her. At her first cries, as the pulsing throbbing of her reached a crescendo, he entered her.

His fullness consumed her, filled her, stretching her as he moved deeper then deeper still. She knew this was when he would hurt her. Closing her eyes against the pain, feeling all of him gliding deeper than even farther into her. She didn't immediately realize his mouth closed over hers again.

She whimpered then purred as her arousal once more built, her fever climbed. He touched her everywhere; her breasts her belly, between her legs. He slid his fingers through her finding the spot that seemed to drive her to the highest of highs.

Once more she cried out in pleasure, in the magical enchantment of what he was doing. When he heard her cry of ecstasy, he thrust deep, breaking through her barrier. This time the scream was one of pain. Frozen, so deep inside her she thought he became part of her, he held still. His groan was deep and rough, contained the pain he felt at hurting her.

With light gentle strokes, he kissed her lips, brushed them back and forth. His fingers continued to massage, deep inside she felt the inferno build again, igniting once more. The pain seemed to vanish almost as soon as it began. She wondered if this was the end of the pain then, if this was all there was. She hoped so because what she felt was not so bad.

He was moving again, deep, and deeper still, strong hard thrusts that sent that fever blazing anew. Hawk was so very deep she was certain he must touch the very essence of her. As his thrusts continued, she found her body once more splintering into a thousand fragments of pleasure. She wanted him, needed him. This time he would certainly find his pleasure within her. When she looked at him, his face was strained, his lips drawn back from his teeth as if he was in pain.

His low harsh growl encompassed her. He growled again as his body plunged one more time. She felt warmth flood her core. She saw his nails turn to claws. They dug into her shoulders. The agony was like nothing she'd ever felt before. She screamed her pain. This was not akin to the breaching of her maidenhead.

Pictures of times long past flashed through her mind. He was running as his cat. Then he was himself, tall, proud, and so very self-assured. Sobs then more sobs she couldn't hold back echoed in the small room. She pressed herself against him, seeking the protective shelter of his big body. Maisie didn't know how much time passed, a few seconds or an eternity. Unable to release Hawk, she clung to him.

As time passed, she became cognizant of the ticking clock, of Hawk's deep labored breaths, his heart pounding so close to hers they seemed to beat as one. Everything was completed now. She was his through eternity then beyond.

He lay so very still above her, motionless deep inside her. He rested his forehead against hers. Maisie felt a tear slide onto her face. "I'm sorry, little one. There was no other way. If there had been I would have found it. How are you feeling? Wine?"

She managed to brush the lock of hair that was always in the wrong place from his eyes. "It is done then? How am I feeling?" she mused as she asked the question of herself that he asked her. "Sore everywhere. All will pass."

"Yes. It is done and yes, all the pain will pass. There will be no more for you to endure. I'm so sorry."

He brushed his knuckles down her neck, touched the pulse point at the base of her neck that still beat hard and fast though the beat was now slowing.

"You are still inside me," she said, her voice hushed wondering if there was a reason. When he moved, she flinched from the pain that small attempt to withdraw from her caused.

"Yes," he murmured his voice gruff, his body stiff above hers. "You are sore?"

"I don't know? You are very big," she told him. "I would like a glass of wine now, something to eat as well. Seems I'm hungry."

The comment seemed ludicrous since her husband was deep inside her body with no attempt to remove himself. Even so, her body pulsed around his length, tightened as if inviting him to stay. She wasn't at all certain what it was she wanted.

He laughed yet the sound didn't seem real. "You can have whatever you wish."

With infinite care, he began to withdraw from her. She grimaced as he left her.

His smile when he looked at her was hesitant, a bit apologetic. "I'm sorry. You are *verra* small. Such a *wee* lady." He stood. Walked to the table with the wine and food. He poured glasses of wine for them then selected some treats, heaping them upon a plate.

As she watched, fascinated, she saw her blood on him. The sight of his member covered in her blood caused her to gasp. He looked down then back to her. "We will take care of this in a minute."

The bed dipped where he sat. The wine he gave her was delicious. She wondered what he meant when he said they would take care of this. Maisie knew him well enough to realize he meant that he would take care of the blood. He handed her a piece of cheese coupled with a small piece of bread.

"Eat, drink... We can talk later."

The meal at the feast had been elaborate. All kinds of Scottish delicacies were laid out, adorning the table in a delicious display. She ate next to nothing. Hawk used her time well, used his time well to ease the fears of the wedding night. She understood better why he seduced her that way. Heat flushed her cheeks at the memory. Now, she found she was famished. Could eat the entire plate he brought to the bed. A bit light headed from the experience or lack of food, she didn't *ken*. What she did *ken* was that she needed sustenance. Earlier, he told her they would spend the entire night making love. Well, perhaps they would maybe they wouldn't.

The plate of food he brought her vanished as did the goblet of wine. She set the empty glass on the table then waited.

"You have this expectant look in your eyes. What are you waiting for?" he asked her seeming to have forgotten what he told her a scant ten minutes ago. Nonetheless, the blood on her shoulders was drying.

She decided she should speak her mind, "I would like to wash." She held out her hand to stop him when he rose. "Myself, I would like to wash myself."

"Would you now? I believe I'll do the honors. It is my husbandly right."

The basin of rose scented water was close by. Before he came to her, he washed himself. After that he filled a second basin with water that was also scented. He strode to her. His grin showed his even white teeth. He appeared very pleased with himself.

She backed up against the headboard. "You don't..." She didn't entirely believe him when he told her he would see to the blood. "No, I'll do it..."

Now he was spreading her legs, sitting between her thighs. He could see all of her, every part of her. Somehow when she wasn't aroused by his gaze, this all felt so different. She felt humiliated, embarrassed to the tips of her toes, humbled. Once before he looked at her this way.

"I *ken* what you're thinking."

She didn't see how he could possibly comprehend what was in her mind. "No...you don't have a clue as to the direction of my thoughts. You've no earthly idea. You're...you're a man."

He laughed at her statement, arching one of his wickedly dark eyebrows toward the ceiling. "Recall also that I'm a doctor. I will deliver all our children with the help of Houston. You are my wife and you will grow used to me looking at you touching you, every part of you. When he finished with her virgin blood along with his seed, he turned his attention to her shoulders. "You will have five marks here for the rest of your life." In awe, he washed the blood from each claw mark. "Would you like to tell me what you saw when I claimed you."

With his question, he blessed her with a tiny amount of power. She would withhold examples until she could temper her embarrassment.

He was still looking at her. Her legs were still spread wide. His legs held steady between them. He wasn't going to allow her the ability to shut herself off from his avid gaze. She lifted her shoulder giving him the smallest shrug. "Just more of the same. You know. What I witnessed during the clan ceremony."

His frown told her he didn't like her reply. He wanted to know everything she saw. That wasn't possible until she decided he should deserve the privilege. If he wanted to act highhanded with her, ignoring her wishes, he would have to wait for enlightenment. His hand flattened on her belly; his fingers splayed wide just as he'd done at the bonfire. She didn't understand the gesture.

"All the same," he murmured as he bent toward her, touched his lips to her stomach. "You could even now carry our child. Would you like that? You could be increasing."

"Yes. So, you mean it?"

She was confused now. She wasn't stupid as she understood what they did could create a child. Shawna became pregnant with Mac with just one time. Anything was possible.

"As when we were wrapped in the cloak?" he asked as if he wished to give her a few ideas. "All you saw were the same scenes? From all I've heard that is unusual. You must have seen something different."

It appeared they were in the midst of two different conversations. "I saw you several different times in your cat. You are just as beautiful each time. I know we are meant for each other. This has to be good and right. What more can you wish to know?"

Hawk looked so frustrated she was tempted to laugh. Instead, she held her amusement in check.

With more wine in their hands, they settled back against the headboard. It seemed he gave up on discovering more about the pictures that were granted her when he claimed her. "Are you going to love me again?" She asked wondering if she wasn't perhaps too daring and shameless.

Even though she was a *wee* bit sore, she wanted to find this pleasure with him inside her again. Wanted to feel all that he could give to her without the pain.

"If you wish me to do so, I'll have to think on it. You are very tiny. This time when I come inside you, you should feel only the pleasure of the joining."

"I don't know. You are too big for me."

She felt his annoyance grow. To hide her grin, she looked away.

"I'm not too big, *lass*. We will fit perfectly. It was just the first joining. A woman's body must stretch for a man's member to fit. Just as the woman needs to stretch in order to give birth."

His words startled her. Was he like his cousin? Did he know she was pregnant? "Perhaps later," she murmured touching his shoulder with her fingertip, running it along his collarbone until he groaned. "I would like to see your cat. Since you are purrfectly naked, you are in the purrfect condition to show me," she purred for him, testing him telling him she was ready to see all of his different sides.

The diversion seemed to work. His grin was broad as well as arrogant. "The purrfect condition you say? I am naked."

"Doesn't that make it purrfect? You won't rip through any clothing." She found her words shivering from behind her teeth.

"You will not be afraid?" he asked as he placed a quick kiss on her lips. "You comprehend that I would never hurt you, cat or human."

She drank deep then waved her hand in the air. "Mayhap this is too soon." She persisted. Despite his previous words, she asked him, "You won't hurt me, will you?"

The silver of his eyes darkened to a deep pewter. "I would never hurt you. I might play with you, tease you until you might want to scream. I would tell you screaming would only bring the clan running to see what was happening in here. I might want to cuddle up against your beautiful breasts. Have you ever had a small cat cuddle with you when you were naked?"

She lowered her lashes before looking back to him. When she was tiny, there was her favorite cat. He did snuggle next to her when she slept. He liked to crawl beneath her nightgown to lay on her belly, "You can't...you know...when you are a cat?"

His jaw gaped open but only for a moment. "Wait." He held up his hand. "Are you asking me if I can make love to you when I'm a cat?"

He sounded astonished. No, more than dumbfounded.

Embarrassed by her question, Maisie studied her thumbnail clearly self-conscious with her question. It wasn't fair since she had no idea about any of this. With sound resignation that this wasn't the first stupid question she would ask, she said, "Yes, that was what I was asking. By your tone of voice, I understand that would not be possible. Think no more about my foolish thoughts."

"Only if you were also in cat form. Since that is not possible, well then, I suppose the answer is no. Doing so would be physically impossible. I can still tease you, caress parts of you, touch you in different ways. Only if it would be something you would like."

He had to be teasing her now. "You wouldn't!"

"Try me...tell me yes."

"No...I'm not going to try you. I'm going to trust you not to tease me so outrageously."

She hoped that was enough to get through to him that she would be horribly uncomfortable if he did what he was implying. Somehow the small tabby cat who liked to sleep on her belly was different.

"Forgive me, Maisie. You are so adorable and so easy to tease. You need to learn you cannot believe everything I say to you, at least not on this topic. Though I promise I will always, in time, tell you the truth."

"Alright. I understand you mean what you say."

"Now? Would you like me to change now?" he asked as he pushed himself onto all fours. He didn't wait for her nod.

As she watched he began to shake, his body trembling in front of her, quaking as his body transformed. While the change seemed to take forever it was also over in a few seconds. He stood over her, his front paws on either side of her body. Before she could swallow her astonishment, he licked her nose then jumped from the bed.

Hawk sat on his haunches on the floor looking at her, no, looking her over, thoroughly examining every inch of her lingering on her breasts then her woman's mound. She brought her hands to cover her breasts, then thought she should cover herself lower. He was teasing her just as he said he would do. The grin he flashed her was huge, his teeth seemingly larger. White. Pointed. Threatening.

"Oh!"

When she reached for the dressing gown on the floor, Hawk snatched it away from her taking that as well as the negligée to the far side of the room. He dropped them in the corner before sauntering back to her. The tilt of his head, the swager in his stride were all familiar to her even though she'd never seen his cat. After he jumped onto the bed, she shrieked. He curled up next to her, his head on her left breast. No, this was nothing like the tabby.

Maisie wasn't at all certain what she should do next. Curious, she stroked his head then down the length of his back. His purr rumbled deep in his chest vibrating across her. When he lifted his head, he brushed her nipple with his chin. He did tell her he would love to joke with her.

Gracious, his head was on her breast, his chin on her nipple. She didn't know what to think or do. Other than that, he didn't do anything else. Hawk said he would tease her. At this moment he was making her feel more uncomfortable than ever thought would be possible. He would have to know that. He should stop.

"Can you understand me?" Maisie asked hoping the answer would be yes.

She wanted to tell him what she was feeling. He wouldn't listen. He tossed her petticoats in the fire. Took her under clothing off while they sat at the feast. He would do as he pleased.

Hawk lifted his head, his eyes darkening just as they did when he kissed her. He nodded his head.

"Good, then I want you to turn back to your human. You've quite shown me enough of your cat. This is all I can manage now."

With a shake of his head, he bounded off her. She clutched the covers to her chin as she watched him saunter around the room. When he was back near the bed, he cocked his head to one side. All she did was look away for a second. He was normal again.

Just as he did when he was his cat, he pounced on the bed tugging at the sheet she held so tight to her breasts. "Now days we only turn into our cat when we are safe from harm. Over the years being a shifter has been dangerous for the Clan Chattan." He moved the sheet so he could touch her breast, sent his palm across her nipple. "I'm not sorry I teased you. I know I said I would. There was so much more I could have done, could have aroused you. Did you know that?"

"No, no...I don't think so. I was terrified."

"Not of me, but of your reaction to me, to my chin resting on your nipple. Shifters can sense moods of their mate, can tell when you are pregnant. You are not by the way, which means I need to try harder."

"What if I'm not eager or enthusiastic about increasing?" she asked knowing the question implied something that wasn't true.

"I will wait."

"You would? You would do that for me?"

She was surprised then not so surprised. Hawk seemed to always care about her moods along with her needs. "I want a child of yours. The sooner the better. Is your father in contest with Alistair and Connal about the number of grandchildren?"

His laughter echoed around the room. He snorted before he replied. "There is hardly a competition where my father is concerned. So far, my father has no grandchildren to speak of. I'm his only child who is married. Who knows. Once we have a *bairn*, he might take part in the competition."

"So..." Maisie plucked at the covers understanding he wanted to remove all of them, wanted to make love to her again. Wanted to see her naked, to tease her body until she responded wildly. "You say that you will know when I'm pregnant even before I *ken* the fact? I'm no certain I like that knowledge. The mother should know first."

"Most likely." He tackled her, ripping away the meager quilt she covered herself with now. Rearing up on his arms, he gazed upon her.

Lowering his head, his lips brushed across hers until she opened for him. He pulled her on top of his body, her thighs touching his flanks, cradling her hips between his legs. She felt him beneath her, against her, touching her. His body magnificent underneath hers, she caressed his chest, ran her hands down his hard belly. She delighted in his low harsh groan of pleasure. She hoped it was so much pleasure he couldn't live without it for the rest of his days.

"You are a vixen," Hawk told her when she brazenly closed her hand around the hard length of him. He stopped her. "If you keep that up,

I will explode too soon."

He flipped her. She was on her back, her legs spread to frame him between them. He pushed her feet along the bed so her knees were bent toward the ceiling. She was completely, entirely open to him once more. She was vulnerable. In this instant she didn't care. With his hands beneath her, he lifted her. She screamed when his mouth settled on her. His tongue danced along her with intimate precision, found that same place where his fingers excited her. He slipped his tongue inside her once, then twice then some more.

She bucked, pushing at him, pulling at him until she thought she would yowl with the pleasure. Her moans of delight drew more magic from him. His weight settled against her. He lifted her legs over his shoulders just as he plunged into her. He drove his body until he touched her womb. Her body broke into pieces of glittering delight of ecstasy so intense it was almost agony.

"Hawk."

She ran her hands along his sweaty back as his last thrust resulted in a severe hushed growl of satisfaction from him.

His voice low and throaty, desire evident in the tone. "Maisie..." The weight of his body fell upon her, covered her. After a few seconds he braced himself on his forearms. "You are a delight. My enchantment." He rolled off her bringing her with him, tucking her head in the hollow of his shoulder.

His fingers lightly touched her arm, her back. He touched her nipple with a slight reverent caress. "Did I hurt you?"

"No," she said understanding now all the joys he would bring her. "Am I pregnant?"

He set his hand on her belly. "We will have to continue to work on this matter. Will you like that sweet lady? I will."

~ * ~

Harris paced the small glen where she first met Ashton so many months ago. He was late. He was always late. She should leave. The man could have the respect to be on time, a time he set. This meeting had been his idea. She told him no, she didn't dare be seen with him several times. Now that her parents understood she cared for an Englishman, a Sassenach, they kept a more careful watch over her. There was always someone following her. Today, she noticed no one. Didn't mean she wasn't shadowed.

This afternoon, this last day before he returned to London, her father had been busy with repairs to the fence bordering the south pasture. Her mother was baking bread, her hands in the dough when she waltzed into the kitchen then kissed her on the cheek.

Where are you going?" her mother asked sounding a bit distracted. "I would know. You can't just—"

Harris interrupted. "I have a few errands to run in the village. Don't worry about me. I'll be home before it's dark." She danced from the kitchen ignoring the fact her mother was calling her back.

She heard the pounding of hooves. Turning, Harris smiled as Ashton leapt from the horse, taking her up in his strong arms. She recalled Crissie McKenna fell in love with a Sassenach. She lost her virginity the very day he left. On that day she got with child. Harris vowed that wasn't going to happen to her. She would wait either for the wedding vows or a ring, a promise of marriage. She wasn't about to leave this to chance.

"Harris, oh, how I'm going to miss you." Ash whirled her around in his big strong arms until she pounded on his shoulders.

"You *ken* you're making me dizzy. Put me down, you big oaf!"

If he was going to miss her, he could marry her then take her with him. He'd said nothing along that line. There had been no words of love either. She didn't dare give in to her desires. Letting him have her virginity would solve nothing. Would complicate her life.

Ashton stopped twirling but didn't set her feet on the ground. His lips found hers, touched upon them. With his teeth he tugged on the bottom lip until she opened for him. His tongue swept inside so deep he touched every part of her.

"I want you," he told her, his voice husky with passion. "Don't want to wait another second to have you. Don't want to wait until I come back to collect you. Let me love you."

More than anything she wished she could tell him yes. When he kissed her, her body burned. "You know I cannot. Let's walk."

She would not fall under the spell he so wanted to weave around her. She would not melt in his arms until she could not make rational decisions. She would not!

"The last thing I want to do is walk. Dear God, the other night strolling with you in the garden, redolent with roses, I thought...well...I never thought you would want to see me again. You told me you wouldn't wait for me to return. You intended to see other men. If you found one who appreciated you, you would commit."

"I did, didn't I?"

She was pleased with herself. A man shouldn't have so much confidence that he wouldn't have a worry or two when he just up and left the country without a proposal or a promise. He was going home to London or Cornwall or wherever he chose. His family was there, not hers. He never invited her.

"I won't be gone long. As soon as I clear up some business, I'll return for you. Don't you dare see another man." He held her hand as they strolled along a path that led deeper into the forest. The grass was green, the sky bluer than blue today. With the air crisp against her skin, she pulled her shawl around her. Two deer dashed across the path in front of them. Surprised, she jumped. He pulled her closer as if she needed protection from deer.

She wondered how long he expected her to remain steadfast. Harris couldn't help but recall Crissie's plight. Walker didn't return for a year. By that time her child was three months old. She didn't want that for herself. He wasn't going to have her today or tomorrow. He wasn't going to leave her increasing as well as shamed. She was too proud to allow him that deed. She would control her emotions today as she had for the past months when he kissed her senseless. When he touched her in places he had no business caressing.

"That remains to be seen."

So far, she still heard no words of love, none at all. This man expected her to wait sitting on her hands until he decided to return? Never. He would have to give something in return. A promise of his own.

"That's not good enough, Ash. I won't become a victim you leave behind."

She was adamant. She didn't need the men who'd been following her to make certain she didn't fall under the spell the big man wove. Harris had her pride.

"I will come for you. We both know we belong together. Don't see anyone else who is good enough for you."

Even though his voice was soft the tone was harsh and unforgiving. She'd never heard that attitude or tone from him.

No one else good enough for her except him? "Do we now? You arrogant sod." She questioned everything he told her wishing she could put his command behind her.

For the longest time, she did believe Ash was her mate. The facts didn't line up. He was Sassenach. Ashton looked for shifters, tormented the families living in the area even though she heard no rumors with his name attached. What would he feel if he knew she shifted. He would hate her. Would never understand who she was. She would never be able to tell him.

"Yes." His one words held a great deal of anger. "I should take you with me. Keep you close so you cannot find trouble. You've a penchant for trouble."

"I wouldn't go with you."

She was adamant of this. Would not leave her home to follow a man no matter how much she loved him, not without a wedding. Marriage to this man seemed impossible. Her father told her she was too young. Perhaps she was too stupid. Only a foolish woman gave her heart to a man who would leave her.

"I could take you," he told her bending close, nipping at her ear, laving with his tongue, teasing a response. "I could sweep you into my arms right now. You could struggle. You could yell and pound on my shoulder. If I chose to abduct you, there would be nothing you could do to stop it."

She shivered from the explosion of sensations within her. "You don't play fair," she admonished him.

He was so big, even bigger than the rest of the clan. While she wasn't a tiny woman, she didn't reach his shoulder. He outweighed her by so much. What he said was true. If he wished to abscond with her, she would have no choice.

"Neither do you. With your slender body, your lush breasts that tempt me, you deny me. I've done naught but kiss you. I need to make you mine. To brand you with the sensations only I can give you. Don't deny me."

All he said was true. He stopped, turning her to face him, his hands cupping her bottom. He pulled her up to kiss her again. "Wrap your legs around me." With her in his arms, his mouth caressing her he walked to a tree. Her back was against the trunk.

"What are you doing?"

"Loving you." His hands roamed beneath her dress.

When his hands slid along her thighs and his fingers cupped her with intimacy, she didn't give permission. She gasped for air. Her heart thundered against her ribs. "Ash! You cannot! No! Stop!"

Harris was terrified she would lose her virginity. He had to stop. She wriggled and fought. Pushed on his massive shoulder. She could do not against his great strength.

"Yes. You know you want me."

He deepened the kiss, his tongue probing inside. It seemed to her he meant to seduce her. She had to be stronger than the seduction. Could not give in to the potent attraction between them. Today, she didn't intend to lose her virginity. He'd given her no reason to say yes to all his sweet-talking charm.

"No!"

With all her strength, she pushed against his muscled chest saying the one word she didn't mean. If he didn't stop, she would never be able to push him away. He must understand that.

"Yes..." he spoke softly to her. His words more charming than she'd ever heard before. "You know you want me. Don't deny yourself. Don't stop me today. We need each other. I want to bind you to me before I leave."

Oh, but he was a smooth-talking devil. Yes, yes...she did but she wasn't about to tell him so. Unfortunately, with one hand he held her, the other gave attention to the buttons of her gown. With far too much ease, he was flicking them open. Beneath the gown she wore little protection, only her chemise. Even with her squirming, it didn't take him long to reduce the lacings to nothing.

"Undo my shirt. I need to feel your breasts pushing against me."

The soft mewling sound coming from her lips she didn't recognize. She started to refasten her gown as the ribbons to her chemise were impossible for her shaking hands. She couldn't give in to his seduction.

"Leave them. I just got them where I want them." Both hands cupped her bottom again. They were large, callused, so warm on her. She wanted to feel what would happen next.

To her surprise, no, it wasn't surprise, she wanted to feel him too, she opened his shirt. His groan astonished her when he pressed one large hand on her back. She felt his chest, the hardness, the crisp hair across her breasts, her nipples. Her body leapt to life, heated, pulsed. Needed him.

"Ash, no, we can't...! You *ken* it's not right. I don't want to conceive a child. You can't...please don't do this to me. You can't treat me as if I'm a whore. You can't take me as if I'm your slave then leave me to suffer the consequences."

He slipped his hand back to her rear, pushing, driving a finger between her legs. She started at the intense sensations he orchestrated. She arched against him. He didn't hear a word she said.

"Who will you be seeing when I'm gone. If you insist on this stupidity, I will make you mine right now. Tell me!" He growled deep in the back of his throat. "Tell me you will not see any man. Promise me this instant. If you don't, I swear I'll make you mine in every way. I will take your virginity. It's mine. We both understand that fact."

Despite the heat swamping her, turning her into liquid she bristled at his audacity. "Tommy, Tommy Brown. He's been wanting to court me for years. I just never said yes to him."

She didn't understand why she told him that. While Tommy wanted her, she'd never been interested in him. She wasn't now nor would she ever be. The only man she wanted was Ashton. She couldn't have him. Harris didn't want him to shame her.

His mouth closed around her right breast, sucked until she was in a frenzy her head thrashing back and forth. After that his teeth grazed the tip. "You won't see him, Harris. You must promise me. I will take you right now if you can't give me some assurance."

Her body pulsed and throbbed. She couldn't think or talk as she arched against him, begging him for more. He knew just what to do. Without a moments warning all of her broke, fragmented into shattering sensations that convulsed within her. Time stood still while her body reacted to all he did. It was over. The mindless excitement, the devastating contractions that wracked her body.

She lay against him, limp, gasping for air, her heart thundering. "Ash?"

"Promise me?"

"Or what? You'll do that to me again? Life could be worse. Why?"

"If you don't, I'll take all your choices from you. Promise me you won't see that little boy or anyone else."

"I promise," her whisper seemed to satisfy him.

Ash adjusted her clothing then, taking her hand in his he walked with her back to the horses. "I'll be back as soon as possible. I trust in your word. If I hear otherwise..."

"You'll be in London." Defiantly, she tilted her chin upward. "What could you do?"

"If I hear otherwise," he persisted. "You'll regret defying me."

The sod, she wanted to toss something at him, wished she could rail at him. He was gone though, riding away from her. She would do whatever pleased her. Curse him.

# Chapter Six

Hawk settled into his practice with Houston. With the help of the family, their office now sported two more rooms, his office along with another patient room. The waiting room was made larger. Maisie worked as his organizer of all things. She took messages from folks who needed a doctor to come to them. She alphabetized all the drugs along with all the medical supplies. When she wasn't at the office with him, she spent her time modernizing his home, giving the bachelor abode a woman's touch. All the rooms now had new carpets or rugs along with stylish draperies.

When the bell above the door rang, it caught Hawk's attention. He looked up to see who was walking into the office. An older man walked through the door. His salt and pepper hair was pulled back in a que tied with a black ribbon. Age lines radiated around his eyes. He was short and thin, dressed in the latest fashion. His black boots shined impeccably. The little man had a pompous air about him. Outside the door, Hawk saw a carriage with a crest blazoned on the door.

When the stranger spoke, it was with a sneer. "You Hawk Fraser?"

Hawk looked up from the article on heart disease he was reading, shuffling the papers for a few seconds while he searched his mind for something nice to say to the man. "Yes." He didn't like the way the man stared at him. "Something wrong. Do you need a physician? I'm certain this isn't a social call."

The stranger cleared his throat before stroking his neck with long slender fingers. "Nothing's wrong. I'm looking for a woman. Heard you might know her. Came here to see if you could help."

The man was trying to look over his shoulder into the other rooms. Hawk stacked his papers together. "Who?" He stood. This was the kind of man who rarely came to this part of the highlands. His motives needed to be scrutinized.

"Miss McKenzie was her maiden name. Don't know if she's married or single. Tracked her to a manor house outside Inverness. After that her trail led this direction. I've a proposition for her, one a long time in the making. I knew her mother very well. Over the years, I've been concerned about the *lass*. Her wellbeing is important to me. I tried to find her but was unsuccessful."

As Hawk stood, he was shaking his head. Even if he did recognize the name, he'd hold any information about this woman to himself. "Don't know a Miss McKenzie. As you can see this is a long way from Inverness. Now, if you don't have a medical problem, I've work to do. Best be on your way."

Hawk thought he'd dismissed the man. He had not. This arrogant stranger rocked on the soles of his feet, his gray eyes cold as well as calculating. He didn't appear pleased with the dismissal.

Hawk's gut instinct kicked in. The man was not someone he would want a woman who he cared about to speak to him. The man was evil. The devil incarnate. Walking with his hands behind his back, he strode around the waiting area looking over his shoulder now and then into his office as if searching. To Hawk, it was clear the man didn't believe him.

"Don't lie to me, boy. If you do, you'll regret it."

The threat was very real. Nevertheless, to Hawk the words were meaningless. Hawk never took orders from self-important strangers.

Following the man, his hand on the man's arm. "It's time to leave. This is a private office. If you don't need a doctor's service then you need to be gone. You'd be wise not to consider me a mere boy. I can't be pushed around."

He shook it off, his glare was as frosty as the glacier farther north. "Tell her the Earl of St. Blevins is asking for her. She might need a protector. Someone who would take care of her, see to her needs. I would treat her well just as I did her mother. I keep my mistresses in fine style. They don't want for anything." He stroked his chin as he seemed to think about her. "The *lass* is more beautiful than her mother. It was a stroke of good luck when I happened on the woman, desperate to keep the roof over her child's head along with food on her table. I would help the poor woman out now. Tell her, tell her if you see her that I'm looking for her."

Sorting through all he knew about Maisie's life before Shawna discovered her, he couldn't place this man. Nor had he heard the name McKenzie. To his knowledge there was never a mention of anyone, or was there. Perhaps he dismissed the knowledge as unimportant. He would have to question her again about those last days before her mother died.

It was then that Maisie walked into the office using the back door. With his senses kicking in, Hawk knew the moment she saw the man she would want to speak to him but would ignore her impulse. Until this stranger was gone, he wanted to keep her in the back and out of sight. Perhaps she should stay home the next few days until he discovered some more information about this earl fellow. He held the distinct feeling that Maisie was the woman the earl followed from Inverness. He always thought her maiden name was MacRae like Shawna's.

At the front door, Hawk gave him a slight push helping him on his way. "I don't know a Miss McKenzie. Can't tell you anything about her. She's never been a patient of mine."

He wanted to holler at him not to come back. Hawk didn't believe he'd seen the last of the man. Blevins was part of Maisie's life, not a particularly good part.

Once the door was shut, Hawk turned the latch to make his way to the back. "Maisie...," he called out.

She was bent over, searching for something among the boxes that just arrived. Her adorable rump was tilted high into the air, tantalizing all his senses. Ah, but that sight gave him endless ideas. It had been nearly a month since their wedding day. So far, he hadn't felt the new life he suspected grew inside her womb. He would have to try harder. Houston lectured about giving her time to adjust to married life. Told him they needed to get to know each other better before they had children. Once there was a child, their time together would be divided.

As if Houston waited with his wife Leah. As far as he was concerned, Houston's words were empty.

He'd taken no precautions. Setting his hands on her hips, he pushed a few straggling strands of hair from her neck with his chin as he nuzzled her nape. "You smell of oranges and woman." Couldn't get any better than that.

"Hawk." Her voice warbled on a high note.

She tried to turn her head to see what he was doing. He touched her ear with the tip of his tongue, bit gently, nibbled along her gorgeous white neck. After that he listened for the soft sounds, she showered him with when he pleasured her. Maisie was pure delight to all his senses.

"Yes. What would you like? A little bit of this and a little bit of that? Do you want me inside your heated damp core?" He brushed a light kiss on her neck while his hands roamed beneath her skirt traveled up the silken flesh of her legs to more intimate places. Just as he liked, she wore nothing beneath her gown. "I locked the doors. No one can interrupt my plans for the next few minutes. We can take this slow or fast. Tell me what you want."

"What are you doing? It's the middle of the afternoon." She pushed her rump against him, wiggled delightfully. Must certainly feel the bulge in his pants, the hardness he couldn't deny, the length of him growing even as she questioned his intentions.

"We've never made love this way. As you well know, the time of day has never stopped me."

His long fingers wandered, explored soft flesh, slipped for a second into her damp cleft, moved higher, stopped to caress her belly, spreading his fingers from between her hipbones. It was then he felt the tiny life hiding within her. Joy swept through him. His *wee bairn* was now part of her, growing in the warmth of her womb.

Maisie seemed to be just as delighted with this as he was. She squirmed against him, brazenly pushing back, enticing all his male parts, telling him she was not averse to his plans of seduction. With his hands curving her hips, he held her still while he tried to catch his breath. "Hawk, this doesn't seem right. We can't...just...in your," she gulped air, "in your storeroom."

Hawk didn't see why not. No one would be the wiser. "Ah, sweetheart, I want you now. Can't wait to find a bed or my desk. Now." He touched her heat, found the honey flowed from her. He undid his pants. Slowly, ever so gently, he pushed inside her core. Just as gradually, withdrew then thrust again. He needed to make this last forever. Knew that wouldn't happen. He was ready to detonate though he wished to see to her pleasure before he exploded inside her.

She whimpered. Gulped air. "Hawk," whispered his name as her need escalated at a pace he wished to ease. Thinking about her rising passion he stopped, held her still as she writhed and coiled against him. The soft flesh of her fanny cupped in his hands.

He needed to prolong this, take the moment with languid ease.

Covering her breasts with his hands, he continued his tender assault. She cried out, then purred softly as she found her pleasure. In seconds he erupted inside her, felt her spasms, circle him, pull him deeper, mercurially kissing his length.

Atop the box she'd been hunting through, her head rested on her forearms. She was panting, gasping for air still excited by the act. She was always so responsive, so enchanting. With measured ease, he pulled out of her then brought her into his arms. She snuggled next to him, her cheek against his chest. "You couldn't wait?" she murmured in a thin voice, her small slender fingers caressing his chest.

"No, could not. Not when I saw your little butt in the air calling to me. I prayed you did not wear anything beneath your gown I would have to push away to make room for my explorations. If you did, I would have had to burn whatever you wore. You obeyed me. Possibly because you wished for me to find you then take you."

"I did. When I dressed this morning, I had this in mind."

Her breathing was now moderated. She pulled his shirttails from his britches, curiously exploring his chest. He found he was hard again, needing, wanting. Yearning.

"You will have to wait for another time. Oh..."

Hawk groaned when she circled him with those sweet fingers of hers. Not hesitating, he set her atop the boxes. Her legs wrapped around him. He was inside her again. This time the mating was hard, faster than he wanted. When they finished, he fastened his pants or there would be a third joining. He wanted to go home with her, find the time to charm and love her in every way possible. When she looked at him questions in her eyes, he could only say in his defense, "What did you expect. I'm only a man, with a man's needs. Should we go home? Close the office? Houston left an hour ago. I want to do this with you sitting on the kitchen table, your legs spread around my flanks. What do you say?" Lifting her chin, he kissed her tenderly. We can have something to eat then explore each other more thoroughly.

He was lost. Could never get enough of her. Holding out his hand to her. "Let's walk home. There are no patients in the office, nothing that can't wait until tomorrow for us to attend.

The walk took less than ten minutes. Silence stretched between them as he tried to figure out what he should say as well as what he should not. If she knew, she should be the one to tell him about the child. To his misgiving, he already told her he would know almost the moment the *wee bairn* was conceived.

She stopped at the door, turning in his arms and lifting her face to him. He kissed her with tender sweetness, evocatively. She smiled, placing her fingertip on his chin. If she continued to kiss him, he would take her on the front porch. They had neighbors. He groaned, the rumbling husky sound coming from the back of his throat.

It seemed she understood his predicament. "I've a venison stew cooking. I'll put biscuits in the oven. There is jam made this summer if you can keep your hands to yourself." She laughed, a small giggle that he adored while she dodged to the left. He missed her by inches. Smiled as she walked inside then headed to the kitchen.

"I will try."

Hawk loved to watch her. She would understand he would never try very hard to keep his hands to himself. When they were alone, he found he always wanted her, pictured her naked with her legs spread, her arms outstretched to him.

She was so graceful and calm, the picture of serenity itself. He supposed that was part of what caught his attention that first time he saw her, that, and her innate shyness, not to take anything away from her breath stealing beauty. She vanished into the house that day, leaving him curious about her.

Even then with only a brief sight of her, he sensed she was his mate. Like a man driven, he went after her. In the process of heated courtship, he frightened her away.

Maisie wasn't like any woman he'd ever known. She was his through all eternity. During the rituals, she saw them together.

He thought about the man in his office today. Recalled her mentioning the second protector her mother found after her father died. The thought that the man wanted her even as a little girl of no more than thirteen or fourteen crossed his mind turning his stomach. There was more going on here than met the eye. He would have to be alert. It seemed this man still wanted her.

The Earl of St. Blevins...he would have to send out feelers to Inverness, beyond if it became necessary. The McKenna would lend a hand. Needed to discover as much about this man as possible. What the devil did the earl want with Maisie? Would the man pursue her even if he knew she was wed? He hoped not.

They walked into the kitchen. Maisie still dodged him. He understood that was prudent. The way he felt now, if she didn't, they might not eat until later, much, much later. She puttered around the room, stoking the fire, stirring the stew while he remained lost in thought. The last rays of the dying sun shone through the window warming the kitchen sending muted light dancing across the floor. He wanted to take her to the bonfire, hold her in his lap, caress her until she cried out his name. Ah, not tonight, this evening they needed to rest. He needed to make certain she understood she conceived. She needed to know important things about her health.

Standing beside him, she placed her hand on his shoulder, garnering his attention. "What has you so involved you didn't even notice me? Could make a girl doubt herself."

Maisie set a goblet of wine in front of him. After that she set the table while she waited for him to answer. Seconds ticked by turning to minutes, "Hawk?" she queried still seeming to want an answer.

He tossed her a half-hearted smile clearly undecided. How much to tell her about his visit with the earl was the most prevalent question in his head. Frightening her was not something he wished to do. Keeping information from her that might be important was also not something that would be wise or prudent. She needed knowledge so she could be prepared for any possible event. An event that should never take place. His fist tightened around the wine glass, sending a few drops to slide downward. He wiped the glass with the tip of his finger still engrossed with his thoughts.

Now, his hand shook when he lifted the glass of wine to his lips. He drank deeply wishing for time so he could sort out his feelings.

Setting his drink down, he sat back in the chair, his hands fisted on the table in front of him. Reaching out for the goblet, he slowly twirled the stem between his fingers, thinking, considering each and every scenario he could create.

Seconds passed, sifting in a deep breath of air, he felt ready to give an answer to her question. "Rest assured I noticed you. Always notice you." Pausing for a few moments to give further consideration, "Did you have a good day today?"

He thought to change the subject in his head to something more mundane so he could sift through his every-vacillating emotions.

At the table, she rested her elbow in one hand then placed a finger on her chin. Tapping one finger, she began to speak. "Let me think about this. Perhaps you would know how my day transpired since I spent most of my time in the office, counting bandages along with newly arrived medicines. Now, tomorrow, I'm going to lunch with Leah. Won't be in the office, except for the morning hours. Hawk, we've things to talk about. I saw someone. At least I thought I did. Wasn't at all certain it was the man I remembered."

That brought him to attention. His gut tightened. Did she see the Earl of St. Blevins and recognized him? He wondered if she guessed about the baby. Maybe she just had a few questions about the office work for her friend. Now she walked to the stove two bowls in her hand. It seemed she never sat still.

With the ladle midway, she spoke, smiling as if there was nothing, no secrets, no babies, no earls, "We're going to pick out some fabric to make new dresses. Mine seem to be getting tighter around the middle. Not a lot, but enough to be uncomfortable. I must be eating too much."

Hawk stifled the laughter bubbling up from the back of his throat.

To Hawk it was now obvious, she didn't guess at the truth of her expanding middle. He wondered if her breasts were more tender or larger. Through the fabric of her gown, he held them today. The devil, he held them last night. After they retired for the night, he meant to discover that truth. Damn, he held them every night. He should have noticed sooner. Sensed the babe's presence sooner. He would concentrate on their weight and size, not just the delightful softness he encountered when he attended to them. Either that or she kept the information from him. "You do need a few new things. Make sure you leave plenty of room in the bosom. Pick out something that the waist won't make a lot of difference if you grow larger."

She stopped dishing up the bowls of venison stew to turn to stare at him. "You're confusing me."

Bewildering her was not on his agenda. It was apparent she didn't realize her increasing bosom and waist were due to the conception of their child, not eating too much. After she set the bowls on the table, she retrieved the biscuits from the oven.

"These are delicious." He hoped once more to change the subject to something that would not bring her thoughts back to her tender breasts. He supposed he should tell her all he knew. Since they'd been wed, she'd not had that time of the month. That course of events would have stopped their lovemaking. Wouldn't she have noticed something so important? Tonight, while they were in bed he would experiment, see if he could draw the conclusion from her agile mind. He could tease her with subtlety.

"Thank you." She shook the spoon she'd been using to eat the stew at him. "What about my breasts and my waist. What are you intimating? You cannot get away with saying such nonsense and not be held accountable."

His sigh of displeasure was long and drawn-out ending is a slight wheezing of his breath. He didn't think there would be anyway to prolong the conversation now that he'd stuck his oar into the mix.

"If you must know, at this very instant you are increasing because my seed took root. You are pregnant."

He blundered his way through the telling as he watched her face turn pale before suffusing with sudden violent color.

"I'm pregnant?" Her eyes almost crossed when she said the words that seemed to cement his accusation into her mind. The vivid silver-mauve of her eyes darkened to purple. She ran her hands down her dress.

Well, it wasn't just an accusation, it was a statement of fact. "Yes, when we...a...when I touched your soft white belly about an hour or so ago, I felt the *bairn* inside. It was almost as if he spoke to me. Knew his warmth that he was comfortable because your womb is very cozy. The boy will be a shifter."

When he first mentioned the fact, she'd been standing. He wasn't certain why. Now, she sat down hard on the chair. "A boy, a shifter, this is a lot to take in on such short notice. Are you certain?"

She downed all the wine in her glass then poured herself a bit more. She sipped air for a few seconds.

His grin grew wide. He'd meant to forestall the tell-tale smile, keep the grin hidden until she digested the information he spouted at her. The action was simply impossible considering the great joy he felt. "Positive."

A man well pleased, he wanted to pull her into his arms, kiss her soundly then toss her skirts. He wanted to make love to her on the kitchen table with her legs tight around his flanks or over his shoulders. He truly didn't care where her legs were just that he was inside her. Needed to feel the *bairn* again. The way her lavender eyes darkened even more gave him reason to believe she might be thinking the same way. Her tiny pink tongue swept across her bottom lip before she tucked it beneath her teeth.

Well, hell!

He changed his mind when she suddenly fled to the back door. Her footsteps pounded down the steps until she reached the lawn. Curious to learn the reason for her flighty departure, he followed at a more sedate pace. As he stepped onto the back porch, he heard the violent retching. The devil, Maisie was losing the contents of her dinner on the new rosebushes that were planted only two weeks prior. Leah would undoubtedly be upset to learn about this since the roses were one of her wedding gifts to them.

He wasn't going to be the one to tell Leah.

Running after her, he knelt beside her. Smoothed one hand along her back while he held her hair away from her face. He wished he had a damp cloth in his hand. He would wash her face. The fact she lost her dinner told him that the babe was farther along than he originally thought. He smiled, pleased with the endorsement of his sixth sense. He wondered why he didn't sense the child sooner. Riley knew the instant his second child was conceived.

"This is perfectly normal," Hawk meant to reassure her, to ease her mind if she had any fears about what was happening to her. "Women many times have morning sickness."

"Easy for you to say. This isn't the morning. Not even close," she bit out just before dry heaves took over her slender body.

He was pleased with the added confirmation of his diagnosis though not too happy with the agony. There would be more pain as well as discomfort before this was all said and done, before he held his babe. When he was certain she was finished, he assisted her into the house, helping her to a seat at the kitchen table. "You will begin to lighten your work load."

He was grinning while he was imagining her increasing, thinking how her belly would feel, how his son would feel beneath his hand when he moved inside his mother.

Hawk poured her a cup of tea, doctoring the brew with milk and some sweet honey from the hive the clan nurtured in the hills near the McKenna keep. "Would you like lemon?" he asked when he stepped back to watch her. He lifted her chin so he could see if she was listening to his advice. "No more wine for you, my dear, until the babe is born."

When she looked at him, staring at him, strands of sweaty hair plastered to her face, he believed she thought him a *wee* bit crazy. While Maisie seemed to be mulling over his dictate, she closed her eyes, to concentrate on breathing.

Maisie nodded as she opened her eyes, "All right." Her voice was paper thin when she spoke the two words. "No wine. Why?"

Pulling his chair around so it was close to her, he straddled it, resting his hands on the back. He meant to be honest with her. She could choose to do what she wanted. Nonetheless, he felt strongly about this. "I don't know."

"Another sixth sense?" she asked her tone soft tilting her head just a bit sideways as if that view gave her a better perspective. "I would think if it affected a person negatively when there was too much imbibed, the potent drink would also affect the baby. Perhaps this way of thinking is just common sense."

Pleased that she agreed with him, even going as far as to give a reason that he could not, he proceeded to say, "Did you toss your dinner up because I told you about your condition? Is this the power of suggestion?" He didn't stop for an answer. "You should have another bowl of stew. It might stay down this time."

As she looked at the pot of stew still simmering on the stove, she turned green again. Her face paled as if she thought about the consequences of more stew. "No, maybe I'll just stick with the tea."

If she was going to be tossing up her meals, she needed to eat when her stomach was calm. "A biscuit couldn't hurt. Don't want you to go to bed hungry. Besides, you've got to eat. Losing weight is not a good idea in your condition. Not best for the mama or the *bairn*."

The biscuit she collected from the serving plate she nibbled. Broke off a small piece. After eating the small crumb, she seemed to wait to see if the morsel would stay where it belonged. When she finished the biscuit, she lathered another one with butter along with the jam. Now, she looked eager.

"It's good," she managed to say between bites. With measured calm she chewed. "I do feel better...oh no!" Once more she fled outside to the rosebush that was the recipient of her first episode equated with pregnancy.

*Well, hell.*

This time, before following her, he stopped for a damp cloth along with a glass of water. He cleaned her face, offering water to drink. Once more and after a few minutes, more minutes than he wished to admit, he eased her inside. More food would not be a good idea unless she decided she could handle it. He helped her up the steps to the bedchamber. Once there, the nightgown was the first order of business. He didn't suppose she wanted to sleep naked with him tonight. Though she might feel just fine in another hour or two. He would weigh his chances.

No, she needed her rest. He could make it through the night without holding her in his arms and loving her. That small deed was up to him to accomplish. Her green face vanished. Now, her cheeks were pale but with a tiny bit of color.

"More tea?" he asked.

Maisie shook her head, her hand at her throat. He brought a basin to her side of the bed. "I'll be back in a few hours." When he left the room, he blew out all but one of the candles. He would have to examine her tomorrow, glad that he was a doctor and that the next person examining her wouldn't be Houston. His wife would be under his care throughout the pregnancy. The only way Houston would be involved was if he needed a second consult or if an unusual problem developed.

His son would be a shifter, he mused as he made his way down the steps to the kitchen. He poured himself a generous snifter of brandy to celebrate today's good news then sat back to think over the events of the day. Maisie carried his child. She had to be at least a month along. He didn't think women lost what they'd eaten unless they were at least that far. He would have to ask Houston or look for a journal. They'd only been married a little over a month.

Good news. He could hardly wait to tell everyone.

That thought struck him hard. Houston always warned expectant parents not to say anything until they were at least three months into the pregnancy. Miscarriages happened. At that thought pain shot straight through to his heart. No, Maisie wasn't going to lose the baby. He wouldn't allow something to threaten his child. He would know, would feel his child's distress and...he would guard against accidents. Maisie would have to curtail her work load. That was all there was to this.

She would argue.

He would win.

The knock on the front door startled him out of the melancholy thoughts. He wasn't at all certain he wanted company tonight. There was so much for him to think about. When he opened the door, he was surprised to see his little brother, Cameron. He stepped through the door, a frown on his handsome face.

"Where's your wife?" Cameron pushed past him then on into the drawing room, looking around as he walked. "Don't want to speak of this if she is nearby. Private, you know. Not for a woman to hear."

While Hawk watched, his brother poured them both a snifter of brandy. He turned, lifting the glass high before sitting down to look as if he brooded. He set one foot on his knee while he sipped staring into the small fire that blazed in the hearth.

"What is it? Your latest lady love kick you out?" Hawk asked with a laugh thinking he might enjoy this diversion. Someone else's problems would take his mind from the Earl of St. Blevins which now that Maisie knew she was pregnant was his next order of business. He needed to discover the man's intent and if it concerned his wife.

From thoughts of his wife, Hawk's attention turned back to his brother. Cameron never took life seriously. Why should he? He was only twenty-five. The boy had a great deal of growing to do, some seasoning so he would mellow then become a good husband and father. His brother did like his women as they all had at that age. What was the trouble now? If Cameron lost one ladybird, he would easily move on to another.

"No," Cameron guzzled the brandy as if the drink was water and he was lost in a desert, his throat parched from the dryness and lined with sand. "She lost weight. Doesn't have what she used to have. The nerve of her...I thought...believed when I took her from LoraLee's she would remain the same."

Hawk chocked on the brandy in his mouth, spitting out a small measure as he gaped at his little brother. When he had himself under control, he said, "Isn't she the same person inside? What does it matter if she's different on the outside?"

"No! Well, yes in some ways. Now she is different both inside as well as out. Don't know how to explain all the changes she made with herself. When we make love there just isn't enough of her to hold onto. Her hips, her breasts, her luscious butt, all of her is smaller. She no longer overflows my hands. I have nearly nothing to hang on to when I plunge inside her to give us both our pleasure."

The boy always had a penchant for curvaceous women, very curvaceous women. What did it matter if he liked the girl. Of course, the woman was his mistress, not in consideration for marriage. She was supposed to please her protector. Hawk shrugged with a small frown as he pulled out a handkerchief then wiped the errant drops off his shirt. If he didn't like her any longer, he could dismiss her.

"You should buy her chocolates. That would put some meat on her bones. Sugar has the knack of it. Chocolates coupled with wine. Lots of it."

Hawk never considered a woman's form to be that important. He'd always been attracted to the woman's mind. Well, maybe not always. No, not even with Maisie. He coveted her body before he knew enough of her to enjoy her nimble mind.

"I tried that." Cameron was now pacing around the small room, stopping to look out the window from time to time. "She threw the box at me. Chocolates everywhere, on the floor, some smashed against the wall. Others were stepped on smearing the carpet. After that she yelled at me, shaking her small fist. Even her fists are smaller. Her fingers are no longer pudgy. Don't even like to kiss her toes. They aren't the same. Skinny toes *dinna* have the same appeal."

"You don't have to keep her. If you no longer appreciate her womanly charms, find someone else you like better," Hawk said laughing as he watched his brother. "The woman is just your mistress. There are more amply endowed women out there. I'm certain with your boyish good looks you could have your pick."

"I can't. I took her from the bordello, from LoraLee's. Promised her she would never have to go back to that life. See how she repaid me? Her breasts don't move the way they used to. She doesn't even jiggle the tiniest bit. Well, perhaps a tiny bit." He rubbed his temples for several seconds. "I don't know what to do. Want her back the way she was."

"You could try loving her body the way it is now." After giving the idea a few seconds to mature, he said. "Perhaps you shouldn't be so obvious in your attempts to fatten her up. Maybe tell her how much you liked her when she weighed more. Praise the way her soft breasts filled your hands." Hawk was groping. The devil if the woman didn't want to be over endowed in every way, she didn't need to be. "It's healthier for her to weigh less. Don't you want her to live a long life?"

Cameron shot him a scowl that told him he could go to the devil. "Of course I want her to live a long time. What happens when she is over the hill isn't going to be part of my life. What she's like now is. By the time she is old enough to expire, I'll be married to my mate. She is simply a pleasant diversion until then. A woman who I care about."

"There is that," Hawk conceded while thinking about his wife increasing. Yes, he would enjoy the extra bounty, of her breasts, her belly, her hips. Soon, because of her pregnancy, her breasts would grow, become more tender. They would be so sensitive her soft purrs and mewls of ecstasy would come earlier. She would waddle delightfully when she walked. He might have to help her stand when she was sitting. Maisie wouldn't like that but he would enjoy every special moment of her pregnancy. He wanted her to think of each part of these next months as a new adventure.

"She asked me not so very subtly for a new wardrobe because nothing of her old one fits. I'm not made of groats. As far as I'm concerned, she doesn't need to wear a thing when I'm around. As to when I'm not around, she has sufficient clothing. Aren't women supposed to be able to sew? She could take some tucks in here and there. Ones that could be let out when she succumbs to my plans to plump her back up."

"Bring her other foods to fatten her up to your liking. She might not be able to resist her favorites. Make certain they are in abundance when you are with her as well as when you are not. When one eyes a coveted delicacy, it is terribly hard to resist succumbing to temptation. Your lady might not have a sweet tooth. That's why she could toss the chocolates at your face."

"Such as?" Cameron appeared eager to learn of foods that might put some weight on her now slim body.

"Wine, spirits of any sort, a large glass of ale to go with dinner capped off with brandy would do wonders. If she likes bread, you could go to that bakery in Inverness, buy some delightful pastries, some of them filled with jelly. Not a lot mind you. Just enough to tempt her pallet. Cheese if she likes it, to go with the fresh bread coupled with lots of butter as well as jam. Even bacon, if she smells that tantalizing aroma, she might not be able to resist."

"You're wicked, big brother. I'll try all that as you say. Subtlety coupled with temptation are the key words in this scheme."

"I would also not leave her for long. If she's a mind to take the pounds off, she will do so each time you leave her to her own devices. Each time her special treats are not lying in front of her. You need to keep her in your bed and feed her tenderly. Tempt her pallet with deliciousness. Let her watch while you devour her favorites. Don't impose. Just tempt."

Cameron stopped pacing to sit in a plump chair by the fire. "I like your ideas. Where is your wife. It's still early. Did I stop you from bedding her?" He hooted then grinned seeming to be pleased with himself. "You did put a bug in my head. I'm trying to think of all Katy's favorite dishes."

Hawk looked to the room upstairs wishing the conversation could have continued around Cameron's mistress. If he ignored his brother, he still wouldn't go away even though he changed the topic back to where it had been. "She is feeling poorly."

"Ah, another way to say your seed is firmly planted in her womb. I'd say belly but you would correct me. Am I right?"

He inhaled a long deep breath. "Yes." Hawk held up his hand as Cameron appeared ready to dart out of the house to spread the word. "We're not mentioning any of this until a few months have passed. Houston advises this caution. I, for one, will heed his advice. When we are certain she will carry to term, we'll tell mother and father first then Shawna and Riley. You will promise not to say anything until then."

He held up both hands as if silently promising with the gesture. "Won't open my mouth. Besides, it is up to you and Maisie when it is to be common knowledge. If mother and father spend much time around Maisie, they will guess the truth."

That was perhaps more reality than Hawk wanted to hear. Secrecy around his parents was difficult. "When will you go to Inverness?"

"First thing in the morning." Cameron sat back, a contented look on his handsome face. "In two days, I'll be able to begin fattening her up. Don't know why women want to starve themselves so they can be skinny. I like to watch all their female parts, touch caress, sway. If there is nothing there to watch or hold, what fun is that?"

Neither did he. It just seemed that some women were built that way. He didn't care how much Maisie weighed. He'd feel the same way about her no matter her size. Hawk suspected that once Cameron found his mate, how many curves she possessed wouldn't change the way he felt about her.

Hawk leaned forward, realizing his brother just presented him with the solution to his problem about St. Blevins. Clearing his throat he began, "When you are in Inverness will you do something for me?"

"Certainly." Cameron's brows drew together as he thought about the unusual request. "I would have time on my hands. The family shipping business prospers. None of us need to spend much time in the city."

"I'd like you to send out a few queries into the Earl of St. Blevins. I need to know everything possible about the man. Who he spends time with, his mistresses. How he makes his groats. Any homes he owns. Everything."

~ * ~

If Hawk possessed a sixth sense, so did she. Maisie understood he wanted to talk to her tonight about something important. She believed her pending pregnancy was one of the topics that seemed to be niggling on his mind. It wasn't only one subject that seemed to be bothering him. Both the look in his eyes, along with his strange silence, told her as much. His mind took a different tact after she showed him her first symptoms of pregnancy.

What was his second theme? She didn't have one notion as to what could be bothering him. Everything here had been peaceful since their marriage.

After he brought her upstairs, she slept for a short time. When she woke, her stomach settled. Since it was making noises, she could use some food in her belly. Now, she was wide awake. Wouldn't be able to sleep again. It had to be the tea that kept her eyes open as well as her mind busy. The drink was not something she could ever sip at night. To wash the vile taste from her mouth, she drank two cups. When she did, she didn't fall asleep. She smashed her hand into the pillow wondering if he would return soon.

Earlier while she was counting the moonbeams that filtered in through the lace curtains at the window, she heard someone come into the house. The low rumble of male voice and laughter sifted its way up the stairs to her room. After listening with quite a lot of diligence, she realized the man in their drawing room was his little brother, Cameron. She should put on her robe so she could see him, greet him properly. She didn't want to see Cameron this evening. Harris came to see her yesterday. She is sweet and so innocent, so in love. His sister spoke quite a bit about Ashton. Ash, she called the man. Harris was falling in love. He was gone though, gone back to London or Cornwall. Harris hadn't been certain. Maisie was afraid her heart would be broken by the Sassenach captain.

Well, she didn't want to see the little brother wearing only her nightgown and robe. Other ideas roamed through her head. Maisie waited until she heard the front door bang closed, heard Hawk's footsteps wander into the kitchen. He would be heading there to clean up the dishes from the evening meal. Her stomach grumbled for the second time in just a few seconds. She wondered if she could eat and keep the food in her belly that now felt very normal.

Smoothing her hair in place before doing the same with the robe she walked down the steps then into the kitchen. She was naked beneath the robe. He would appreciate that fact when he discovered it. She wouldn't tell him or perhaps she would. She wanted to see the look in his silver eyes when he learned. His back was to her as he was running water into the sink. A kettle sat on the stove heating more water to rinse with.

When she stood directly under the door frame, he turned. The smile he greeted her with seemed to reach his ears. Ears she'd like to nibble on for a few seconds. Biting his chin just to get his attention might be fun. She thought of the way his hands felt when he caressed her breasts, breasts that were tender as well as larger. He was always so gentle. Nerves shaking, she swept her tongue across her lips, moistening them as if she wanted him to kiss her. She did.

"You're feeling better?"

He looked worried. His eyes were narrowed as if assessing her.

After that they stopped at her bosom before dropping lower to continue until his gaze rested on her bare feet then lazily moved upward once more. She wondered if he could tell what wasn't beneath her robe.

"The tips of your breasts are pushing against the silk of your robe," he told her his voice soft, throaty with desire.

The look on his face told her he wanted her. When he gazed at the kitchen table still filled with bowls of stew as well as a plate of biscuits, she understood he'd planned this scenario. Her sickness got in his way. Was he going to continue with his plan? There wasn't any room on the table. She imagined her long braid covered with the broth from the venison stew, crumbled biscuits there too. She shuddered. Wrapped her arms around her pushing up her breasts.

He noticed. Groaned low and rough in the back of his throat.

She dropped her arms to her sides. "Yes, much better." Her heart pounded. "I'd like something to eat. Want to see if the food will remain where it belongs." *Before you play with me. Before I play with you.*

Maisie didn't know when she'd grown so bold, she could even think of something like playing with him. She sat down to wait for him. Knew he would bring her food. Understood that as soon as she finished, if she wasn't sick, he would proceed with his earlier plan. Deep between her legs, her body thrummed, ached as it heated and grew damp in anticipation. Only her wicked thoughts caused her body to pulse. So far, Hawk had done nothing expect look at her. She understood what he did to her so easily, how she became a violin to be played in the orchestra he directed.

With his back to her, he dished up a bowl of hot stew to replace the congealing bowl on the table. She wanted to look at his crotch, needed to see if he was reacting to her the way she was to him. When her stomach responded to the heady aroma and grumbled, he grinned at her, an all-knowing masculine grin. She swallowed, hoping this was a good idea. Her gaze slanted downward. Seeing the swelling in his pants she smiled wickedly, at least she hoped it was a wicked smile.

"Glad to see that you want to eat." He sat down at the table with the brandy he must have brought with him. He buttered a piece of bread for her, no longer warm but fresh. "You need to fatten up. Well, I suppose that will all occur quite naturally."

When he chuckled, she wanted to toss the buttered bread at him.

"Cameron was here?"

Her stomach calm now, she dug into the stew. The food was delicious. As she chewed on a piece of venison, she thought she had died and gone to heaven, the taste divine. After she finished almost half the bowl, she looked up to question Hawk, "What did he want?"

"Advice." Hawk chuckled while his eyes rolled upward to stare at the ceiling. "He was asking for advice from his older brother. I find that thought refreshing."

Maisie wished she understood what was behind that expression. "Would you tell me his question if I asked?"

He slipped his hand across the table to take her into his. "Tell you that my brother likes his women to have generous curves. While I was thinking about how your curves will appear in another couple of months, I decided your body is a beautiful work in progress. Perhaps there is something to be said for plump women."

This time she wanted to toss her cup of tea at him.

He rubbed gentle circles on her wrists. "Will your breasts overflow my hands? I wonder. Will your belly be so round that all I will want to do from one night to the next is stroke and caress the white flesh. While I stare at you, imagine you naked beneath that robe, you are as flat as this table. If I splay my hands on your belly, my fingers will touch your pelvic bones." He stared at the table, a wicked look in his eyes. "I still want to caress and stroke your belly even though you are still quite flat."

Heat flamed on her face. He was outrageous. She stiffened her back, tilting her chin as high as it would go. "You, Sir, will have to wait to discover the truth of that. I would not know. If I did comprehend the truth or falsehood, I would never tell you."

Seemingly unable to help himself, he howled with his laughter. She tugged on her hands. He held them tight. "Your breasts are already larger. Are they not? I want to kiss them. Delicately bite the tip. Nuzzle them against my cheek. Would you like me to do so? Your belly, well...that brings on new very pleasant images for me to think on. I want my tongue inside you, tasting you." He stepped forward, so close to her she could feel his breath ripple across her cheek.

One handed he picked her up, holding her close, guiding her toward the table. She knew this would happen. That was more than half the reason she walked down the steps this evening, why she waited for Cameron to leave, why she wore nothing under the dressing gown. She wanted to tempt him, knew how to charm him with words. She did want to feel his tongue inside her.

With his free arm, he moved the clutter on the table to one side. When he was satisfied, he set her on the table. She stared into his face, saw the lust in his eyes, the masculine desire raging just beneath the surface. He pushed her knees apart, separating them before stepping between her thighs.

"I've naught on beneath the gown." She had not meant to tell him. Her breath rasped from her parched throat. "I knew you wanted me on the table but I lost my dinner. Your plans changed. Cameron distracted you. Now...now you can do as you please."

Her fingers rested on his shoulders. She toyed with the laces on his shirt before spreading her fingers so she could move them across his chest. "I want you to take your shirt off."

"Soon."

"Now."

"You feel fine at this moment?" he asked as he untied the ribbons holding her robe in place. The back of his hands played across the tips of her breasts as he separated the fabric. He stepped back to look at her from a new angle. "Yes, the color of your nipples is different, a different hue a subtle difference. Perhaps they are darker, dusty pink. They are also a *wee* bit larger." His big body shook. "Maisie, I want you naked. My imagination has created this scene too many times for me to count. Don't know how long I can wait to see all of you, to fill you then empty my seed into you. When you reach your climax, your body will kiss my penis."

The cool night air rippling across the tips of her breasts hardened them. He touched each pinnacle with his mouth before licking them. After that he blew his breath whispering across her. She trembled. Her body ached. Her heart raced. He picked her up so he could slide the fabric of her robe down her arms. The material pooled around her hips. He stood between her legs, pushing them farther apart, then farther so he must be able to see every part of her. His fingers fondled her breasts, tugged then pulled on each tip until she gasped for a snippet of air.

"Take your shirt off. You should also be naked. Just as you are doing, I need to look my fill." Her voice was so gravelly she didn't recognize it as her own. "I also want to caress you, wrap my fingers around your penis, lick and kiss you with my mouth."

It didn't take long before he was hoping on foot to remove his shoes. Once his boots were vanquished the rest of his clothing joined the pile. Hands on his hips he stood back so she could look her fill, to see all of him that was so different from her. In all the times he'd made love to her, she'd never had her chance to stare at him, to absorb all that he was into a picture she could hold onto. As if to touch him, she reached out, thought better of the act and pulled her hand back.

Hawk waisted no more time. She was flat on her back. He settled her against the table, her legs dangling over the edge. When she turned her head to the left there was one bowl of congealed stew staring her in the face. Her stomach lurched. The plate of biscuits a bit farther north. "Oh, my, perhaps you should move the old food."

He pushed the bowl to one side as he bent over to kiss her, to touch her in all the ways it pleased her. Cupping her breasts in his hands, he was kneading them, massaging, them fondling them as if he never wanted to stop. He stared at the ceiling for a moment seeming to gain control. With a moment of what seemed to be resignation, "Do you think by the time you are ready to give birth these beautiful jewels will overflow my hands even more?" His hands moved lower, lingering on her belly, heading farther south to cup her mound. "You are so soft, so silken. You will stay that way through all our lives together."

She had no idea how to answer his questions or reply to his comments. She needed to tell him yes, she would, "I suppose that whatever you want, Hawk, you will receive."

She gasped then when his finger swept within her cleft. At the same time he tugged on the tip of her breast with his teeth. Her body spasmed.

He spent many more moments kissing his way from each breast

before moving down her body to the midline of her torso to her navel then lower. His hands under her hips, he brought her to his mouth. Her fingers dug into his shoulders. He sipped on her intimately, licked, bit with gentle concern. She squirmed and twisted against him, arching her back needing more than he was giving. Whimpering...mewling...as he continued to stroke her intimately. Her back arched off the table when, for a second time, he nipped her, laved then bit again.

"Over my shoulders or around my flanks?" he asked his voice a deep harsh panting sound. For several seconds he pulled back, staring down at her, looking his fill.

It seemed he didn't search for an answer from her. Startled by his quick movement, the backs of her legs now rested on his shoulders. Her fingernails scraped across his flesh as he continued to tease her into ecstasy. She pulsed. Throbbed with the pleasure of him. A soft fragmented sound bolted from her.

"Hold me..." he whispered. When she didn't respond he continued. "My penis sweetheart. Hold me in your hands, stroke me, caress my length."

She circled him, did exactly as he told her until his groan stopped her for a moment. "I want to kiss you there, suck you into my mouth. Can I? Is that something that would please you?"

"Later, when we are done here," his voice thick with desire.

As if to put her comments to the back of his head, he sucked on one breast, held the other in his hand twirled the tip between his calloused fingers. Just as he had this afternoon he entered her slowly, deliciously as if he had eternity. There was so much time between each languid movement that she pounded on his shoulders asking for more of him.

"We're going to take as much time as possible." His unhurried movements sent her heart racing. The time mercuric, heating, ravishing. Her insides clenched around him, begging him for more, more of the magical enchantment she was oh so close to experiencing. It seemed he meant his words. In then out, again and again while she spiraled higher but not high enough to send her over that pinnacle to the blinding spasms that would soon encroach upon her. This was torture.

Suddenly, he thrust into her, harder and faster. She cried out a wail that she could not hold behind her teeth. "Hawk...Hawk...! Oh...oh...God...please..."

She was moving in time with him, arching, spiraling, writhing. Her body jerked when he thrust one more time. She felt his wetness enfold her. She gasped in a straggled breath of air. His weight fell on top of her, pressing her against the table. He moved her legs downward so that they enclosed his hips. She locked her ankles behind his back.

"That was nice..." he murmured taking little nips on her chin then down her neck to rake his teeth across her nipple. "I love the way you taste. Should we try this some other place? Where would you like? Where haven't we made love? Perhaps a guest room? What do you think?"

No response came to her mind. She was utterly limp, wrung out with no energy. What now? Her mind was filled with several different scenarios. They couldn't stay on the table much longer. Her back was getting sore. The wood was hard. His weight pressed down on her. The remnants of the stew seemed to be closer. Her stomach recoiled again.

As if he guessed her feelings, he lifted her to a sitting position, lightly touched her swaying breasts with the tips of his fingers.

"You came down here for this. I find that fact delightful." He placed a finger on her lips. "No, don't deny the fact. You can ignore the question but don't refute me. You waited until you heard Cameron leave. You wore nothing beneath the robe so I could touch you sooner, enter your sultry heat sooner." He lifted her in his arms. "Keep your legs wrapped around me. One more place to make love to be checked off my list."

She thought they would go upstairs. They didn't. Now, both naked, they sat in the drawing room. She sat on his hard thighs, straddling him. Her breasts sweeping against his naked chest, feeling the crips hair on his torso tantalize her over stimulated body. His fully aroused member pressed eagerly against her core. "What are we doing? Anyone could come by. Could peer in through the window." She had the sudden image of Cameron or Harris waltzing up to the front porch to visit. The time was still early. Anything could happen. "I don't want to be naked anymore."

"I'm going to hold you. After that we will probably make love in the drawing room. We haven't done that yet. Perhaps I'll hold you against the door. Hush now, no one will come by to say hello. It is, after all, almost nine o'clock. Much too late for visitors."

The horrible feeling that he might be wrong swept through her. "I'd like my robe. It's," she gulped air. "It's still on the floor in the kitchen."

She tilted her chin in the air thinking a bit of stubborn pressure might get her what she wanted. Sitting in the drawing room with nothing on was something she'd never believed she would do.

"No..." He was grinning shamelessly, shaking his head at her. "No, I want to hold you in this room while you are clothed only in your beauty. Wish to make love to you here as soon as you are more relaxed. Don't want to have to disrobe you again, since I've got you exactly the way I like you best."

"Once each night is more than enough times."

"Never enough."

She sighed softly as Hawk proceeded to do exactly as he told her he would do. He was, once more, deep inside her, tantalizing her, enchanting all her female senses. She wondered what he would do next. In his arms, she climaxed. Her body once more was limp from the satisfaction he heaped upon her. She closed her eyes, letting all her weight settle against him. Hawk was so close to her; she heard the even cadence of each breath he drew into his lungs.

When he turned her in his arms, her lashes fluttered open. Before she realized what was happening, they were half way up the steps. He carried her. After that he set her on their big bed and came down atop her.

"Maybe we should do this in the usual way."

"Again? I can barely breathe or move."

"One more time."

When she woke in the morning, Hawk was gone. There was a basin lying on the bedside table, a note sitting on his pillow meant for her to read.

*Good morning, sweetheart.*

*Hope you are feeling wonderful. Just in case your stomach decides to rebel I've left a basin on the table along with a fresh glass of water to rinse your mouth.*

*I will be at the office. Sleep as long as you wish. You can join me later or not at all. Enjoy the luncheon with Leah. Put whatever you purchase at the dressmakers on my tab. You can ask Leah all the pertinent questions you want. You know, about the pregnancy as well as giving birth. I understand we are not supposed to spread our good news this soon. Nonetheless, Houston will have to know. The man keeps nothing from his wife.*

*Tonight, I will need to examine you. We might both find that enjoyable. There are certain things I need to look at as well as learn from you before I can determine when the child might be born. I would that you relax today as much as possible. Take a nap before dinner.*

*If it's nice this evening, would you like to go to the bonfire, roast a few marshmallows? Make love. If you recall the first time at the cabin, all I did was pleasure you. Promise you won't catch a fever this time.*

*If you want when you've finished your business with Leah, you can come see me. Our lovemaking last night kept me distracted from a few questions I have about a man who visited yesterday. You should know about him especially if he is looking for you.*

*See you soon,*
*Hawk*

Maisie wished he ended the short message with *Love, Hawk.* Of course, he did not. She thought she might ask Leah if shifters always loved their mates. Perhaps loving their life partner wasn't a prerequisite. She wanted to find out the truth.

Her hands on her belly, she felt fine. Maybe she wouldn't have morning sickness but afternoon sickness. She would ask Leah about that too. Hawk should know. He was a doctor. Would he tell her? Would he have Houston examine her. No, he said that he would look at her. It was something that would have to be done soon. Did he tell her that he would be her physician throughout or just that first time?

So much happened yesterday she didn't seem to be able to recall anything. Was that also a symptom of pregnancy? A muddled brain? Pregnancy brain? She hoped not. She didn't want to go so many months not being able to recall simple conversations. Stiff from her exertions last night, she rose from bed. She stretched to relieve a few aches and pains caused by his ardent lovemaking.

She took a few minutes to look over her wardrobe, selecting a gown that had always been large on her. Her petticoats, she left in the armoire. She wouldn't see Hawk this morning. The time already passed ten. By the time she ate breakfast then tidied up the kitchen, she would meet Leah. They planned a luncheon at the Tea and Crumpets lodge that was located a block from the dress shop. The cook there, Mrs. Brown, was one of the best in the small village. The haggis she made melted in the mouth. Her fresh bread was light and fluffy.

With no warning, her stomach rebelled. Bile rose to her throat. A mad dash to the bedside table and basin was made just in the nick of time. She lost the contents of her stomach which wasn't much since she ate little last night. She wiped her mouth with a soft damp cloth. She sipped a small portion of the water he left in a glass.

Hovering over the basin, Maisie waited until she thought her stomach calmed. She wondered how long this unwanted and sporadic illness would continue. A woman could only pray each day that each time she threw up was the last. Hawk caused this, curse his soul. She wanted to shake her fist at him. If he stood near her, she would do so. As for doing so now, the act was a waste of energy.

She bathed and dressed, ate a small biscuit that was left over from the night before, tossed the contents of her stomach in the basin once more. Sitting at the kitchen table she sipped a cup of tea laced with all her favorites. The brew was more milk and honey than tea.

Last night, Hawk told her she shouldn't drink wine. What else should she eat or drink? She would try to use logic to make her decisions. Strong tea always made her a bit flighty, skittish. Milk was fed to babes. Well...breast milk. She would think that milk and honey couldn't hurt the *wee* one. Perhaps old Gregory, the goat's milk, would be good for the *bairn*.

Would Leah have any ideas about what would be best for the child? Something else she would ask. After she cleaned up the dishes, she wrapped a shawl around her shoulders. It would only take her between five and ten minutes to walk to the inn.

The air was brisk. Fall colored leaves adorned the trees, the leaves shimmering and gleaming in the full sunlight. While the morning was frigid, the sun was beginning to warm the earth. She breathed in deeply, scenting fall, anticipating the winter months ahead then the birth of their child sometime this spring.

A stray cat darted in front of her. She gasped as she sidestepped to avoid the animal. When she opened the door to the inn, warm scents assailed her, bread fresh-baked from the oven, tea, even coffee that had become a staple of the inn after Kit Stuart and Roby McKenna traveled to the colonies to locate their mates. It was there they learned to love coffee. Enough so that they kept the stores and cafés supplied. Neither were successful in that endeavor. Hawk adored his coffee. In the month they'd been together, she hadn't acquired a liking for the bitter drink.

The devil, they'd been married a month. She carried his child. So much in her life changed in such a short time.

"A table for two," she told a cute, young serving girl.

Maisie thought she might be one of Mrs. Brown's daughters. The girl was well-endowed. Her hair was red, tight with curls that bounced provocatively around her face. She possessed the most incredible green eyes, eyes that were the color of the moss near the waterfall Hawk took her to two weeks ago. Her dress fit her tight across her bosom, revealing soft rounded breasts that seemed to be pushed up high. For a moment, she thought she saw the dusky pink crest of one of her nipples.

Maisie shook her head setting that image to the back of her head.

The girl nodded then led her to a table near a window where she could look outside to the main street of the village. "What can I get you?"

"At the moment, just tea with milk and honey."

Maisie wasn't certain her stomach would take anything else. She didn't want to toss the contents of her stomach here.

Setting her chin in her hands she stared out the window. The small town bustled with energy. From what she learned from Hawk, at least half, maybe more of the people who lived in this area were shifters. She was in the minority. She couldn't shift. When she saw an older man walking on the other side of the street, a small tremor rippled down her spine. She didn't understand the sensation or why. The man was not familiar to her. There was just something about him that stirred a memory.

Her hands on her belly, she thought on Hawk's proclamation last night. She carried a boy who would also be capable of shifting. How would she handle that? She didn't know. Hawk would have to teach the lad all that he knew. So lost in thought, she didn't notice the man standing beside the table until a shadow fell across her.

He cleared his throat then asked, "Miss McKenzie? Thought it was you. Was certain I would find you in the village. How fortuitous?"

Startled, she looked closer. Fear slithered down her spine. Dark images gathered in her head when she looked upward, stared into eyes she knew she should remember. He was small, not nearly the size of Hawk. His lean figure was well-dressed in the fashion of the time. The black frockcoat he wore was tailored impeccably for him. While he stared at her, his dark brown eyes turned dark, nearly black.

When she first saw the man, she didn't recognize him. Several seconds passed while she searched her mind for some hint of who he was and why the sight of him caused her to shiver. Shaking her head, she bristled at the thought he was intruding. Leah would arrive soon. She wanted no more to do with this man who surveyed her as if he owned her. "No, I don't know you."

She did though. It might take a few minutes to recall the time and place.

He smiled at her. "Your memory has failed you. I knew you when you were small, just a girl. You were lovely then. Now, you would rival your mother's beauty. You always had this way of holding yourself, so still, so very proud. Somehow even as a girl, you were able to show no emotion. Nothing phased you. When your mother passed..."

He would see the recognition in her eyes, the dread, the terror. She shuttered her eyes, forcing her gaze to her hands that she held clasped in her lap. This wasn't happening. Couldn't be. Once, just weeks ago, she thought she was in full control of her life. She felt rage simmer from the pit of her stomach.

"My mother's protector. You weren't there for her. Where were you when she needed you? You owed her after all the things she did for you."

There was a wealth of accusation in her voice coupled with the increasing anger. She thought that he'd done a horrible job protecting, seeing to her needs. Her mother died because there was not enough food for both of them. She gave what little food they had to her. After they both sickened, her mother gave the medicine they were able to buy to her. "Mother..." The single word ended on a soft sob. She clenched her fists tighter. "Go away!"

Watching her, he stroked his chin, his eyes narrowing in on her. He shifted his feet as if he meant to say something but changed his mind. "I was away at the time of her passing. Had business elsewhere. If not, I would have been there for you. I've regretted that."

"What about before you left on this so-called business? Why did you never provide enough for us? She never asked for anything. All she wanted, for what she gave to you, were the necessities. I heard the two of you arguing at night. You forced her to have sex with you for your promise that you would see to our needs. She didn't want to sleep with you. She believed you would at least give her enough to feed herself as well as me. You did not." Her anger seemed to grow faster and harder. "Where were you!"

"Excuse me. Am I interrupting?" Leah asked as she pulled out the chair meant for her then signaled the serving girl. She looked from one to the other seeming to read the situation accurately. "Some tea, please. We'll tell you what else we need as soon as we decide."

"I will speak with you later, Miss McKenzie." He bowed turning to leave.

"That's Mrs. Fraser."

~ * ~

"The nerve of the little twit," Farlan, the Earl of St. Blevins muttered as he strode away from the young woman, he thought to make his next mistress. What the devil did she mean, Mrs. Fraser? She wasn't married. She couldn't be. If she was, he would figure out how to do something to get around that deplorable fact. An affair might be pleasant. He wouldn't have to arrange for a place for them to meet where they wouldn't be discovered. He could have her whenever or wherever it pleased him.

Of course, there were more ways to get around a husband.

He smiled benignly at the young serving girl he wanted in his bed tonight. Since Maisie wasn't available to him this evening, he would make do with this one. She even flaunted herself in front of him, dipped down so he could see her sweet accessories beneath her gown. For the budding whore, the gown was modest. He imagined the rest of her, plump and sweet, her flesh soft and white. She would taste of the kitchen along with the ale she would be serving later in the evening. The aroma would have to do. He preferred a woman straight from the bath, perfumed just for him. He preferred the scent of roses. Anything delicate would do.

Finding a place in a far corner that gave him direct line of vision to the two women, Farlan sat. The girl brought him a platter of meats and cheeses as well as a few slices of the fresh baked bread. He needed a light repast. There were errands to take care of before this evening's entertainment which he had yet to procure. Maybe, he could take a bit of the serving girl's time right now. She might have some information that would help him learn how to go about seducing and even acquiring Maisie.

When she hesitated a moment, he patted the place beside him. "Join me? Maybe you can answer some of my questions?" he asked as he watched her tilt her head toward the kitchen where her mother worked.

"I'm not too sure if I should. What can you do for me? My time here is important."

She slipped her tongue across her lips leaving a path of moisture behind.

Farlan understood she was bargaining for his time. She would earn extra money if she complied with his wishes. "What is your name, girl? I'm Farlan."

"Rosemary." She paused a moment, posturing then moving her long braid over her shoulder. "It was my mother favorite herb. She uses it to make all the meats taste better. I've work to do. You know. I can't just sit and idle away the hours. My mother would be angry with me if I dallied and there was no money forthcoming."

"I'll make it worth your while."

He set a coin on the table as incentive. With a slow-eyed look toward Farlan, she placed it between her breasts.

"Thank you."

Farlan patted the spot beside him again, smiling at her. "Sit for a while. There are only two customers now. Surely the other woman can bring the women their food."

That was true enough.

She nodded.

Farlan grinned when the girl sat next to him. He placed his hand on her thigh, moving it down then up as he watched for her response. He didn't want a virgin whore. Experience is what he wished for. "Have some of my ale." He shoved his glass her way. Hesitating a moment, she sipped before handing the glass back to him. "Is this all you do here? Serve? Do you have a room upstairs? Do you entertain customers up there?"

He decided bold was the only way to go about this since he needed information. Wasting time was not a priority. With privacy he could get more questions answered as well as a bit of entertainment to go along with the newfound knowledge.

She blushed as she looked up the steps. The rose color was a becoming shade on her rounded cheeks. She licked her plump bottom lip again. "I just started," she whispered looking at her hands then back to meet his gaze. "I've only had one customer. If you're hoping for a knowledgeable *lassie,* it won't be me. So far, as I told you, I've only had one customer. I'm willing, also eager to learn. You can teach me."

"No, I don't mind someone who is new to the sexual games we men like to play. I can teach you everything I like. His hand slipped higher to just below her rounded breast. When he cupped one, he found she wore nothing beneath the gown. He liked the way her bubbies felt in his hand. Yes, she would do very well for one night of pleasure. "Tonight, you'll do just fine. For now, what can you tell me about the women over there, Maisie and the other lady?"

She turned to stare in the direction of the women. "Oh, they are so beautiful. Maisie is Doc Fraser's wife and Leah is Doc Houston's.

They help in the office from time to time. Leah does more because she is also a healer."

So, Miss McKenzie was truly wed. He'd wondered if she'd lied to him. Farlan trailed a fingertip along the top of her gown, dipping lower to touch the hardened nipple. Her gasp was one of pleasure. Her flesh was soft. He wouldn't mind bedding this budding young whore. "What else can you tell me? Extra coin for the information."

"Which one are you more interested in? Not that you could have either."

Farlan thought if Maisie betrayed her husband, he would have a better chance to provide for her. Perhaps he could find her alone sometime. Her mother had been willing at first, more than willing. It wasn't until later that she protested.

"Maisie, I believe. Tell me about her first."

While he watched Maisie, he chewed on a piece of cheese, his heart pounding. The devil, but Maisie was so serene and calm. Every move she made was as if she was royalty. Her name should have been Duchess. Lust spiraled straight to his groin. Maybe he would have to take this little Rosemary upstairs before this evening.

His plans for Maisie began to take shape.

# Chapter Seven

For Hawk the day seemed to drag on forever. He thought of his wife. The image of her long white legs over his shoulders while he thrust into her, when she straddled him while they were naked in the drawing room, after that when she spread her legs waiting to cradle him in their bed. He thought of tonight at the bonfire and the way she would taste, a little bit salty combined with the sweetness from the marshmallows they would roast.

They would make love tonight in front of the bonfire. Before that happened, he would tell her everywhere he would have her. They'd only touched on a few of the places he had in mind. He wanted to take her to the mossy glen surrounded by trees where little sunlight made its way through the dense canopy. After she was thoroughly seduced as well as pleasured, he would examine her. He gazed down the long hallway to Houston's office. A second opinion would be nice. Houston told him he should not be Maisie's doctor.

He wondered if she kept her breakfast in her stomach this morning. This musing had to stop. He was losing track of what he was about. The Morrison boy was in his office with a slight concussion. He would have a headache for the next day or two. The incorrigible boy would forget his discomfort then find some new way to torment his poor mother. This was the boy's third visit since he returned to McKenna land to share the practice with Houston.

When he gently opened the boy's eyes with the pads of his thumbs, they were vague a bit dazed over. Hawk smiled, shaking his head, laughing inside as he recalled some of his exploits in his younger years. "No, don't go to sleep. I know you want to but it's not a good idea. Your mother will give you a list of chores for when you've recuperated. You will memorize them."

Hawk chuckled when the boy grimaced with displeasure then immediately moaned.

Hawk turned to his mother who was standing beside the boy wringing her hands, moisture filling her eyes. As if her nerves controlled her, the woman was moving from one foot to the other. This boy would be the death of his mother. Soon her hair would be white from the worry he inflicted on her. The worry lines around her eyes would grow.

"Is he going to be alright?" she asked as she smoothed the brilliant red hair on her boy's head with a trembling hand.

His eyes were deep, dark green. They looked the color of oak leaves. While the boy was gangly, all arms and legs, he was also tall for his age.

"He just doesn't have one bit of fear in his bones. He thinks he can do anything and survive. How can I convince him he can't do whatever his little boy's mind decides to do? That adventures don't always turn out as expected."

All Hawk could do was shake his head. He knew that he and his best friends had all been the same, jumping from one misguided escapade to another. "Tell me again what happened? How did he get a concussion?" Hawk moved a finger in front of the lad's eyes hoping the boy would follow the movement.

"He and the Halsey boy were baiting each other, challenging, daring each other to do something stupid and dangerous. They do that from time to time when they get bored. You are right. He needs more chores. Needs to be more responsible. I need to keep him so busy he can't get into trouble." She sighed then seeming to think about how impossible that quest might be. "The other boy challenged him to climb to the top of the old oak tree on our land. That tree has been there for at least one hundred years. No one should climb to the top. The branches are weak at the highest point. That's what happened. The branch wouldn't hold him."

Hawk knew that all the little boys in the surrounding area had climbed, not to the top but as close as they could get without breaking a branch. No, they had not made it to the top of that same tree, but they'd done justice to the challenge. "So..." he urged Mrs. Morrison to continue with the tale.

"According to Jacob he went too high. The limb gave way under his weight. I'm just glad I was not there to see it happen."

"He fell." Hawk supplied the rest of the story, remembering other times when the climb to the top was not successful for one or the other boys.

She nodded at him to confirm his suspicion. "Hit his head on a rock. He did. Always thought his head was as hard as a boulder. In this case it wasn't. Didn't even crack the devil-rock. When he gets home, I'm going to have his da tan his backside."

The boy squirmed then groaned. His eyes cleared a bit while he tried to push himself to a sitting position. "Doc? My head hurts."

"It will serve as a reminder of what little boys should not do. Tell me how many fingers you see," Hawk said as he held up three.

The boy shook his head then blinked a few times. "Two?"

Hawk grimaced realizing the boy would have to stay a bit longer. "You understand that tree won't hold anyone's weight at the top. Is that what you did? Climb all the way to the top?"

"Don't ever back down from a dare." His little fists were clenched tight. "I want to go home now. I'm hungry."

"Can't let you go anywhere until I'm certain you are going to be fine. When I am positive, I'll give your ma some laudanum with instructions to keep you in bed for the next day at least."

Hawk felt certain his mother would want him to advise bedrest for the next week. Unfortunately for her, the boy should be back to normal in a day. Keeping him in bed would be more work for the mother than a punishment for the boy. Even if it did keep the lad out of trouble for a few days.

The thought of his boy doing all this foolishness turned in his stomach. All boys were reckless at some time. He imagined they were all lucky to have survived completely intact.

Once more time he held up fingers. "How many?"

"Four?" was the mumbled reply. He closed his eyes. "Yes, it's four."

"You were right with four. Now," Hawk tested him further, making him track his finger with his eyes, having the boy touch his nose then his finger then several other tests. He turned to the mother, smiling as he knew the boy would be fine. "Keep him awake for a few more minutes. I've got another patient waiting. If his eyesight is still good in the next fifteen minutes, I'll send the two of you home with instructions on how to continue. This time the correct answer could have been a lucky guess."

"He is going to be fine. Isn't he?"

Her hands settled on her swollen belly. The woman was pregnant again. She was rubbing her belly, massaging the small bundle that would soon be born.

His concern was now more for the mother than the son. "How are you? You will make certain to let us know when the labor starts. Since you've had multiple children, the labor could be fast. You will see Doctor Houston soon."

She was nodding, complying with his wishes. He touched her belly, found that his instincts kicked in. The child seemed fine, was growing at a normal rate.

Mrs. Morrison was nearly six months pregnant with her fifth child. Houston lectured her but all she could do was shrug then tell him she had no control over her husband. When he felt the urge, then he did what came naturally to all men. Hawk hoped he would have more sense than Mr. Morrison when it came to taking precautions with Maisie. Though, if it wouldn't hurt Maisie, he would have a dozen children if that was what she wanted too. No, he wouldn't do that to the woman he loved. It was tantamount to signing her death warrant.

Because of her husband's selfishness Mrs. Morrison would most likely die before her time. Childbearing held multiple risks to a woman's body. In addition, these two parents couldn't afford more children. Though that was not his business. Hawk wished he could give her something so she wouldn't conceive. That wasn't a choice. Her husband would never let her use a sponge. Told her it wasn't natural. Mr. Morrison also told Houston he would never withdraw. That also wasn't natural.

At the door, he turned to her. "I'll be back in a few minutes. Make certain he stays awake. You've still got that list of chores to give him. When he's ready to run around with his friends, give him something else to keep him occupied."

Striding into the waiting area, Hawk groaned when he saw the young lady waiting for him. Before he arrived to share the practice, she tormented Houston. Previously, the woman came weekly with one complaint or another. Now that he was married, her visits slowed. Houston teased him that she wanted him. Would take him as her lover if he ever gave her reason to believe he was tired of Maisie.

"Miss Jersey, what can we do for you today?" Hawk asked wishing Houston had been free to see her this time.

Even now that he was married, she continued to visit the office with one bogus complaint after another. He watched her run her tongue across her bottom lip. The gesture did not have the desired effect on his body. She was too blatant. The ploy too obvious.

She smiled then stared at her toes for a few minutes. When she looked up to meet his gaze, she thrust her breasts outward. As far as breasts went, they were ordinary, nothing exceptional. She stared at his crotch. He thought he'd vomit.

"My stomach." She rubbed the area. "This morning it hurt something awful. When the pain didn't go away, I knew I had to come see you. You can fix it can't you?" She looked hopeful, her dark eyes shimmering.

When she looked at him again, she was batting her eyelashes. She was a beautiful girl, her body slender though curved in all the necessary places. Her hair was a deep, rich brown with shades of red mingling within the long strands. Today she wore her hair lose curling around her slim shoulders. She lifted them as if to shrug. Her bosom swayed slightly with the movement.

Since he married, Hawk didn't understand why she was always conjuring maladies so she could visit the office. He told her more than once he wasn't interested. Her blatant invitations continued. "Come with me. I'll take a look."

He started for the second room, heard the soft tread of her slippers behind him. If he frightened her, he wondered if she'd stop coming to see him with different symptoms. Didn't think that was possible. He could call her bluff. Give her a complete exam. Rumor had it that she was no longer a virgin. In most cases, he didn't listen to gossip. In this situation, it behooved him to do so. The stomach problem might be very real. His thoughts turned to Maisie and her pregnancy.

"You can sit on the table." He turned to collect his stethoscope.

"I can take my gown off if that would be easier for you," her words, sultry and murky, purred from her lips.

Hawk's gut clenched. He needed to remain both calm as well as patient with her. He needed to call on his best professional manners. She might need a doctor this time. "No, don't need to have you do that. Your malady most likely stems from something you ate. If that's so it will be gone by tomorrow morning."

Either that or she was increasing. Until he examined her further, he didn't want to believe that possibility. "How old are you?" That was truthfully none of his business.

"Seventeen." She smiled at him then tilted her head a bit sideways. "Why? Does my age make a difference?"

The thought of his wife on that table, her legs spread while he thrust inside, swamped him so hard he almost groaned. He would have to make love to her, not on this table but on one of the others.

"That's young. Do you have a boyfriend? Someone you see on a regular basis?" He meant to ask a few pertinent questions.

Her slight complexion turned a brilliant shade of red. Awkwardly, she moved on the bench. "No...no one. I don't have a boyfriend."

"When was your last monthly?" If she wanted him to help her this was something he needed to know.

She gasped seemingly startled by the question. This time her face drained of color. Something was going on here.

"That's...that's none of your business."

"Very well."

Getting to the truth without offending her would be next to impossible. He needed to ask her who she was seeing. Her mother lived alone. As far as he understood there had not been a father figure for at least ten years. Was she seeing men to help put food on the table? Was she just a brazen flirt. "I'm going to listen to your heart as well as your lungs." He set the end of his stethoscope on her chest, listened. "Take a deep breath."

She giggled. Her large bosom rose then fell. He heard nothing amiss. He would have to wait and see. In a few months if she was pregnant, she would return. There was nothing else for her to do.

"You are so handsome. You and Doc Houston are the most handsome men in the village." She played with her hair, holding the length then draping it over her shoulder.

"We are both wed, Miss Jersey. Though...thank you for the compliment."

He backed away from her certain she would do or say something more that he would not like. His mind raced with a dozen different scenarios.

"Joan," she murmured softly. "Call me Joan. Everyone does." Her breaths were heavy now almost as if she'd run a few miles. She fingered the buttons near her throat, playing with them. "I will take my gown off so you can examine me more thoroughly." She sounded as if she pleaded with him.

"No!" He opened the door to the room. "Maybe more information is needed here. When was your last monthly?" he blurted again. "This is your doctor's business. I need the truth."

Her hand flew to her chest to the row of buttons dancing down the front of her corsage. She'd managed to unfasten two. When her fingers left her to settle on her lap, two more were open. He could see the lace of her chemise as well the tops of her breasts between the separated fabric.

The blush on her cheeks deepened. She looked away for a second, seeming to compose herself. After that she stiffened. "Why do you ask?" She blinked a few times. "I do believe it's time for me to leave." She scooted forward, her feet now touching the floor.

"Your stomach?"

"Is much better!"

She jumped from the table before stalking to the front door, grabbing her shawl on the way out.

Hawk leaned on the framework of the door, his arms crossed in front of him. He imagined he wouldn't discover the truth about her condition. Who the devil would come through the door next? The day had been long, exhausting. All he wanted now was to join his wife for dinner then take her hand to walk up the hill to the bonfire.

Sitting down in his office, he drank the cold coffee left in his cup. Cold coffee was just as good as hot. He tried to convince himself. As he leaned back, he closed his eyes listening to the sounds outside the office. He pinched the bridge of his nose, feeling the frustration of the day eat at him. The little boy who had no fear and the young woman who was willing to give herself to him.

Hawk longed for the peace filled days when he traveled in the country encompassed by the silence of the trail. No, he would give up all that for Maisie. The office was quiet. They were far enough away from the hustle of the village so they didn't hear the wagons rumbling down the streets or the people laughing and chatting as they went about their daily routines. All he heard was Houston puttering around in the workroom along with the wind whistling then whispering around the eaves of the building.

Houston stepped through the door with two cups of steaming coffee in his hands. "Heard the Jersey girl leaving. What did you ask her that put her in such a huff that she slammed the door on her way out? I'd like to know for the next time she sees me instead of you."

"Thanks, asked her when her last monthly was. She said she had a stomach ache." Hawk held up the cup that held hot coffee, steam rising. "Where did you get this?"

"Leah made a fresh batch before she left to meet Maisie. They were going to the dressmakers."

"Eating first at the Tea and Crumpet Inn." Hawk sipped. No, hot was much better than cold. "Maisie is pregnant. About a month along. Her stomach is upset all the time."

Hawk wasn't at all certain why he told Houston. Perhaps he needed to confide in someone. Maybe he needed advice confirming that at least for the moment he was doing the right thing.

"Do you want me to look at her."

"No, not yet. Maybe when I can convince her that while her husband is a doctor, she would be better off seeing someone else. It's so early. The *bairn* is healthy though." He knew he was too quick to answer.

"Just discovered the fact last night when I touched her stomach. The child warming in her womb is a boy and a shifter. I'm both pleased as well as terrified of pending fatherhood. Seems I've waited so long for this moment, I want to burst with the news."

Houston shuffled a few papers on Hawk's desk. Replaced a pen to its holder. When he looked up and spoke, it was to reiterate what Hawk already said. "You understand it is not prudent to doctor your wife. However." He tapped long slender fingers on the cherrywood of Hawk's desk. "I'm certain Maisie will come to see things our way in time. When the labor starts, you should be the father, nothing more."

"Yes. This will take a few months for her to come to terms with another man looking at her. I will examine her tonight. When I've finished with the basics of the exam, I will start to explain to her what is yet to come. She is very innocent. Other than watching the farm animals, she has no idea about what will happen to her woman's body."

"Who else knows?" Houston asked as he rose to walk around the room stopping at the window to look into the distance. His hands behind his back, he stood perfectly still.

"Cameron." Hawk held up his hands in supplication, shaking his head as he studied his friend who turned from the window. "The boy guessed from something I told him. Mother and father will also come to the same conclusion when we see them. Since Maisie is meeting with Leah today, I told her to ask her any questions she might have. So, Leah will know. Other than that, no one knows. Swore my brother to silence."

"Good."

A noise, a knocking of the door, footsteps pounding on the hard wood alerted them they had a new patient.

"Doc Stuart, Doc Fraser, anyone here? She's hurt real bad." It was a woman's voice calling out to them, seeking help.

The door banged shut. Both men stood, the conversation they were having forgotten. "Mrs. Brown?" Hawk asked then he saw the lady in a man's arms. She was slumped against the man, her head pressed against his chest. "He beat her. That's no way to treat a woman. I would have done the same to him but he got away. My Rosemary's hurt bad," Mrs. Brown repeated. "It was only her second time. Told her we didn't need the money that bad. She insisted. My sweet Rosy wanted to help. Now look what has happened."

"Set her on the table." Hawk stood back to study the girl. She wasn't very old. He understood though that she was practicing. Someone used her harshly then left her. Her gown was shredded and tattered. He needed to discover if she was torn internally. There was blood on her legs.

"What happened?" Hawk asked wondering if Mrs. Brown would tell her the truth. "What did she insist on doing?"

His stomach clenched tight as his mind created new images ones that were as old as time and far from pleasant. Women sold themselves. Mostly to put food on the table. Not because they enjoyed the invasion.

Houston ushered the man from the room closing the door behind him. The three were alone. Tears ran down Rosemary's round cheeks. The bodice of her gown was ripped, hanging around her breasts.

"He's new to town. At least I've never seen him before. A real gent, dressed so fine so perfect. All decked out, a smooth talker that one. He convinced her he wanted her. Forced her he did. She's also bleeding, not a lot but he tore her," Mrs. Brown explained.

"It wasn't that fancy earl who came by earlier? Don't know this one's name. At the time he didn't give it."

"Farlan..." Rosemary said softly. "This man...he said he would pay me." She held out her hand. It held one coin. "I suppose he did. Thought there would be more. He looked wealthy."

"Does he have a last name?" Hawk asked his mind once more racing to the Earl of St. Blevins.

That didn't make sense though. A man wouldn't hurt a woman when anyone in town could identify him. No, he would have too much to lose. Could there be two wealthy men in town, new to this village? Unlikely, though he supposed anything could happen.

"Said his name wasn't important," Rosemary rasped out her eyes closing as she seemed to be stealing each breath.

Her small body was beginning to bruise. Hawk didn't like this. He turned to Mrs. Brown, handing her a gown. "Will you help her from her clothing? I need to look at her more closely. You will stay in the room with us?"

Mrs. Brown's face was the color of death. She nodded. "Yes."

"Open the door when you're ready for me."

He stepped into the outer office, stuffing a hand through his hair. Houston was there. "Someone beat her. She is bruised and battered inside as well as out. Her lip is swelling as are her eyes. In a few more hours, the right side of her face will be more than colorful. Need to discover where else he beat her. Her mother told me she is bleeding and that the man forced her."

"This won't be the last time for her. You know that. Women in the profession..." Houston's voice drifted off. "She is so young."

"I understand. There is a man here, looking for Maisie. At least I think my wife is who he is looking for. This man who hurt Rosemary is most likely one and the same. He would harm Maisie too if given the chance."

Hawk was terrified for his wife. He wanted to find her this instant. Needed to make certain she was idling away the day at the dressmakers.

"Would you like me to take this case?" Houston asked, his voice soft as he placed his hand on Hawk's shoulder. "I'd be more than happy to step in on this one. You did save me from the wiles of Miss Jersey."

"Yes," Hawk said his voice cracking with the terror racing through him. "I need to find Maisie. Besides, it's almost time to go home. She will either be at the house or still at the dressmakers. On his way out the door he grabbed his coat.

As he walked toward the village center, he tried to remain calm, tried to keep himself from running. To steady himself, he pulled in a few deep breaths of air. This was not the way he expected the afternoon to transpire. He stepped along the boardwalk that ran in front of the businesses. When he stepped inside the intended door, he held onto his breath for an extended length of time.

The modiste looked up. Tilting her head to one side, she smiled. "Doctor Fraser, what can I do for you? Your wife and Mrs. Stuart left about fifteen minutes ago." She tapped a finger on her chin. "No, it was more like an hour. Got lost in my thoughts. Your wife purchased two ready-made gowns. They also ordered several new gowns. Would you like to see what your wife chose?"

"Alone?" he queried his voice soft.

One more time, he found himself holding his breath as he waited for an answer.

"No, seems that Riley's wife knew they were here. They all left together, going to get a cup of tea at the inn nearby before heading home."

"Shawna? Shawna was here?" Relief washed through him. Shawna would guess that Maisie was with child. The two women shared everything. If Shawna guessed and said anything, Leah would also know. So much for keeping the fact a secret. Well, he did tell Maisie to ask questions of Leah. What else would he expect?

"Yes."

With the confirmation, Hawk sprinted from the store, striding down the front of the businesses to the inn. His heart rushed as he saw his wife along with the two other ladies sitting by the window. He calmed himself before walking to her. They each had a cup of tea. A plate of scones sat in the middle of the table.

"Maisie," he said and was surprised when she jumped from her chair to give him a hug.

He stumbled back a step amazed at her reaction. She kissed him on the cheek then bit his chin. After that she licked the small hurt.

"I've missed you," Maisie said her voice vibrant with passion even though she whispered.

Well, hell, he missed her too. He always missed her when she wasn't with him. His hands were around her waist. Against his chest, he felt her breasts push against him. He wanted to cup her bottom and pull her so close she would be able to feel his need. Wanted her to wrap her long legs around his flanks. Next to her softness, his body turned to steel.

He let go. Tapped a finger on her nose, wishing he could kiss her as he wanted to kiss her. Needed to taste her, taste the sweet tea and the scones she'd been eating.

"Hawk, I didn't expect you to come here. Do you want tea? Something to eat? I forgot. You don't like tea." Her slender hands with perfectly manicured fingernails were still flat against his chest. She moved them higher to circle his neck.

He stopped her quest. Holding her hands in his own, he smiled at her. "I came to walk you home. Are you finished here? Do you have a few packages. The modiste told me you purchased two ready-made gowns."

Until this man left, he didn't want her out of his sight. He would stay with her, keep her close. He was so afraid the Earl of Blevins would find a way to get to her.

Smiling, she nodded then turned to her friends. Before she spoke, she bit into her scone. "I'm going now. Where is Houston?"

"Seeing to Rosemary. She was hurt upstairs. I'll tell you more later."

He turned to Leah, speaking plainly. "You should go to the office. He might need your help with the *lass*. She was banged up inside as well as out. A woman there would help the *lass*."

Leah set her napkin on the table, her brows furrowed together. "All right. I'll go. What about you, Shawna?"

Maisie set coin to cover her food on the table. "Since it's on the way, Hawk and I will walk you home. We're going to have a bonfire tonight."

After he cleared his throat, he spoke to the women. "That wasn't an invitation. It's a private affair not a party." Even with those words, if the women told their husbands he wouldn't be surprised to have visitors. "No one else allowed." He tried to make his voice stern. The women were nodding as if they understood. He could never let this go without a few more parting words. "Don't tell your husbands!" with that shouted, coupled with the expression on the wives faces, he knew he was doomed to have visitors.

As they walked out the door, Maisie whispered to him while he bent to hear her words, "That is a for certain way to make sure we have company tonight. Could you have been more obvious? Maybe we should go to this bonfire on another night. We could have a cozy time in front of the fire in the drawing room."

"No," he laughed while he pulled her closer, so close he felt her heat, caught the sweet scent of her. "No one except us will be there. Houston as well as Riley will *ken* what we are about. While it might be fun to tease, they won't show up. If they did, they would set down a precedence they would not like. The bonfire has always held a wealth of memories. If one couple lets the other know they will be there, why then it is taboo to show up. We did not usher invitations."

"All right, I will have faith in what you tell me."

He wished he trusted what he said. He thought Maisie was right in that he overreacted. By the words he said, he sent out a blatant invitation that would never be refused by his friends. He wouldn't be surprised if more of the clan showed up.

~ * ~

Her back against his chest, they sat in front of the fire. She was cross-legged between his thighs. His warmth settled into her. Flames raced heavenward; embers popped floating skyward while the dry wood made a nearly smokeless fire, crackling in the flames. She reminisced about the first time she sat in front of a bonfire in Hawk's arms. That evening seemed weeks away, months. That night, he taught her a woman's pleasure.

In that small amount of time, so much changed. She was pregnant now. He liked to stroke her belly seeming impatient to feel the beginning curves that would increase with time. Beneath her skirts his long fingers caressed her, stroking intimately. Arching against him, she struggled for air. She heard the soft rumble of his pleasure against her back.

Her mother's protector had come to town to find her. Farlan didn't understand there was nothing he could do or say that would separate her from her husband. She didn't understand why he could possibly believe she would turn to him. Well, she did comprehend more than she wished to admit. The man knew her mother as his mistress, he would assume since she was the daughter, she was cut from the same cloth. All she needed now was the way to tell Hawk what happened at the inn. How she felt about that man.

Her head was set against his chest, his hands splaying across her belly then lower to stroke her in more arousing places. He alternated his attention. She looked to the velvet black sky sputtering with bright stars. A sliver of moon sat low on the horizon casting a small amount of light.

As far as she could tell tonight there were no clouds to speak of. She closed her eyes breathing easily to the same cadence as her husband. There were moments she thought they were one with each other, hearts beating in synchronization. She loved him more than anything else in her life.

With fingers still sticky with the marshmallow they indulged in, she licked her fingers. The sweet taste lingered. She thought of tasting Hawk's fingers. Earlier they were sweet and sticky. She wanted to bring each one to her lips then suck them deep into her mouth, play them with her tongue. Bite then sooth. Now, his long fingers were preoccupied with enchanting her. She didn't need seducing. When he looked at her, she was always ready for him, needing him, wishing for the mercuric feeling of his fingers upon her. He bewitched her with his smile. Created magic with his kiss.

His fingers worked the buttons of her gown open then closed over her breast. "We need to talk, Maisie. I've something important to speak about with you. Wanted to speak of the man last night but was sidetracked several times. Wonder how that happened? Did you like it when we distracted each other?"

He pulled her closer as she turned to look into the depths of his silver blue eyes, captivating eyes. She reached up to touch the dimple by the side of his mouth.

On her belly, his fingers massaged, the caress gentle. She coiled against him, moving with each stroke of his fingers. Her breath raced.

"Yes," she sighed reveling in the warmth he generated. He was orchestrating this scenario to his whim.

If he wanted, he would cause the distraction before he spoke. She pulled the blanket he wrapped around them both tighter. If she didn't hold it tight, the breeze would caress her, touch her nipples. "Found out I was pregnant. Suppose losing one's dinner can sidetrack the best intentions."

"Lost your dinner several times." He chuckled light-hearted as he seemed to remember seeing her huddled by her new rose bushes. "Not that it is funny. Don't want you losing what you eat. Nonetheless, the night was most enjoyable for both of us once your stomach settled. What do you think? Should we do the same tonight? When we return, I could take all your clothing off and make love to you in my office. Perhaps on the desk with your legs around my flanks. Need to taste you again."

"Your brother visited you. You told him about me."

She tried to ignore the seductive statements he was making. No matter how she answered, he would do as he pleased. Whatever he did would also please her.

"You waited upstairs then came to me nearly naked. Beneath your pink robe you wore not one stitch. I liked that just as tonight you wear nothing except your gown. I didn't even ask you to forego your chemise yet you did. We made love on the kitchen table."

"Then in the drawing room. Anyone could have seen us. I sat on top of you." She turned to punch him in the shoulder. "I didn't like that."

"No one saw. Your moans of pleasure coupled with the soft sighs tell me you are not telling the absolute truth. If I made a manly guess, I would believe you loved all that I did. That you did. You stroked me, touched me with your mouth. Should I go on? If it pleases you, you can do so again. I almost exploded when the warmth of your sweet mouth closed over me."

"You don't know that. Someone might just have been polite. If they saw us naked, they would never knock on the door. Interrupt us." His hands roamed higher to cup her breast, rolled the tight crests between his fingers.

She wore nothing beneath the gown, no chemise or petticoats. As he just told her, he would appreciate that. First though, they needed to talk. She heaved in a long breath of air, searching for courage to talk about a distasteful subject. She imagined that she would have to begin the discussion.

"I saw a man today...from my past. He is loathsome. It took some minutes before I realized who he was."

She couldn't stop the shudder even though she tried to hold herself still. A slow breath in then out of her lungs helped. When she closed her eyes, she saw him with her mother.

"The Earl of St. Blevins?" he queried with contempt in his voice. "Yes, I saw him yesterday. He came to my office searching for a Miss McKenzie. Is that you by any chance? Is your sur name McKenzie not

McRae? I wondered what it would be when I learned about your parentage. Does he believe he can get something from you?"

"My mother's name," she said her voice raspy with the distress she was feeling. Yes, he wanted her just as he had her mother. "When Shawna found me, she insisted I take on MacRae as my last name. Shawna always wanted to believe I wasn't a bastard but family, real family. She always considered me her sister, never her half-sister. For a short time, she made me feel that way, even loved. David never acknowledged me. Always reviled me. In ways, I think he blames me for what happened to his son along with his wife."

"You didn't argue with her?"

"As you might have realized one doesn't argue with Shawna. Once she sets her mind on a course, she sticks to her decision. Yes, well...after father died and the money stopped coming, mother accepted a new protector. With me so young, she didn't want to leave me alone in the house so they came to see her, paid her with gifts most of the time, rarely with the coin she wished for. Men, she always relied on someone. I vowed I would never be like that." Her breath left her in a soft sigh. "Shawna saved me from that destiny. I owe her my life. Did you know that David threatened to give me to a whore house if she didn't comply with his mandate to marry Riley."

"They?" Hawk asked. "Was there more than one man who visited your mother?"

"The earl along with his manservant."

"Oh? Only it wasn't Riley she wed," he murmured, nuzzling her long hair from her neck, kissing her, grazing his teeth across her flesh.

"No. Suppose we both *ken* the long story. Mac is fortunate Riley was his true father not the other man."

"It seems the earl wants you back. Remember we talked about this once before. Even as a child he coveted you. You were probably just as beautiful then as now. I'm surprised he didn't search for you before this. It would have been easy for him to take you from the manor house. All he would have had to do was wait until you were alone."

"Me too. I wouldn't have had a chance against the man." Maisie shuddered when he traced her nipples with his thumbs, still running his teeth along her neck, still arousing her. She wanted him to kiss her. "He confronted me today when I was with Leah at the inn. I don't think he intends to back down just because we are wed. He makes my stomach churn even more than the babe."

He shouted a bark of laughter at her words. The sound of his amusement eased the tension they were both feeling. She supposed she would have to take every precaution. She wasn't like Shawna. She didn't care if she was flitting from one place to the other. She possessed no restless energy. No, she was content to stay at home or work with Hawk in his office.

"I held that impression also. Having you is his intention. One way or the other, he will attempt to coerce you to his will." He played with her, teased her until a low moan caught in the back of her throat. "You must not go anywhere alone. He will try things, deceptive things."

"I don't want anything to do with the man. He forced mother. I heard her cries, sobbing in her room after he left. What are we going to do?" Her breaths were slow and even. She knew that would change when Hawk set his mind on truly seducing her not just teasing. "I don't like him."

His fingers played with her nipples rolling them between his fingers, fondling her, seducing her. She wondered if they were now finished talking. If they were, they would move on to more pleasant endeavors.

"Do you know if he forced Mrs. Brown's daughter? Would he treat a young woman that way? Someone did today. It was a man who fits the earl's description; an aristocrat, well-dressed in the fashion of the time. There aren't many men who come through the village who are aristocrats."

She turned to look at him, her body tensing with the knowledge it couldn't have been the earl. "When did this happen? The earl was in the dress shop while Leah and I were there. He seemed to be watching me, studying me. He was there for more than an hour. I think he even purchased a few gowns. Hawk, he gives me chills. His eyes are so dark and fathomless. Cold. The man is chillier than arctic ice. Mother used to stoke the fire when he was coming to see her."

"So, there must be someone else though Rosemary implicated the earl. She called him Farlan. Would that be his first name?"

She lifted her shoulders wondering the very same thing. She found that she was searching her memories. Something she should know but couldn't bring it to the forefront of her mind. "I don't know. Don't think I ever knew the man's name. Just knew he was an earl. Mother never spoke of him. When he would come to see her, she would call him earl. That was all I knew." The memory snagged her, she turned in his arms to look at him. "He did have a bodyguard who was always there with him. Believe he took mother into the bedroom almost as often as the earl. Sometimes the two men went in there together. Mother hated what they did. She wouldn't speak of what happened."

Hawk hissed in a breath of air. He stroked her, caressed her belly then lower. "You must take care. Don't want you going anywhere by yourself until the man leaves. Believe you could be in danger."

"I will go to work with you in the morning then walk home with you when you are finished for the day."

She moaned when his nimble fingers found tender, sensitive flesh. He stroked her, caressed her. He sent raw passion pummeling through her with infinite ease. She pushed back against him, her fingers winding around his wrists.

"If I'm gone on a call, you will keep the door locked. You won't answer to anyone. Maybe I should ask for help from the clan." He brought his hand up to touch her cheek. "I would have the house guarded. Would you mind that terribly. I recall when the Stuarts guarded Kit's house when a mad man was after Aila. Kit hated the guards, refused. His father saw things in a different way."

"I would not like that. Guards." His fingers tightened around her breast. She gasped with the pleasure. She wanted him now. Didn't want to wait until this was resolved. "I know. I will do as you ask. Whatever will ease your mind."

"Since we have that decided, how did you feel today? Did you keep all your food inside you where it belongs? Did you feed the roses?" One hand roamed along her thigh while the other continued its ardent attention on her breast. "Ah, I see you followed my directive. I like that.

Your food belongs inside your belly."

"I like it too. As to my food, all but breakfast remained inside me. The marshmallows are doing well also. I drank lots of milk in my tea. In fact, the drink was more milk than tea. What do you think? Do you think milk is good for me? Leah seemed to think so when I asked her. She also told me that birthing a child is nothing to be afraid of, not with Houston as the doctor. I thought you would be the doctor."

"I can't be the doc. I'm the father. Houston and I have discussed this. I will, however, be with you when it is your time. I will not be stashed away to drink brandy and wait for the blessed event. I will be there if you need me."

"If you want my opinion, I don't like that. I haven't agreed to anything. Hawk, I don't want him looking at me. I want you there maybe Leah too. Not Houston. Never Houston."

His sigh was long, heartfelt. She felt his agitation with the conversation. "Your opinion is important. In this circumstance, what you want will give way over more sound minds. You will get used to another man looking at you. Your safety along with the health of our baby is more important than your shyness. A father cannot be an objective doctor."

"What can I do to change your mind?" she asked feeling the heat as his fingers moved ever more into intimate territory. She was gasping as he touched more evocative places, found the seat of all her pleasure. "Hawk..." her moan seemed to spur on his questing fingers.

He turned her so he could kiss her. His mouth surrounded hers, his tongue dancing, prodding deeper into her. A broken sound filled the back of her throat.

"Nothing, there is nothing you can do."

That was it. He decided. Her feelings didn't count. What to do? She didn't want Houston to touch her or see her. Who delivered Leah's child? It wasn't Hawk. At least she didn't think her husband was the doctor. He must have been in Selkirk.

The noises coming from down the hill told her that Hawk was wrong about the invasion tonight. His words created an invitation that wasn't refused by his friends. He'd told her he would examine her tonight to see how far along she was. She was certain that would have to wait until they were home.

"They are making enough racket to wake the dead," Hawk muttered. By the tone of his voice it was clear he was displeased. "Didn't believe they would come here. I suppose our evening here will have to be put on hold."

"Do you think they brought their own marshmallows and sticks? Suppose we could share the sticks. Oh, my, I do believe if I ate any more sugar, I would be sick."

Tonight, she enjoyed herself, eating and laughing with Hawk. She stepped outside her usual calm serenity.

They would have company. Beneath the small covering she was very nearly naked.

"Keep the blanket around you." His voice was thick, sounding different to her, strained. "Don't want anyone to get the wrong idea." Well, hell, they would know exactly what they'd been about. It was something all his brothers would do.

"Yes...why...the blanket..."

She started to button her gown. She wasn't intending to sit in front of these people while he fondled her breasts and touched her in the most intimate of ways. He wouldn't do so. Would he? Of course, he would do just as he pleased. He would embarrass her. She would be mortified when she thought on his behavior even while he pleasured her.

A hand on hers, he stopped her. Whispering close to her ear, sending a myriad of shivers weeping throughout her body, "Don't. I've spent most of the night undoing your gown getting it in the exact way that it pleases me. My friends are not supposed to be here. I fully intend to ignore them then hope they will go away."

"I..." She swallowed hard, "I cannot ignore them. They are not going away until they get what they've come for."

She wondered what that was. Her humiliation? They already succeeded with that. Why were they here? Perhaps they were showing their support, their solidarity in the face of her impending issues.

Leah and Shawna picked up the sticks, waiving them in the air, grins on their beautiful faces. Neither Shawna or Leah would wish to embarrass her. She didn't imagine their husbands wanted that either.

What they must want would be to tease Hawk. When they accomplished their goal, they would leave.

"We brought marshmallows," Houston said a slight snicker accompanying his words. "The girls love them. Don't you?" He turned to his wife who nodded her agreement.

Leah and Shawna roasted marshmallows for their husbands. Houston sat cross-legged, leaning against a boulder. Leah sat in front of him, his hands resting possessively on her stomach. For a while the conversation lagged. Finally, Houston began. "It was not Farlan who forced the girl. It was someone else who purchased her for an hour, though the two men, according to Rosemary, looked and acted much the same. The man told her they shared women. If she was very good to him, he would share her with Farlan."

"His bodyguard, or driver. I don't know his exact job description. When he visited mother, the man was always with him," Maisie said, her voice quivering as she tried not to let her thoughts roam into the past. "They both used to come to mother's home. At times, they would go into her bedroom together. They never beat her. Though I believed they forced her. Imagine it couldn't be called force since she let them come to her. She was in ways, willing. Though she couldn't refuse the money. Perhaps if she didn't have me to support, she would have chosen a different path." Massie wished she could push back time. Even if she could, the outcome would be no different.

"Rosemary will not name the person who attacked her," Houston went on to say. "No one can prosecute if the exact man cannot be identified. If she did make an accusation, the word would be hers against theirs. Women stand few chances when it comes to the law."

"A threat had to be made against her. They are holding something or someone in peril who she holds dear. She would do well to remain with her mouth closed. The girl is terrified," Leah continued speaking, shaking her head. "After you left the inn, I went to the office to help with her. She cried, sobbing that she could not tell who it was. The girl will do the same, again and again. Even if these men don't stay, we will be seeing to her baby before long. Seems she has chosen her profession."

"How are you going to keep Maisie safe, Hawk?" Shawna asked.

"She is vulnerable at home alone. The only place where she will be safe is with you. She cannot remain at the office all the time. There are always errands to run. The two of you have a life that cannot be abandoned. You cannot be with her night and day. Those two men might not leave for months." Shawna was rambling, the list of problems multiplying with each new thought.

Riley was staring at them, his eyes narrowed with concentration. "You should bring in the clan. Both Connal as well as Alistair will make certain you have enough men guarding the house. Farlan will not be able to get close to her. If she needs to run an errand, one of the men will go with her. Someone will be nearby night and day."

"Maisie doesn't want the guards," Hawk said, his voice cracking on the words. He stiffened as he made a decision. "I will override her on this if she insists. She won't do so. She also doesn't want you for her doctor. When the times comes, if necessary, I'll make the final decision on that topic. For now, I'm all she needs."

With her husband's words, Massie squirmed. He was right on all counts. He did know her well.

"Very well," Houston said, a half-smile on his face, appearing to give in to their wishes. "I was Leah's doctor. With Leah's pregnancy, there was no one else to assume the duties. There were also no complications. We will see what transpires. If there are any difficulties, I expect to be called in as a consult."

Yes, they would see. She would stay strong in her convictions. Hawk was the only doctor she needed. There was nothing Hawk could do if she refused to see Houston. He wouldn't tie her down or force her to his will. "I wouldn't mind the guards as long as they remain distant. If they hover, I'll scream," Massie said, her meek nature seeming to disappear as she spent time with Hawk.

"Have you ever screamed, Maisie?" Hawk chuckled softly touching her beneath her chin. "Would you do that for me? I'd like to hear you."

As she turned to look at him, her eyes blazed with fire. Embarrassed, she felt heat pour from her, stain her cheeks. Before she showed her fury, she calmed herself, sifting in a few deep breaths of air.

It wasn't easy. Beneath the blanket covering her so completely no one would see what he did, his fingers were traveling over her, caressing her, slipping between her legs. She shuddered. Her head fell back to settle on his chest. She closed her eyes turning into him. "No, I have never screamed," she admitted with a soft sigh as he continued on his desired path.

While Hawk seduced her, chatter filled the little clearing, the couples laughing and talking now that Hawk decided her fate. She sipped a breath of air as his fingers slid slowly inside her core. She was going to do something that would give her away. She arched against him, twisting with pleasure with the need he so expertly orchestrated, closing her eyes to the raw hungry passion that was building within. He'd been seducing her for more than hour. Her body wanted release.

"Hush," he whispered by her ear, his tongue caressing the lobe, his teeth touching gently to send more ripples of ecstasy within. "You don't want the family to know what I'm doing beneath the blanket. How you are almost there, almost finding the sweet release only I can give you. In a few seconds, possibly sooner, you are going to climax. Not a peep from your sweet, kissable lips."

No, she didn't want anyone to know what he did. She fought the raw desire pummeling her body. Turned her face so it was against his broad chest. It seemed though the couples were now wrapped in blankets of their own. The chatter turned to soft sighs and tiny moans as pleasure was being given as well as received. There was a soft gasp, a gentle please coming from one of the couples then another.

When she opened her eyes, she saw Houston lead Leah from the small clearing into the woods beyond. He swept her into his arms, his lips molded to hers. Leah's arms encircled her husband, pulling him close to her.

"Oh, Riley," her sister sighed softly as Riley did the same to her. "We can't. Not here. What will they think?"

"Why not. We will go to the other side of the bonfire. I want you, now. Don't want to wait until we get home. Do you want me? Ah, I can feel your heat, the dampness of you. You can't wait either. That's my girl. Come with me now. Come a little closer. I'll take you so high you'll reach the sun."

"They are gone, sweeting. No one is here except us."

He kissed her hard and deep. She wanted him desperately. She always wanted him.

Inside her, his fingers moved so slow she wanted to yell, bringing her to that point where she would forget everything. Where all control was lost. Where her body hummed. He turned her. She sat on top of him. He was inside her. Deep inside. So far, she gasped with the pleasure of it all. She felt the length of him, moving, teasing, and taunting as her body wanted and needed him. She tossed her head back, her breasts touching upon his chest.

When his fingers found her again, she cried out. His lips were pulled back as he emptied himself inside her. She moaned, pulsing and throbbing. His hands roamed along her back, calming her. Her head fell against his chest. "Hawk..."

"Should we go home now?" he asked as he once more touched her, fondled her, tugged on hardened tight buds until her heart once more raced with the pleasure he generated.

She sighed, purred, burying her face in his chest, biting him on his shoulder. "In a few minutes. I can't walk right now. Can you?"

She wondered if a man was affected so thoroughly as a woman. She was limp, week kneed, breathless as the list went on. To walk now would not work too well. She ran her tongue along his collarbone, nipped his shoulder.

"Unless you want me to ravish you again, you should stop." He chuckled while he pulled her tighter. "I could do so if that is your wish. One more time would not be difficult. You're moving against me, pulsing, crying out for me to enter you again."

"Do you want me to stop?"

She found him with her fingers, enclosed his length. After moving along his shaft a few times, she cupped him, fondled him, delighted in his deep husky sound of pleasure.

"Perhaps not." He groaned again as she tempted him more. Sparks flew from the fire in front of her as well as within. "Maybe I just want to hold you in my arms for a few more minutes. I don't want you to stop what you are doing. If you don't, I will come inside the warmth of you again. Doesn't make a bit of difference if we can't walk. We can do other things. Ah..." he exhaled as she changed her attention to his shaft once more, moving her hand up and down. "If we try to leave, the attempt would undoubtedly fail. Oh, the devil...they will return and wonder where we have gone off to. Should we stay until they come back to the bonfire? Should we finish what you started? Would you like that?"

"Does any of that matter? They will probably go to their homes after they are done, not to the bonfire," she said thinking this was wonderful, believing she didn't care what anyone thought. She wanted to continue what she did, wanted him inside her one more time before they left. "Wouldn't they guess?" His hands centered on her waist.

"Sometimes I forget you are with child. Can you do this again? I should be more careful."

"I'm fine. I forget too." She purred as his mouth found her then suckled one breast then the other. He worked his magic, touched her, heated her. "Hawk..."

"Yes?"

"Come inside me."

When he did, they both climaxed again. She fell against him, her head on his chest. The crisp hair there tickled her nose. When she touched his skin with her tongue, he tasted salty and damp. She heard Leah and Houston leaving, walking down the hill immersed in themselves. Not caring what anyone else was doing. He carried her, her head resting on his chest. After that, Shawna and Riley left. Once more they were alone. She closed her eyes. He was still deep inside her, hard, needing.

"You're still...."

"Hard as steel."

A few minutes later she screamed his name. He caught the sound inside his mouth. "Massie..." he whispered.

Hawk kissed her forehead then her nose. He pulled her gown down to her ankles then gently touched her breasts. "They are larger. It has only been a month." He sounded as if in awe. "I would like to feel a bump here." His hand once more caressed her belly splayed his long fingers from hipbone to hipbone. His hand cupped her, and she lost all thought of leaving.

"I'm certain the bump will come soon enough. A few more minutes, Hawk."

"Very well, I'll wait until you are ready to walk."

At home, Hawk did look at her, did examine her. He seemed to realize that doing so was very difficult. She understood he wanted other things when he looked at her. With no compunction or hesitancy, she opened her legs for him, allowed him to clinically examine her. Maisie didn't want Houston to see her, not when Hawk could do the job. He was trained. Had read almost as much as Houston on childbirth.

"I would not let another man do that to me." Maisie felt strong, fearless now in her conviction. Hawk would not gainsay her on this. She wouldn't let him. No, she did have a say in her health. Leah told her to stand firm as did Shawna. Though, a woman, Bonnie delivered Mac. What would Shawna do now with these two demanding men hovering close, giving her advice.

"I understand."

She braced herself on her elbows, her legs spread to him, her knees in the air while he gently touched her, looked at her. Maisie realized he was looking at her differently. She wondered so many things about his past. "How many children have you delivered? How many women have you looked at this way?" Jealousy exploded inside her. She knew she was not his first lover; understood he'd even had a mistress or two. The fact made no difference to her feelings.

He stepped back from her, tugging on her dress to cover her. "I don't know. Enough to be competent."

"More than ten?" she asked, her voice soft. Not only was she discovering that she didn't want another man looking at her this way she also didn't want him looking at other women. Considering his profession, her thoughts and wishes weren't rational.

"Yes...I don't know, Maisie. A lot. I've been delivering babies for a very long time. The husbands were always thankful there was a doctor available to help their wives. More than ten births under my belt. More than ten lovers. What I can promise you now is that you are the last of my lovers."

Finding she couldn't stop the questions, "What did you feel when you examined the women?"

Her voice cracked at the end of the question. She had no business asking him something so personal. Though she didn't regret the question. She would ask until she received a legitimate answer.

There was a long silence before he answered. "Not the way I feel when I look at you. With other women, I'm a doctor first. Be assured the feelings when I am a doctor are not the same as when I look at you."

She wasn't at all certain about what he said imagining she would have to listen to him. Would have to believe what he told her. She had no experience in this.

"Maisie." He touched her chin with a finger, bringing her chin high. "There is no one else but you. What more can I say?"

"Promise?" she asked as he brought her to a sitting position, her hair tumbling around her shoulders.

"Come let's go to the drawing room. I want to make love to my wife." He pulled her dress over her head. "I want to feel your breasts against me. Need to feel your body pulse against mine. Wish to be inside you so we can forget all this nonsense."

*Nonsense?*

~ * ~

Farlan stepped back to look better at the outside of the home he purchased. He steepled his fingers beneath his chin, tapping them together a few times. He had plans for Maisie as well as this fine home. He would give her whatever she wanted. She would come around to his way of thinking. He wanted her. Had wanted her since the first time he saw her in her mother's home. It was just a matter of time. He was a patient man. This would all turn out for the best even though he understood he had a lot of convincing in his future.

Images of her as a small child swam in his head. If her mother had not passed, he'd decided he would have her when she turned fifteen. Somehow, she got away from him. The MacRae girl stepped in, finding her before he could take her as his. Her last name had been McKenzie.

He would have set her up to wait for him. No, he would have taken her as soon as he had her in his possession. She was a fire in his blood. So beautiful, he could barely breathe when he looked at her.

Ah, he recalled the times she sat on his lap. Even then she was more than lovely. Her face was one of an angel, her demeanor always so calm and serene. She rarely smiled or showed emotion. As a twelve-year-old, her body gave promise of womanly curves to match her mothers. Her breasts were filling out, her hips widening. Massie was lovelier than her mother.

His body hardened while he thought about Massie. Now, she was a married woman. Another man won her maidenhead. He regretted that miniscule fact. A persistent man, he would wait, would prepare everything to his liking before he went after her. In a short time, she would become his.

His first step had been to purchase a place for her to live. He gave his solicitor the task. The home was not in the small village near the McKenna keep. No, it would not do for her family to be close enough to render aide if she sought them out. Distance was necessary. This home was five miles south of Inverness, very accessible for him.

His friend, Gawain, met him inside. The rooms were spacious. Over the last few weeks, he had all the furnishings updated. The rugs were all new as were the draperies. The bed in the master suite was large enough to accommodate three people when it suited him. She would learn how sweet it was to have more than one lover at the same time. A threesome was more exciting than anything he experienced individually. He had thoughts of finding a third man who was compatible. First and foremost, his pleasure would be seen to. He would give her whatever she wished for, except his permission to leave him.

First, Massie needed to learn how to appreciate all the little things he could do for her. He would introduce her to the ways of armoire at a slow pace. She would learn what he liked. She would learn what Gawain liked. If there was a third partner...she would have to accommodate his likes as well.

He turned to Gawain, "Show me upstairs." They walked. "Have you purchased a suitable new wardrobe for Massie?" He wanted to see her in exquisite negligées as well as other fashions. He didn't intend to be niggardly. He would take her riding through the countryside. She wouldn't be a prisoner in the home. Inside, in the depth of his heart, he grinned. She could come and go as she pleased. There was nowhere for her to go, miles to walk to reach anyone. Ah, but she wouldn't want to leave this new home of hers. It was so beautiful. Much more than the country doctor could afford.

"Yes, all is in order. The negligées are exquisite as are all the other garments. You will savor every moment taking them off, revealing her more thoroughly. As will I when it is my turn to taste her sweetness."

Inside the room, he stopped at the armoire. Opening the doors, he touched each gown, let the silken fabric slip through his hands. "Have you taken care of Hawk?"

"Not yet. The plans are still in motion. All the little details need to be done with precision so nothing goes awry."

"Quite right. Not one thing can be left to chance." Farlan sat down on the bed, moving his hands with languid strokes along the fabric, imagining Massie beneath the covers with him, both naked, both writhing with sexual need. His body flexed, tightening. He needed a woman now, not in a few weeks. He understood it might take that long to get her here as a willing participant in his plans.

Somehow, he didn't believe she'd ever be totally enthusiastic. Nonetheless, if she thought Hawk's life depended on her agreeable compliance that might have a different meaning for her. If she was as much in love with her husband as he thought she might be, well then, it would not be difficult for her to see things his way. He could manipulate her emotions. Hawk's life in exchange for her sexual favors. She would have to understand she couldn't hold anything from him. He would know if she did. Maisie would have to give all of herself or the deal would be null and void.

He tossed his head back, roaring with laughter. Her mother had been dealt with in much the same way. She was so much in love with Damian MacRae she was prepared to give herself to him when he threatened the man's life. Unfortunately for him, MacRae rescued her from his possession. Not, however, before he married Shawna's mother.

233

Once the man died, little Miss McKenzie was his. She had no other means to support herself. With MacRae gone, she had no monthly income. The grandfather was too distraught over the deaths to investigate his son's financial holdings. Either that or he just didn't care.

# Chapter Eight

Hawk's feelings were convoluted. Two weeks had passed since the bonfire. Maisie was growing restless staying in the house along with his office. Isolation couldn't be good for her. She looked pale, frazzled from nothing to do. She paced. She arranged then rearranged the pillows as well as the pictures on the wall. The cupboards had been reshuffled at least three times. Everything cleaned more times than he was willing to tally.

He wouldn't even allow her to go to the barn without someone who could accompany her. On one very sunny warm day, they rode to Glen Cove. This was one of his favorite places. Especially when he remembered that first time, when he kissed her then stole all her petticoats along with her corset and stays. After he disposed of her undergarments several times, she ceased wearing them. He wondered if she wore them today. All that soft white flesh for him to touch and caress.

Last night she yelled at him, told him that she was done with this nonsense. At first, he adored her show of temper so unlike herself. Once he saw there was more than temper involved, he felt more remorse and self-reproach than ever before. When she finished yelling, she tossed the dishcloth on the floor. After that she raced from the kitchen tears in her eyes. Guilt swamped him. The unfortunate thing about all this was as long as the earl seemed bent on having her, he had to continue in this manner even if she thought it to be nonsense.

When he found her, she was kneeling close to the rosebush that took the brunt of her sickness that first day the *wee bairn* took over her body. It was the day she learned she was pregnant. He had a fondness for those roses.

Now he sat across from her at the breakfast table. To his adoring eyes, she looked apologetic. She had nothing to apologize for. He wanted to take her into his arms. No, he wished to haul her up the steps to their bed.

"I don't want to hem you in, to keep you from living your life," he murmured as he clasped her hands in his lightly rubbing her wrist with his thumb.

With a dazed expression she stared at him as if he'd gone mad. Perhaps he had. He didn't know how to make this right for her. Despite tender feelings coupled with wishes, he had to keep her safe. "Will you come to the office with me today? It's been two days since you were there? You could reorganize everything there. Well, Leah would most likely come along and change everything back to the way it was."

She looked up from her plate, a huge grin on her delicate features. "I'd like that. Do you want me, truly? I would come with you." She let out a long slow breath of air. "I don't mean to be difficult."

"You have every right to your feelings. I would not like to be jailed in my home. What I hope for is for you to be happy and content. If coming with me and working pleases you then it pleases me. How are you feeling? No more morning sickness?"

"I'm tired sometimes. Is that normal? I'm still sick in the mornings." She cocked her head to the side, her eyes hinting of mischief. "When am I going to stop losing my breakfast? The rosebush...well..."

He yowled with the laughter that had been sparse the last few weeks. Between her sickness and the confinement caused by the earl there had been too many frowns and furrowed foreheads and not enough smiles. He didn't think the rosebush would suffer too terribly.

"Let's go for a ride after we've closed the office for the night. We can go to Glen Cove." He watched her with tender concern, knowing she didn't like to ride. He changed his tune. Thought the ride to the stream would not suit his purposes. He needed her to relax. "The bonfire...would you like that? Roast some marshmallows. Make love in front of the flames?"

Her smile was demure. She'd been looking at her fingers. Now she looked at him. Her eyes glimmered with an idea. "There's the inn in town. We could go for dinner. I don't have anything to fix tonight. Would have to go to the market along with the bakery. If I'm working, I won't be able to bake bread today or make anything for dinner."

She works too hard. He wished... "We should hire a cook. Someone to help you with the chores around the house. You would have a person to talk to besides me."

"With just the two of us, I don't need either a cook or a maid, but thank you. I would not wish to waist the money."

It seemed she worried about money. There was no reason. While he wasn't wealthy by some standards, he made more than enough with the crops along with the horse breeding his father began. His practice brought in enough groats to maintain their household. The family shipping business thrived. There was always money left over. "The baby will take up a lot of your time. We should plan ahead. Both Houston and Riley have help. I will post a notice in the next paper."

"I'll think about it. Not sure if I want someone cleaning my house. Now, about dinner?"

She smiled at him again. He brought her hands to his lips. Kissed her knuckles.

Her smile brought his heart to this throat. He wanted her now, on the kitchen table. Too bad there wasn't time. "We haven't finished breakfast."

He laughed as he looked at the plate of half-eaten food.

The pounding on the door took him by surprise. "Hawk! Hawk! You've got to come...come quick. It's Jessie. He fell. Can't move. Think it's his back."

He rose, striding to Massie before kissing her on the forehead. He let the man into the kitchen. "Sit down. Tell me what happened. After that we'll decide what is to be done."

If he needed to go with Benjamin, he wouldn't be home for dinner or breakfast the next day.

"He was fooling around. You know, like Jess always does. Isn't afraid of anything. He was riding one of our mules when he hit his head on a tree branch. He went down hard. Didn't move. A few of us carried him to the hut." The man was wringing his hands. His voice wavered with emotion. "Took me three hours to get down the mountain."

With that bit of information, Hawk groaned. He would have to leave. "Suppose you had to move him."

He nodded his head. "Didn't have much of a choice. He couldn't stay there, too cold, the ground too hard. I know you've always told us not to move someone..." The man lifted his shoulders, shrugging away the wrong doing as if it didn't matter.

"You say he can't move?" Hawk queried as he began to gather supplies he would need. He turned to Massie. "Will you bring down a change of clothing. This may take more than just the day."

He didn't want to leave her this way. He would have to talk to all the men before he rode out. They would guard her, keep her safe.

"When I left, Jess was unconscious. He groaned when we moved him. I was sent to fetch you since my little horse is the fastest."

Massie returned with the requested items. Hawk grabbed his slicker from the coat hook at the kitchen door.

"I've got to go. I'm sorry, but you'll have to stay here until I get home. Don't go anywhere by yourself. You should move in with mother and father."

In the back of his mind, he wanted to send the man to Houston. He couldn't do that. Jessie and family were regulars of his. They lived on the trail running farther north into the highlands. There, the terrain was rugged and harsh. He traveled that trail once every four months. These people were his patients. While he was there, he would have to take some time to visit a few others.

"No...Hawk, I'll be fine here. Don't want to move in with anyone," Massie said. "I could go with you," she told him her voice quivering with fear. "I could help. You know that I could. I would be there for you to see as well as protect. You wouldn't have to worry about me."

The devil how he wanted to take her. He couldn't. If he gave into his basic wishes, she would be miserable. This wasn't something she would enjoy. "No, stay here, bake some bread. Send one of the men to the village to pick up whatever staples you need. I might have to spend the night or a few more days."

He regretted that. He didn't want to endure one night without Massie. Even while he made plans they changed.

"Bake some bread?" She bit off a piece of toasted bread. "Think I'll work on some clothing for the *bairn*. Your mother brought a stack of cloth two days ago. Suppose I should do something I enjoy."

When he gave his ultimatum, she looked both relieved as well as disappointed. He imagined that was also how he felt.

"If I must stay longer than tonight, I'll send someone to let you know. There are plenty of boys up there who would like to earn a few extra groats for taking a message to my wife." He pulled her into his arms, kissed her forehead then her nose. Pulling back from her to stare into her beautiful eyes he hesitated only a moment.

"Don't wear any of your underwear while I'm gone, especially the corsets. Not good for the child. I want to be thinking about what isn't beneath your dress while I'm away from you."

His lips found hers, kissed her deep and hard. He didn't want to say goodbye. Didn't want to turn around and look at her after he let her go. If Benjamin wasn't standing at the door waiting for him, he'd lift her skirt to see if she wore anything beneath.

When he strode away, he did turn. Looking over his shoulder as he followed the man from the kitchen, she was frowning. *Well, so much for making her happy today.* What they planned might have been fun. Once in the stable, he sent the stableboy to his parent's home to tell him he was leaving for the hills. Massie would be by herself. He couldn't help himself; he raced back to the house. He found her still standing in the same spot, her fingers clasped tightly beneath her chin.

"You are staying the night."

"Yes." He hated the answer but it would save him time in the long run. "I might as well do rounds with the families while I'm there instead of making another trip. What do you think? I could get the wagon...you could go..." He couldn't subject her to the long ride in a lumbering wagon. Winter was fast approaching. The hardships on the trail were something a woman who was increasing should avoid if possible. He reassured himself she would be safer here with the men guarding the house and with his parents along with the relatives close by to turn to for help. Despite all that, he would worry.

She was shaking her head, her pretty curls dancing around her face. "No, that would not be pleasant. I'll stay here where it's warm and dry, where I have a real bed to lie down in at night. Don't worry about me."

She touched his face with her hand. He leaned into the soft flesh, wishing the day could start over. With a last hard kiss, he left.

Hawk stopped at the office to tell Houston he wouldn't be in today. Maybe not for the next two or three days. Hawk left with the reassurance that Houston and Leah would check in on Massie. Houston told him they would have her for dinner tonight. Tomorrow night would be Heather's turn. All would be well.

He'd been on the trail for two hours, Benjamin riding just behind him to his right. The beauty of the highlands never surprised him even though it always stole his breath. The long rolling hills, the craigs, the streams coupled with the fact that he always felt as if he could see forever when he crested a hill. Sometimes he wondered why he ever changed his ways and set up practice in Selkirk. He'd always enjoyed riding through the countryside, seeing the crofters, the simple folk who eked out a living from the land. Every day was different from the one before. The life for these folks was humble. Nevertheless, most were happy. They took great enjoyment from working together. They played together during holidays, labored together during the days. Sang and danced during harvest and planting.

When he thought of his clan as well as how they formed strong bands, he understood in the end with Massie this was right for him. Massie...his thoughts centered on his wife, on his half naked wife. It was almost dinner. They would have strolled arm in arm to the inn where they would have eaten. After they finished, he would have made love to her on their big bed. Next, he would have spread his fingers across her belly to see if he could detect a tiny bump. His son grew within her. When he touched her, he felt the *bairn's* heartbeat.

He was a man well pleased. This was the right life for him. He had much to look forward to as well as be thankful for.

Yes, life was good to him. He had his mate, the woman he loved and a child on the way. Even though he nearly bungled the task. He'd been stupid. That was all in his past.

What more could a man want?

They passed beneath a canopy of trees. His hair stood on end. His hand clutched around his sword. The cry of battle rang in his ears. A man landed on top of him dropping from overhead tree limbs. Air rushed from his lungs as he felt the brunt of the blow. He was dazed. The ground spun beneath him. Sky blended with the earth. He gasped, drawing in a harsh breath, replenishing the wind that had been knocked from him. He concentrated on the attack. He and another man fell to the ground wrestling to gain the upper hand. He tried to clear his head. Started to shift despite the threat.

A shot rang out. The sound stopping him. "Cease! I don't want to kill you. No one wants you dead, just out of the way."

The man he was wrestling with hauled him to his feet by the front of his shirt. He stared into dark brown eyes. "Ah, the good doctor will go with us, yes. He has no recourse but to do as we say."

The attack ended before it began. If he shifted, he thought he would be dead. "Where? Where is it that I'm to go with the likes of you?" Hawk questioned.

Benjamin was gone, nowhere to be seen. The man was part of this. Why? Massie, was she now being held? He should have never left with the man. Hindsight. He stiffened his shoulders taking on all that went on around him, searching for a means to end this. "What is going on here? I'm seeing to a patient. If you're looking for money, I've none with me. You're out of luck."

"Got what we want. You. Been paid to deliver you." The man turned him, while the second man kept his musket pointed at his chest. "Put your hands behind your back."

Hawk found that he was tied then hefted onto his stallion. He found himself doubting what was happening to him. His thoughts centered on Massie. He needed to know the part Benjamin played in all this. Something was amiss and he didn't know how he was going to change that fact. "I will go along with the three of you. You do understand there is a young man who has a bad injury. A man who is waiting for my help." Hawk questioned that fact too. If Benjamin instigated this, Jess might not be hurt.

"He will have to wait longer for your attention. No doc is coming his way anytime soon."

"What is it you want?" Hawk asked his voice harsh.

He didn't know how to fight these men. He needed to get to Maisie.

"Got what we want. You." The man sneered at him, tugging his horse forward. "Been paid to make certain you are indisposed for a while. As I said before, don't want you dead just out of the way for as long as it takes."

With those words, Hawk had a great deal to think about. They wanted him. Why? An hour must have passed before they rode up to a small hut. His mind reeling, he didn't understand what anyone would want with him. As far as he knew, he had no enemies.

After the two men ushered him into the one room hovel, one man started a fire. "To keep *ye* warm," the man laughed. He untied him. "Everything you ever wanted and more is here for your taking. You won't be running away. If you step out of this place without one of my men, the guards have orders to shoot. Not to kill mind you, but to maim. You'll be findin' yourself in a great deal of pain. Will have to be seein' to *yer* own doctorin'."

The fight had not lasted long. He was miles away from home or finding anyone who would help him. He didn't know why he was here. He sat down on a pallet near the fire. The warmth radiated out to his cold, numb hands. He tried to work the unresponsiveness from them.

"What is it you want...besides me?" he asked now holding his hands closer to the heat.

"Just you. We were told where you would be and that we needed to bring you here. As I told you, keep you here. When we did, we would be paid." The man seemed to be repeating himself.

"Who told you?"

The man with the musket lifted his shoulders in an indifferent shrug. "The lord in question never gave a name and I never asked for one. All I needed to see were the golden groats he offered. Said there would be more when the job was finished."

"Well, do either of you know anything else?" Hawk searched for information. Seemed that every time he asked, he learned a bit more.

"Suppose it doesn't make no difference if we tell you. We're supposed to stay here with you for a week. After that, we're too leave with the horses and all your supplies. This lord what's his name said it might take longer than a week. He'd let us know."

*They would leave him here.*

Hawk searched his head for enemies, men who would see him dead. He very well could be dead if they left him alone in this rundown shack. While he had survival skills, he would also need a weapon other than the knife in his boot. His gut turned sour. Massie, he thought about her perfect soft body, growing with his child. This was not at all what he wanted.

"Imagine Jess wasn't hurt at all. Was he? What part did Benjamin play in this?"

Hawk felt certain the man's family would have had to be threatened for him to turn on him the way he did. Hell, he delivered three of the man's children. Saw the family through several illnesses where they all survived.

"Don't know."

The man pushed his hat back from his forehead. He spit into the fire. After he turned, he scratched his belly. "Suppose that friend of yours who got you was just supposed to bring you to us. That was all. We were told exactly where to be waiting. You was easy pickings, easy money. Didn't suspect a thing."

The gut feeling rolling around inside him cried out that Massie was in trouble. He needed to get to her. Why the devil did he ever leave her? For some reason, his capture was meant to bring Massie to the man who coveted her. If the earl threatened her with his life, she would do whatever he asked. Cold sweat broke out over his body.

He prayed she would not fall into the trap being set, vowing that he would get to her. She would not go with Farlan in order to protect him. She would think about how much was at stake, the child. His relatives and family would stand by her. If something happened to him, she would have the babe. Houston would deliver the *wee* child.

A drop of blood slid down the side of his face. Above his eyebrow, he'd been cut by one of the blows inflicted during the brief attack. He couldn't think about Maisie going with the earl to protect him. Before anything happened, he would return to her. These men were only staying for a week. After the week was over, he would be on his own. He knew this country. Understood he could get help from most any person he ran across. All he needed to do was set his path south.

He leaned against the wall, closing his eyes, gathering energy, soaking up the meager warmth. These men were fools. They would make a mistake. When they did, he would have his chance. Either that he would bide his time. He was a patient man.

As the days passed, he planned for the moment the men left him. His stallion would never let either man ride him. Windwalker would be close. All the scenarios he plotted in his head were just his imagination. Nothing was grounded in reality. He wondered if they would bind him before they left him. They might still kill him.

It seemed whenever he dosed, someone would kick him. His ribs were bruised. He felt battered as well as bruised from the inside out. After the second day passed, he discovered there were two more men. He was constantly guarded. There was no chance of escape.

He counted the days that passed. A week had come and gone. He heard the four men arguing outside. They were yelling at each other. He imagined something went awry. That thought pleased him despite both the constant hunger and the fear for Maisie. Even though they fed him occasionally the food wasn't enough to fill his belly. They answered none of his questions as to the purpose of his abduction. When he walked, he felt dizzy. His head still pounded.

"I'm for going now!" One man hollered. "Been waitin' here like an old lump on a log. What fer? There will not be more groats. The fancy man lied to us!"

"No!" the other cried out. "We have to wait for the go ahead. What happens if we leave him here and it's too soon? If he gets away and ruins all the plans that have been made? We won't be getting' more money if that happens. He told us to be keepin' him here until he sent the message."

"The man told us a week. The week is gone. I'm going home. Need to see my wife. Need a good meal."

"You won't be paid if you leave."

The threat was clear.

Hawk wanted them all to go to hell. Getting back to his wife was his only concern. He should be there for her. He'd offered to pay them more than the earl. His clan would do anything to get him back. They might search for him now. They might not. When he traveled into the highlands, he never knew how long he would be gone. He told Maisie he would send a message to her, if he was going to be longer than three days.

She would be worried.

Hawk had to keep reminding himself that his family would never let anything happen to her. They would protect her. What if she didn't go to them for help? If Shawna were around, she would speak to her. Shawna lived outside Inverness. She and Riley planned to leave the same day he was captured.

The door creaked open, the four men walked inside. The leader, the man who'd held the gun at his chest a week ago, who made certain he understood there was no escape, spoke. "We'll be leavin' you now." He slid a rope through his hands eyeing him thoughtfully. "Won't tie it too tight. You'll be able to get free in no time. Heard tell he got what he wanted."

Those words slammed Hawk hard in the chest, his breath catching. He would be tied again. A mad dash through the four of them might be possible. If he could reach Windwalker, none could catch him. The man seemed to guess his intent.

His broad grin showed yellow stained teeth. "Your stallion, that mean devil, is gone. Bucked off that one, he nodded to the man who landed on him that day a week ago. After that he took off down the mountain. If you're thinking of escaping on the horse, you won't. Nay...you'll be walkin' down the mountain. Will take you a while. Who knows you might get yerself lost."

A tug of relief coupled with hope swept through him. Good for Windwalker. The stallion wouldn't have gone far. The two of them had an understanding. One didn't leave the other behind. Windwalker wouldn't be far from him. The problem was getting untied if they did mean to bind him.

He kept the smile forming in his heart behind his mouth. That might not take too much effort. His knife, a wicked blade, was still inside his boot. When he was attacked, he didn't have time to retrieve it. With the musket held on him, he decided prudence was the best idea. So far, he'd done nothing to enrage these men. A few more minutes, even an hour wouldn't make a difference.

When the men left, he was tethered hands as well as feet. He waited until the sound of their horses leaving vanished. With a great deal of twisting and turning, a few grunts combined, he managed to get his hands in front of him. For a big man, he was agile. Once he accomplished that, he retrieved the knife then cut the bindings.

Rubbing his wrists, he forced circulation into his hands. Working feelings back into his feet, he walked around the room until he could move without limping. This was it. He would return to Maisie, find her then love her. Check out the *wee bairn* growing inside her.

Stepping into the open, he inhaled the raw, fresh air in a deep gulp. Bringing his fingers to his lips, he whistled. The sound brought a nicker along with pounding hooves. He saw Windwalker rounding the hut at a fierce pace. The saddle bag Massie packed for him a week ago was still attached to the saddle.

"Good boy," Hawk rubbed Windwalker's nose, scratching him then praising him. "You waited for me. Didn't think you would go anywhere."

Unfastening the saddle bag, he rummaged inside to find some trail mix savoring the small amount of food as the nuts and dried food hit his stomach. A change of clothing was packed in the bottom.

Before he left, he wanted to wash then put something different on himself. One of the times they let him outside to relieve himself, he'd heard a stream nearby. There had always been fresh water to drink. A half hour later he was riding down the path that led to the hut. Looking to the sky, he could tell it was the middle of the afternoon. He figured he had at least three hours before nightfall.

Hawk recalled that two days passed before the men brought him to this place. He also remembered having the distinct feeling they were traveling in circles. While he was blindfolded, he listened to the sounds of the forest. Now, he listened again. He was stymied, didn't have an inkling as to his location. He looked to the sun then the trail and decided.

Hawk backtracked. Finding the stream, he decided to follow the water as it tumbled downhill hoping to begin to see recognizable landmarks. If he continued on that path, he would have water to drink. Before the sun dipped behind the horizon, he made camp. He ate more of the mixture in his bag.

As always when he closed his eyes, images of Massie floated around in his brain. He saw her clearly. In each room of their home where he made love to her, he recalled the way she welcomed him into her arms, coupled with her secret warmth when he was so *verra* deep inside her. His body tightened. Her laughter always filled the home. Her sweet words comforted him. She was a delight.

He missed her.

Prayed she would be fine when he returned home. He wanted to walk up to the house and see her in the kitchen cooking or the drawing room sewing. Maybe stoking the fire with her pert little bottom high in the air. Life would go back to normal for them as if he hadn't been kidnapped, as if the earl didn't want her. The devil, how long would it have taken him to get back to her if his horse wasn't so loyal? Would he get back to her? Too many questions buzzed in his head.

When he dozed, he heard her crying, soft sobs. His heart wrenched in two. He understood the tears were for him. She believed he was dead, that he wasn't coming back to her. She was pacing a room that wasn't familiar to him. Where was she?

He was too late. It seemed she spoke to him. He heard her thoughts. Felt a renewal of hope in her. She looked up, startled as if she understood he was listening to her. Twirling in one spot she seemed to search for him.

*Hawk...Hawk are you there?*

She called to him walking to the door to search the countryside. She stood on the porch, a soft breeze whispering through the silken strands of her hair. He felt as if he was beside her, listening to her, soothing her fears. He needed to touch her, calm her. When he reached out, he felt nothing. "Be strong, sweetheart. I will be there for you. I'm coming. Don't give into that man. I'm not dead." He didn't know if he said the words aloud or if he just thought them. It seemed she heard him.

She was nodding, still looking out over the countryside. He needed to hold that picture in his mind. He would need the images to find her.

He sat back, leaning against a log, his legs stretched out in front of him while he sipped the fresh spring water. Windwalker nickered. The night breeze chilled. He brought the blanket he always kept with him around his shoulders trying to gather more images, more of her thoughts.

*I'm trying. Where are you? I thought you were...no, he promised me you were only dead to me. He told me he wouldn't kill you. Told me I'd never see you again. I ken he was wrong. Did they send you through the Kinnel Stones? Is that why you are missing. If he did, you must come back to me. Kit returned through the stones. You can too.*

Fear for Massie swept through him. This plot was instigated by the earl. He guessed now he felt certain his assumption was correct. The earl must have threatened his life unless she agreed to go with him to become his mistress. She was in a new home, a place the earl planned to put her. His clan had to be looking for her. They must be searching for him too.

"I'm coming for you, Maisie. I wasn't sent into the stones. I'll be there as soon as I can find where he took you."

*No, if you do, he'll kill you. Stay safe. I can endure anything if I know you're alive. Don't come for me, Hawk. He told me he wouldn't take me unless I'm willing. I'm not willing. Don't ever forget that.*

Hawk couldn't see him. He knew the earl was in the room with her, felt the new presence. He felt revulsion sweep through her. Knew the man touched her cheek. Understood he spoke to her. She jerked away from him, striding across the room. He could no longer hear her thoughts.

Hawk felt as if he would explode. He wanted to kill Farlan. The earl held his life over Massie's head to bring her to this home? Despite trickery, she would never willingly give herself to him. The man must understand he would search for his mate. No stones would go unturned.

The earl was a stupid man. He didn't kill him. He wouldn't because he would *ken* he would never get away with murder. Whatever happened with Massie the earl would claim that she was willing. Nonetheless, she'd been coerced. That, too, was against the law.

~ * ~

Massie dined with Houston and Leah that first night just as they planned. They were wonderful, the food amazing. She missed Hawk, counted the hours until morning light. "Do you think he'll return tomorrow?" she asked Houston as he escorted her to his home. The house was two stories and close to the office.

"No, won't be expecting him in the morning. When we first decided to share the practice, Hawk volunteered to travel to the outlying settlements. He loved that part of the work, meeting new people, breathing in the beautiful countryside. Since he will be there, Hawk would go to the other settlements as well as see to the crofters. He will be back soon."

Houston tried to give encouragement even while her heart was reeling. She didn't want to be alone with her fears. Didn't want to see the earl on her doorstep. Though it seemed he'd been gone for several days.

Nothing either Leah or Houston could say to her made her feel better. Once during the meal, she leaned forward, staring at Houston, her heart pounding hard in her chest, "Hawk is in trouble. Something isn't right. I don't understand why I'm thinking this. Nevertheless, the feeling is *verra* real. It's as if he's calling out for help."

She sat back, chewing on her lower lip as she searched her mind for reasons, her hands on her belly.

For a moment, Houston looked away. Clearing his throat, he returned her gaze. "Hawk can take care of himself. If he's in trouble, which I'm certain he is not, he will deal with the problem." There wasn't a lot of conviction in his voice as it wavered with the last words he spoke. "I'll talk to Elliott on the 'morrow if that makes you feel better. We can decide then. You are the one who needs protecting, not Hawk."

"Something has happened to him. Yes, speak with his father. I will too. I'm due for dinner at his parent's home in the evening."

Maisie was convinced of the fact. She wanted to shake Houston until he agreed to look for him. It didn't seem that he would.

"No, I'm certain he is just fine. He's going to see people he's always seen. Nothing is going to happen," Leah tried to reassure her. Her words didn't have the desired effect. "You don't need to worry about Hawk."

She did worry. Shaking her head, she wanted to scream that they were all wrong. Something happened to him. Just as she knew she was sitting here; she knew he needed their help. It seemed her words fell on deaf ears. As the minutes ticked by one after the other, she became more certain Hawk needed her help or his friends. In her head, she heard his voice. He was telling her to take grave care. He would come back to her. The last thought she heard was not to do something foolish.

"Come, let's have desert then I'll see you home," Houston said placating her fears.

He nodded to Leah who rose. She returned from the kitchen with slices of chocolate cake for each of them.

When Houston left her in the kitchen, he said, "I'm worried about you. You should go to Shawna's and Riley's place. I think Hawk's father would take you."

"If nothing has happened to Hawk then he would be home at about the same time I reached Inverness. You don't make sense."

Maisie understood what Houston told her wasn't rational unless he thought the same as she that Hawk needed help. He must want to send her some place where she might not worry so much.

"It's all right, Houston. You don't need to concern yourself about me doing something stupid. I'm not going to ride into the highlands to search for him. I *ken* I would get lost."

"Stay at home tomorrow and rest."

"Doing so will not help my husband."

She was tired of the argument, exhausted from trying to convince two stubborn people she was listening to Hawk, understanding his fears.

Houston didn't have an answer. He simply sighed then wished her good night. "Lock the doors, Maisie. Bolt them. I will stop by in the morning to check on everything. I'll light the stove for you."

With that said he was gone. Shawna watched him walk down the porch steps then into the night.

Leaning against the frame of the door, she stared at the moon, thinking that Hawk could see the same moon. He would feel the night breeze on his face. If he was alive... No, he wasn't dead. She would sense that if he was. Her hand rested on her belly, that didn't have a bump. Perhaps some of the shifters sixth sense she was feeling was orchestrated from the baby. Not knowing anything about shifters other than what little Hawk told her, she wondered if she might be right. The *bairn* missed his father and wanted him home, possibly as much as she did.

Talking to herself and to Hawk, she poured herself a generous portion of his best brandy then continued upstairs with the drink. After changing into a dressing gown, she sat on the bed, sipping her drink, studying the swirling amber colors knowing she shouldn't be drinking the potent liquid.

She didn't know how she was ever going to fall asleep tonight. She would find herself beset with dreams, nightmares. In her imagination, she saw him lying on a dirty pallet in front of dying embers. He was cold, hungry too. She knew that. He wasn't tied yet she understood he was held prisoner. His frustration ate at her as she felt it soul deep. Repeating the action even though nothing changed, Maisie touched her belly understanding it was up to her son to keep her in contact with his father.

Maisie wondered if she could convince Hawk's mother and father that he needed them. They should search for him. They might know the places he traveled as he made his rounds. She cursed herself. If she was more like Shawna, her sister, she would look for him herself. She would ride into the highlands. The others be damned.

Despite the need, she understood she couldn't race to the highlands. She saw herself getting lost. Watched as she groped around for some clue as to her whereabouts. They would have to search for her along with Hawk. If impulsiveness took over, she would make everything harder for the clan as well as put her life and the babies in danger.

When dawn came and sunlight flowed through the window, she made up her mind. She would go about her day as normal. This evening, when she went to his parent's home for dinner, she meant to voice her fears for their son. They would tell her he could take care of himself. She imagined he could. Maybe he would save himself.

Elliott drove a buggy to get her. They lived too far away to walk. "Houston told me you were afraid for my son, your husband. Do you think something has happened that is keeping him from returning home? You do understand he could easily be gone a week."

She wasn't going to deny anything. "Yes. I saw him last night in a hovel, lying on a dirty pallet. He was a prisoner, both hungry and cold. Something happened to him on his way to see that young man. He was abducted. People he thought of as friends led him into the trap."

"You didn't tell Houston that. Do you have the sixth sense? Your accusations about entrapment are serious."

"No, I didn't tell Houston. I was gifted with the images after he left me at home. I saw Hawk. Talked to him. As for the sixth sense, I believe it comes from the babe inside me. Never experienced anything like that before. As for the accusations...I'm repeating what Hawk told me. He doesn't blame them. Believes they were threatened by a man wielding power. This is my fault."

"You talked to him? What else did he have to say?" Elliott asked as he watched her carefully. "I'm curious that he isn't talking to anyone else." He rubbed his hand along the back of his neck. "Yes, he would go to the woman he loved. Never mind what I said."

"Do you believe me?" Her heart leapt. She didn't want to start telling her story if the man would think her crazy. "I'm not going to be telling you things that aren't true. If you're going to laugh at me or tell me it's my imagination, I won't say anything more."

"Don't go and get your back up. Yes, I do believe you. You would never make up anything like that. You would never try to send us out to look for Hawk if you weren't terrified. He is a capable man. Well able to see to his needs."

"So, it has to be true?"

She cocked her head to the side trying to study the man's expressions. He was a lot like Hawk. The way he frowned, the tilt of his lips when he was concentrating, even the tone of his voice when he questioned. The silver-blue of his eyes turned to pewter.

"Yes. As a shifter, I must believe in the supernatural. You are right. My son is in danger?" He lifted an eyebrow that reminded her so much of Hawk. "We would have miles and miles to search for him. The hunt might take days even weeks."

"All I *ken* is what he showed to me. He was hungry as well as cold. When I saw him, he didn't appear to be in danger or injured. Though I *ken* his life was threatened. Hawk is a prisoner. The issue is deeper than that. I think it has something to do with me."

"That earl who is after you? He's threatened you?" Elliott pulled up on the reins. When they came to a stop, he focused on her. "Hawk would want me to protect you at any cost to him."

"Not yet. Hawk told me the man will come to me with a proposition."

At this point she didn't want to tell Elliott more. She would decide how to handle the suggestion when it was made.

"We're here." Elliott pulled the horse to a stop. "We should continue the conversation where Heather can hear what you have to say. Believe she had some of those same powers when the *bairns* were inside her. She is better suited to listen to you."

"She would understand?"

After the night with Houston and Leah, she didn't want this one to transpire in a similar manner. She needed someone to come to the aide of her husband. She was tired of hearing how he could take care of himself. In this instance, he needed someone to give him aide. To take care of him.

"More so than me or Cameron. Harris won't be here for dinner tonight. She is eating with a friend. A girl friend. Though we all know she is enamored of the soldier. He has been gone a month now." Elliott didn't seem to like the change of topic.

"I was in love with Hawk for three years. Believed he didn't want me. When we finally were able to talk, we discovered the truth. I love your son. I would die if anything happened to him." Maisie reached out to place her hand on his arm. "If they love each other, you have to forget the fact he is Sassenach."

He seemed to ignore her statement about Harris still concentrating on her and Hawk. "My son has a way of using the least number of words as possible. I'm not at all surprised you misinterpreted what he meant to say. He would have never asked you to be his mistress in a letter nor would he have asked you if he could court you if you weren't standing in front of him. He is a man of great honor and was deeply hurt when you never responded to him."

He gave her too much to think about. Hawk hurt her too. They were moving on with their lives. Maisie saw no reason to rehash the past. Elliott helped her from the buggy before handing the reins to his stableboy. With his hand on the small of her back, they moved up the steps then into the house. When she saw Hawk's mother, she sensed both their concern and belief in her concerns. Maisie felt as if she would get through to them tonight. They would understand her fears and accept them as truth.

Heather hugged her, "Good evening. I'm glad you could come for dinner. Wish my son was here too."

Unable to stop herself she was nodding her agreement. "So do I. He is not. In this case, I must make the best of this situation. He was too trusting."

Unless Elliott brought up the topic during dinner, she would stay away from the subject. As it was, she was holding her breath in anticipation of the upcoming discussion.

At the dinner table it seemed no one wished to bring up the subject of Hawk. She pushed the food around her plate, chasing the fresh peas with her fork, unable to eat more than a few bites. Her stomach was not pleased.

When they cleared the dishes, Heather spoke up. "You believe Elliott should send someone into the highlands. Doing so could be dangerous. That was stupid of me. Of course, it is risky. Hawk understood the dangers though he didn't believe the people he knew so well would turn on him."

"We don't know if they did," Elliott said, looking to the door, seeming to wish for Hawk to walk into the house so this conversation would end.

Maisie nodded. "I do *ken* he needs our help. I know Hawk told me he would send me a message if he would be later than three days. This is the second day. Though it is early, I've not received any note or timeline that he means to adhere to. He would know now if he was going to be gone longer. Wouldn't he?"

"You should look for that written word tomorrow at the latest. Perhaps when you arrive home this evening, there will be something for you. If Hawk can, he will write. If you don't receive some clarification of his intention by tomorrow afternoon, let my husband know. He is also worried. Elliott knows where Hawk will be traveling. He's accompanied him on his rounds just to keep him company. The people would never turn on him."

"They would if they were threatened," Elliott said his voice harsh. "They would...any one would if their family was endangered. If lives would be lost."

Maisie didn't want to think about his last words. She nodded sending the conversation into a new direction. "I will send for you." Turning her attention now to Heather, "I did start sewing clothing for the babe. Hawk says it's a boy. I'm trying to relax as Houston told me last night. Relaxing is impossible. Nevertheless, keeping my hands busy does help pass time."

Heather held up her hand, quickly leaving the drawing room where they retired. When she returned, she had two beautiful baby blankets with crocheted edges. She displayed two small gowns for the boy. They were different shades of blue. They chatted until she couldn't stop yawning.

Elliott took her home. At the door, he kissed her forehead. His brows drawing together, he began, "Tomorrow, if you don't hear anything by noon, I'll ride into the highlands at least as far as Benjamin's home. He will tell me what happened to Hawk. Perhaps nothing. Rest assured we will find him. The man might shed some light on what has happened here. I hope this is nothing but I do fear the worst."

She cringed at Elliott's words. He feared the worst. Maisie didn't want to think about the worst or the best scenario. She just wanted to talk to Hawk again...tonight. Following the same routine as she did the previous evening, she sat on the bed, sipping brandy. Maisie knew she shouldn't drink the brandy but the alcohol helped her sleep. When Hawk was safe, she would make up for this.

With her eyes closed she could almost feel him. Nothing changed though. He was still in the hovel, still hungry and cold. There was no one else in the room with him. The fire was mere embers.

*I've not been able to discover anything new. While I don't have solid reasons as to why I was abducted, I sense the explanations revolve around keeping me from you. Has the earl threatened you? If he does anything to make you believe he will harm me, rest assured I will take care of myself. The earl cannot hurt me. If he tried to make you believe I'm dead, I'm not.*

She wanted to believe his words. So far, he wasn't doing a very good job of rescuing himself. Maisie understood she would have to trust in herself as well as her husband.

*I haven't seen the earl in days. Rumor has it he left the village. You know I don't go there without someone guarding my back. Hawk, your father is going to see Benjamin tomorrow if I don't receive a message from you clarifying where you are and how long you will be gone. I'm hoping the man will shed some light on this mystery.*

*Benjamin betrayed me. Father should take care.*

Her heart stopped when she heard his thoughts. She didn't know what to think of those words. The crofters, the people who lived such solitary lives were loyal to Hawk. He visited them, healed them, delivered their children. If Benjamin betrayed him the world had gone topsy turvy. No, it had to be something else. Hawk had no reason to lie she told herself as she attempted a one-sided argument. Benjamin lied to him then set him up to be captured.

She closed her eyes. *I will tell your father. He believes as I do. Houston didn't. He thought I was just worrying overmuch because of my pregnancy. Houston didn't say as much but the thoughts were clear in his eyes. I'm not imaging this. While it isn't the child that makes me worry, it is the* bairn *who helps me see and speak with you.*

She clenched her fists wishing Houston would have accepted what she told him. As she pulled the covers across her, she heard him again.

*Maisie, if you get a paper message from me, it's not from me. I've not written one. If my captors come to me with the request to write something, the words will be false. I'm certain they will tell me what it is they want me to say.*

That was all. The image vanished. For the longest time she stared out the window, watched the stars twinkling in the night sky. Somewhere an owl hooted, crickets hummed. He was in a hovel, starving. She couldn't do anything to help.

She sipped her brandy, her mind in chaos.

Tomorrow, she would go to Kit. Tell him what she thought, what she felt. Perhaps he could convince Houston or assure her Hawk wasn't lost in the stones. Hawk might need a doctor. Maybe she should walk to the keep. Surely Connal would be interested in Hawk's well-being. Connal was head of the clan. He would set things right.

The soft sigh whispering from her lungs left her frustrated as well as confused. The men would all tell her he could take care of himself. She felt backed against a brick wall with nowhere to go. With his family she was treading in deep water. If she didn't get aide soon, she would sink.

The next morning, she slept too long. When she woke, she was exhausted from the nightmares that plagued her. Her eyes were swollen from the tears she cried. The ache in her head throbbed along her temples. The images floating through her brain while she slept were of her mother with the earl. The things he did to her. She thought of his hands on her body. Debilitating shudders swept through her.

"No!" She sat up with a start. No...she needed a bath then she needed to walk to the office. If she kept busy her mind might not wander to Hawk quite so often. She especially didn't want to see images of the earl and the way his eyes lingered on her breasts, sending shivers of revulsion throughout. She didn't want him to touch her, let alone bed her.

Dressed and bathed Maisie wandered down to the kitchen. She put a kettle of water on the stove to boil. Houston must have stopped by, to set the fire in the oven. She sliced a couple of pieces of the bread she baked yesterday. After the water boiled, she sat down to eat, her mind once more on Hawk.

"Maisie, it's Leah. Want to talk?" Leah was knocking on the door, smiling as if nothing untoward had happened, as if Houston hadn't refused to believe her.

Maisie didn't know if she wanted to hit her head against something hard. Didn't know if she could stomach talking to Leah when she would ignore all her concerns. She unlocked then unbolted the door so Leah could come in. "I brought some fresh eggs if you're interested. A peace offering. I know you need to hear from Hawk. I would feel the same if Houston was missing."

"Set them on the counter. Perhaps I'll have them for dinner." She played with her napkin before she could speak. "Would you like tea? Oh, I see you're helping yourself. Elliott said he would go see Benjamin today if I don't get a message. Hawk said he'd let me know what he was doing and where he was. He hasn't. That fact alone should tell everyone there is something wrong."

Leah sat down at the table helping herself to a piece of bread. She put butter and honey on the slice then looked at her thoughtfully. "That is a good idea. You do know that Houston is concerned. I think after some second as well as third thoughts, he believes you."

"He doesn't seem that way to me. I thought the clan stuck together. Oh," she waved her spoon in the air, "I'm not truly clan, now, am I? So, no one thinks I can sense my husband. I can. I did last night too. He is with me even now. I can feel him through our child." She placed her hand on her flat belly.

"I understand. Houston has this way of holding himself back. He likes to make certain he knows all the facts before he jumps into the fray. He would go with Elliott if he wasn't leaving the town without a doctor. As it is, Kit has decided to travel with Elliott. If something has happened to Hawk anyone looking for him might also find dangerous territory in front of him."

Maisie felt the blood drain from her face. It was almost better when no one believed her. Now, the men were giving credence to her visions, to all her fears. They would head into the unknown. She sucked in a breath of air. Leah's hand rested on top of hers.

"You will come with me to the office?" she asked her voice soft. "You should have something to occupy your mind while the men are away."

Maisie found herself shaking her head, not wanting company

now. "No, I've chores to do. Since Hawk left, I've not had the energy to tackle much. The kitchen needs cleaning as does the laundry. Everything needs dusting as well as sweeping."

"You shouldn't be alone."

"I feel better knowing someone is looking for Hawk. I need to have my thoughts to myself. Perhaps I will receive a message today from him. Though he told me that if I did receive a statement, the words wouldn't be his. I shouldn't believe what is written down."

She was far too aware of the earl as she thought on the past. The man had a way of bending people to his will. His power along with his wealth gave him strength. She didn't know what she would do if he threatened Hawk's life. Understood he wanted her. He told her as much. If Hawk was in his possession, he wielded untold power.

After Leah left, Maisie stayed at the kitchen table, sipping the now cold tea, staring out the kitchen door, wishing she would see Hawk striding through it. She didn't have the heart to work or the energy. When she finished the tea, she walked through the house then onto the front porch. Wrapping a blanket around her, she sat on the swing. Hawk seduced her on the swing, kissed and loved her here. She wanted to walk up the hill to the bonfire where memories were ripe and potent. Time there was precious. She might never get that back. Her hands framed her belly.

"Nice to see you, Maisie." His gravelly voice surprised her.

She sat up, her eyes wide, knowing the moment the man spoke who he was. "You..." She didn't hear him approach. His buggy was tethered in front of the house. He stood at the bottom of the steps staring at her as if he owned her.

"Yes, me. We need to talk about Hawk, about our future together."

He sat down next to her on the swing. His leg touched hers. He was trying to possess her, to tell her he owned her. She swallowed hard, willing courage to rise.

When she tried to get up, his hand on her shoulder held her down. "I don't want to talk to you. Nothing you can say is of interest to me. There is no future for us."

"You will. I have Hawk. No one will find him. He's alive for now.

If you care for your husband, my dear, everything I have to say to you should be of the greatest interest. If you come willing, your little hand in mine, nothing will happen to the doctor."

Her worst fears were coming true. Everything she was afraid would happen...no, I'm going to believe in my husband, my family. She needed to trust in her husband. He was a shifter. He could take care of himself. "What do you want, Farlan. I won't be your whore or your plaything? I'm not yours to possess. I don't need money or food. I've a family who care about me. There is nothing you can coerce me with."

She jumped to the foremost question in her mind even though she felt certain she knew the answer.

"My willing mistress," he told her running his hand along her shoulder, touching her as she'd watched him touching her mother. The gesture was meant to control her. He meant to have his way with her. She would never go to him in any capacity.

"Never!"

She wanted to run from this man. She should have gone with Leah. Maisie understood it would have only delayed the moment. He would have shown his face in her home this evening. "I won't be your mistress. I'm a married woman. I'm expecting Hawk's child. My mother needed your money. I do not. You cannot have me."

"That fact is a bit of a disappointment. Though if the child turns out to be a girl as lovely as her mother, I would be able to use her in another thirteen years. What do you think of that? Hmm... I find I quite appreciate that notion. The mother then the daughter, after that the granddaughter." He ran his knuckles along her cheek then down the column of her neck. "So soft. I would never make the same mistake. A girl can become a woman at thirteen. She doesn't have to reach the age of fifteen. I won't wait to make the granddaughter mine. At thirteen or maybe even twelve, she will be malleable. Your daughter or your daughters will all be mine."

Maisie shuddered, her body vibrating with both revulsion and rage. She would fight him to the bitter end. He would not have her. "I'm not going with you. The clan will search for Hawk. They will find him."

"Dead," he interrupted her. "If they find the good doctor, he will be dead. That is...if you don't come with me. If you decide to let your husband live, you will get in the buggy with me this instant. You show yourself to me soft and willing, your breasts falling into my hands after you undo the bodice of your gown. I won't have anything less."

Her throat was parched, so dry she couldn't swallow. By the look in his eyes, he would kill Hawk if she didn't do as he said. Farlan had the power. She looked down the road, saw nothing that would help. She turned to him, resigned now to do what he bade. Her heart fell, dejection along with hopelessness set in to the deepest darkest parts of her. He presented her with no choice. She loved Hawk. She couldn't let him die.

"If I go with you, Hawk will live? Do I have your promise?" she asked hoping, *nay* knowing he would tell her what he wanted her to hear even if his intentions were to the contrary. Hawk could have been killed before Farlan came to her doorstep. She wouldn't know. Once she stepped into the buggy, he could give the order for his death.

"He will live. I'm not a murderer. However, I do want your promise that you are coming with me of your own volition. I will not take an unwilling woman."

Hanging her head, ashamed at the fact she was giving herself over to this man without a fight left her bitter. "I am willing to ride with you," she murmured as she rose.

In a daze she walked to the buggy then waited for him to help her.

"To become my mistress?"

"Yes."

She had to buy Hawk time to escape.

~ * ~

Elliott stopped at Hawk's place to see if Maisie received information from her husband. She wasn't there. He thought she must have gone to the office. If so, she was safe there. He called to one of the guards to see if that was true. He couldn't leave until he discovered where she was. If he left without knowing, Hawk would never forgive him.

Taking off his hat then rubbing his jaw, the man said, "I don't know where the missus is. She had a visitor a while ago. She was sitting on the swing just staring out at the road. Not moving, mind you. Saw the man leave in the buggy. Haven't seen Mrs. Frasier since."

Elliott's gut tightened his mind focusing on the earl. He didn't want to ask when he was positive, he knew the answer. All kinds of scenarios swarmed in his brain. "You didn't see Maisie with him?"

"No, just saw the back of the buggy. Didn't seem in any hurry to leave. This man was sittin' with her on the swing. Just assumed all was fine. If Mrs. Hawk had been there, or if there'd been something wrong, wouldn't she have called out for help? No, ask Michael, he's around the corner. He might have seen something."

Not if she thought her husband's life depended on her leaving with the man. No, she wouldn't have said anything. Not a peep to call attention to herself. No one would have seen her leave. Under that circumstance, she would never call out for help. "How long ago?"

"Couple of hours..."

What to do? He cursed. Then set off to find Kit. The two would have to look for Hawk first. After they found his son, he would make inquiries about Maisie. During the interim, Maisie's life wasn't in danger. Hawk's life was.

Elliott and Hawk rode hard for the two hours it took to reach Benjamin's crofters cottage. Dismounting, they strode to the door. His wife answered, wiping her hands on a dish towel, appearing startled to see them. She was small, plump in the bosom. Her green eyes looked weary. Bits of bright red hair poked out from beneath the white cap she wore. Her smile was genuine. She might not know what her husband did, what he helped put in motion. What was the price asked of Benjamin for him to betray Hawk?

"Where's Benjamin?"

At the moment, Elliott had little patience. He was frustrated as well as angry with himself. During the long ride he realized he should have left this morning. Should have seen that Maisie was better protected. He failed at both. His son was not going to be pleased to discover his wife missing.

They would find Hawk. If his son was dead, he would feel the loss bone deep. He would know beyond a shadow of a doubt. Hawk still lived.

All shifters felt the loss of their *kin* when they passed. Just as the *wee bairn* Maisie carried told Maisie what he was sensing. Seemed the baby also had the sight. He'd never truly thought about an unborn child possessing such amazing attributes even though Heather swore that it was true.

"In the fields working," she told them her voice curt as if she realized this was not a typical visit nor was he friendly. "What do you want? He's a busy man trying to put food on our table, earn a living too."

With sudden insight, he realized the woman did know what he was asking about. Benjamin must have confided in her. "Have things to learn that we believe only Benjamin can tell us, unless you care to shed light on the whereabouts of my son."

Understanding she wouldn't answer, Elliott bolted back on his horse. He saw the man working with his sons. Saw him bend over to speak with the smallest of his boys.

When Benjamin saw him, he sent both boys to their home. His back stiff he waited. After they reached him, he spoke. "Wondered when you would turn up lookin' for the doc. Thought I'd see you yesterday. What took you so long?"

No, Hawk's father was too stubborn to truly listen to Maisie as were the rest of the clan she pleaded with. "What do you know about his disappearance. It's evident, you do know something," Kit asked, leaning one elbow on the saddle horn. "From what we understand, you're the last man to see him. In good faith, he took off with you in order to help one of your own. He's a doctor first. Will always come to the aide of his patients. You knew that...took advantage. Now you owe him your compliance. Tell me all that you know."

Benjamin's face was redder than a beet. He cleared his throat, holding up his hands. Shaking his head, he began to speak. "The men told me they wouldn't hurt him, just hold him until some gel did what she was supposed to do. When that happened, they were going to let him go. Promised me the doc wouldn't be hurt."

"So, you lied to him to get him to come with you. Was Jess hurt? Was that a ruse also?" Elliott asked his voice deepening with anger as he *kenned* the truth, the betrayal, the loss of loyalty they all took for granted.

If Houston had believed her the first night, they would be that much closer to finding Hawk. The trail would not be as cold. Perhaps Farlan would not now have Maisie doing his bidding.

"They threatened my three boys along with my wife. Said they would take all four of my *kin* north, so far north they would never find their way home. Said..." The man stuffed his hand through his thinning hair. He heaved in a huge breath of air as if seeking the strength to continue. "Said they would die. What choice did I have? I'm sorry. Truly, I am. Hawk can fend for himself. We all know that for an absolute fact."

Elliott didn't see a reason to make him more uncomfortable than he was. He was blubbering, tears in his eyes, running down his nearly gaunt cheeks. His thinning brown hair was plastered to his head from the sweat of his labors. His blue eyes pale. The distress clear in every movement.

"I understand. Now, if you wish to make amends, you will take us to the last place you saw Hawk. Get your horse." Elliott whirled his stallion in the direction of the ramshackle barn.

They rode for another hour in a northeastern direction. The few trees gave way to rolling hills devoid of anything but rocks and heather. A few deer grazed in a valley below. When they turned to the west, they moved south. Elliott felt as if they were riding in circles. He was losing track of the landmarks.

Benjamin pointed a dirty finger toward a group of trees. The trees seemed to be abundant, a good place for a surprise attack. "One of the men jumped him from the tree. There were just two of them. After Hawk fell off his horse, the second man held him with his pistol pointed at his chest. There weren't nothing I could be doin' to help. I left. Don't *ken* what they be plannin' for the doc. Nobody told me anything like that. Just told me to bring him here and take a roundabout way."

Elliott understood the man would fight for the lives of his sons as well as the life of his wife. Even so, he was outraged after all that Hawk did for these people. The sacrifices he made. "Hell, Hawk delivered your last child. This is the way you repay him?"

"They were going to kill my wife and *bairns*. What did you expect me to do? Hawk can take care of himself. The devil, all who live here know that for the truth. There be nothin' going to happen to the good doc." He was blubbering, sputtering saliva as he spoke.

"Can you tell us anything else?" Kit asked, as Elliott rode toward the trees bent on finding a clue that might tell part of the tale. "We need to know what direction they took."

He could hear their voices. His intent now was to find tracks to follow, a trail that would lead him to his son. Once he found Hawk, they would go after Maisie. Thinking of Maisie, his stomach turned over. He didn't know what the man would do to her. Hawk mentioned that the earl wanted her from the time she was just a girl. Maisie had been thirteen when Shawna found her. Maisie's mother had been the earl's mistress.

The guards he hired had not done their job. All they needed to do was make sure she was never alone except inside her house. The men failed. They let her ride away with the man who meant her harm.

Kit caught up with him after only a few minutes. "Do you see anything?"

Elliott shook his head still staring at the small trail leading west then the bushes. "We will have to ride home. Tell our wives and Houston what we believe happened. These men would not have been able to sweep away all the tracks. We will find him."

They would need supplies for a week at least, food as well as clothing.

"It will be late when we get home," Kit said while he rubbed the back of his neck, staring down the path Hawk must have taken as a captive. "We can meet up in the morning. I'm sure you're right, we'll find a trail."

Elliott wanted to stay put, to keep tracking his son. He didn't have provisions. He'd started out in haste, still doubting Maisie. He cursed. "Tomorrow then."

Angry with his lack of foresight, he whirled his horse around, heading down the mountain. If he'd not been so pig-headed, they would have the necessary supplies with them now. All this time would not have been wasted.

# Chapter Nine

Hawk followed the river downstream. He camped at night, hunted by setting traps. The first night he ate well, a tender rabbit roasted to perfection. The second night, rain sluiced from the sky. He took shelter beneath a rocky overhang, the river rushing by him on one side while water dripped from the ledge. He pulled his great coat close, huddling to ward off the incessant water. By the time morning arrived, he felt soggy as well as disheartened, felt as if moss grew on him, he was so damp. Maisie always the focus of his thoughts, filled his soul. He hoped the earl did not persuade her to his way. How many days...more than ten. Anything could have happened. Deep in his heart, he knew she went with the man to protect him.

So far, he didn't see any landmarks he recognized, or people. This wasn't his home turf. There wasn't one crofter's hut or small cottage in his sight. No one to ask information from. All he wanted were directions to Inverness. He supposed southeast would get him close to the city. Downhill, at least that was the direction of the stream, toward the ocean, east toward Inverness.

The third night a stiff breeze blew from the north. He wrapped himself in his blanket and tried to sleep. He'd eaten mushrooms earlier in the day, a few wild potatoes and onions. After he stopped for the evening, he found a nest with eggs. He had boiled eggs for dinner along with some trail mix he packed before he set off with Benjamin. His stomach still grumbled.

He was closing in on the seventh night on the trail when he saw a small hovel. An old woman stood outside with an ancient blunderbuss pointing his way. The weapon was clearly as old as the woman holding the firearm. Her thin graying hair seemed to stand on end. Her face wrinkled; her eyes brilliant as if she'd been a beauty when she was younger. She moved the weapon to the right then back making certain he understood what she held. Hawk wondered what would happen if she fired the thing. It would most likely explode in her face. He wasn't worried. She was just protecting herself. She wouldn't fire unless she thought he meant her harm. He didn't. From him, there would be no unexpected moves.

He held up both hands. "I'm a doctor who has lost his way. If anything ails you, I can help. If not, you could point me toward Inverness."

She spit on the green leaves of a bush near her feet, cackling at him. She lowered the gun. "Don't have anything that ails me, at least not something you can fix. Old age isn't something a doc can be fixin'."

"Directions then?" he queried, his grin growing. "To inverness?" One eyebrow lifted, speculating what she would tell him.

"If you share a meal with me, I'll tell you whatever you be wantin' to know. Tired of talking to myself every day. You look mighty hungry." Chortling again, she set the gun on a stool near the door to her home.

"A meal would be nice if you have enough food for yourself. Don't want to take something you can ill afford to give."

He dismounted then followed her into the one room dwelling. A large cat sat on the bed. The cat stared at him before jumping off the bed. He rubbed against Hawk's legs, purring before curling up in the corner of the room.

The inside was gloomy with only one candle lit. A bit of light came in from a lone window. There was one pallet, a chair by the fireplace, a kitchen table along with two more chairs. In the corner there was a bed for the cat.

"He doesn't usually take to strangers. It's unusual that he would like you," the woman said staring from the cat to Hawk then back. She held out her hand, "My name is Anice, the cat I call Worthless. Except as a mouser he's does nothing except sleep and eat. Course he catches his own food."

Worthless would sense his alternate form. They were both cats in one way or the other. That's why he took a shine to him.

Something bubbled in a huge black kettle that hung over embers in the fireplace. "Smells good."

Hawk wasn't at all certain he wanted to eat what she cooked. She must have guessed his hesitation when she replied again. To answer his uncertainty, his stomach rumbled.

"Been a while since you ate?" she asked as she bent over to stir the cauldron. "It's venison. Got a neighbor about five miles down the hill who brings meat. Out back I got an herb and vegetable garden. Everything else I scrounge from the countryside. We exchange." She turned to him as she picked up a bowl. "You have a seat over there. As you can see, there's two of them. Biscuits are on the table. You showed up at the right time."

Hawk didn't realize how hungry he was until he started eating. Since the first night, hunting had not proven beneficial. He'd been able to trap one more rabbit. Except for that he'd had very little. He bit into a biscuit that was flaky and light. He thought he could eat the entire batch. She had fresh churned butter. When he lifted an eyebrow to question the wonderful food, she cackled.

"Neighbor has several goats. Sometimes he leaves them with me. Got goat milk as well as butter and some cheese. I do fine out here. Everybody helps everybody." She handed him a glass of fresh goat milk. "You a real doc? Or are you just blathering to this old lady."

With a mouthful of stew, chewing the venison, he answered, "I am a real doc. I'll mark your place as one to come to when I'm doing my rounds up here. Though I'm not at all positive where I am. Do rounds three or four times a year."

"I'd say about ten to fifteen miles give or take northwest of the McKenna keep." She stopped talking to look at him. "You're not one of them shifters, are you? That must be why old Worthless took a shinin' to you." The old woman squinted at him as if she tried to see his cat.

If the question, half accusation, wasn't so series he would have hooted. He could never tell her the truth even though she guessed as much. "I'm not a McKenna. I'm a Fraser. Not related at all. That wasn't entirely true. He supposed they were related by marriage. Nothing else. Do live close to the keep. Fifteen miles you say?"

"Not too good with directions or distance. Could be wrong. Will you be staying the night or high talin' it out of here to get home?"

"Who is this neighbor of yours?" he asked while he chewed thoughtfully wondering if he knew the man. "Could be one of my patients. Might have delivered a child..."

"*Nay.*" She took his bowl to refill it chortling as she walked away. When she returned to the table she continued, "He be too old for siring children. Still a good hunter though. Eyesight's keen."

"Does this hunter have a name?" Hawk asked wishing she would be more forthcoming.

"Likes to go by Mort. Doubt if you know him. The man is never sick. Wouldn't be needin' a doc."

"I'd like to meet him though. How often does he stop by?"

She sat down next to him, sipping on the rosemary tea she brewed. "Once a week, just to sit and talk with someone. He doesn't talk to himself like I do. Though sometimes I talk to Worthless. The cat doesn't have much to say in return."

"So..."

Though he wanted to laugh, Hawk needed to learn more than she wanted to tell. He supposed she needed to keep her secrets just as he did.

"Was here yesterday. You got cause to hurry down the mountain?" she asked now seeming content to sit and watch him eat. "Got a little missus you be missin'? Ah, that's the way of it. Now, isn't it? Your eyes are telling me everything."

Thinking of Maisie, he nodded. "More reason than I want to think about. Part of my trouble is hers. I wasn't there to protect her. She's going to need me. The sooner I get myself down the mountain the better for her. She isn't at home. I will have to find her."

After finishing the second bowl of stew, he leaned back, stretching his legs in front of him replete for the first time in nearly two weeks.

"It's a woman. Always is. What she done? You say you didn't protect her like you should?"

Nothing that he wished to talk about now. "Think I will head out. Got at least two hours of daylight. How far can I follow the stream before it heads away from McKenna land?"

"About two more miles. Like I said though. I'm not too good at estimating distance. The water will run east. You need to go south. You really goin' to come see me next time you do those rounds of yours? I'll be lookin' forward to the company."

At least he understood that fact. He stood, nodding his head. "Thank you for your hospitality. The food was delicious. In four months, I'll be back doing rounds. I'll stop by." He would bring her provisions along with his medical expertise if she needed it. "Is there anything you need that your friend doesn't bring?"

"*Nay*, don't be needin' much that the land *dinna* give."

By the time the sun descended and the moon showered the earth with some light, he'd traveled about six miles. He laid out his bedroll near a boulder then started a small fire. When he closed his eyes, he saw Maisie. She was no longer in his home, hadn't been for days upon days. His gut churned with fear for her.

*Hawk?*

*It's me. I'm safe. You can leave him. Walk away. I understand by the room, you are no longer at home. You dinna need to stay there.*

*Your father and Kit left to find you. It's been more than a week, closer to two. Where are you?*

*About seven or eight miles from home. I'm coming for you.*

*It's strange that I know things I shouldn't. Seems this little one I'm carrying has the sight. He will tell me how you are.*

He sipped in a breath of air. The earl walked into the room, his smile wicked. He watched as Maisie backed away from the man. Farlan strode to her. She was pressed against the far wall in the room, trembling. Hawk felt her fear, sensed the revulsion she felt for the earl. His stomach churned. He couldn't help her. All he could do was watch.

"No!" he screamed, his fists clenched. "No..." he said more softly as the vision faded. She was no longer in his head. He could no longer see what was happening to her. He rested his head in his hands. A sob tore from him. Tears slipped down his cheeks.

"Hawk?"

Startled, he looked up. "Father?"

"Kit and I, we're here. We've been looking for you for days. Followed the trail to the cottage where they kept you. Saw the old lady a little more than an hour ago who gave you dinner. She told us where to find you."

They embraced. "She's in trouble. The earl has Maisie. I don't know where she is. Feel so damn helpless. Can't do anything to stop the man. He's going to hurt her. She'll fight him now that she knows I'm alive and away from his hold over me."

"The earl took her the third day you were gone," Kit said, his voice gentle. "I'm sorry. We divided our resources. Houston along with the others from the clan are looking for her. They'll find her."

Hawk paced around the small campfire. He wanted to change to his cat, to run until exhaustion would let him sleep. Elliott brewed a pot of coffee, handed them each a piece of venison jerky. Hawk waved the food off then thought better of it. He stuck the jerky in his mouth slowly chewing on the end.

"Can we be home tomorrow?"

He thought that perhaps later tonight he could see Maisie again. Talk to her. She might know where the earl stashed her. If she could give him some direction, he would find her.

"Easily," Kit said.

"We'll find her," he said again as if to not only convince Hawk but to convince himself as well.

His energy soared, restlessness possessed him, body, and soul. He was so close to her he could feel her, sense her and the babe. It didn't matter. He was too far away to help her. "If it wasn't so dark, I'd take off. I want to ride until...until I can see her, hold her in my arms."

"The earl threatened Benjamin's family. Told him his wife and children would die if he didn't do as he told him. The man had only one choice. In a similar situation, we would all have done the same," Kit told him.

Hours slipped by as the night slowly began to lighten. Hawk thought of Maisie. It wasn't until near dawn that she came to him again.

*All is fine with me, Hawk. If you are safe, I will leave this place. I don't know where I am. Nonetheless, Farlan let slip that the home was south of Inverness. I'll walk north. If I can find the MacRae townhouse in the city, I'll try to get inside. The weather is turning. I pray the earl doesn't come after me. He will though if he thinks he can find me. If you try to prosecute, he will say that I was willing. Yes, it's true. With your life in his hands, I was prepared for the accusation and agreeable to his plans.*

*No, stay where you are. I'll find you. Don't leave the protection of the home. You don't know what will happen to you on the road. It's dangerous out there. Anything can happen.*

*I can't do that, Hawk. Next time he comes he will force me. So far, he's wanted me willing and in his bed. I'm not. Now, he says he doesn't care. He will have me even if I lay on the bed unmoving. Even if I fight him. His friend, his driver, will take me too. I cannot bare either of them.*

He cried out at the thought, his mind closing. She vanished.

As soon as sunlight filtered across the craigs, Hawk was stamping out the fire, spreading the embers and pouring water over the coals. She would be at the MacRae townhouse. If he could, he would fly there. He didn't think he would stop at the cave though. If he had company on this trip, he felt certain they would insist. He felt his father's hand on his shoulder. Understood that he would try to make him think rationally. Urgency of this situation plagued him.

"You must slow down."

"If it was Heather in trouble, would you?"

"You cannot fly off the handle. You must use your mind. Remember what happened to Kit when he didn't use the common sense God gave to him. He ended up in the Kinnel Stones trying to find his way home."

"She's not at the stones. She'll be walking to Inverness. Don't know what road she will be takin'. Anything can happen to her," he gritted out through clenched teeth seeing her in his mind struggling along the road. "I couldn't convince her to stay put. Damn stubborn woman."

"How do you know all this?" The question hovered unanswered for several seconds. "It's as if you've spoken with her."

Hawk found himself nodding as he searched for words, any words. "Yes, seems the child in her belly wants me to know all her foolishness. I saw her this morning clear as anything I'm looking at now. She is resigned to her fate. I couldn't change her mind. She told me next

time he visited he would force her. Told me she had no choice left to her."
He rubbed the back of his neck, tension building, nerves fragmenting,
unraveling with each passing second. He'd never felt so stretched thin
before. "Not that I would want to change it after what she told me Farlan
meant to do. I must get to her."

"If you are hurt or ill, you will do her no good," Kit said getting
in on the conversation. "We will pack more provisions once we are home.
You can start out then. When you reach the cave, it will be late. Wait
there, rest, sleep a few hours then start to Inverness. You will get there
with a clear mind. We will follow."

"All true," Hawk mounted the horse feeling the frustration
escalating. "I'm going. I'll see all of you when I have my wife back."

"I will meet you in Inverness. While you search for her, I'll keep
the old townhouse in observation," Elliott said. Houston will give me the
address. "God go with you."

Hawk nodded. If he could, he would race his horse, race until they
were both heaving. He could not do so. He had to take care. Even though
his father didn't believe he listened to his sage advice, he did. The plans
in his head changed by the second as he mulled everything over in his
mind he knew then weighed it against everything he did not.

He reached his home late afternoon. He gathered supplies then set
off. He didn't intend to stop though he did. He reached the cave by
midnight then rose with the beginning of dawn. His morning meal he ate
while he rode.

~ * ~

"You look wonderful, my dear," Farlan told her when he strode
into the drawing room where she now resided. "Are you rested? Your
face is pale. You've dark smudges beneath your eyes. You must take
better care of yourself along with the babe. The pale face, the shadows
are hardly appealing."

Maisie sipped her tea. She didn't want to acknowledge the man's
existence. Didn't want to know that he would sit with her, eat dinner with
her then expect her to sleep with him. She wasn't willing but she wouldn't

fight him. Every time he came to her, she lay on the bed unmoving, refusing to touch him, to respond to overtures he made. Maisie loathed the man. He seemed to hate the fact she wasn't moved by his suggestions. Hated the fact she didn't respond in any way. She didn't even struggle.

Perhaps she should fight him. Mayhap he would stop, understanding she would never allow him to bed her. She shuddered in a long breath of air holding the lump of oxygen tight in her lungs until she could hold the breath no longer. If she fought him, he would kill Hawk. She didn't doubt that for an instant. Until she knew he was safe and at home, she had to remain unmoving.

When her eyes were shut tight, she saw Hawk sprawled on the filthy pallet. Knew he was hungry and cold. Understood his life depended on her. This was the third day of her captivity in the home Farlan purchased for her to reside in. This was the third time he visited her.

"What do you want, Farlan," she said in a tight voice even while she tried to soften the tone. She hated this man, reviled all that he was, all that he assumed he could take from her. "I've given you all I possibly can give. There is nothing more left. I can't give you what you're asking of me no matter the threats you hold over my head."

He sat back, the glass of brandy he poured resting on his soft belly. He looked her over, his eyes settling on her breasts, seeming to disrobe her. He'd yet to take her. "Believe you *ken* what it is I want, my dear. I will come every night until you comply with my wishes. On Hawk's life you promised. I'm the man to make certain you live up to those vows."

Her body vibrated with the growing nausea. "Willing. Don't know if I can do that," she spoke, her voice soft, trying to keep her serenity and calmness intact. "I came with you a willing *lass*. Doesn't mean I can let you take from me that which is Hawk's. I cannot abide your touch. You are repulsive. Hateful. You are a small, weak man."

"You must figure out how to do so." He sipped as he reached out with one hand to touch her chin. He lifted it. Stroked the contour with his thumb. "Your husband's life depends on your complacency. I must be satisfied with our little arrangement, treated as the man who pays your way. You do understand the terms of our bargain. If you don't, you will come to regret your decision. I can always find a place for you in any of the many whorehouses in Inverness. Would you like that better? To be used by any man willing to lay down the groats to come between your white thighs. If that happened Hawk would never want you back."

*A bargain made in hell.*

Her eyes blazed. She was shaking, trembling so hard she could barely breathe. Now, she was back to what David wanted from her. If Shawna had not married the imposter, he would have sent her to a whorehouse. She sat up straighter, twisted her chin from his grasp. "I'm trying. You must give me more time. Seconds, minutes, hours, just a few of them. That's all I need."

"Good. I have every confidence you will succeed. Now, time, this is a different matter entirely." He stroked the length of her neck, stopped at the pulse that was beating so hard, so frantically. "So white and soft, is the rest of you this soft? I would like to discover this for myself. Should we proceed to the bedroom? Perhaps you should don one of those beautiful negligees I purchased for my enjoyment. Yes, go put the lavender one on then come out and sit with me. I'd like to spend a bit of time enjoying your company before we take our pleasure this evening."

His hand settled beneath her breast, cupped it as he seemed to savor her. He closed his eyes as he caressed her, flicked his thumb across her nipple.

She stiffened starting to pull away then remembering what she needed to do to keep Hawk safe. Needed to yell at him that she detested him, that she wouldn't do what he asked. She wouldn't ever lay down with him. "No... no, I find nothing pleasurable about any of this. I don't want you, Farlan. Don't want you to touch me or look at me."

She saw his expression turn to rage, his face turning red. Watched as his eyes darkened, until he heaved a beath of air seeming to set his emotions back into an even keel. His Adam's apple bobbed up his neck then stilled. He set a finger on the swell of her bottom lip.

"You care so little for your husband? I've men stationed along the route to the little hut where he is captive. Again, do you not care what happens to him? If he lives or dies?" he asked as he leaned forward to run a fingertip along the top of her bodice dipping casually into the valley between her breasts, taunting her with his actions. "I do want to see if you're as wonderfully endowed as your mother. I remember her with a great deal of fondness. Her breasts overflowed my hands. I liked to suck on them, tug on her nipples with my teeth until she moaned her pleasure. She would be hot and damp for me. Will you moan my name, Maisie? Will you scream Farlan when you reach your release? I would like that. The thought makes me swell with need for you. I could take you now. Toss up your skirt and plow your white belly. Would you like that?"

She held her breath, willing her mind to a place where she felt nothing. If he took her, she would go to that place where daisies filled the fields where soft summer breezes swept across the flowers. Now though she needed to confront him. "I heard mother crying. I never heard her moaning with pleasure or with your name on her lips. She loathed you as much as I do. The problem was that she needed your money. Not you, never you...nor your driver. He took her too, didn't he? Is he going to force me? I don't have to be willing with him. He is not part of our bargain."

He sighed deeply as well as loudly. Shaking his head, he pushed her off his thighs. She landed hard on the floor. "You disappoint me, my dear. Go now, get yourself perfumed and bathed for me. I'll wait here, a patient man. Wait to see your sweet curves. Your bath is drawn. I saw to it as soon as I entered here. As to my driver, it matters not to me what he does to you. Our bargain doesn't include him. With you he has *carte blanche*. He can do whatever he pleases. Willing or not. Gawain likes a woman to fight, to struggle while she lies beneath him. Likes to subdue her to his will. He calls the process taming."

She stood resigned to the inevitable. She couldn't let him touch her. She wouldn't do this freely. He wanted agreeable or Hawk would die. Her mind was embroiled with confusion.

What to do? She had no options left to her. She caught her bottom lip between her teeth, biting, hoping the pain would help her forget all that was happening to her.

Maisie took as much time as she thought he would allow. While she was bathing and vulnerable, she thought certain he would walk into the chamber. He would humiliate her. Pull her naked from the water.

He did not. When she was finally bathed and perfumed as he

asked, she put the gown on then walked into the drawing room. Her body was stiff, seeming to resist him even before he approached her.

Every part of her could be seen by anyone who wished to look. She hated presenting herself to him in this fashion. When she peered down, she saw her nipples pressed against the soft fabric. When she looked lower, she could see her woman's mound, the curve of her thighs as well as her hips.

She thought of Hawk.

There was no alternative to this.

"Come here," he said beckoning her with his finger. He smiled as his gaze lingered in various places. "Come here and let me see you. I've waited years for this moment. I'm certain I won't be disappointed. You are truly lovely, my dear. More lovely than your mother. She was a beautiful woman. Pity, she had to die so young. Thought I would have you sooner. If I had, you wouldn't be so hesitant with me now. Ah, but I can't retrieve the past, only move forward into the future. You are my future, Maisie, as my goodwill is yours."

Maisie's feet didn't want to move. She stood frozen to the spot, her eyes wide. She saw his anger growing. He was used to women obeying him.

"Come here then turn around so I can see all of you. Don't disobey me. If you do, you will regret the action," he repeated himself.

Still, she didn't move. "I c-can't. I don't want to come to you, n-now or ever. Y-you are a horrible man. I despise you!"

"If you don't, you'll regret it. You are but a woman. You have no say in this now that you left with me, eagerly became my mistress, my whore. You're a little harlot, Maisie, just like your mother. I've always known that fact. When you watched me with your mother, you wanted me then even as a young woman."

His voice was smooth and soft. She understood he would make good on what he said. She didn't know how or what he would do. She already regretted him, regretted walking to his buggy.

Her footsteps hesitant, Maisie moved toward him, her heart lodged in her throat. She was nothing to this man, nothing except a means to assert himself, proclaim his power over someone who was helpless.

When she stood before him, she looked at him, at the lust shining in his eyes. Her breath wobbled into her lungs.

"Turn around for me." His hand rested on her hip, slipped to her buttocks as she swayed from one foot to the other. She didn't want to turn. Wanted to run back to the bedroom then lock the door, a door that had no lock.

Closing her eyes, imagining this was not happening, her breath heaving, catching in her throat, she turned just as he asked. Her hands fisted at her sides.

"Stop." He placed his hands on her buttocks, moved them, caressed then squeezed hard. He pulled the skirt of the negligee up until she felt the coldness on her, felt his hand stroke her, felt his finger slide down her inner thigh.

She gasped for air, stunned by the pain and humiliation he caused. Maisie had not thought he would humble her. Had not thought he would scrutinize her in this fashion. She needed to offend him.

"Face me," his voice purred with what sounded like satisfaction. "You please me, Maisie. Your compliancy pleases me. I don't mind some fear or a bit of maidenly reluctance. After all, you've been with only one man. I will change that. After you've accustomed yourself to me, why then you will also service my bodyguard, my driver as well as any other man who will pay me for your body." He tugged on her so she sat on his lap again. His hands circled her waist. "Kiss me."

She jerked. "What did you say?" Her mind revolted with displeasure. "That was not what I promised. I'm not servicing anyone."

"You know what I asked. By accompanying me here, you've lost all choices."

He brought his hand to surround her breast, to flick lazily across one nipple. He pinched her hard. Once more she jerked away from him. His hands held her still. "You will accommodate any man I choose with your beautiful woman's body. Many will pay very well for you. I will charge an exorbitant fee. You see, you are so very beautiful. You are every man's dream. Men will line up for their chance at you."

This couldn't happen. She couldn't allow him to force her or to make her see other men. If she didn't do something soon, he would violate her. Tears slipped from her eyes. Her stomach rolled in upheaval. She felt the bile rise to her throat. Instead of looking away or running for a chamber pot, she vomited on him.

Farlan jumped to his feet, cursing, swearing foully. He dumped her on the floor again. She landed hard. The pain felt right. Somehow comforting.

"What the devil do you think you were doing?"

He stared at her while vomit slid down his face to slither across the pristinely white shirt he wore. He picked up a cloth, rubbing it across his face, wiping his hands.

She grimaced after holding back a small smile. Even with the nausea she still felt, she couldn't help feeling glad she stopped him. She lifted her shoulders in a small shrug. "Isn't it apparent? You make me sick to my stomach."

The words were far too brazen. She cringed when she saw the rage reflected in his eyes. His hand fisted as he threatened her. She thought he would hit her.

Angrily, he strode from the room, still wiping the vomit from his shirt and jacket with a handkerchief. He returned a few minutes later. Pointing his finger at her, he shook it then spoke. "Don't think you will get away with this. I will return tomorrow. See that you are not sick a second time. I won't tolerate this resistance of yours."

She gained a day and to what good would that do her. The earl would return. Hawk remained in the hovel somewhere in the highlands. A rescue would not be forthcoming by tomorrow night. All she could be grateful for now was the fact the earl left. One more night she was safe from his attentions. In relief, she pulled in a deep breath of air. She would have to take this one night at a time. Perhaps, she could think of something else to keep him from her bed.

Five days passed without seeing the earl or Hawk. Maisie spent her days wandering outside the cottage to figure out where she was. Nothing would help her. There were no landmarks she recognized. She'd never been south of Inverness. As far as she could walk, she saw no sign of other people. The lane leading to her home must come off a large road. For the entire time she'd been here, there had been no traffic except for

Farlan arriving in his little buggy then leaving the same way.

Now, she sat on the porch, plucking on her skirt. Idly, she pushed the swing with a foot. The gentle movement lulled her. She closed her eyes, enjoying the soft scent of the fresh air. It would be time to fix something to eat. Farlan kept all kinds of food in the pantry for her. He would bring packages every time he came to see her.

Unfortunately, she wasn't hungry. Because of the baby she needed to keep food in her stomach. She had to think of the *bairn* first.

Thoughts of Hawk filled her head. She missed him, missed the sound of his voice, of the tread of his footsteps when he walked up the porch coming home from work. She missed the way he tenderly held her and kissed her, how his body felt when he covered her before sinking deep inside her.

All she wished for was to be home, cooking dinner for her husband, waiting for him to return from his practice. She wondered if he was still in the cottage. It was strange to her that she wasn't locked inside the home. The earl left her free to move about. Clearly, he wasn't worried about her leaving.

She could walk to Inverness. It couldn't be that far. Hawk would yell at her when he discovered what she did. Confronting the possible dangers to be found on the road was better than having Farlan sully her. After that his driver or bodyguard, whatever the man was to him. When they were done, any man who was willing to pay for her.

Thoughts tumbled in her head, confusing and frustrating her, making her second guess her decisions. Hawk wouldn't want her to be alone on the road. Anything, any possible dangers would be better than waiting for Farlan. Twice during this time, he sent her food to prepare. He never stayed to eat. Always left swearing and muttering.

Tonight, she would have some of the fine vegetables he sent. One evening she had mutton, another chicken. There were always eggs for her breakfast. In the kitchen, there was enough flower and sugar along with the other ingredients for her to make bread. One day she made cinnamon rolls, another she made a wonderful coffee cake with apples on the bottom.

Keeping herself busy was the biggest problem she had during the day. At night it was the fear of waiting for the earl to come that set her on edge. She heard the clock on the mantle of the fireplace chime five times. The few days he came to see her, he arrived by five. She rested her hands on her belly, wishing she felt a small bump, wishing too that the babe would connect with Hawk again. Too much time passed since she'd seen him through the images.

Stepping onto the porch she stared down the lane seeing nothing. Another reprieve tonight would be welcome. She sipped in a breath of air, closed her eyes trying to see Hawk, attempting to know what he was going through. Perhaps he was safe. Maybe he was coming for her. She opened her eyes.

It was then she saw the buggy winding its way to the cottage. A shiver of dread rippled down her spine. Goose bumps rose on her arms. She rubbed the spots willing them to vanish. She didn't want him to be here.

What could she do?

Nothing...absolutely nothing.

Two men stepped from the curricle. Her body tightened with dread. Two men to see her, to use her. Perhaps he meant to force her with threats of the bodyguard taking her instead of him. What difference would that make? She loathed both of them. Hawk told her what they most likely did when they were with her mother. They would take her at the same time, sharing her body, using her for their needs with no regard for her feelings. She couldn't imagine any of it. What Hawk briefly described seemed so unnatural.

She wondered if she could lose her dinner on them. Maisie didn't feel sick. She'd not thrown up since that night when Farlan did his utmost to seduce her. He couldn't seduce or charm her. She would never give herself to him in the manner he wished.

"Ah, my dear," Farlan stepped up the porch making his way to her. He pulled her into his arms, kissing her on her unparted lips. His tongue thrust against her mouth while his hands tightened on her arms seeming to give warning that she should submit. She wasn't about to do so, deciding now that there had been enough time for Hawk to escape who ever abducted him. She knew that it would take days for a message to come to Farlan.

She slapped him hard. His head jerked back. She stepped away from him, breathing heavily while she waited for the retaliation that was certain to come.

Her hand print kissed his face, bright red, giving her a feeling of purpose. He screamed at her, spittle flying from his lips. He looked to his man then back to her. "How dare you! You're just a little whore, a slut. Just like your mother. We will both have you tonight. There is naught you can do to stop us."

His bodyguard grabbed her arms from behind, holding her. If he tried to kiss her again, she'd let his tongue inside her mouth then bite him as hard as she could. She spoke with stiff words, controlled words. "Not a whore until you have your way with me. Only a whore because of your inability to have a woman who cares for you. You need to force women in order for your small man parts to act the way you want them to."

He stepped up to her, his fingers grabbing her chin, tightening until she winced. His man pulled her arms so hard she thought they would pop from the sockets. "You came willing, no eager, knowing full well what I expected from you. You want this, you little slut. You want me along with what I can give you. Admit it. So far, I've been gentle with you. No longer. He will hold you down, your arms above your head, while I take you then he can have you. Perhaps we will take turns ravaging you tonight. What do you think? Will you like that? Both of us pounding into you? I tried to be tender. Wanted you to adjust. Gave you time. You spurned me, rejected me, your protector. I give you everything you have." Farlan stared at the rise and fall of her breasts.

"If you want enthusiastic or even agreeable, this evening won't be the night. I loathe you as well as your man. Mother did too. She never wanted you or him."

The man let her go with a push. She stumbled, turned then marched into the cottage, her chin in the air, her back stiff and proud. Poured herself a glass of wine before drinking it down. She poured more, saluting the two men with the glass high in the air. "Go to the devil, Farlan. I'm not complacent. Never will be. You coerced to get your way. It's over now. I'm doing what Hawk would want. I'm refusing you.

Telling you that you can go to hell."

His face whitened until it appeared a death mask. She didn't understand how her words would have an effect on him. He was the man. With little effort he controlled the scenario. Bile once more rolled in her stomach. It was the baby. The *wee bairn* understood and was helping her fight this man. She felt as if she was turning green.

"Don't you use that ploy with me again!"

He marched toward her. Grabbing her by the shoulders he shook her. After that he seemed to understand that perhaps he should be smarter than to get too close. He stepped back.

Maisie rushed to the chamber pot, emptying her stomach with horrible gut-wrenching heaves. When they stopped for a moment, she sat back, pushing damp tendrils of hair from her face. Sweat beaded on her forehead, running down her body. A few seconds later dry heaves ripped through her stomach. She had nothing left to toss into the pot. Still her body tried to do her in.

"That's quite convenient of you, a hidden talent," Farlan told her, his voice smooth and ugly. "You only get sick when I come to see you? Have you been ill? Should I call a doctor?"

It was the babe. True also that the vomiting occurred when she saw him. Seemed to be a symptom that wouldn't go away. Maisie hoped it wouldn't go away. Being able to vomit on Farlan came in handy.

"Don't need a doctor." She stood. "If you and your helper want to stay and eat, there is food in the kitchen. If not, you can see yourselves out."

She sat down by the fire, in front of the clock that was ticking away her life. She hoped she would see Hawk again tonight, hoped he would come into her mind and talk to her, give her hope where there was none.

"Perhaps you will feel better in an hour or so. We shall see, now, won't we?" He walked into the kitchen. She heard the rummaging, the talk between the two men. They would stay for a time.

She was certain he would eat. After that he would expect her to feel better. She drank more wine despite the fact she didn't think it was good for her baby. She needed her stomach to be full if she was going to throw up again. Needed the wine to vanquish the vile taste in her mouth left from the last time she vomited. There were pieces of cheese as well as sausage on a plate she'd brought out earlier in the day, bread too.

Maisie ate a piece of cheese along with a slice of bread. She'd put them in the living room until the meal finished cooking to help ease her hunger pains. She wasn't hungry. The food was to provide protection for her from the men.

Maisie heard the two men talking, listened to the sound of dishes along with silverware clattering. Wanted to know what they were saying. Undoubtedly, it was about her. What they were going to do when they finished eating.

Tonight, she was going to think only of Hawk. If he came to her in her imagination, she was going to tell him again she would walk into Inverness to the townhouse her grandfather owned, that Shawna and Riley owned now. She would explain why she had to do so. For her, there was no other choice. She would rather take her chances on the road than in this home with these two men.

The men walked through the door. Farlan stood over her, hovering. His grin was wicked, evil. He stood so close she felt the heat from his body. Smelled the food on his breath. The sweat along with the cloying sent of the rest of him. "I'll be back in a few days in hopes the sickness will have vanished."

"Don't you understand it is you who makes me sick. The sickness will never be gone." She looked to the bodyguard, "As well as your friend. The sickness won't go away. It is not something I can control. Every time you come; I will puke on you. Never doubt that. I don't want you."

"We shall see."

They were gone, walking out the door seconds after the short curt words that were said between them.

He came to visit three days later, backing her into a corner. Once more, she tossed the contents of her stomach, this time on his immaculately shined boots. Before he attempted to kiss her, she saw Hawk. In that instant, knew he was safe, alive, and well. She made up her mind that tomorrow morning, bright and early she would begin her next journey. She wouldn't wait for Farlan to defile her. Wouldn't wait for Hawk to save her.

Her child saved her from Farlan. The little shifter would also lead Hawk to her. She had no doubts.

The morning wasn't bright the next day, not at all. When she set out with her one change of clothing along with a small bag of food, heavy mist coated the ground. She could see about ten feet in front of her. The cloak she brought with her was warm, comforting, keeping her dry. She wrapped the fabric tightly around her, pulling the material close. Almost an hour passed before she left the lane leading to the cottage. This was the road leading to Inverness, she didn't doubt that.

She heaved a silent sigh of frustration as she didn't know which way was north. While she could tell by the position of the sun, today there was no sun. Placing her hand on her belly then relying on instinct she didn't possess but she prayed the child did, she turned to the left. What seemed a few hours passed, the sun dried the heavy mist. The sun beams warmed her chilled body. She figured she walked far enough to see Inverness.

She had not.

The devil, her feet hurt. Her legs were sore. Her back ached. She needed some nice person to drive by then offer her a ride into town. How the devil would she *ken* if the person was nice?

She sat down beneath a large oak tree, delving into her bag of food. The shade cooled her as did the slight breeze which must have helped chase the mist away. She loosened a button on her dress then two more. She fanned herself trying to ease the heat. Her skin was slick with moisture. Finding a slice of ham then tearing off a chunk of bread, she ate slowly, relishing each bite. She sipped from the water she brought in a small leather bag.

For a few seconds she closed her eyes. A soft breeze ruffled the leaves on the tree she was leaning against. She could stay here forever. She was so tired, exhausted, and bone-weary. Maisie wanted to close her eyes and sleep forever. She jerked. Farlan could drive by. She needed to stay alert. Once more she placed her hand on her belly, thinking perhaps the child could instill some energy in her wearied body.

Maybe he did. Perhaps he didn't. Maisie knew that she had to continue. She had to stand then put one tired foot in front of the other. The city couldn't be that much farther. Had to be around the next bend in the road.

The sun was sitting low on the horizon when she reached the outskirts of Inverness. For the first time in hours, hope blossomed. Maisie would make it to the townhouse where she could finally sleep. All she had to do now was find the home. She knew the address. Some nice person would point the way. Once there she would sleep for twenty-four hours.

~ * ~

Farlan slammed the heavy oak door behind him. He stood in the middle of the entryway, breathing hard. He knew, oh, he knew she left. He had a premotion of this. The place was too quiet, too still.

"Maisie!" he yelled her name at the top of his lungs over then over again as he marched through the cottage opening doors then slamming them again. "She's gone. Who the hell would have thought she would leave? She's always been a little mouse." He turned to his man who lifted his shoulders. "Hawk...*nay* even if he rallied and found his way down the mountain, he could not have reached her. He didn't know where she was.

"She's just a frail little woman. You should have taken her, shown her who was in charge. Now, you must figure out how to get her back. If you ask me, even though she is lovely, she's turning out to be more work than she is worth. You could find a more willing mistress. Someone biddable. Someone like her mother."

"You wouldn't say that if you remembered her mother as I do. Her breasts would overflow even your large hands. I want her. No other woman can replace her. Where the devil do you think she went? It's miles to the city. She couldn't walk that far."

"She could. She's a determined little thing. Figure once she set her mind to doing something, she will accomplish the feat. Who does she know in the city?" His man lifted his large burly shoulders. "She would go to someone she knows."

"Don't know..." Farlan paused as he sifted through his confused, angry brain to answer the man's question. A few seconds passed. He snapped his fingers then strode to the front door. "We'll have her back by this time tomorrow. As far as I know, she has only her half-sister and her husband to help her. They live to the north of Inverness. She won't be able to get that far walking."

"You *dinna ken* when the foolish woman left. It's been three days since you walked out on her. You should have taken her. Shown her you weren't going to be worried about her tender sensibilities. She used your words against you. You *canna* let that stand. If you still want her, teach her a lesson she will never forget."

Farlan knew the man was right in his assessment of the situation. He left her when it would have been so easy to take her. The devil but she puked on him twice. He could have taken her from behind, mounted her, let her smother her face in her vomit. There were many things he could have done. Should have done. When he got her back, he would do whatever was necessary to teach her a belated lesson in propriety.

Unable to help himself, he was hard as steel thinking of Maisie, he rubbed his crotch. He hit his fist on his palm. "She's mine. What's mine I keep! I will have her back here. When I do, she'll be under lock and key. Maisie will never leave."

Long angry strides took him to the buggy then waited for his man to join him. He whipped the horse into motion. "MacRae has a townhouse in the city. I'll go there first. If she made it to her sister's home, we'll have to find a way to nab her when no one else is around."

He meant to have her under his thumb again. This time he would lock the doors and shutter all the windows. He misjudged her, underestimated her determination and tenacity. Had never thought she was stupid. Stupid, stupid woman, all manner of things could have happened to her on the road where she was alone and vulnerable.

She could have been raped!

When he pulled up in front of the townhouse, no lights shone through the windows. The night was black. Someone should have been there. Lights should be shining. Anger swept through him. She'd made it to her sister's home. He would have the devil of a time getting her back.

"What do you think happened to her?

"Blind luck," his man said. "Let's go to LoreLee's place. Need a woman."

# Chapter Ten

Maisie's heart sank to the pit of her stomach. Her body trembled while her knees threatened to give out. She'd been so close to victory. She tried every door along with every window she could reach. They were all bolted against her. She supposed if she could climb up the trellis, the window next to it might be open. Too afraid of heights to try something so daring, she crossed it off her list of possibilities. Setting her head against the frame of the last window she tried to open, tears fell from her eyes. She was so exhausted. A place to sleep, a soft welcoming bed would all be wonderful. They weren't to be, at least not tonight. Highland Manor was too far for her to walk. She didn't have coin to send a message to her sister to come get her. Hawk could be anywhere.

What to do?

A stiff breeze careened through the trees surrounding her, chilling her bone deep. Rain began to fall, softly at first. Recognizing the building as her last hope for shelter, she stumbled to the small carriage house where they kept the vehicles they used to come and go. She imagined Riley still used the small structure when he came into town. This door was open to her. She crept inside imagining rodents and spiders infesting the space. In the rafters, she heard tiny scurrying feet. She cringed. A shudder of revulsion swept through her. She knew her fear to be irrational. She hated mice.

Inside, she was out of the wind and the rain, warmer and drier than the outdoors, she had to keep telling herself. She would have to sleep here. Would have to suffer the spiders along with the mice. A few seconds ago, when the last of her energy faded, the rain began to fall in earnest. The water falling from the sky was thick and hard pummeling the earth as well as her body. She walked inside the carriage house, thanking the fates that the door was not barred against her. Finding a blanket by the door she wrapped herself in the musty fabric then settled down to rest. Her eyes closed for a few seconds while she tugged air into her lungs. Her stomach rumbled hungrily. She pulled out the last of the food. If she ate it all, there would be nothing for her in the morning.

She would have nothing.

What did it matter? She didn't know anyone in the city. Couldn't go to anyone for help. Had no coin to purchase food. She rationed the food before eating the portion meant for tonight. She wanted Hawk to come to her.

He didn't.

She slept.

When she woke the next morning, the rain still thrashed the earth in sideways streams. Peering out the door she shuddered, frustrated that she couldn't leave, frustrated that she had nowhere to go. It wouldn't do for her to feel sorry for herself. She had no regrets about leaving the cottage. She was free of Farlan, at least for the time being. Given the circumstances she would do so again. Told herself one day at time. Now it was up to her to make the best of this horrible situation. If she couldn't get into the townhouse, she needed to think of another way to save herself. She had to get a message to Shawna. There was no one else for her. Her hands rested on her belly. She closed her eyes, wishing to see Hawk. He might be able to help her. Tell her where she could go for refuge.

With no coin or friends to her name, she didn't know how to do that.

It was just she didn't know how to do anything. She should have been bolder, learned to talk to more people instead of pulling into herself when there were visitors. Since she left the cottage for Inverness, she'd not spoken to Hawk. The babe seemed to be resting quietly. Wasn't telling her anything she needed to know. Perhaps if she slept. It seemed to her the *wee bairn* always liked to play inside her when she slept.

Maisie once more, sat on the floor of the carriage house. She brought out the last of her food and ate. She sniffed then sneezed. With the back of her hand to her forehead, she felt hot to the touch. No, she couldn't be sick again. It had to be her imagination brought on by stress. She sneezed as a fine trembling took over her body. Exhaustion consumed her while she felt her body giving in to fatigue and hunger.

Once more she slept. This time when she woke sunlight slid through the small opening of the door to the carriage house. The wind no longer howled nor did the rain pound the building. She felt better. Her head was no longer hot to the touch. Hunger rumbled deep in her belly. There was nothing to do. She ate the last of the food she brought with her this morning. At least Maisie thought it was the same day. She had no way of knowing.

How long could she have slept? The entire day and night? A few hours? She had no idea.

Understanding something needed to be done, she pulled herself to her feet. Her grandfather spoke often of LoraLee's place. She would tell the madam who she was then ask for help. Yes, she understood there was gambling as well as women at this home. Understood she might put herself in more danger by visiting. Nonetheless, David talked highly of the madam. The woman was kind, he said. She took in women who were lost or abused, he told her. The madam would know Riley. Perhaps Hawk had been there from time to time. She didn't like to think of her husband partaking of the women there or gambling. A wave of jealous anger swamped her. Maisie understood it would do her no good to dwell on those thoughts. They were in the past, unchangeable.

Maisie was neither lost or abused, just alone with no viable resources to her name. That didn't make a difference. Desperate to find someone who would understand her plight, she needed help just as any woman in her circumstances would seek aide. The night that Shawna stole the vouchers in hopes of keeping some of the debt her grandfather acquired at bay, her half-sister told her where the establishment was located as well as the Campbell residence which is where she ended up.

It wasn't far.

Well, she would go there, inquire about work. She could do chores as a maid or a cook until Hawk came for her. The establishment would need competent servants. Sifting in as much air as she could, Maisie peered out the door. The sun was bright, blinding her. She gasped as she blinked trying to allow her eyes to adjust. Maisie had forgotten about Farlan. Now the thought of him following her blindsided her. He might even now be looking for her. He would come here first just as she did. She would need to slip through the side streets to LoraLee's place of business then go in the back door.

That scenario was plausible. Perhaps her luck would hold.

Stiffening her spine, she left the property. As she strolled along the walkway in front of the stately townhouses, she felt as if someone looked at her. Shivers of fear spilled down her spine. The feeling was the same as when Farlan stood over her staring at her, taking inventory of her body. She picked up her skirts as she walked faster. When she hit a pebble, she cried out. Pain tore up her leg to her hip. Her feet were blistered and sore from her long walk yesterday. She had to go on. Stopping and giving up were not options.

After she turned down the next street, she saw the stately building that was both a gambling establishment as well as brothel. It was a dwelling profiting in male entertainment. No respectable woman would be caught here. She gulped air. Vacillating, she held back afraid to go forward, terrified of turning around. Her only option stood in front of her. It was up to her to take her chance.

While the front of the building was terrifying, when she reached the gate to the back door it seemed as if the place was a regular home. Maisie ran her hands along her wrinkled, dirty gown, smoothing out the creases, whisking away what dried dirt she could. She tried to finger comb her hair, finding a bit of hay in one of the strands. She wanted to look presentable, not a beggarly waif.

It's now or never, she whispered to herself as she unlatched the gate to step into the backyard. Don't chicken out now. She was surprised a residence such as this had a backyard. Though it was pleasant she didn't see a reason for its existence. There were tables and chairs, umbrellas to cover the tables providing shade on days that were too hot. There was a fountain off to one side. Water poured from the statue landing in a small basin surrounded by brilliant flowers. She saw a bench placed to watch the fall of water as the liquid landed in a small pool. A few seconds passed before she could step over the line between the walkway and the yard. When her foot hit the green grass on the other side, she heard the yell. She jerked then hiked up her skirts turning just to make certain this wasn't also her imagination.

"There she is!"

Oh, Lord. When she saw him, she nearly wilted. She would recognize that foul voice anywhere. Her knees wobbled. Farlan, no he couldn't have found her so fast. Torn with despair along with fear of the reprisals that would come her way when he caught her, she raced to the back door.

Pounding hard she cried out, "Help! Someone please help me!" Unable to stop herself, she kept pounding. "Please!"

Much to her surprise and almost immediately the door swung open. The biggest man she'd ever seen stood between her and safety. His eyes were a deep dark green, greener than the moss in Hawk's favorite spot, Glen Cove. When he smiled at her, she saw compassion in his eyes coupled with curiosity. The devil, he was even larger than Hawk, his arms as well as his thighs bulging with muscle. "What can I..." his voice faded off as it seemed he saw the two men chasing her. Grabbing her arm, he tugged her inside. He said, "Stay behind me, little Miss. Whatever you do, don't move."

Maisie didn't intend to do anything else. Behind him, she froze, her knees stiff. Her breaths wheezed in then out of her lungs in terrifying gulps. She tried to slow the tempo, attempted to ease her heartbeat which pounded as frantically as a hummingbird's wings. Found the task impossible. She was beholding to this man. From behind the man, she peeked around his beefy arm. He must be the man who kept the ladies protected.

The earl came to a skidding halt when he realized he wasn't going to be able to grab her then run. His voice was commanding, belligerent. "The girl is with me. She is mine. Hand her over." He wasn't yelling yet the sound was very close.

The big man's voice was harsh and low. He growled, a noise that came from deep and muted in his throat. "Doesn't seem to me she wants to be with you. Now, by my way of thinking, a woman's got a choice. She chose to run from you. Now, I choose to keep her with me until she says otherwise."

Farlan puffed himself up, smiling as if he was going to get his way, grinning as a besotted man might before he won the coveted prize. He pointed a finger directed at her. "I'm her guardian. You can't keep her from me." He stepped forward reaching out a hand as if the man would hand her over to him.

"He's lying," Maisie panicked wondering who this man would believe. "He's nothing to me except a worm. He's never been my guardian. David MacRae was my guardian but he's gone now. I'm married to Hawk Fraser."

"Got the papers to prove your words?" the man asked Farlan. "You got the papers, I won't have a choice. You be showin' them to me, I'll hand her over to you. If'n you dinna have those papers, I'll be calling the constable. Got one inside the premises enjoying a *wee* drink on the house."

Farlan was backing away, shaking his head, frowning as he thought. "They, the papers are at home. I'll get them." He turned once more to look at him. "You stay here where I *ken* where you are. Tired of chasin' after you, my dear. It will not go well for you if you leave."

"No threats," the big man said. "Won't be havin' you threatening one of the girls under my protection. This little gal is now under the safeguard of this home as well as me."

Maisie squeezed his arm to get his attention. She wanted nothing more than to leave. Still, this was her only chance. She had to convince this man that the earl was nothing to her. "I'm married," she whispered softly, repeating her earlier words. "Married to Hawk Fraser. If you know him or of him, you understand this man is not my guardian. He is lying to you."

Farlan hmphed and sputtered for another minute before he turned on his heel then left the place, his shoulders squared. Maisie understood unless something drastic happened, she had not seen the last of him. He would return. She would have to think of some way to dissuade him.

The man turned holding her at arm's length, studying her. "You do not have the look of a whore or a mistress. Who are you? I am Rolo. You said you are married to Hawk Frasier? The truth of that is easy to discern," he told her as he took her by the arm to lead her to a back room, an office she guessed. "You will have to explain why you are here at Miss

Lora's. She will decide what to do with you though I doubt if she will give you back to the earl. The man is despicable. He is banned from this place of business because he abuses women."

Maisie nodded feeling her heart lurch with dread or fear, she wasn't at all certain which was the predominant emotion. She stopped. When she looked at him, his smile was gentle. Her confidence soared.

"Rolo." She set her hand on her chest as if that gesture might slow her racing heart. "My name is Maisie Fraser. If you recall my grandfather, he was David MacRae. He lost a lot of money here, signed more vowels than he could repay. Riley Stuart married my sister, Shawana."

"Ah, so you are not a whore. Why are you here? Why does that man chase you? No, save your breath along with your energy. Tell Miss Lora. I will hear the tale then\ too."

She nodded then followed Rolo into the office. The madam sat behind a big desk, pouring over what appeared to be ledgers. She heard them walk into the room and looked up tilting her head to the side as if that would help her decipher the situation. "Who is this, Rolo? A new girl? What can I do for her? I know that you wouldn't be bringing her into my office if she doesn't need something. She's a pretty little thing though she appears a bit worse for wear. Would you like a drink?"

Maisie's head spun with all the questions. She didn't *ken* what to answer first. "Please, all I need is a *wee* bit of help. I've no coin and I'd like to send a message to my sister, Shawna Stuart. I'll pay you back as soon as someone comes here to get me."

"Mrs. Stuart will pay me back. Now, tell me why I should do this or believe you. You are nothing to me." She was tapping her pen on the desk, looking both irritated and put out at wasting good work time.

"You know my husband. At least I believe you do. He is Hawk Frasier. He will be here for me as soon as he can, as soon as he knows where I am. I was kidnapped when he left to see to a patient up north. He is coming from McKenna land to find me." Maisie went on to tell her about the earl as well as what he wanted from her. "I can't leave here until either my husband comes for me or Riley. Please let me stay. I won't get in the way. I'll work for you, not as a..." she wasn't certain what to say. "I'll clean, sew, cook..."

"I see. Farlan wants you that bad, does he? You are a lovely young woman. Old, Farlan has always scented out the most beautiful ladies. Years ago, I remember..."

She rose, walking to the sideboard. She poured two glasses of sherry, handing her one. Turning she began to speak again, "A woman who had a young daughter. You have the look of that woman."

Miss Lora knew about her mother. Understood that she wouldn't want to go to the earl for any reason. Maisie breathed deeply sensing a small victory. "I will work. I can cook and clean," she repeated.

"Ah," Lora took a sip of her sherry then nodded to her, "You look as if you need a drink. She leaned against the desk. "So, you don't work on your back. Pity, you'd bring me top dollar. I see why Farlan doesn't want to let you go."

"Will you help me?"

Her hand shook. Drops of sherry slid over the top, to slide down the face of the glass. A second ago, Maisie thought the woman understood everything about her. Maybe she didn't believe she was the daughter. Maybe she did and believed she worked on her back as her mother did.

"Well, of course I'll help. First, we need to see to your feet. You can barely stand. Either you are petrified of me or your feet need attention.

"Rolo," she said looking to him. "See to her then get back to me. We'll discuss what is to be done with her until we wait for her knight in shining armor to arrive."

"Both," she answered honestly as her voice wobbled.

"You don't need to fear me," Lora spoke softly then nodded to Rolo who stood perfectly still during the interview not volunteering a word waiting as it seemed was his want.

He bowed low, his eyes gleaming in the light cast by the fire. "I'll get her fixed up, bind her feet so she can't do herself any more damage. Foolish woman. She doesn't take care of herself. The doc won't be pleased. After that I'll be in the gaming room. Wouldn't be surprised to have a visit from the earl this evening. He will be back with forged papers claiming he is her guardian. Don't doubt it."

"If that is the case, we will have to double her protection. Put her on the third floor. No men are allowed there." She turned to Maisie. "All understand the women who live on the third floor are maids who provide cleaning services not women who entertain. You will be hired in that pretense. It will not take more than a day for Hawk to retrieve you. He will come as soon as possible." She paused then for several seconds seeming to think over her words. "You chose the right place to come for help."

She nodded. Maisie understood that for the truth. She had prayed. "Thank you. If I ever can, I'll repay you the debt."

"I will write a note. My errand boy who rides like the wind will be at Highland Manor and back before dark. It will take Riley longer, certain that he would have to bring his wife and child along with a suitable vehicle to take you home in. There will be arrangements that need to be made. All take time. While Hawk won't be here, Riley will protect you when your husband cannot."

A giant weight was lifted off her slim shoulders. She followed Rollo through the hallway to the long flight of stairs leading to the rooms above. With a look of desperation at the steps then to Rolo, "I don't think I can do that. Walk up those steps."

"May I?" he asked, his words soft studying her, seeming to realize what she was implying. "Doubt if your bruised feet will allow you to walk all that distance. You can barely take another step as it is."

Before she could answer he scooped her into his big arms. To her bruised nerves along with the fears of the past week, his strength fed into her. She wrapped her arms around his huge neck burying her face in his shoulder while he strode through the house to the third floor. He found the room he wanted at the end of the long hallway. Kicking it open with a foot, he strode to the chair in the far corner.

He set her down, "There you are. Don't move," he warned her.

The room was pleasant and clean, sparse in its furnishings. The bed was covered in a soft light blue quilt. The window was draped in the same color. The chair was wide the back high. It was comfortable. Other than that, there was nothing in the room. She hoped she wouldn't have to spend the night on the bed. The madam seemed to think Riley would not be here before dark.

She looked up, surprised when three men walked into the room carrying buckets of steaming water. "We will be back in a minute with more. Miss Lora said you would like a bath. She is offering a clean gown for you along with a few underthings. They will be along in a moment."

Rolo nodded, a smile on his lips turning his attention back to her. "Now, Miss Maisie, first, let me see to your feet."

Without a second passing he reached under her skirt and slipped her stockings off. He let them fall to the floor. Minus a second look, he pushed her skirt out of the way.

She gasped, surprised. Stared at him, tried to move away. Didn't like a man other than Hawk looking at her. He only appeared to be observing her feet. When she looked at her feet she gasped again. Not only were they bruised but they were torn, bloody as well. The bottom of each foot bled.

"No wonder you could barely put one foot in front of the other. You were foolish to walk all that distance. Where did you say you came from? Never mind. It must have been miles and miles you walked. After I clean your feet and you take a bath, I'll put salve on them to keep the infection at bay." He sat back on his haunches. "No, desperate might be a better word. I'm surprised you didn't walk to Highland Manor though by the look of your feet I *ken* you wouldn't have made it that far. Foolish woman, if you tried, you'd be lying on the side of the road. Maybe not."

"If you pay attention to what I did do, it's obvious I'm not foolish since I didn't try to continue on to my sister's home," she bristled at him knowing full well that she would have tried if she'd not thought about LoraLee's place.

Going about his business without further word, he poured hot water into a basin. He whistled as if he was a man without a care in the world. Perhaps he didn't have a care. Rolo picked up her feet one at time before setting them in the water. He grinned at her, seemingly pleased with something. She wanted to know just what that was.

"It's hot!"

She jerked, trying to escape the heat. When she tried to remove them, he held her feet in the steaming liquid.

"No, they need to soak. The heat is good for them. Don't want an infection to set in. Your husband would reprimand me if I allowed that to happen. He taught me much of what I know so I can tend to the girls when something happens. The doc here in town doesn't like to make house calls, at least not to LoraLee's Pleasure Palace. No worries, Hawk is a real gentleman. He will come for you. I will see to you in his absence."

"I see," she spoke grimacing with the heat, the sting of the water in the ripped blisters. "Hawk used to come here?"

Once again, jealousy hot and very real swamped her, ripped into her heart. She didn't like to think he saw some of the girls in this place, touched them the way he did her. She wanted to know who they were. No, that wouldn't be such a good idea.

Rolo soaped one foot methodically rubbing the soap across the bare skin while he spoke again, "Haven't seen him in a long time. Seems it's been about three years since he visited. Even then his visits were rare. He usually came with his brother Cameron to gamble. Cameron had a favorite girl, Katy, or Kate was her name. The lad took her away, made her his mistress. Guess he didn't like sharing." He continued to talk while washing her other foot. "Suppose not sharing is always a good idea if a man wants to stay healthy."

Systematically, he rinsed each foot taking great care. More hot water was brought for her bath. She found that Miss Lora did indeed give her clean clothing to wear. A small girl with brilliant red hair brought the items then set them on her bed. Maisie wondered who the clothing belonged to. Well, it didn't matter. She would make certain to return the pieces when she had her own clothing back.

Rolo stood, his large hands on his hips as he stared at her. His voice rang with authority. "I'll return in thirty minutes to wrap up those tiny feet of yours. Other than to walk to the bath then after that to the chair you will stay off your feet."

The command in his voice surprised her for a second. She fought the urge to salute him then struggled to keep a sarcastic stream of words behind her teeth that threatened to unloose. After all, his advice was sound. There would have to be a fire in the building for her to walk any farther than where he commanded. She nodded at him then watched his broad back disappear out the door.

In quick jerky movements, even though she knew she'd be

finished in less than thirty minutes, she closed the door then stripped herself of the rest of her clothing. The steaming hot water felt divine as she slipped into liquid heaven. She closed her eyes before setting her head on the lip of the tub thinking once more of Hawk.

She wished she could soak until the water grew tepid. She could not. Rolo would return. It just wouldn't do for Rolo to find her naked in her bath though she didn't doubt in this profession he'd seen his share of naked women.

Washing in haste, she finished by ducking her head under the water to scrub her hair. She soaped it then found the extra bucket of water. Once her hair was rinsed thoroughly and with a look to the small clock that sat beside the bed, she decided she had time to soak. The water felt heavenly.

With her hands on her belly, she closed her eyes breathing in the fragrance of lavender that was left behind from the soap. The clock ticked the seconds away. She ran her hands along her stomach then higher. She thought of Hawk doing the same to her, caressing her in intimate places.

*I want you to come to me, Hawk. Need to talk to you, to tell you what I did was necessary. You will not like it but I could never have born having Farlan or his bodyguard force me. He told me they would hold my arms over my head and spread my legs since I'd fought him. He doesn't like a woman to resist. Either that or they would put me on my stomach so if I tossed up my food, I would smother in it. Don't know what I would have done. I couldn't stay. I only did what I had to do. You must understand.*

Even with her eyes closed when the images came to her, she always saw him as clear as if he stood in front of her, always thought she could reach out and touch him. He was only part of her imagination. Touching him wasn't to be. All she could do was hear his thoughts.

*You're right about what I would think. Reckless woman. You risked your life and that of our child's. Yet...I don't' feel as if I can reprimand you for doing so. I understand why you did not wish to be forced.*

Her gasp surprised her. She had not expected him to come to her mind. A long draught of air filled her lungs. She let the oxygen out at a slow pace.

*I'm glad you are here with me, Hawk. Even though it is just in my imagination. While I'm safe here in this hot bath and protected by Rolo as well as Miss Lora, I dinna care what you think about my behavior. Nothing happened to me other than sore feet. My feet do hurt. Other than that, I suffered nothing untoward. Well, I'm hungry too. A bit tipsy from the sherry Miss Lora gave me to drink. I needed food not wine. I'm hoping she will provide something else when Rolo comes to finish taking care of my feet. He's going to wrap them up. Rolo told me you taught him everything he knows about doctoring. That was nice of you, Hawk.*

*You can eat your fill later. What did you do to your feet? Hold them out of the water so I can see better.*

She did.

*Suppose women's slippers aren't made for long walks. It took me all day yesterday to get to the townhouse. Once there it was all locked up tight. Think Riley must take more care of it than David. I couldn't get inside. Had to spend the night in the carriage house with the spiders and rodents. Hoped you would talk to me last night. You didn't. So, I had to figure out what to do next.*

*I'm certain Riley would never leave the building unlocked. What else happened, Maisie. I'm sorry I haven't seen you for a few days but I've been busy. I came as soon as I could. For a while, well, let's just say it took me some time to get my bearings. Ran into an elderly lady who fed me then gave me directions.*

*How busy?* She didn't understand how being busy could keep him from coming for her. This was all just a mind thing.

*First, I had to find my way home. Was lost if you can imagine such a thing, Hawk Fraser lost in the highlands. No one will believe that tall tale.*

She felt a fingertip run along her collarbone, the feeling delicious. When a hand wrapped around her breast, a calloused fingertip teasing her nipple to hardness, her eyelashes opened with a jerk.

"You!"

~ * ~

301

Hawk spent the day racing to the cave. He alternated between a gallop and a cantor. Windwalker was tireless. He reached the safe haven just after midnight. The full moon cast plenty of light on the small path he used. He didn't want to stop. Had to do so. Mentally and physically exhausted from the depravation he faced for the last weeks, he knew he couldn't keep going. Reaching Maisie was too important to leave to chance. After brushing his horse down, feeding the animal and whispering how good he was, Hawk left Windwalker tethered just inside the cave.

After he sat down in front of the warm fire he built to keep the chill of the evening from settling into his bones, he pulled out the food Leah packed for him. Trying not to rush, he chewed on the piece of bread then the cheese and meats while he thought about tomorrow. Maisie told him she would go to the townhouse if indeed she left the cottage. The earl would also look for her there. He searched his brain. Maisie just didn't know anyone in the city or out of it. She'd spent such an isolated life at Highland Manor, always a recluse.

He thought of Maisie waiting for him at the townhouse. Thought about her walking to Inverness. She would do so, there wasn't a doubt in his mind about that fact. She would put her life on the line in order to avoid the earl.

He didn't want her to risk one hair on her beautiful head.

If the earl forced her, it would never make him change his mind about his beautiful wife. He would ease her through the humiliation and pain of the event. He loved her. He needed to tell her that every day as well as night for the rest of their lives. Right now, the most pressing thing was to rest so he could find her sooner.

Ah, he leaned back, sipping the hot coffee. He should have wine for tonight then coffee in the morning. From experience he understood that coffee had an adverse effect upon sleeping. One cup shouldn't keep him awake too long. He stood, wandered to the cave opening. As he stared into the night, he hoped Maisie was safe and sound looking at the same nearly full moon as she was. From the breeze heading down from the northern reaches, tree branches rubbed against each other, scraping, making eerie noises. Somewhere in the distance an owl hooted then hooted again. He heard soft scurrying noises as night animals sought shelter from predators seeking them out. The cycle was endless. He breathed in deeply, letting the slow breaths calm his racing pulse. Taking one more look to the night sky clouded over with heavy clouds, he emptied his coffee cup.

With a heavy sigh, Hawk walked inside the cave, sat down in front of the fire. He wrapped a heavy wool blanket around him then stared at the flames, embers popping. He placed another piece of wood on the fire. Time he should be sleeping seemed to tick by at a rapid pace. Even as exhausted as he felt, sleep would be elusive for him. He thought about Maisie, tried to find her in his mind. All he saw was emptiness.

Strangely, she was absent. This evening, she wasn't going to make an appearance. He prayed that it wasn't because she was hurt. His heart raced at that thought. Through this entire ordeal, he'd never had this feeling of pain stab at him. There was something irrevocably wrong. He wasn't there to fix it or change it. He was helpless. Hawk didn't like the feeling.

The problem wasn't with the earl. He sensed that. No, Maisie was frightened and hungry. She was cold too. Here he was eating and he couldn't give her food, nourishment for her along with his unborn child. He clenched then unclenched his fists.

In a world that should not be this way, he felt powerless to change the events to his liking. He wanted to find Farlan, beat him to a pulp then push him into the Kinnel Stones so he could send him on his way to some other time. He sucked in air, knowing that he wouldn't do that unless it was a last resort. When he righted these events of the last few weeks, he would pursue Farlan until he gained his word, his promise that he would never seek out Maisie ever again. If he would not do so...then and only then would he enlist the help of his family.

The noises outside didn't surprise him. He looked at his pocket watch. More than an hour passed since he reached the cave. The horse nickering, the soft soothing sounds made by the riders, followed. Swaggering, Kit and Elliott walked into the cave. He looked up, smiling, welcoming the company.

"You're not asleep yet," Elliott said bending over to pour himself a cup of coffee. "Thought you'd be here sooner than this." Seeming to realize that his son was farther ahead, he asked, "You couldn't sleep?"

"Imagine that my body had different ideas from my head. Couldn't race the wind as I wanted. Had to stop several times just to catch my breath. When I got here, my mind took over. You're right. I couldn't sleep. As it happens, I've been here over an hour. What took the two of you so long?" Hawk wasn't at all certain he'd wanted to sleep. What he wished for was to talk to Maisie. If he slept, he couldn't do that. If she slept, he couldn't do that.

"You're going to need us tomorrow," Kit said with a pointed look to the pallet that Hawk made for himself. "Do you think you'll find her at the townhouse as you said? Wouldn't the earl search her out there too?"

Hawk found himself shaking his head, wondering the same, "Would surprise me. Riley isn't someone that would leave the doors or the windows unlocked for anyone to walk inside. He's not like David. Maisie probably thought it would be easy to get inside then climb into a nice warm bed."

"She wouldn't have anywhere to go," Elliott said as he steepled his hands beneath his chin. "What then? What would your wife do?"

"No," Hawk sighed having realized the same things. "That's what bothers me the most. When she discovers she can't get into the townhouse, what would she do? I'm not a foolish woman so I can't think like one. She would do something stupid." Hawk didn't have any idea what that could be.

Maisie wasn't typically foolish. She did have this way of thinking she could fight a man and come out on the winning end.

She could not.

Where did she get those strange thoughts? She wasn't that way when he first met her, first held her in his arms three years ago. Ah, but time had this uncanny way of changing a person's life. "She might be able to take refuge in the carriage house for a night. That won't feed her but it would give her shelter out of the rain that was buffeting us an hour ago," Elliott stared at Hawk then looked to Kit.

"That's part of what held me up. Windwalker doesn't like rain much. He balked every mile or so, refusing to go further. By his mind, he believes he deserves a warm stable along with a good brushing down. In any case, I would never have made it to Inverness this night despite how much I wanted to do so. It's a good six hours more of a ride. While I might push myself that hard, I'd never ask it of Windwalker."

He'll get that warm stable as soon as we reach the Stuart townhouse tomorrow," Kit said as he hooted with laughter. "So will we. First, we'll check out the MacRae place then we'll go home. I want a soft bed to lie on tomorrow tonight. It's been a while since I've had one. Since any of us have had anything to lie on other than a dirty pallet or the ground." Kit was rubbing the back of his neck, easing his muscles.

Hawk found he was tight everywhere. Stress along with worry for Maisie stretched all of him to a breaking point he didn't like to acknowledge. A hot bath would work wonders. Nothing though would ease him more than finding Maisie safe and sound. Once that happened, he would have to make certain Farlan understood the benefits of leaving her alone.

When Hawk woke the next morning, the sun was shining. There was no mist on the ground. He felt rejuvenated even though it was later than he hoped. He'd wanted to be riding as the sun peeked its head over the forest. That wasn't to be the case. Coffee simmered on the fire. Bacon sizzled in a pan. Biscuits sat on a tray. Elliott woke early fixing the breakfast that would rejuvenate them. He wondered if Maisie had anything to eat this morning. A moment of guilt swept through him as he filled his belly. He tamped the emotion down understanding there was nothing he could do about that fact.

Hawk helped himself to the food knowing full well the necessity of eating before he left. If he couldn't help himself, he couldn't help Maisie. She would need him. There wasn't a doubt in his mind about that fact. Scene after scene played itself in his brain each one worse than the last. After he closed his eyes last night, he hoped to see her. If he spoke to her, he would have a better idea of what she was going through or even where she was. She didn't appear in his mind.

The afternoon was hot, scorching. The rain from the day before vanished leaving a soft mist in the morning. Now a brilliant blue sky was overhead, a few clouds high in the sky didn't threaten rain. Three abreast they rode the fastest streets to the MacRae townhouse. When they pulled up in front, anticipation seethed within.

Not surprising to anyone, she wasn't there. Disappointment hung in a cloud around his head. Hawk dismounted. He checked out the carriage house to find the remnants of food, a bag that had held bread and cheese.

She wasn't starving.

Where was she?

"As we all guessed, the doors as well as the windows are all latched firmly in place," Elliott told him. "She did not find a way inside the home. If she found comfort from the storm it was someplace else."

Hawk spoke, his voice riddled with pain as well as guilt. He knew he should have taken more precautions when he rushed to the aide of the crofter. From now on, he would look at the people in the highlands with a different perspective.

"She spent some time in the carriage house. Where would she go now?" Hawk asked, shielding his eyes from the brilliant sun while he stared down the street understanding she was out there somewhere, alone, and vulnerable.

"The earl might have found her," Kit said his voice a whisper as if he didn't want to think about that scenario. "The man might have her once more despite her efforts to the contrary. We cannot avoid that exact consequence."

"No...no he doesn't. I would sense it if he found her. She's gone some place she feels safe. The misfortune of it all is that I have no idea where that could be. She's never spent much time in the city. To my knowledge, she doesn't know anyone. We never spoke of people or of friends she might want to see." Hawk's stomach turned sour. Thinking about this sent him on edge. "She would try someplace she has heard of either through Shawna or her grandfather, possibly Riley."

"Doesn't that leave the doors wide open? Who could possibly know what has been said to her, what people or places have been mentioned?" Elliott said pointing out the obvious disadvantages here.

"We can't run blindly around the town. That would waste time as well as energy. Maybe you'll sense something," Kit said hopefully to his cousin as he mounted his horse to move on.

He looked at them. "I'm going to the Stuart townhouse. We can hash over the possibilities after we've made ourselves more comfortable. Baths along with food are on the top of my agenda. After that a brandy while we discuss the choices she might make. You must think back in time. Remember every conversation you've ever had together."

Kit was right on all counts. They needed to see to immediate needs then go over in their heads everything Maisie might know about Inverness. Hawk did remember three years back when he courted her for two wonderful days. He'd been called back to Selkirk before he could settle anything between the two of them. Shawna was wed to the wrong Riley Stuart. Maisie attended the wedding.

What did he know? Not a hell of a lot!

Would she take refuge in the church where Shawna married? She'd been there for the ceremony. The minister was amiable. He'd helped Shawna and Riley when they tried to annule the first marriage. He felt certain the minister would give aide to her.

Scenes were running through his head as he mounted then followed the others back to the townhouse. Her grandfather had been gambling and drinking. The vowels he wrote were putting the manor house in jeopardy. Shawna searched for a way out of an unwanted marriage. There was little he'd known about that time except for the excessive gambling done by David MacRae, some done at private residences but most, according to Riley, at LoraLee's fine establishment.

At the townhouse, they lounged in chairs in front of the fireplace drinking the Stuart's fine French brandy. During the following minutes, they weren't talking each enveloped in the sweet sounds of silence. Hawk searched his mind for anything that might resonate. He closed his eyes, once again going over everything he could remember from those days, making a list of places to search for her. The Methodist church would be a safe place to start. The Campbell residence would be better to look for her there than at LoraLee's place of business simply because that was where Shawna stole the vowels. She wouldn't feel safe at the Campbell's or LoraLee's.

Kit rummaged in the pantry for food. It seemed Riley kept the storage area full of necessities. There was ham along with bread. Fresh eggs as well as loaves of bread were in a basket on the counter.

"How often does Riley come into town?" Hawk asked as he sunk his teeth into a large slice of ham set on top of freshly baked bread. He reached for the platter that held several different kinds of cheese to place one on top of the ham after that he splashed the top with a tomato. The bread had to have been made just this morning.

"Not often. He does, however, employ a man to make certain there is food here so there is something for an impromptu visit. The man along with his wife keep the shelves stocked each day. What isn't eaten is taken home as partial payment for them. So," he paused thoughtfully, "if we didn't eat this tonight, the couple would take it home tomorrow morning."

"Kind of like what we do at the hunting lodge," Hawk said enjoying the wine then thinking about Maisie who might not have anything to eat. "I'm going to take a bath. After that, I'm going to visit a few places she might go to seek help. I've some in mind."

Hawk rose striding toward the kitchen to get hot water for his bath. Kit set some on the stove to heat the moment they got here. A few trips later, Hawk settled into the steaming liquid. Closing his eyes, he concentrated on his wife. There was nothing. Only vague sensations that the earl found her. He saw her stepping through a white picket fence. It didn't make sense. Then the feeling that perhaps she was safe. He felt relief yet he didn't understand why.

Someone saved her.

A big man.

Maisie clung to the large man. He lifted her in his arms. He was carrying her to a bedroom. Her head was pushed against his shoulder. Hawk gasped in air, now seeing the man and building clearly. Eager to be off, he dipped underwater, rinsed his hair. There was no longer fear in his gut. Maisie was safe but to what purpose? Why did she present herself to the madam? Was she offering herself as the next woman to be sold at the Pleasure Palace? No, Maisie would never do that. She wasn't a whore. She couldn't be that desperate.

When Maisie tuned into the big man, he felt no fear emanating from her. What he felt was relief as well as fatigue.

Before a few minutes passed he was dry and dressed. When he passed Kit and his father still sipping brandy in the drawing room, he nodded his head. "She's at LoraLee's. She's hurt and I'm bringing her back. After she's safe in this house, I'm going after the earl. We will have to put enough fear in his small mind that he won't dare venture close to Maisie again. Suppose there are several ways to do that."

Elliott spewed his drink. Kit stood up so fast his chair was pushed aside. He waved his hand in the air. "Wait for us. We're right behind you."

Their request was left hanging in the air. Hawk wasn't about to wait.

Hawk strode into LoraLee's looking for the madam. She wasn't in the main room with curling blue smoke and gamblers losing their money. She wasn't supervising the women as she always did. That didn't surprise him, since it was still too early for the business to be booming. A woman clad in a gown meant to entice a man, hooked her hand over his shoulder. Impatient, Hawk brushed it off. He passed by one of the bouncers while looking for Rolo. He found him. The man nodded down the long hall Hawk knew would end up in LoraLee's office. This man was the one he saw. Rolo would know where Maisie was. Decorum insisted he speak with the madam first. Hawk headed in that direction.

He stepped into a hallway that would lead, he was certain, to offices. One door was open. A movement caught his eye. The woman stood, her hands resting on the top of her large, cheery-wood desk. Her eyes were a deep, very dark brown, her hair the color of dark brown velvet. She smiled.

"I've been waiting for you, Hawk," Miss Lora walked toward him extending her hand in greeting. "Seems I have something you lost. You need to take better care your wife. As to why she came to me, I've no idea. Come in and sit down. We can talk."

"Where is she?"

After all that happened, he didn't mean to waste time chatting with the madam of a bordello. He did, however take her hand in his. Did hold it for just a second before kissing the back. He needed this woman's good graces if he was going to find his wife, sooner than later.

"Well...that's just the thing. She was hurt real bad. Rolo is taking care of her. He came downstairs to grant her some privacy."

Miss Laura poured them each a glass of brandy, ignoring him for the moment. She handed him the glass.

He downed the burning liquid in one gulp. "Hurt?" His tongue caught in his parched throat. "How?"

"Her feet, mostly. Her spirit not at all. She's a feisty little thing. You knew that though."

No, he didn't think of her in that light. She'd never been feisty before. He imagined the circumstances might have broken through the soft fragile shell she cloaked herself in. "Where is she?" he repeated, rapidly losing all sense of patience with the woman.

He needed to go to her, see for himself that she was well.

"As I said, you need to keep a closer eye on your woman. Seems she was a bit foolish. However," Miss Lora paused dramatically, "knowing the earl as I do, she did the only thing she could. She ran when she got the chance. You understand you will have to take care of that man. Farlan cannot be allowed to get away with snatching a woman from her husband. He's not a nice man. He's hurt several of my girls, threatened them as well. We no longer allow him into this establishment."

"I'm losing patience with you. It's been hell for two weeks. I need to see her, take care of her."

He thought he would shake the madam until she told him what he needed to know. His fingers curled into tight balls. His gut twisted hard. Patience was a thing of the past.

Miss Lora smiled an all-knowing smile, one that seemed to radiate from her. In that instant, her features changed, softening. She nodded. "On the third floor, the last room. As I said, Rolo was attending her. Presently, she is bathing. Rolo is waiting with bandages as well as salve for her feet. He also has food for her. Don't think she has eaten much in the last few days. She needs the care of a loving husband. Do you love her, Hawk?" As if sensing he'd never said the words of love to Maisie, she continued, "You need to figure that out. If you love her, tell the woman. She deserves to know."

"I'll take it all...."

He turned on his heel, to head to the stairs eager to see her, to talk to her. He needed to hold her in his arms, to touch her everywhere just to make certain she was safe.

Her feet, her bloody feet were hurt. Well, hell, of course, they were. Stupid, foolish woman. She knew he would come for her. "Why didn't she wait?"

"You tell me." Rolo stood in the doorway his arms laden. He handed everything over to Hawk. "She's a mighty lovely lady, Hawk. You need to guard your woman better. She could be under that man's evil thumb again. Take better care of her."

"Thank you, both of you for taking her in," He growled out as he grabbed the items from Rolo's beefy arms.

Rolo's words hit too close to the truth.

Rolo called out to his retreating back, a hint of caution in his deep voice. "The earl was after her. She got here by a squeak and a promise. Made it through the front door and behind me just before he almost got his fingers on her arm to tug her to him. He's coming back with forged papers saying he's her guardian. What do you say about that? You got any papers saying you've married her?"

"Don't need any. Maisie is my wife. Carrying my child. Got nothing to prove."

Hawk raced up the steps. When he stepped into her room, she was naked in her bath. Her eyes were closed. She seemed to be dreaming. She never looked lovelier. He saw rose colored nipples bobbing on the top of the water. Her long white neck was ready for his attention. She adjusted herself, her beautiful breasts swaying softly on top of the liquid heat surrounding her. He clenched his hands willing himself to hold back a few more seconds.

She spoke to him through her mind. He grinned, a man more than pleased with the sight in front of him. He held his breath, not wanting her to know he was in the room, at least not yet.

In his mind Hawk answered as he set the items on a table then made his way to her. Kneeling at the bath, he ran his fingertip along her collarbone. He cupped her breast in his hand teasing the tight hard bud.

She moaned softly the sweet sound of pleasure emanating from the back of her throat.

"You!" She sat up splashing water over the tub then on to him. "Hawk!" Without using up another second, she threw herself on him. He held her tightly, drawing her out of the water. Kissing her, feeling the length of her against him. His tongue entered her warm sweetness. "I need you, Maisie. More than you could ever know. I was so afraid for you." He held the back of her head with his hand.

"I need you too." She moved away from him, looking at him, studying him. "You're not hurt? I was so worried. I was afraid they would kill you."

"Not as worried as I was about you. Why did you run from him? I would have found you today. Your feet..." He set her aside. Placed her on the chair. "Let me see them." He studied each one, murmuring for his benefit. Without speaking to her, he dried them, put the salve on then bandaged each one. All the time she was naked in front of him. When he lifted her feet to wrap them, he was treated to the sight of tender flesh. Her legs were parted for him. He ran his hands along her thighs to the apex. "Are you cold?"

When he looked at her, the tips of her breasts were tight hard buds. He lost all rational thought. Lifting her into his arms he strode to the bed then came down on top of her spreading her legs with his. Hawk needed her more than he needed to breathe.

The heat of her entered him, warming the coldness that had been part of his soul over the last weeks. He missed her. His hands rested on her hips, then rose the ladder of her ribs until he cupped her breasts in his hands. He touched upon her soft white belly with his lips and teeth before following the path of his hands.

Hawk sucked first one then the other nipple into his mouth, tugging on each one until she cried out. She moaned and heaved. Her body arched while her hands pushed at his clothing tugging at his shirt. She ripped two buttons trying to unfasten his shirt.

"Hawk, please..."

Her hands found the fasteners on his buckskins. She pushed until they slipped down his narrow hips to finally stop at his boots.

"A second..." He was tugging on his boots, unable to rid himself of them as quickly as he would have liked. Hawk came down upon her, his length stretched out against hers. She was so soft everywhere. "Maisie..." he growled her name. "Are you ready for me?

Maisie nodded. The small gesture was not enough. He stroked her between her thighs, found the jewel that brought her so much pleasure. She was hot, so very wet that her nectar poured from her while he brought her to a fast hard climax. After she screamed his name, he took his time filling her, stretching her as he moved inside. When he reached her womb, he held still enjoying the violent contracting of her body. Within her he was kissed by the pulses of a new wave of pleasure building within her.

He yelled as he pumped his seed into her. When he was done, he fell upon her, blanketing her. She clung to him, her hands smoothing down his back to settle on his buttocks. She squeezed him there. On his forearms he rose above her, smoothing damp tendrils of her hair from her face.

"How is the babe?"

"You should know. It was because of him you came to me in my mind. It was because of the *wee* one, that Farlan didn't force me. Even though he knew I carried your child. He told me if the *bairn* was a girl, he would have her too. You do know the little shifter caused me to vomit my meals on the man. Twice. The boy will be a handful. You do *ken* that. Other than those times, I've not been sick at all."

"Good, we will go to the Stuart townhouse where I will keep you locked inside until we can go home."

"Hawk..." She pounded on his chest. "Let me up. I going to..."

He saw the look on her face the slight green tinge. He moved off her, helping her to sit. She rushed to the basin on the floor near the bathtub. While she tossed the tiny amount food she'd eaten this morning into the basin, he held her hair to the side.

"I don't want to venture a guess as to what all this means," he spoke softly thinking about what she told him of Farlan. "Do you not appreciate my attentions?"

She moaned softly. "'Twas my bragging that I'd not been sick except when he tried to force himself on me. The *wee* one is now acting as all babes do. Oh..." she moaned again, heaving nothing into the basin.

He hated this sickness of hers. Disliked the fact that women would lose what they ate just because of a man's lust. Well, with him it wasn't just lust. "I will get you home, well, not home but to the townhouse where you can rest. We won't return to Carnoch until I'm satisfied with your recovery. You say Farlan knew you were with child?" He'd hesitated to ask that question.

For a few seconds, she stared at him puzzled with his question. Deciding to ignore the fact she answered his question before he asked it. She shook her head, "No, I decided not to say anything. He could have done something, hurt me to try to get rid of the babe. Couldn't risk that. Didn't want to lose our child."

Fury swamped him. She risked the long walk. He couldn't judge her, wouldn't. "Come, let's get dressed then say our goodbyes to your hostess. I need to see Farlan."

~ * ~

Hawk sent his message to the earl that evening. There were threats to be made, some things to be made clear. He stood on ground owned by Riley Stuart. Highland Manor was now restored. The land was private. If he needed to change to his cat, he would. No one would see because loyal members of Clan Chattan guarded the small area.

The stormy sky echoed Hawk's mood. Wind howled around the few scraggly oak trees. Intense rain would fall within the next hour. Hawk was furious with this man who orchestrated his abduction so he could snare his wife as his next mistress. He needed to be taught a much-needed lesson. A show of power would be needed. Even though Hawk didn't want to show the man his cat, he might not have a choice.

"Do you think he will show up?" Riley asked as he stood beside him watching the trail leading to the place they selected for the encounter. "The man is a coward, always having others do his work that is not above the law."

"He will show. I gave him little choice. If he doesn't, I'll go to him. He won't like the consequences if I do. Here we can have a

314

gentleman-to-gentleman conversation about his future if he refuses to believe me. If I must seek him out, believe I've got the Kinnel Stones in mind for his demise.

"Yes...though we do *ken* now that people can return to the time they left," Riley said while he seemed to stare fixedly down the small rutted road.

"True enough but I think that only worked for Kit because he wasn't supposed to end up in them in the first place. The stones helped him get home back to the destination where he was supposed to be."

"Even so, I don't like that idea. We've been there one too many times. We all understand how it can backfire."

"There he is." Riley said pointing down the road. "Do you want me to leave you? I could step just far enough..."

"No," Hawk interrupted. "I'm certain the bodyguard will be with the man. Gawain won't leave Farlan alone with me. Seems they are never far apart. Last night Maisie told me much about what happened to her mother. Some she remembered, some Farlan taunted her with. Both men forced her mother. She had no choice, no say because she wanted to keep Maisie alive."

"Maisie is safe at the townhouse?" Riley asked. "She won't try to come here, will she?"

Riley voiced his fears. Hawk didn't want to think about her coming here on her own. His father wouldn't allow her to do so. With her feet so badly torn she couldn't walk. She had no money to hire someone to bring her. "Should be well-protected. Both my father and Kit are there. They promised not to leave her since I could not be certain Farlan would not take this as an opportunity to snatch her again. Though he'd be a fool to try."

"Here they are. Just as you predicted there are two men. I'm assuming the second one is his man."

The buggy moved along the dirt road. By the time it was close enough to see the occupants, it was evident the bodyguard was with the earl. Hawk curled his fingers tight against the palms of his hands, needed to hit the man. Wanted to stuff his fist down the earl's throat. He didn't intend to change to his cat. He would though if all means of persuasion failed. He didn't believe it would. There was not much size or strength to the earl. While he wasn't overweight, he was slight in proportion, his arms and legs lacking muscle. Maisie was almost Farlan's height. Maisie didn't reach his chin.

When Farlan stepped out of the carriage, he paused for a second. He strode, swaggering toward them, the bodyguard following at a slight distance. Farlan's face was mottled with anger, crease lines around his eyes as well as his mouth.

Farlan stopped several feet short of him. He turned to the man who seemed to be his shadow. He nodded as if this situation was in his control. "This will be over in a minute. Doubt if I will need you."

Hawk offered a half-smile at the man's audacious words. Of course, this would be over within minutes, but it would not be the earl who succeeded. He wanted to hit his head with the palm of his hand so he could figure out what was meant by his overconfident statement. He spoke to him. "You will leave Maisie alone. She is not for you, Farlan. Maisie is my wife." His voice commanded over the scant distance between them. Farlan gave no sign of fear or comprehension that he was in this over his head.

"Or what?" Farlan asked with a sneer. "What will you do? You have no power or say over my actions."

Hawk was both annoyed as well as infuriated with the insult to him. He didn't want to bring up the Kinnel Stones, not just yet. He didn't want to change to his cat in the process making himself too vulnerable. "Maisie is my wife. She carries my child. You will not go near her."

Farlan waved his hand in the air with more confidence than he should have had. "Makes no difference to me. You won't be around to take care of her. As for the child, I can find a good foster home for the babe. If the *wee bairn* gets in my way, I can get rid of the brat. If it's a girl, I'll use her as soon as she is old enough. Perhaps when she is around ten. I've been told the younger the better. We shall see."

His eyebrow lifted at the lofty statement. His stomach somersaulted. "I won't be around? Perhaps, you won't be around, Farlan." Hawk loosened his shirt, unfastening a few of the buttons, giving in to the anger as well as the fury seething within. He'd brought along a change of clothing just in case he needed to shift before he could disrobe. Hawk looked to Riley, a curious expression on his cousin's face almost as befuddled as the way he felt. Had the world gone topsy-turvy? The earl was now threatening him.

It was then that Farlan began to quiver. He too had loosened his clothing, tossing his tie to the ground then his jacket. His small male body vibrated with the force of a minor earthquake. Hawk understood what the earl was doing. He just didn't believe what he saw. Had never suspected or heard about anyone in this area other than family being shifters. The earl was having difficulty. His shirt ripped at the sleeves, after that the buttons popped. Hawk followed each one as it landed on the ground. With a lift of his shoulders, he turned to Riley. A huge grin lit up his cousin's face.

Hawk imagined he should shift too. He didn't feel the need to do so. Being a small man, Farlan would also be a tiny cat. It was fascinating to watch what should have happened in a blink was taking way too many minutes. After endless minutes of shaking and shuddering, the earl was naked, still twitching, still trying to force his body into a different shape. When he finally became a cat, he drooped, exhausted from the effort.

Riley stood his legs braced apart, clapping at the unusual performance, grinning from one ear to the other. His amusement obvious, Riley hooted with his laughter.

If the situation wasn't so serious, Hawk would have laughed too. As it was, he needed to make a decision. The small panther lifted his head and roared. The man wasn't a black panther, he was yellow and spotted. Even his roar sounded pathetic. If the cat wanted to fight rather than talk, it would be horribly unfair of him to shift. In his cat form, Hawk could demolish him with one swipe of his paw. Hawk decided he would stay as he was. No reason to give this man something to hold over his head in the future. He never intended murder where the earl was concerned. He just wanted to come to an understanding as it concerned Maisie.

When Farlan ran toward him and leapt, Hawk caught him mid-air then grabbed him by the throat. Holding his arm straight he let Farlan dangle from his hand while the cat swished his legs around trying to reach him. His cat's tale twitched back and forth, a sure sign of anger. He barred his teeth at Hawk who was now laughing. He roared his outrage.

Hawk sipped in a small breath of air, chuckling. "I could strangle you. You know that." Hawk shook the cat, once then twice trying to send home the most pertinent message. Farlan was weak. "I could swing you around like I would kill a chicken, swing you until your neck broke. Would you appreciate that? I might. When I think about your plans for my wife...well perhaps we should try just one swing and see how your neck feels."

Farlan's cat eyes bulged. He swiped the air again and again in a feeble attempt to sink his claws into Hawk. "You will leave Maisie alone." He shook Farlan hard. "Now that I know what you are, well, there are other avenues I can approach to get rid of you. Stay away from anyone I care about. Sassenach have plans for shifters. I do know a few who would love to have you."

Another solid shake brough a mewl of pain from the pathetic animal. Hawk never took kindly to a person who abused animals. This situation was different.

Riley was behind him, still hooting with laughter, holding his jacket and tie. When he could finally get a few words out, he said, "Do you truly want to humiliate him this much? He doesn't have much to wear once he changes back to his human."

"Yes, after all he humiliated and embarrassed my wife without a second thought. Why not?" he repeated. "I'm certain the Sassenach would like to know about you. I could keep you in this form until we could fetch a soldier. What do you think? If I hold you, you would have difficulty shifting back." He grinned again. "Can you shift back? It took you a ridiculous amount of time to change the first time. Will it take longer for you to show your human form? Can you change back?"

He shook the animal again. Small gurgling noises emanated from his cat. Now Farlan hung limp from Hawk's outstretched arm.

"No don't think too long. You might decide to do something even more foolish. That wouldn't do. Now, I want you to change back." Hawk tossed him hard to the ground. He looked at the bodyguard who stood frozen to the spot. Riley was beside the man, smiling as if he wanted the man to change too.

"Ah," Hawk directed his words to Riley. "I see you're hoping this man will change also so you can do what I am doing. You're a jealous man, Riley Stuart. Admit to the fact. You want to show your strength."

"Aye, in this case I'm jealous." Riley looked to the quivering form on the ground. "Is it going to take you as long to change back?"

Hawk imagined that it might take longer. He was looking forward to viewing this transformation. Farlan didn't have clothing to wear. He wondered what he'd thought. Did he plan on shifting to terrorize him perhaps. No, the clothing extras must be in the buggy. Riley seemed to have the same idea. He started for the vehicle retrieving the accessories then holding them high over his head as if they were a trophy.

"Should we give them back to the sniveling coward?" Riley asked, his grin stretching across his face.

"No, we'll keep them. If his man wants to share, well then, they will share. Only one will get the pants though. What do you think the fine people of Inverness will think when they see the good earl naked, well almost naked riding through town in his little buggy."

A naked Farlan stood in front of them, shivering, holding his hands in front of his manly parts. "You weren't surprised that I could shift?" He sounded outraged at the very idea.

Hawk shrugged, lifting his shoulders, and thinking that showing Maisie his cat was all important so many times she would be at ease with him. Farlan might have tried to intimidate her.

"Surprised? We all know about the rumors in the highlands pertaining to shifters. Figured there must be some shifters about the land for the tales to continue," Hawk told him smoothly without even one snicker. "Now I know they aren't tall tales. How about you, Riley? Though I would never fear a cat as pathetic as the likes of you. Now..." Hawk paused again. "You will stay away from Maisie or you'll regret it more than you probably regret showing us your true colors."

The earl nodded, looking fully humiliated. "Yes."

"Good, then we can part company."

"Riley...Riley, where are you? I wondered..." Shawna stopped, the look on her face one that Hawk wanted to remember forever. She doubled over with laughter. She was staring at the man, pointing now. "I see what you were doing. There is not much to him. Is there?"

"Not all of it sweetheart. Nonetheless, I'll enlighten you as soon as we are home. This will be another story we can tell our grandchildren," Riley said pulling her into the comforting embrace of his arms.

# Epilogue

The fire crackled and sparked. Orange and yellow flames danced toward the heavens. Earlier rain sluiced from the sky. Now the clouds vanished to leave the dark velvet of the night twinkling with stars coupled with a sliver moon casting light upon the ground. A brisk breeze blew into the highlands, down from the north, chilling the air. The days were growing shorter, the nights longer. Winter would come soon. Snow would fall. The nights would last forever.

Just as she had the first time Hawk brought Maisie to the bonfire, introducing her to marshmallows, she sat cross legged between his massive thighs. As he wished, she wore no underclothing. He would burn her petticoats if she wore them. Maisie believed him now after losing several. Together, a soft warm blanket wrapped around them, he held her, fondled her breasts, drawing out the hardened tips, rolling them between his fingers until she moaned with the pleasure he created. Maisie squirmed against him, curved, and arched, wishing he would stop teasing her. As always, she wanted him now, not in a few minutes when he deemed the time right.

His chuckle of delight gave her good reason to turn in his arms her bared breasts pushing against the solid muscle of his chest. She would give him what he gave her. She ran her hands across his chest, over the hard nubs she found delightful as she pushed his open shirt away from the skin she wished to caress. Her hands roamed down the ladder of his ribs to his hard belly, slipping beneath his half open buckskins. His groan of pleasure pleased her. She bit his shoulder while she wrapped her fingers around his swollen penis.

"Maisie," he growled his voice husky and deep. "You're playing with fire."

"As were you. What comes around goes around."

His long fingers wound around her wrist, holding her as she smoothed a fingertip along the smoot hot skin she found so intriguing. With every reason to entice, she pushed away from him, bending over to capture him within the heat of her mouth. She licked him, nibbled on the tip while her fingers pushed his pants lower so she could stroke all of him with her mouth. He groaned seeming to enjoy the attention.

When she looked up, he was smiling, a wicked expression on his handsome face. His strong white teeth shown prominently in the darkness of the night. "You have the look of a contented cat about you. Is that what you want? Do you want to bring out my cat?"

"Not contented yet," she told him, her voice purring deep in the back of her throat. She moved the blanket so she could see his heavy arousal. "Soon I hope we will both be satisfied. Will you see to my needs? Will you please me?"

"Yes..." He pulled her up, lifting her high in air so he could turn her. His lips were drawn back from his teeth, his brows furrowed with concentration. "Straddle me, sweetheart. You know what to do."

Oh, she did know what he wanted, what she wanted, too. When she settled on him, taking him deep inside, he filled her, heated her through to her core. She let her head fall back, moaning softly as he moved with slow precision. With his hands on her waist, he surprised her when he stopped. In the firelight his silver eyes turned to pewter, as concern seemed to overpower the passion he was feeling.

"You are ready for me? This is not too soon? You just gave birth a few months ago." he asked her, questioning his afterbirth instructions.

Biting his chin, then lifting her head to stare at him, questioning, Maisie tilted her head. "I'm fine, as you well *ken*. There is no pain, only immense pleasure. It has been almost three months since your little shape shifter was born. Do you wish to wait longer? Would you like that? I wouldn't."

She understood he always thought of her needs first.

"I don't want to hurt you. We need to take precautions," he mumbled then groaned as she began to move on him. Again, he stilled her, his fingers squeezing against her waist. "You could get pregnant. It's too soon."

"I won't. You won't. We can take precautions next time as well as the time after that. I couldn't bear it if you didn't stay deep inside me this first time since the birth. How will we ever manage these safeguards you speak of?"

Only a few seconds later, they both cried out their pleasure. Maisie fell against him, her head on his shoulder. He was still deep inside her, not filling her as much as before but still hard. She knew if she allowed it, he would make love to her again.

He did. After that he pulled her clothing together, tying the ribbons to her chemise, covering her legs with her skirt, running his fingers along tender flesh. She fastened his clothing, letting her fingers dance across his skin as she did so.

"You're wicked, a little minx. You know that though. Don't you? Had I known you were so passionate when I first met you..."

He looked up to the stars, seeming to need the conversation ended before he could say more.

"We both regret the miscommunication. Going back in time would not serve a purpose." Maisie only wanted to look to the future.

Hawk stretched out, pulling her with him, her head nestled against his shoulder. "We need to get back to the house. The babe will want to suckle just as I do. You realize I'm a bit jealous of the attention you give to the little shifter. I'm not used to sharing you."

Laughing, pleased with his words, she ran her fingertip down the line of his chest to his now fastened pants. With a sigh, she brought her hand back to his chest. He lifted her hand, kissed each fingertip.

"We do need to be careful now. While another child in nine months, give or take a few days, would be nice, it would be exhausting for you. I won't put your health at risk."

"What if I conceived tonight?"

"We will deal with whatever happens. As for our future lovemaking, I will take great care with you. Rest assured, this spontaneity won't happen again until we decide we are ready for that second child."

While the night sounds sifted through her head, she listened to the breath of the wind while embers hissed and spit from the bonfire. She thought back in time. Thought of the earl and what he tried to take from her. Thought of all she had here with Hawk. She'd never been happier.

"Farlan is a shifter. Did you have any idea? I certainly didn't. I expected all shifters to be big and strong. Thought them to be good people," Maisie spoke, her voice soft.

"I was shocked when he tried to shift. For at least a minute, I didn't believe he would be able to do so."

Hawk was running his hands down her hair, holding different strands to his nose. He pulled her so she lay on top of his chest. "It smells of oranges, citrus fruits. You make me hungry."

Her favorite scents, she always bathed with the oil of oranges or lemons. "He's left Inverness, at least that is what Houston told me. Heard he is living in Glasgow now. I'm glad he left. Hope he never comes back."

"Yes, as I am too." He sat up with her, holding her tight. "I love you, Maisie. You create magic in my life. Should have told you a long time ago. I think I loved you the moment I saw you. What I did *ken* that first time, was that you are special." He kissed her softly, nibbled on the corners of her mouth before she opened for him, accepting him once more inside her.

When he finished, she touched his chin, caressed along his jaw. "I love you too, Hawk Fraser. You are the magic in my life. Now that we have loved, I do *ken* the magic of you, the magic of Hawk. I will love you forever."

Coming Soon
by the Author
At Rogue Phoenix Press

*Roc's Steadfast Heart*
Sweet McKenna Book Nine

"Come back. Sit for me. I'm almost finished," Rafe Fraser called to Dallas, a soft chuckle hiding the frustration he felt. He understood Dallas felt some of the same annoyance. The irritation wasn't because she was tired of posing for the painting he was working on but was because of their bizarre relationship. As much as they liked each other, the association was going nowhere.

Wearing a robe of pink satin belted at the waist, Dallas looked over her shoulder at him, her lips thinning to a small pout Rafe recognized. She huffed for a moment, "I'm tired. Can we put this off until tomorrow?" Her long copper colored hair picked up the dying rays of the sun filtering with soft golden tones in through the window. There were so many different shades coloring the silken strands, he always believed her hair to be the color of a sunset. Her lips were the nearly the same color as her nipples, with just a tinge more pink to them. Her eyes the color of blue-buttons, focused on him, pleading for him to relent. He had the devil's own time forcing his way on her. For some reason he couldn't comprehend, this time he felt an urgency to complete this painting of her.

"Ten more minutes." Holding up both hands then wiggling his fingers, Rafe bartered for more time knowing full well that ten minutes could turn into sixty once she returned to her pose. This respite was meant as a short break not a cessation of the session. She promised him she would stay until he finished this last sketch of her. He was farther than that. Rafe was poised to begin adding the oil colors to the drawing.

The scrunched-up face told him what she thought of his

proposition. Her tiny chin pointed into the air a notch higher than it had been the previous second. "A glass of beer, after that I'll stay as long as you need me."

With that comment Rafe understood he had won her over. She too had trouble telling him no. He nodded. "That's fair. I'll bring up two glasses. You relax in the over-stuffed chair while I'm gone." Rafe headed out the door, hoping she meant what she said. Sometimes Dallas was so flighty, she didn't remember her promises after he made the concessions.

Before he could get past the door to the third-floor studio, she walked beside him, linking her arm in his. She moved closer, her soft scent of citrus flowers teasing his nostrils. "I want to get out of this stuffy room for a minute. I'll walk down the stairs with you."

"You're restless tonight?" he asked accepting the fact Dallas would do as she pleased. "I'm surprised you were able to sit for me at all."

She turned so she could place her hand on his chest. Her smile showed beautiful, even white teeth. She spent three years after she turned ten wearing braces. "Very restless. I feel as if someone or something is calling to me. Don't understand that feeling. It's too bad you aren't the man seeking me out." She leaned into him, her head resting on his shoulder. He placed his hand on her cheek.

He felt the softness of her breasts pushing against his chest. Once they thought they would suit each other. He'd always been drawn to her. After their first experimental kisses, Dallas pushed her hair from her face to stare at him with those beautiful blue eyes of her then say, "Rafe, there is no spark. I don't feel anything when you kiss me. Shouldn't there be something more?"

The unfortunate truth of the matter was that he didn't feel the spark either. Ever since that day, they'd been friends, good friends. She told him everything as if he was her sister. He spoke of all his fears along with his dreams. Dallas was a remarkable model. He'd painted her several times. This was the first time she wore nothing at all. The sight of her naked, day after day, stole his breath yet he felt no quickening. The sight of her wearing nothing at all didn't cause an erection. In every way except sexual they were perfect for each other.

Her happiness meant everything to him. Dallas was a remarkable photographer. The woman sported a natural eye for what would be the best picture. "Tomorrow, you should go into the hills. Spend the day taking pictures. If you like I'll go with you. We could spend the day together, take a basket lunch. It will be good for both of us to get away from my studio. What do you think?" Even though he offered, Rafe wasn't certain it was a good idea. They both needed to stretch their wings, find a partner for life.

Her trilling laughter left him feeling amused. Dallas was going to refuse his offer. "You don't have to go with me. I'm not a little girl who needs to have her big brother take her places." She pushed away from him a smile on her lips. "I'm independent, a modern woman."

Big brother…little sister…he supposed that was the best and only way to describe their unique connection.

"I like to go with you. Enjoy spending time," he said as they strode down the steps. "You're more fun to be with than most of the females of my acquaintance. You haven't mentioned Seth Peters in a long time. You stop seeing the man? In my estimation he isn't good enough for you." He lifted an eyebrow in speculation before he spoke again. "No spark?"

"Not even a *wee* bit of heat."

Still arm in arm, they walked into the kitchen. He pulled out a chair at the kitchen table for her before ambling to the refrigerator. When she sat, she pulled the lapels of the robe closer. Deep inside he chuckled at her modesty. He just spent several days looking at her buck naked. After they finished the beer, she would uncover herself, pose in the nude. What was between them was simply platonic.

"Only saw him once. Seth is an animal. I can't be with a man who doesn't understand the meaning of the word no." She crossed her legs, the pink of her robe slipped down the side exposing her slightly tanned skin.

"Oh? He took what you didn't want to give." Silently Rafe cursed. His fists tightened with the need to protect Dallas.

This was her time to smile, "No, after the man tried to kiss me then groped my breast, I pepper sprayed him. His eyes must have been red for at least a week. I didn't stick around to see."

He set a glass of Guinness in front of her. "Still your favorite beer?"

Dallas lifted her shoulders, unfettered breasts swaying slightly beneath the robe she wore. Her nipples poked against the fabric, tightening with the slight friction her movements caused. Despite the fact there was no electricity between them, he loved to look at her breasts. They were lush, very full. The round globes could probably invite any man who wasn't a saint to want to taste. He read the invitation loud and clear. He wasn't going to take when he couldn't give back the feelings she needed. He could never give her love. She deserved a man who would love her not just care for her.

Her hips were wide. Her stomach rounded. If any female possessed an hour glass figure, Dallas did. It was nearly perfect…no, her figure was the perfect hourglass. All her womanly curves were generous. Rubenesque always came to mind when he looked at her. Dallas hated her body. Was always dieting to make herself smaller. Even when she lost weight the roundness would not go away. She would never have one of those concave bellies that women nowadays wanted. Her breast would never be less than generous mounds a man could lose himself between.

"I like Guinness. Can't say favorite…"

"What about you? Are you still seeing…" she drummed her fingernails on the wood table where they sat her expression pensive. "Can't seem to remember the girl's name. She's pretty but an airhead. Doesn't have a brain. If she does, she chooses not to use it."

"Shelly Grant? Is that the name you were looking for? You're right, as for brains she was sadly lacking." Idly, he leaned back, stretching his long legs his hands clasped together on his lean abs. "No, no spark with her either," he told her before she could ask the question. "Don't know if I'll ever find the woman I'm looking for."

The sigh parting the softness of her lips seemed to surprise her. "What are we? Too picky for our own good? What is it that we're looking for? Does love exist in this modern world?"

"Don't know about picky. Thought you were the one for me. Still believe you are. Nonetheless, there is no denying the fact there is something wrong between us, something illusive that is keeping us apart. Until I figure out the missing component, we can't be together as lovers. Won't take your innocence." Rafe held up his hands to keep Dallas from commenting. "You would have told me if you found that special guy."

"You think so?"

"Know so."

To Rafe's ears she sounded hopeful. Hell, he was always hopeful where it concerned Dallas. Undying love wasn't there for them. Since they were kids in grade school, they'd been attracted to each other. In high school, he dated her a few times. He took her to a concert in London when they were in college together. It seemed the harder he tried to find that elusive thread that would bind them together through eternity the more convinced he became the thin filament didn't exist for them.

"I do." He punched his fist into the palm of his hand. Damn, he wanted to find his mate, to go through all eternity with her. If he didn't find his mate in this lifetime, what then? Were the rumors true? Would he forever be kept from her?

There were too many days to count where Rafe wondered if he would ever find his mate. He would never hold his woman in his arms or show her his cat. Sometimes he wondered if that happened to him before…in another life. If somehow, his mate illuded him. How did one go backward in time so he could fix the problem? If he understood the complexities of time travel, he would do whatever was necessary to secure his mate.

With absentminded thoughts ruffling in his head, Rafe cracked the knuckles on both hands. The act seemed to relieve tension while he watched the woman who should be his but wasn't sip her beer. He never told Dallas about his clan, Clan Chattan. She didn't know he could change his form to a black panther. It was something a man didn't show just any woman. Even though in his mind, Dallas wasn't just any woman, he could never let himself be so vulnerable. Only for his mate could he risk so much.

Sometimes at night, desperate fears filled him. He tried to see backward in time. Never was he ever able to do so. Conversations with his parents didn't help. What could they do? They could not scavenge a mate up for him. All they ever said was to be patient. In time, he would find the woman meant for him.

With a wistful gush of air, she finished the glass of beer. "Shall we finish upstairs? I'd like to get home tonight before…well…I suppose it will be dark. You're going to want to work until you can't work any longer." Dallas stood, hugging the robe closer, outlining her breasts along with her hips.

Damn, but he wished there was something tangible between them. There just wasn't. When he looked at Dallas, he saw a beautiful woman with generous curves. That was all. "All right. I'll walk you home when I'm done. Don't want you walking the streets by yourself in the middle of the night."

"I appreciate that. Though I'm certain I can get home by myself. As we both know, nothing much ever happens in Carnoch."

"Of course you can. The fact that remains is that I'm not going to allow you to go by yourself." He headed up the steps behind her, staring at the delicious butt she presented to him...eye candy. She was that. She checked off all the boxes he had for a partner. All the boxes expect the one that counted the most.

They stepped into his studio. The lighting needed to be just right. What he never told her was that the rest of the sessions would have to be at dusk so he could get the light exactly the way he wanted it. Just as the sun shone through the window now. Rafe needed to see the golden tones light up her hair.

When she stood by the couch, her small hands on the belt, she appeared reluctant to remove the garment. He watched the rise and fall of her breasts beneath the silk cloth. Too many seconds passed while he felt the upsurge of guilt for keeping her, for even suggesting the nude painting. He'd wanted to paint her naked, needed to capture her spirit on canvas. Rafe didn't understand the reasons why but the need wrestled within him. Sometimes the thoughts kept him awake at night. Resting would not be possible until he put her form on the canvas.

The robe slipped to the floor. Nodding her head in the direction of the table, her long copper hair spilled across her breasts hiding them only to reveal them a second later. She arranged herself on the markings put there so they would remember where she was to place herself. While he studied her, he stepped back. A flash, a fleeting glimpse of something so close yet so far away swamped him, nearly sent him to his knees. In the ensuing moments, it was as if he was seeing her for the first time. He blinked focusing in on her. Whatever he thought he saw or felt vanished.

His Dallas was a beautiful woman. She should be his. Would

never be for him. Leaning over, he placed the long tendrils of hair so they covered her in just the right way. When the back of his hand brushed a hard tip of her breast, he should have felt lust surge to his penis. To his disappointment Rafe felt nothing but a tiny sensation that didn't reach his loins. The feeling was in his heart.

Loss.

Pain.

She should have reacted to his touch against her nipple. Dallas didn't.

"What is it?" she asked looking at him as if she could see all the way through him to his soul. "You look, you look as if you saw your death…or someone's…mine? You're creeping me out. Don't look at me that way."

Rubbing his hand on the back of his neck thinking he needed to control his wayward thoughts better, he told her, his voice taking on a husky tenor. "Nothing…nothing at all for you to concern yourself with. What I…my imagination…that's all. I thought I saw you in a different way. I didn't."

God she was beautiful. Why wasn't Dallas his mate? Over the years he asked himself that same question so many times he couldn't count them all on both hands. "Let's get on with the business at hand." The sooner he finished this painting the better for both of them.

He stepped back, picked up the paintbrush along with the oils he laid out for this particular moment.

"You don't look as if this is nothing." She sounded hurt that he wouldn't confide. If there was anyone, he could burden with his thoughts it was Dallas. With this he couldn't. Simply because he didn't understand.

She stiffened.

"Relax, sweetheart." Rafe didn't like the way his voice sounded just then. She'd done nothing wrong. He was treating her as if his changing mood was her fault.

The room heated to an inferno. Sweat beaded along his collar. He opened a window. Evening sounds made their way into the small upstairs studio room. A small drop of perspiration slid between her breasts leaving a trail behind. In the distance a car backfired. People chatted as they walked along the sidewalk in front of the house. Everything seemed normal, except in his studio. To his fine-tuned cat senses, there was something different here.

Dallas' lashes drooped. He shouldn't push so hard. She needed a break, to rest. They'd just returned from the kitchen. The need to remove her from the studio catapulted through him. He didn't understand. He wasn't one to ignore the sixth sense that was always an integral part of his life.

"We need to stop for the night," he gritted out as he saw the rise of exhaustion fill her blue eyes. She wouldn't even take money for modeling. He promised that no one would see the painting except him. That was a lie. The commission he was promised was in the thousands for this painting. What he would do is be certain her face would never be recognized. What he didn't know was if he could part with it when he finished.

"If we work for another half hour, you will be that much closer to finishing. I'm not too tired. The beer made me drowsy. That's all. Do as much as we can, please, Rafe."

Rafe knew he could probably finish this without her. The sketch was finished. He put a lot of color on the canvas tonight. The final painting was so close to completion. If he tried to finish without her though, the painting might not be as authentic.

"Another half-hour," he agreed, half-reluctant, half-pleased. "No more. Don't want to wear you out." He dipped into the copper color he mixed for her hair adding some of the tints of the sunset. That was what the color of her hair reminded him of…the setting sun…maybe the dawn of a new day. Rafe loved her hair more than her lush curves.

The ensuing time passed more swiftly than he could imagine. When he stepped back to look, he felt the warmth of a smile grow within. This was the best painting he'd ever done. Deep in his heart, he understood it wasn't his skill that made the painting so good, his model was the reason.

"We're finished for tonight. There will be some finishing touches to be made at another time. Need to step away for a day or two."

"Ah…" She stretched out her arms, lengthening her muscles, shoulders, back, triceps. Easing muscles that had been in one position too long, she moved her legs, testing them on the floor before she stood. "I'm stiff as a fire poker," she mumbled. She stumbled when she tried to stand.

He was beside her, holding onto her arms. She leaned against him, her curves pushing against him. This was his Dallas, so trusting. Good God, she was naked. He was holding her. He didn't have one carnal thought in his head except for the fact there were none.

Letting her support herself on his body, he bent over to pick up her robe. He wrapped it around her. "Go get dressed then I'll take you home."

Brushing back hair from her face, she nodded. Stiff movements hindering her steps, she walked to the small dressing room in the corner of the studio. She didn't bother to draw the curtain. What would be the point? As if she was now in a rush to get home, she slipped into a pair of cutoff shorts and a tank top. Her bra and panties she stuffed into a bag she brought with her. Rafe had to laugh at the fact she was going *sans* underwear. It was just like his Dallas. She hated constricting bras. Didn't realize she disliked wearing panties too.

Dallas finger-combed her hair, pulling it back into a ponytail. With her hands she scrubbed her face then shook her head as if she tried to wake up. The hour was almost midnight. This wasn't the first time tonight he was besieged with a strange sense of *deja vous*. When he looked out the window it was almost as if he saw Dallas standing on the sidewalk. The hazy woman he saw for an instant was Dallas though she could be her twin.

"Can we walk? I need to stretch out some more, loosen up my stiff muscles. If I don't, I'll never get to sleep tonight."

"Whatever you would like." Hand on her elbow, he ushered her to the door. "Did you bring a coat?" Rafe asked as he stared at her long, naked legs. They were slightly tanned. When she posed for him, he noticed the tan lines marking her skimpy, thong bikini. When she sunbathed, she didn't wear much. In order not to have tan lines, she untied the top when she was lying on her front, then pulled down the tiny shoulder straps when she was on her back. The lavish curves of her breasts were outlined in tiny white triangles.

He didn't like to think of other men seeing so much of her. Whenever his thoughts veered in that direction, he always made a point to remind himself he wasn't her mate. Would never be her husband or lover. Jealousy would never be tolerated.

All his thoughts and feeling conflicted with each other. She pulled a lightweight sweater from her bag to put around her shoulders tying the sleeves so the they knotted over her breasts.

"What have you got in there?" Rafe took the satchel from her as if he meant to search through to see the contents. Enough items to live through the week?" he asked laughing as she scrunched up her face to show him what she thought of his question.

"Just what every girl needs in an emergency. That's all. Nothing exceptional." She smiled at him as she took the bag back into her possession then slipped the long strap over her shoulder. Not waiting for him, she walked.

Once he caught up to her again, he wrapped his arm around her shoulder pulling her close. By her ear he whispered, "I always wanted to know what a lady would need in an emergency."

"Did you now?" She laughed seemingly lighthearted for the first time today. "Does that mean you are going to search my bag?"

"Tell me," Rafe coaxed sensing her playful mood and hoping to exterminate the tension. "What do you have in there."

"If you think about it, you might be able to guess as to a few things."

"Yes…well…" Rafe could make a few stabs in the dark. He did know her well. Probably better than anyone except her mother and father. "I would say you've a change of clothes…even two different outfits…underwear…maybe a bikini, one of those skimpy ones you so like to wear."

"True, obvious guess though. What else?" She winked at him, understanding he could probably relate the entire contents of the huge bag she always carried with her even though he'd never seen the contents.

"You could take the suspense out of this and give me a list." He ran his hand along her arm then back to her shoulder. She fit against him with perfection. He let out a long breath of air understanding that no matter how much he wanted things to be different between them, they were not. He could muddle this over in his brain again and again until exhaustion overcame him. Nothing would change. It was past time to put an end to his musings about the possibility of Dallas becoming someone special to him. Well, she was special just not in that way.

"Where would be the fun in that. Try again." She poked him in the chest. It was a playful poke, not in the least suggestive. The gesture was something a sister would give her brother.

He caught her finger then enclosed her hand within in his. She was meant for someone else. That fact had been apparent from the first time they thought to kiss. Jealousy flooded him at the notion of some other man possessing her. He could no longer hold onto her. Letting her go was a deed he would have to undertake.

"Let me see," he paused while he began to think, tapping a finger against his chin and hoping not to embarrass her. She'd come to him once in tears, the pain of her periods so intense she could only curl into a tiny ball on his bed. At that time, he comforted her the best he could all the while believing if her relationship with her mother was at it should be, Dallas should discuss this with her. He gave her some pain medicine. When she could talk, she told him about her cramps. He took her to the doctor, waited for her in the waiting room. He'd know she had taken birth control pills since she was sixteen to regulate her periods.

She giggled appearing pleased with herself. "It can't be that hard. You do know more about me than anyone else on planet earth."

"No, I just didn't want to cause any embarrassment. I'm certain you have birth control pills in the bag."

"Yes, two months' worth. I'm not embarrassed. A lot of women have to do the same even though they aren't sexually active."

"You could be though." He didn't want to fish for information. Rafe wasn't certain why he suddenly needed to know if she had a significant man in her life. Earlier she told him Seth was not appreciated, her words, 'he's an animal'. Could there be someone else, a man she didn't wish to speak of around him? Most of the time with him, Dallas was an open book.

"Yes....I could be." Dallas lifted her eyebrows at him, questioning his integrity he didn't doubt. "Do you carry condoms with you?" she asked prying into his life with the question.

Just as he pried into hers. "No... If I ever meet someone I would like to be intimate with, I would."

"You should. As a just in case. That's why I keep a box of

condoms with me in my bag. You're not implying to me that you're a virgin? If you are, I won't believe you." She let out a puffy breath of air stopping to turn in his arms. Her hands rested on his chest. "I want to be prepared in case…" She sifted in a deep breath of oxygen. "In case the right man ever comes along. I'm beginning to think there is no one out there for me."

"Geez, Dallas, I've those thoughts all the time too. Since the right person isn't you, I doubt if there ever will be a perfect woman for me. Not that she has to be perfect…without flaws. Hell!" He was managing to confuse himself.

"I understand what you're trying to say, Rafe. I just wish I understood what went wrong between us. I can tell you anything. Speak of whatever pops into my head without one concern you'll gossip. Sometimes I feel that I've known you forever. You even took me to the doctor."

"I don't like you carrying condoms." *What the hell was the matter with him?* She was right on all counts.

"You don't want me to have safe sex?" she asked, her eyes open wide, walking away from him, her back stiff, shoulders squared as if she tolerated him nothing else. He was pretty certain her chin would have risen at least an inch.

The closeness between them evaporated with her questioning. If he could, he would get that lightheartedness back.

He couldn't. At least not tonight.

"Here we are." They stood in front of the door to her apartment. "Can I come in?" Rafe wasn't at all certain why he asked. He did know he wanted to retrieve something of what was lost during that last conversation. The only way to succeed would be to spend more time.

Dallas was shaking her head, her lips turned down in a small pout of displeasure. "I don't see why you would want to. Go home, finish up the painting or don't. Tomorrow I'll go up into the hills. I'll take so many pictures it will take us hours to look at all of them. After that if you need me to pose for you again, I will."

"Sorry I upset you," Rafe mumbled in a whisper that he hoped she didn't hear. Looking up, he brushed hair from her eyes. "Don't like to say things…well, we both understand with time there will be someone else in our lives. We're going to have to get used to that notion. Damn, the thought of you with another man eats at the very heart of my soul."

"It's the same for me when I think about you with some unnamed woman. What are we to do with each other? This can't go on. I should move to another town."

Rafe wiped a tear from her beautiful blue eyes. "Don't cry. Don't move either. I don't know what we are to do. For me there isn't anyone except you."

"There's no spark."

"The connection isn't there."

Opening the door, he waited for her to set her things down. With a tentative smile on her face, she closed the door leaving him standing alone on the porch staring off into the distance at nothing.

With slow measured steps, as if he was going to his execution, Rafe walked home. He didn't understand the feeling but he felt certain, he was about to lose Dallas to a man. Even more prevalent in his thoughts was that after tonight she would be gone from his life.

His gut twisted. The pain sent him to his knees.

~ * ~

When the misty fog covering the ground cleared to brilliant sunshine, Dallas felt as if she was seeing a new world. The spring scented air swept around her. Long grass waved with soft rhythm coupled with the soft breeze blowing down from the craigs. Perhaps she was seeing this world in a new light. She'd driven to a spot about thirty miles from Coronach traveling towards Inverness. She knew of this beautiful spot. Had always hoped to stop here. Until today, she never made the time. The pictures would be absolutely amazing. Rafe would tell her which ones should be enhanced with colors. Which ones to mount then take to the art gallery in Inverness. She had scheduled an exhibition of her photographs for July. It was almost time to prepare all the photos.

Today, she wore a tight-fitting dress. The baby blue fabric molded with love to all her curves, showing off all her best assets. Rafe didn't like the dress. Told her she was encouraging every male who saw her to touch those assets. If not touch to stare. Didn't matter if she encouraged.

No one would dare. She always kept her distance from leering-eyed men.

Too bad, Rafe!

She meant to wear the dress whenever she wished. Her high heels were in her bag. For the photo shoot she wore a pair of jogging shoes. If she had to walk down paths for the pictures, the aerobic shoes would suit her feet better than the heels. Afterward, she planned to dine at this bistro in the city she heard about from a few of her friends, hence the reasons for the heels strategically placed in the satchel. Even Rafe said the cuisine was good. He took his last date there.

*Date.*

They weren't suited. Dallas didn't have to remind herself. She knew all too well the truth. The two of them would never would have that flicker they were both looking for. Though she would be satisfied without the energy, the excitement, or the flames between them. Rafe would not. He was holding out for the best possible woman. So far, she never felt that electricity with anyone. She supposed she should hold out too. Dallas could count the number of men she dated on one hand. She was stuck on three. None of them excited her, left her breathless with longing. None of them generated the desire to have sex. They were dull, witless, fools.

"Wow!" Dallas whistled through her teeth after she rounded the corner of the path to get a full-on view of the water pouring over the cliff. This waterfall was filled to the brim with liquid. It was nearly April. The runoff from the mountain snows and glaciers was filling the rivers as well as all the waterfalls. The roar was impressive tumbling through her ears. Time seemed to stand still while she gazed in awe at one of the most spectacular sites she'd ever seen.

Today, there were two tourists who were taking pictures. At least she thought that's what they were. Seemed they were also planning on photographing the landscape. The time was too early for the tourist season to be at its height. She would have never stayed here if there had been crowds. She detested crowds. Hated waiting for them to clear the view so people wouldn't be in the picture. Disliked using photoshop to rid herself of the landmarks that weren't natural.

Hands on her back, she stretched to get rid of the kinks.

Dallas set up her tripod working on all the setting to get the affect she looked for. When she checked each photo, most were magnificent.

She sent the ones she didn't like into the trash. After she finished, she pulled out her laptop. With the card from her camera, she put them in a folder on her desktop. Pleased with the morning's work, she inhaled a deep breath of the surrounding fresh air. This was paradise to her.

The day was turning out to be better than she expected. There was more than enough time to drive into Inverness to eat before returning home if that's what she decided to do. Curious as to its destination as well as feeling pulled by some unseen force, Dallas decided to investigate a trail that seemed to wander beneath the waterfall. She put her tripod in her car then started walking enjoying the warmth of the sun's rays as they beat down on her face.

"Beautiful day," Dallas said as she passed the older couple who were shooting selfies. She loved to see loving couples who were in their sixties and even seventies. The thought she might never find someone to love her, left a cold shiver trembling down her spine.

"Yes, love…you all alone? You need to find yourself someone who will love keeping you company," the woman spoke to her as she walked past.

"Alone, going to see what's on the other side of the waterfall. Don't suppose there is someone there for me."

"Your camera…we saw you shooting pictures. Are you a professional?" she asked, curiosity in her voice.

Dallas reached into her bag then pulled out her cellphone. "If I see something that warrants a better pic, I'll grab my tripod and camera. Yes, I am a photographer. I've an exhibit of my pictures coming up this summer. It will be in Inverness the end of July. You could come."

"Oh, if we would still be here this summer, we would attend. I love to support talented artists," the man spoke for the first time.

"Thanks," she ruffled in her bag for a few seconds before pulling out her card. "Here, take this. If you're interested in some of my photographs you can go on line to see them. They can be ordered then shipped." Dallas didn't know if the couple were just being polite. Nonetheless, it never hurt her to hand out a card. She'd made multiple sales as well as fans by doing so.

"Have fun and don't get lost. The highlands can be frightening if one doesn't know their way." The woman waved at her as she backed down the path. She waved back, smiling cheerfully despite the sudden feelings of loss as she left the two people behind.

No, she wasn't going to get lost on this path. The trail was well marked even though it wound around the falls. She hummed then cringed at the off-key noise. While she possessed a few talents, carrying a tune was not one of them. Rafe never failed to tease her about her lack of musicality. This coming from a man whose deep base voice never failed to thrill her when she heard him sing.

At the bottom of the falls, she looked up, shielding her eyes with her hand. Mist splayed out from all the rocks the tumbling water bounced off. The sun shining behind the misting, she saw the face and form of a man seeming to float in the haze. He was tall, his hair a burnished blond. Impossible. As if her thoughts were true, he vanished. She was left with the rainbows that crowded the water filled air.

With the palm of her hand, Dallas tapped her head. My imagination is conjuring men…in the mist of waterfalls. I didn't eat anything strange today. Haven't had anything to drink since the one beer last night. I don't think I'm obsessed with men. No, silly, you're only obsessed with finding the right man.

Trying to shake the discordant feelings, she snapped pictures with her phone then strode farther down the trail. A sudden shifting of the ground caught her off guard. Flinging her arms out, she braced herself against a sky-high boulder. The cold rock pressed against her cheek. That was different. Dallas hesitated to use the word peculiar or bizarre. Perhaps a minor earthquake was what caused her to step off balance. She gulped a gallon of oxygen. For the longest time she clung to the boulder, adrenalin racing through her. Once she felt steady again, she continued. She reached what could only be described as a turning point. On one side, the terrain was flat, on the other side the land gave way to a steep slope. In either case her footpath stopped. She would have to turn around, go back to the beginning. Maybe she could find another trail to follow.

This time when she looked up beams of sunlight imprisoned that same man, his smile was wide, laughing. His eyes danced with something he must think amusing. He seemed to stare at her, holding her enthralled. Her heart skipped then stuttered. When his eyes focused on her it seemed to Dallas he summoned her. He asked her to join him. Now, her heart stilled while she remained enthralled with the very essence of this man. The breath she inhaled caught in the back of her throat staying there until she choked. Tremors ceased her. Her body shook so hard she felt the sensations to the tips of her toes.

Captivated, she followed the laughing man, one hesitant foot in front of the other. She didn't understand the reason. It seemed he reeled her into some unknown place. Somewhere in the back of her mind, she understood this was not her usual behavior. While she continued walking the ground shook. She slipped, her feet skidding out from beneath her. Her arms whirled while she tried unsuccessfully to maintain her balance. Tumbling to her rear, she sat on the soft grass, sliding, falling until she was brought to an abrupt halt at the bottom of the incline. Air rushed from her lungs as she rolled to her belly, hitting the earth hard. She took another tumble suddenly coming to rest.

With her legs spread in front of her, her body framing dress hiked nearly to her hips, she leaned on her elbows in order to better survey the scene in front of her. Some point during her fall, the wind was knocked from her lungs a second time. Painfully she inhaled, slow desperate breaths of much needed air. Her eyes couldn't focus. Beneath her the earth still whirled. She saw herself or someone who looked much like her, running through this field with a huge black panther. Dallas tried to shake the nonsense from her head. This time when she sensed a presence and looked upward, she didn't see the man of her imagination. What she saw was very real as well as very frightening.

"Well, lookee what we have here, Scratch. An itsy-bittsy *lassie* just ripe to be tried out. She just sitting on the grass legs spread waitin' for us to be good to her. Should we show her what we got?"

"I get her first, Gordie," Scratch said as he slipped a hand beneath the waistband of his britches. "I'm the oldest."

"You no be makin' sense. I saw her first. So, she be mine first." Geordie walked toward her, his eyes glimmering with the need to possess.

*Damn!*

Dallas crab walked backward. Her body quivering. She couldn't imagine any of this. "No! No, I'm not going to let you touch me!" Her hands searched the small pocket in her bag for the pepper spray she always kept there. She prayed the cannister would work having bought the weapon over a year ago. She bought the spray mostly with the hope of keeping dogs away from her on her daily jog. Praying what little wind there was wouldn't send the pepper her way, she pulled it out. Her arm extended, she cried out, "Stop!"

Scratch roared his laughter. He pulled up his shirt to scratch his belly then lower. His grin turned to a smirk. "Stop? What kind of weapon you think you got there, my *wee lassie*? Whatever that thing is, it isn't going to keep me from what I want." He leered at her stepping forward again. "I want you, little *lassie*. I'm going to have you. After that I plan on sharing you with Geordie here." He cocked his thumb toward the other man.

With great effort, Dallas pushed off the ground. She stood in front of the two men clutching the small cannister. Even she didn't think this would keep the men away from her. She needed divine intervention. Still, she brazened her way. "It's pepper spray. If you take one more step, I'll use it."

Dallas was standing, her arm outstretched, shaking as she looked from one man to the other. Her heart pounded with fear. She ran her tongue across her bottom lip while she searched her surroundings for someone who might help. Divine intervention was a myth.

Scratch stepped forward. "Just want a *wee* bit of loving. That's not too much to ask for. I wouldn't ask if you weren't so pretty."

He needed to take one more step before she could use her small weapon. She wanted a direct line to his eyes. In her wildest imagination, she never thought to be in a position such as this one. Her gaze darted from one man to the other. If they attacked her together, she didn't stand a chance.

*Keep your cool. Breathe.*

The look on Scratch's face changed to something more feral. His lips were pulled back from his teeth in an untamed smile. His eyes came together in a fierce scowl. When he leapt at her, Dallas discharged the spray. His screech of agony didn't give her pleasure only relief. With no hesitation, she turned her attention to the other man, Geordie.

Holding the spray at arm's length, she cried out. "Don't come one step closer! If you do, I'll give you the same dose your friend just got." She was backing away, taking slow steps trying to keep her attention on the men as well as her footing. If she went down, her fate was sealed. They would be on top of her in a second.

"That wasn't wise of you. What did you do to him? I'm going to…" He started forward, his fists clenched at his sides. His eyes were wild.

The applause from behind her caught her attention. She twirled to see. *Not three men.* She heard the soothing timber of his voice.

"If I were you, I'd do what the lady says. Seems to me at this moment, this little *lassie* has the upper hand." The voice behind her was deep and husky holding the hint of amusement. Nonetheless, his meaning was clear.

*Her divine intervention?* She looked skyward to say a silent prayer. Though her family were devout Catholics, she'd never taken to the church.

Trembling, afraid to ask, she blurted the words as if she expected an answer. This new man might want the same things these two thugs did, "Who are you?" the words spoken, her voice trailing off. Dallas understood there wasn't enough pepper spray in the tiny cannister to take care of three men.

"Roc." Geordie was holding up his hands then looking at his friend who was reeling on the ground, "This isn't any of your affair. This *lassie* needs to be taught a lesson. She can't go around hurting men." He snapped his fingers. "Just like that…as we if were naught more but twigs. When we're done with her, we'll share her with you. Certain there is enough of the lady to go around. Just look at those bubbies of hers."

Dallas tried to slouch, to cover herself suddenly mortified by the man's words. While she'd never heard breasts referred to as bubbies, it was obvious what the man stared at while he fondled himself.

"Why not?" Roc had his hands on his narrow hips. To Dallas he sounded outraged at the notion of sharing. "You meant to hurt her…or did I read the scenario wrong? Is she willing for you and Scratch to manhandle her? Or…did she tell you to stop?"

"You want her for yourself," Scratch cried out.

"Seems that way." Roc turned his attention to her, his heated insolent gaze roaming the length of her body. "Get up and stand behind me. You and I are getting out of here." The command in his voice was not to be disobeyed.

Confused. she didn't know what to think. His actions seemed at odds with his words. When she hesitated, her rescuer spoke again but didn't make eyes contact. With a lift to his broad shoulders, he went on to say, "You can choose between them or me. Do it now," he spoke calm, with such calm she knew she would obey. "If you choose Scratch and Geordie, I'll ride out of here and never look back. The decision is up to you." He waited two seconds. His following roar surprised her. Nonetheless it broke the frozen spell she'd fallen under. "Do it now!"

"Well…when you put it that way. Don't have to be so…" She didn't know how to finish that sentence. Picking up the bag that had fallen from her shoulders, she scrambled to his side then stood behind him cowering. Her body seemed to vibrate with the rush of adrenalin coursing through her.

"You'll regret helping her," Geordie threatened shaking his fist at both of them. He pointed a scrawny finger their way. "I'll have my revenge on you then I'll take her. Won't be any sharin' this time."

"Who's going to make me regret helping out a *lass* who's in distress? Not you." He looked at her, a genuine smile on his handsome features. "Can you ride?"

She shook her head wishing she could answer in the affirmative as well as wishing she knew what was going through his head. "Never been on a horse in my life." She wanted to yell at him that her car was just up that hill. For some reason Dallas couldn't fathom, she kept silent.

His encouraging smile turned to a sudden frown, his eyebrows drawing together in concentration. "We'll have to improvise in that case."

This was the same man who she saw in the mist as well as the sunbeams. "Roc? Your name is Roc?" If she could figure out was going on inside his brain, she felt certain she would fare better.

"Stand behind me." He motioned to where he wanted her. "Right there. Don't move a muscle."

What would he do if she twitched the wrong way. Wobbling, her knees weak, she managed to put herself where he showed her. She wrapped her arms around herself, warding off the strange chill that seemed to embody her. Except for the pistol he held in his hand, she wondered why these two men didn't attack him. All they did was threaten.

Roc didn't seem phased at all by the two of them. He was outnumbered. The man didn't seem to care one way or the other.

"You two start walking, keep walking. Don't stop until I can no longer see you." He continued with the gun pointed at them, "Who will get it first? Geordie or Scratch."

Geordie turned, his hands in the air as they would stop the bullet. "Now *dinna* go gettin' impatient. We're going."

Dallas held her breath while the men walked away.

When they were finally out of sight, he took her hand and tugged. "Let's go."

Dallas found herself without a single word or thought. Beside him as well as blindly, she stumbled trying to keep pace with his long strides. He didn't slow to help her. She sensed his urgency. While she didn't want to find herself in this position with a man she didn't know, this man was infinitely better than the other possibility. At least he was clean and he didn't smell of stale tobacco and sour whiskey. Her stomach churned.

When they stopped in front of a horse, she assumed it was his horse. With her hands on her hips and with as much conviction as her frightened self could muster, she said, "Couldn't you just walk me to my car?" Dallas understood this would be wishful thinking. The man didn't seem to be open to suggestions or negotiation.

"Car?" He lifted a burnished, dark blond eyebrow skyward then ignored her questions. "I'll help you up." Before she could utter another word and voice the protest, his large hands wrapped around her waist. The first second after the contact she felt airborne, flying upward. It wasn't a sensation she cared to duplicate. Her breath caught then she found herself astride his horse. Against her legs her dress rose to above midthigh.

The horse shifted position. Terrified, she grabbed on to the animal's neck while she tried to tug the fabric of her tight-fitting dress to cover herself more thoroughly. The horse whinnied its objection. "I c-can't..." She'd never sat a horse before. Her terror rose to form a lump in her throat that seemed to block further speech. Despite her efforts to the contrary, her dress rose even higher to her upper thighs. She heard a small rip and realized the pressure of her parted legs created a slit on one side, baring her on her right side to her hip. There was naught to do about that except try to ignore it. She looked down at him, the steel grey of his eyes darkening as he stared at her legs.

"You can ride. We need to leave before Scratch can see again. I'm getting on behind you. Hold still."

"T-trust m-me he won't see well for at least twenty-four hours. That stuff is potent. Supposed to keep a bear at bay for that long. That man was hardly a bear." Her voice lost all its intended force when she saw his hands on the saddle horn in front of her. Damn, she was riding away with a man she didn't know. She could hardly stay here as he pointed out. In the process risking a second encounter with Geordie and Scratch.

"Good." He vaulted on behind her. His hands once more touched her waist. "Steady there. I'll no' let you fall."

*He won't let me fall... Who's going to keep him from falling?*

That thought was no consolation and held no merit when the horse started to move. The sensation of heat vanished when he took up the reins. The animal picked up speed. She tried to sit up straight so she wouldn't find herself pressed against him. For the next minutes, nothing surrounding her registered except the man behind her, the breadth of him. The heat he generated. Every time she started to relax; she stiffened as the movement of the horse sent her against his chest. She found herself cradled between his massive thighs. His arms brushed hers. She clung to his massive forearms. Unable to watch the forest rush past her, she closed her eyes.

"You *dinna* need be afraid of me." His voice whispered across her neck then her cheek. Heat infiltrated her body. To her dismay, she found her nipples hardening, parts of her tingling she'd never particularly thought about before.

"I'—I'm not a-afraid. I'm t-terrified. More scared of the horse than you." She ran her tongue across her parched lips. "C-can't you just take me back to my car?"

He didn't answer her for the longest time. Suddenly, using his soft husky voice with no amusement in the tone, he asked, "What's a car?"

Startled, she whirled her amazement obvious if he watched her. The motion upset his horse who reared his head back then sidestepped a couple of times. "Easy, *laddie*," he whispered soothing words to the animal, stroking the horse's neck with practiced skill. Seemed he knew how to calm the beast. While she watched his eyes, he spoke to the horse as if the beast understood him. "This little filly in front of me surprises me too, *laddie*. She keeps takin' me off guard. In time, we're sure to get used to her." Then, to her, once more bending close to her ear to whisper, "Don't move so fast. Moonstar isn't used to *lasses*. He wants you to like him but you keep surprising him. That confuses him so much that he doesn't know what to do."

She felt the stubble from his chin caress her cheek. "Oh!" she cried out once again surprised by him. She felt the heat from his words. The sensation swept through her as she was doused in flames from the simple contact.

"Easy…" he spoke again. "Don't be frightened. For Moonstar's sake, don't move fast again. He's not used to riding double. Don't usually share him."

*Riding double? Was that euphemism for something else?*

"Wh-where are you taking me?" She tried desperately not to stutter. Seemed to fail miserably. While she was both terrified as well as curious, curiosity seemed to reign prevalent. Dallas didn't understand why she was beginning to trust this man. "I," she gulped air, "don't ride. Don't know how to ride."

"That's obvious. Perhaps an understatement." He chuckled, his voice slightly gruff yet whiskey smooth. "As to your other question, I'm taking you to safety. Ye *cannae* stay where those men can find you. They meant you harm."

Yes, she knew. They would have forced her if Roc didn't come along. "That's also an understatement. What are your intentions? I…" She lost the stutter. He could be wanting the same as those men. It was replaced with indignation as well as annoyance. He saved her. She should be grateful for his interference even when she thought she had all under control. Under control only if there was enough pepper spray in the cannister to do in the second man. "I repeat, where are you taking me?"

"Carnoch eventually."

"I was planning on going to Inverness for dinner. Thought I might stay the night. So, I would guess you are going the wrong direction. Though I cannot go anywhere without my car." If she expected him to take her to her car, she was beating herself up over something that wasn't going to happen.

"Too far to go before the sun drops behind the craigs. You wouldn't make it there for dinner or to stay the night. I will feed you tonight. We can talk more about tomorrow. I can't take you to Inverness yet. Just came from there. Nonetheless, in a week or so I need to return. You can go with me then if that's to your liking."

Dallas felt as if she was talking to someone who existed in a different dimension or century. "Of course, there's time. It would only take a couple of hours to…" The distinct feeling her words went in one of his ears then out the other met with direct conflict. They were talking on two different levels.

"You *dinna* listen to me. Things will go along more smoothly if you begin to do so. From here the trip will take all day. As I just told you I don't have the time." He spoke with little inflection as if he spoke to a small child he found lacking.

"Then where…" She supposed she would have to concede to his ways.

He interrupted her train of thought. "Tonight, our accommodations will be a cave I know very well." The thoughtful then the ensuing question caught her off guard. "Do you always dress so provocatively?"

Dallas looked down at the expanse of leg she showed. "This isn't…" She looked up, caught the amusement in his eyes as well as the darkening of the color to deep pewter. "My dress ripped." Now she was angry at what he was saying but not actually accusing. Men! "Are you implying my attire was somehow the reason why those men wished to attack me? That's just stupid!" She sounded too prim and proper for her ears. No, she wasn't prim or proper. What she was, was indignant that the man dare reply in that manner. Her short shorts as well as her bikini were more provocative.

"Maybe somewhat stimulating. Though that doesn't give a man the right. I find your attire very fetching. I can see every curve you possess. I find that I enjoy looking at you." Once again, there was a hint of amusement in his voice.

He set his hand on her bare leg. Heat seared her, touched that part of her his whispered words tinged a few minutes ago. "If a woman doesn't want unwanted attention, she would be well advised not to show so much of herself. Whether I agree or not matters little. What I stated is a fact."

Dallas tried to pull her skirt down. Sitting astride this huge animal made the task impossible. "I don't want to stay in a cave. I didn't dress to go riding. If you didn't come along and hoist me up here, I wouldn't be showing so much of my legs. Though I've…well…my short shorts show a bit more," as she confessed, she felt heat rise to her face. No, not when a quick trip to Inverness would get her a nice four-star hotel.

"Short shorts?"

"Yes." Her chin rose to prove her point as well as show him she didn't care for his words of warning.

"Suit yourself. That's where I'm headed though." He didn't act like he was about to give her a choice. She knew from the first command, there were no choices in her future. "Do you wish for me to set you down. You will have to take your chances with Scratch and Geordie."

At this point they were headed away from the falls, away from Inverness. They'd been riding at least twenty minutes, perhaps more. The setting sun was in front of them. Yes, by the slant of the sun, they were traveling west not east. It seemed she was going to stay the night in a cave with this man. Maybe a name would help her adjust to losing her ability to choose. "What do you call yourself?"

He barked with a sharp bout of laughter. "If it's a name you're looking for my name is Cameron Petroc Fraser. Most call me Cameron. A few tend to use Roc." He paused for a few seconds. "You? Do you have a name?"

She sifted in a hard breath of air. Fraser? She didn't know any Frasers by that name in this area. Was he related to Rafe? If so, maybe that little fact would help her get what she needed. "I'm Dallas Elaine Shaw."

"Lainie," he murmured softly, his hand around her waist tightened. "I like that name, Lanie. What kind of name is Dallas?"

Her middle name tumbling from his lips felt like a soft caress filled with warmth. Leaning into him, she sighed as if he stroked her. For all practical purposes, she felt as if he had done so.

"Roc?" He shortened his middle name to something more

palatable than Petroc.

"Yes?" His hand rose on her ribcage then settled on the curve of her hip.

She felt the caress to the tips of her toes. Didn't understand why but she wanted him to do that again. She wasn't about to ask. "Don't you need to use both hands?" While she appreciated the way his hands felt on her, she would feel safer if he kept both hands on the reins.

A small chortle proceeded his next words. "You wish for me to touch you with both my hands? I can be accommodating if that's what you wish."

The amusement in his voice didn't go unnoticed. She stiffened pushing her back against his chest. "No! I want you to use both hands to steer your horse."

"Moonstar," he corrected. "I'm disappointed. Thought you wished for me to caress your beautiful curves. All you need do is ask. I'd be happy to oblige."

"No, I don't want you touch me at all." Her voice was too indignant when all she wished for was to feel more of the heat he generated.

"As you wish." His hands fell away from her but he didn't pick up the reins. "Don't need to use two hands or even one. Can guide my horse with my knees."

~ * ~

When Dallas didn't show up the next day as she told Rafe she would, Rafe drove to the falls. He discovered her abandoned car at the falls. While her tripod was inside the trunk, her camera equipment along with her big bag she always carried were gone.

He tried not to panic. She would be able to explain. Over then over again he told himself she was fine. *Nothing happened.* Dallas would turn up soon. She must have met a friend here. Why she didn't text him though was beyond his wildest imagination. She always apprised him of her plans if she was going to deviate. She always knew he would worry.

Along the way to Inverness, he stopped at stores as well as eateries to inquire if anyone saw her. No one could report seeing a young lady of her description. Later that night when he climbed the steps to her studio apartment, he searched his head for anything she might have told him that would give him a clue as to her whereabouts.

*I should move to another town.*

At the time she spoke those words, Rafe hadn't believed her, couldn't believe she would do something so foolish. Especially without speaking more plainly. No, she didn't move. Her home was not up for sale. Her car was now in his driveway. In the studio, he stared out the window, his heart in his throat.

She was gone from his life, at least for the time being. *Until he could find her.* He would too. He wouldn't not give up his search for Dallas. It would not be so easy to disappear. If necessary, he would hire a private detective. She was not skilled in vanishing. She would leave traces of her passing. Dallas would you her credit card. She would withdraw money from her bank. She could not remain missing for long. Rafe was certain she wasn't attempting to hide from anyone.

After he uncovered the oil painting of her, her body seemed to fade, change in subtle ways. His imagination worked overtime. For the longest time he stared at the painting, remembering her.

No, she wasn't gone. Dallas would come back to him. Yesterday was not the last time he would see her.

He prayed.

*Dallas, where are you. I'll miss you. You cannot be hurt or in need of help.*

As the days passed, Rafe became more desolate. His best friend in the entire world went missing. There was nothing he could do about finding her. At least not any more than he already was.

Every time he passed a woman with copper colored hair, he stared. Now, he painted furiously. Sketched her from memory. Water colors, acrylics, charcoal, were all different medias he used to portray her. His walls were wallpapered with paintings of her.

At times he thought himself a bit crazed. Many times, he found himself staring out the window into the setting sun or the dawning sun. He ate little and slept less.

His friends stopped coming by to see him.

He was disheartened. Rafe visited a therapist. After a session when the doctor hypnotized him, the man pronounced him sane. Rafe supposed that was a relief even though the doctors words didn't bring Dallas back to him.

After several months, Rafe began to recover. The process was slow. He still spent most of his time in the third-floor room, drawing and painting Dallas. She was all that was on his mind. The detectives he hired turned up nothing. It seemed she vanished leaving no trace of her behind.

His mother came to see him. Told him he looked terrible and smelled even worse. He knew her words for truth. Supposed a bath would be in order along with a shave. He didn't like how the unkept beard aged him. He didn't like the fact no one wanted to see him. Rafe understood he needed to snap out of the depression where he floundered.

By the time he finished bathing and dressing, he felt better. Stepping out of his home, he strode along the bustling city streets of Carnoch. The wind seemed to blow in from the sea. The air felt clean and crisp. He felt rejuvenated. The sky was a brilliant blue with few clouds. A weight seemed to be lifted from his shoulders.

For the first time in months, he felt as if he had something to live for. When he caught his first glimpse of her, his heart stopped for a moment. She turned down a street filled with people, tourists…so many tourists. The woman disappeared. Rafe ran after her, calling out her name, waving his arms to get her attention.

Dallas, his whispered word echoed in his head. The woman couldn't be his Dallas. If she was here in town, she would have come to see him. She would not walk from him. Dallas would have sensed his presence then turned to look at him.

This woman sure as hell looked like Dallas. Who the devil was she? An unknown twin?

Rafe decided he was going to find out.

## Also by the Author
At Rogue Phoenix Press

### *Nick's Tender Rogue*
Naughty book One

Once a McClellan lass

Beautiful, naughty and audaciously daring, young Nickie Gray is a McClellan princess through and through—as wild and reckless as the most incorrigible of her male cousins. Now that she has reached a marriageable age, Nickie has set her amorous sights on a most unsuitable male—the notorious rake and womanizer known to all mamas on the debutante scene in London as dangerous. When her chaperone tells her all rakes are off limits, she finds the challenge one she sets her mind to.

Always a McInnis rake

Not expecting to find a ravishing woman throwing herself at him yet blatantly willing to accept whatever overtures she makes, handsome Collin McInnis is thrilled by the brazen escapades of this naïve creature and is willing to experience her high-spirited advances with no expectations of commitment. On the high seas, he is bested by a vivacious beauty whose love of freedom and adventure rivals his own...and by an inescapable tidal wave of passion that threatens to engulf them both.

### *Dream About Lyssa*
Naughty book Two

When Lyssa Andrews sees the earl sitting behind his desk

scowling, she knows she will someday put a smile on his face. The handsome brooding earl isn't playing the same game. He resists her outrageous comments and questions until she is ready to give up. Lyssa didn't come to London with the intent to find a man. Now, though, she is willing to chance love with the stodgy earl of Blackmore.

Raised by the Sioux when his father sought adventure then fell in love with a Sioux maiden, Kane has been betrayed once by a white woman. He isn't about to give his heart to another, especially one who is as white as newly fallen snow. Despite his best efforts, he can't deny Lyssa's intoxicating effect on him. Now Kane will risk his very life to protect the innocent beauty who has seduced him with her tender love.

### *Deke's Magic Kiss*
Naughty book Three

SHE WOULD RISK EVERYTHING TO BECOME A PRACTICING DOCTOR

Annie Lundin's dream of practicing medicine and a life of dignity and self-sufficiency vanishes in the small Kansas Territory town of Denver City. When the men of the town refuse to become her patients, all she has left to fight for is her practice. She is thwarted from every direction. She didn't mean to fall for the dark, handsome sheriff. Didn't mean to ask for his help. Annie needs Deke Sullivan to protect her from the dark secrets that follow her from Boston. In return she offers all she has—herself.

HE WOULD STOP AT NOTHING TO WIN HER LOVE AND TRUST

Raised by the Cheyenne, Deke Sullivan was churlish, overconfident, and dangerously handsome. His life changed when his Irish grandfather discovered him. He was sent to West Point, fought the Seminole in Florida as well as some on the planes where his loyalty was divided. A woman is the last thing in the world he needs. Especially a woman who belongs in Boston, not the rugged Rocky Mountains. He has commitments that don't include a woman. The moment he sees Annie her intoxicating beauty changed him forever. Love has a way of changing the rules.

## Connal's Eternal Love
### Sweet McKenna Book One

A few days shy of All Hallows' Eve Connal McKenna, Laird of Clan Chattan stands on the parapets of his castle. Bonfires line the hillsides while his clan prepares for the upcoming festivities. Drawn by the whispering of the wind, Connal McKenna feels a strange restlessness in his soul. Setting out to discover the wickedness that is calling to him, he discovers his mate. With gentle words and sensuous kisses, the auburn-eyed highlander conquers his mate, the beautiful, defiant Wynnie Adair who he comes upon during an evening ride. She must ultimately put her trust in the only man who can save her from the ruthless plans of her father and succumb to his gentle coaxing.

## In Brady's Arms
### Sweet McKenna Book Two

Forced to run from the only home she knows, beautiful, headstrong Lillian Townsends seeks shelter in the wild highlands where the McKenna clan live. Trying to avoid a betrothal contract signed by her stepfather to an aging lord, she is desperate to find a means to sidestep the inevitable, including a marriage to the oldest son of the laird. Lilly is enamored of the young lord who pursues her with unrelenting determination flashing his devilishly handsome charms. She is hard pressed to resist.

Besotted from the first moment Brady McKenna sees Lilly, he is determined to find a means to coax her into his arms and bed. With only the promise of carnal pleasure as his mistress, Brady relentlessly pursues the woman who has unwittingly forged a place in his heart. She is like no other woman, proud, defiant and enchanting. Despite his father's advice to stay away from her, he cannot. He boldly seeks her out and makes her his own.

## *Nobody but Walker*
### Sweet McKenna Book Three

The Highland Lass...

She was brought up, adored and loved by a doting mother and father ardently protected by her brothers. She was everything sweet and innocent until she was faced with betrayal and an unexpected and out of wedlock pregnancy. When she gave her love to a man who couldn't return her passion and commitment, she was left devastated and furious. Faced with the loss of her child if she didn't comply to his demands, Crissie McKenna followed him to Belfast then on to his country home to discover he was already married.

...The Irishman

Stunned to find out his one and only encounter with the woman he wanted to love forever created a child, Walker Endicott, Earl of Briarwood, claimed his child as his only heir. Walker threatened all her previously held values even while he thrilled her senses. From the moment he first saw her to the second she ran after him begging him to make love to her, his captivating masculinity held her fascinated. In his arms she would know tempestuous passion, bitter despair, and a soaring joy that would humble them both before the power of love.

## *Roby's Moonlit Night*
### Sweet McKenna Book Four

Once she'd been a pampered child with high expectations for her future blessed with love. Then she became an innocent pawn in a terrible game of greed and power. Now, with a noose around her neck, Pippa was to hang before she had the chance to unveil the men who drove her from her home, before she had the chance to live.

Roby McKenna was a man blessed with endless charm and wit. While he searched for his eternal love across the Atlantic in a new land, he would have to come home to find her. His silver blue eyes could sparkle with amusement or harden to steel gray with displeasure. He had all the women a man could want or need. As he grew older, mistresses were not enough. A quirk of fate brought him to the gallows, a spark of destiny made him claim the condemned Pippa as his bride.

## *Made for Houston*
### Sweet McKenna Book Five

Leah Kennedy is as wary of people as she is strikingly beautiful. However, the shocking death of her father that forever changed her girlhood has left her terrified of the very love she desperately longs for. Only in the untamed splendor of the Scottish crags does she feel safe from the feelings she stirs in men and the cruel mockery of Selkirk's villagers.

Debonair, well-educated doctor Houston Stuart has turned his back on social privilege along with professional honors to set up a medical practice in the lowlands of Scotland. There, serving those who need him the most, he hopes to forget the bitter memories and disillusionment that disturb his days.

Coincidence brings the cultured doctor and this fey mountain girl together. Something as bizarre as destiny disrupts the obstacle of birth and breeding, stubborn pride and fear which has kept them apart...as each seeks to heal the other's wounds with a raw passion neither can deny and all the odds against them cannot defeat.

## *Say You Love Kit*
### Sweet McKenna Book Six

Fascinated...

When the woman stepped through the door of the pub, the sun setting her fiery red hair glowing around her delicate features, Kit Stuart finds himself captivated by the sight. The moment he sees her he knows she will be his. Convincing the fire-haired lady of that fact isn't easy.

After she calls out another man's name when he kisses her that night, he is instantly enraged as well as jealous. The road they travel is fraught with secrets that neither can tell. Trust is an elusive quality that neither can give.

Intrigued...

Forced to run for her life, desperate and afraid, Aila MacDuff willingly enters into the Kinnel Stones, a mysterious place where people disappear then appear magically in different times. At the first sight of Kit, she finds herself inexplicably drawn to him. She's been told to search for her mate and that she will know when she finds him. Aila doesn't know what this man's name is or what he looks like. Nonetheless, she is certain he will be similar to her mate from one hundred years earlier. Despite the fact she is falling in love with Kit, he can't be her mate. Her mate is a shifter. Kit is not.

## *It Had to be Riley*
### Sweet McKenna Book Seven

Her anger assured retaliation...

Shawna's only concern with the contemptable scoundrel she had been forced to wed was the return of her dowry. She had not seen her husband in three years, and now Riley Stuart furiously repudiated there had ever been a marriage. He even went as far as to tell his family he'd never seen her before this day.

... Her passion promised love

In the heather clad hills of the beautiful Scottish crags surrounding the small village so near to the Mckenna keep, the ferocity of her loathing yields to the intense hunger of unquenched longing. In the powerful arms of the dark and handsome husband she thought she reviled, Shawna shivers with the honeyed torment of awakened desire and powerlessly submits to the wild, enchanting ecstasy of burning passion. Together they abandon themselves to the exquisite pleasure of the love their hearts cannot escape.

## *My Sweet Broc*
### Bad Boys Book One

He's a bad bad boy...

Broc Wallace is a fun-loving rake who never thought any beautiful woman could melt his heart. He lives life in the present enjoying the camaraderie of his friends and the pleasures of his mistress. When Bliss races into his life, he is ill prepared to deal with her secrets or give up the tenor of his life. When the truth is revealed, he finds himself unable to forgive and forget the betrayal.

...but she's sweet for him

Bliss MacTavish knows she's playing with fire when she refuses to tell this bad boy her name. He tempts her with sweet whispers of seduction knowing her innocent nature will be unable to refuse all he yearns to give her. Deciding to follow her heart, she finds the repercussions more than she bargains for when she gives herself to this bad boy.

## *Crazy for Cam*
### Bad Boys Book Two

He's a bad bad boy...

Lord Cam MacEwen, Viscount of Rosehill, tries his best to be proper and court the lady of his dreams in the acceptable way. The feat proves impossible when the lady in question uses every means at her disposal to tempt him. He fights his jealousy for another man as well as the need to make her his own, finally giving in to her irresistible passion.

...but she's crazy for him.

Chelsea MacTavish wants the bad boy she fell in love with and kissed just before her eighteenth birthday. With feminine wiles and irresistible allure, the sensuous lady plans to best Cam at his game of hearts and make him forget his need to court her properly.

## Falling for Flynt
### Bad Boys Book Three

He's a bad, bad boy...

Fascinated by Hope's loss of memory yet haunted by her sultry beauty, Flynt is irresistibly drawn to the stoic miss—and into her troubles with the sultan who wants her for himself. When he discovers she is the sister of his best friend, his pride keeps him from pursuing her and making her his.

...but she's falling for him.

Raised in a harem but now penniless, alone and without her memory, Hope must discover a way to remember all that she has lost. She finds a way to continue with her life as a servant in Flynt's home. The first sight of Flynt steals Hope's breath as well as her heart. Can she overcome her fears and give herself to the man she fell in love with.

## Dancing With Donal
### Bad Boys Book Four

He's a bad bad boy...

Once a bad boy always a bad boy, Donal Chamberlin's carefree ways come crashing down around him when he meets the ravishingly beautiful Daryl MacTavish, the innocent little sister of one of his best friends. He is determined to win her heart as he sets his sights on marriage and an heir. His past gets in the way of his quest when a woman he once loved threatens Daryl's life.

...but she's dancing with him.

Daryl has seen the control her sister's husbands hold over them. She yearns for a life where she makes decisions for herself. No man will have power over her. But no man kisses her the way Donal does. No man can make her forget all her goals leaving her helpless to give up her dreams. Yet Donal is determined to dance through all the barriers she thrust in front of him, pursuing her until she says yes.


## *Loving Leslie*
### Bad Boys Book Five

He's a bad bad boy...

Leslie Stewart, Duke of Southcliff is stoic, set in his ways, a spy who is used to having his life well ordered. He expects life to continue on in this perfectly conventional fashion. He assumes his bad boy status while keeping mamas and debutantes at arm's length. An heir is needed but Leslie has every intention of finding a woman who doesn't covet his wealth and tittle. He is irresistibly drawn to the headstrong young lady who becomes more beautiful as she develops into a woman.

...but she is loving him.

When Leslie kisses Lacie MacTavish, she knows even at the tender age of fifteen this is the man of her dreams. Forced to wait until she comes of age, Lacie withdraws into herself. Now she is eighteen and Leslie has returned from a mission for the British Government ready to claim her as his bride. She refuses him and he must find a way to seduce her and in the process create a burning passion within her, which she cannot deny.


## *Pleasing Arie*
### Bad Boys Book Six

He's a bad bad boy...

Arie Demir has never been denied anything in his life. He takes what he wants. What he undeniably yearns for is the beautiful redheaded spitfire he sees in a restaurant in Glasgow. At every turn, she confuses him by disputing his power over her. Alison refuses to accept the fact he owns her. While Arie tries desperately with patience and tenderness to drive her wild with new sensations, his scorching kisses ignite the fires of her very soul to make her understand he is all she will ever want.

...but is she pleasing him?

Alison Fletcher never expected to find herself kidnapped and sold to a whorehouse then bought by a Turkish sultan to become his slave. She vows to never surrender to the arrogant man who believes he owns her. She is stunned by the magnificently handsome man who awaits her compliance. Unexpectedly, she finds Arie the lesser of all the evils. The hidden depths of his mesmerizing dark brown eyes hold her into their power; his muscular embrace makes her weak with desire. She is his to do with as he wishes.

## *Graham's Wicked Kiss*
### Bad Boys Book Seven

He's a bad bad boy...

Graham Chamberlin is stunned to find three young boys dangling from the trees lining the drive to Runningmead Manner. On further inspection, he is astonished at their obsession to protect a young woman who has been brutalized by her pimp. The woman he discovers hiding in a third-floor attic room is gravely injured. He takes the silver haired stowaway under his wing. Clearly, Graham's new guest is a lady with many secrets. He is determined to unlock all the mysteries surrounding her.

...But she can't resist his wicked kiss.

The years since Ria left the convent where she was raised have been a nightmare. Her secrets are dangerous—as is the powerful man determined to find her. Handsome Graham Chamberlin is clearly a gentleman with secrets of his own, but staying with him could mean the difference between life and death for Ria. With each passing day, her handsome host turns Ria's convalescence into an increasingly sensual escape. Now her greatest challenge may be imagining anything less than a future in his arms.

### *Feeling Etienne's Love*
### Bad Boys Book Eight

He's a bad bad boy...

Etienne Dubois is the son of a wealthy vineyard owner who craves the excitement of putting his life on the line. Working with the French government and as a confidant of King Charles X give him reasons for living. An encounter with a beautiful young woman in a plush bordello in Paris has him rethinking his roguish ways. Etienne never expects to become a father especially from one encounter with an innocent prostitute who whispers his name and has him rethinking his well-ordered life.

...But she can't help feeling his love.

Elisa Moreau, the only daughter of Angelique Moreau, the owner of an exclusive bordello in Bordeaux, France, has loved Etienne Dubois since she was six. Unfortunately, until an unexpected encounter at a brothel in Paris puts the two of them in the same room, Etienne doesn't even know she exists. Confused but wanting Etienne and this chance meeting to never end, Elisa gives herself to the man who has held her heart in hands for what seems like her entire life

### *All I Want Is Link*
### Bad Boys Book Nine

He's a bad bad boy...

Merry Stewart is wildly unpredictable. Left alone to run wild over the Bordeaux and Scottish countryside she becomes impetuous and daringly bold. Over the years, she's found she can bedevil her softhearted brothers into allowing her exploits to go unnoticed. As a young woman she has learned she can do as she pleases when she pleases. Now, Merry has set her amorous sights on the Duke of Weston—a man she has never met but has every intention of marrying. No other suitor will satisfy her—especially not the exceptionally striking, horse breeder, Devlin Mathews.

...she's the woman of his desires.

Posing as commoner Devlin Mathews to escape a potentially fatal confrontation, Devlin is enthralled and infuriated by the audacious, duke-hunting dark haired vixen. Bedeviled at every opportunity, he finds dealing with the tiny she-devil exasperating as well as intriguing. Without revealing his true identify, the infamous rogue pledges to thwart Merry's plans to wed the man of her dream-never imagining the bewitching strategist would turn out to be the only woman he would ever dream of marrying.

### *Devlin's Angel*
Bad Boys Book Ten

He's a bad bad boy...

Merry Stewart is wildly unpredictable. Left alone to run wild over the Bordeaux and Scottish countryside she becomes impetuous and daringly bold. Over the years, she's found she can bedevil her softhearted brothers into allowing her exploits to go unnoticed. As a young woman she has learned she can do as she pleases when she pleases. Now, Merry has set her amorous sights on the Duke of Weston—a man she has never met but has every intention of marrying. No other suitor will satisfy her—especially not the exceptionally striking, horse breeder, Devlin Mathews.

...she's the woman of his desires.

Posing as commoner Devlin Mathews to escape a potentially fatal confrontation, Devlin is enthralled and infuriated by the audacious, duke-hunting dark haired vixen. Bedeviled at every opportunity, he finds dealing with the tiny she-devil exasperating as well as intriguing. Without revealing his true identify, the infamous rogue pledges to thwart Merry's plans to wed the man of her dream-never imagining the bewitching strategist would turn out to be the only woman he would ever dream of marrying.

## *Needing Gill*
### Bad Boys Book Eleven

He's a bad bad boy...a man with no heart.

Gil Allemand wants to be left alone, especially by the beautiful outcast who's invaded the vineyard where he meant to wallow in his grief. She has a ton of impudence and brazenness, a talent for trouble, and a child who brings back memories better left in the dark recesses of his mind. Yet Jenna's feisty spirit might just be heaven-sent to save a hard, inflexible man.

...she's a desperate young mother.

Jenna Bonnet's bad luck has taken a turn she never imagined. With twenty-five silver francs, a mare that can't walk up the hill to the chateau that is her five-year-old son's birthright, a son she is desperate to keep alive, she's come home to a village that despises her. However, this single-minded young widow with a shocking past has learned how to fight. She'll do anything to keep her child alive—even take on a man with no heart.

## *Just For Michael*
### Bad Boys Book Twelve

He is a bad, bad boy...

Michael Flannigan has burgeoning ideas the moment he meets the woman who has inherited Mayfair. Clare will fit into his big plans quite nicely. Mayfair Plantation is his heritage. Even before the Revolutionary war Flannigans owned this land. No woman is going take what is his. Realizing the only way he can possess the land that is his birthright is to marry the impulsive woman who waltzes into his life, he sets his sights on making her his, slowly seducing her until she unwittingly falls into his scheme.

...but she is determined

When Clare Carter-Brown returns to Mayfair Hall in Virginia after several years absence, she intends to claim her inheritance. Bypassing Leslie Hall, she moves into Mayfair without a chaperone intending to take over from the manager. Michael objects to her tactics. At every turn, he adeptly points out her failings. As the fires rage around them they find a love that burns more fiercely than either could ever imagine.

## Foolish for Piper

The pickpocket...

Piper has spent her life surviving the streets of St. Giles Parish in London, a den of iniquity and crime. Masquerading as a boy she escapes the whorehouses the young girls are sent to as they come of age. The day she encounters Brett MacLachlan begins the same as every other one. When she picks his pocket, she has no idea her life is going to change irreversibly.

...and the mark

Handsome aristocrat Brett MacLachlan has come to London for his amusement only to find his world turned upside down by a thief and her dog. From the moment he spots her, Brett knows there is something intrinsically wrong. In his arms, Piper discovers passion and joy. Yet secrets of her past haunt her, and a scar will tell the true tale as well as her identity.

## Taylor's Destiny

She traveled to another time and place to change destiny...

Enjoying a day of sailing, Taylor Maxwell never expected after a suffering a concussion she would wake up in another century. A resilient independent woman in the twenty-first century, the blond beauty is ill prepared for life in the 1800s. Her first sight of the naval captain who rescues her makes her heart stop, giving her hope for her future.

His life is transformed by a woman who appears from nowhere...

Born to a life of ease, Reid Stewart defies the dictates of those born to aristocracy and chooses a life of adventure in the navy and as a spy for the crown. When he discovers a nearly naked woman on the bow of small sailing ship, his heart warms. His love for Taylor and his need to protect her from a man who pursues her might cost him his life as well as hers.

## Caitlin's Duke

She played a fiddle in an Irish pub...

Caitlin O'Shea Is the most beautiful woman Roc Leighton has ever seen. With her blue violet eyes and long black hair she captivates him. In turn he mesmerizes Caitlin. Caught in the power of his gaze as he watches her, she is wise enough to know he desires her but will never give his heart to her. Caitlin has vowed to never be any man's mistress.

And fell in love with an English Lord...

Roc knows the first time he watches her play the fiddle and dance around the pub, she will be his next mistress. Despite her protest, he will find a way to convince her that her place is with him. While Caitlin's determination to keep her vows, fate takes a cruel turn and she is forced to seek refuge with Roc.

## Catching Meara
### Book One in the McKenna Clan Series

Meara Thorton was a feisty, world-class computer hacker—cornered by the FBI and shockingly given the chance to be their newly acquired technical analyst. Brilliant and intuitive, yet aching with the loss of everyone she has cared about, her restless heart led her to discover a love she fought and a world she didn't know could possibly exist.

## Sweet Sexy Sadie
### Book Two in the McKenna Clan Series

From the first time Sadie's eyes met those of Brody McKenna in the hot Sierra Madre Mountains, theirs was a potent attraction—not gentle, slow, and easy, but hot, hard, and all-consuming. The daughter of a dysfunctional family, Sadie had dreams no man could wrench from her with hot sex and an all-consuming passion. She'd challenge this alpha male with all the strength she possessed. But her red hair, fiery temperament, and indomitable spirit obsessed Brody...and he knew he had to find a way to show her he was more than he appeared and convince her to make a life with him.

## Sweet Misbehavin'
### Book Three in the McKenna Clan Series

Cast adrift after fleeing the home of Jokul, the ice demon, Atantsi, a firestarter, grew to womanhood as she moved through time to keep the demon from finding her. Though stubborn and courageous, she was ill prepared to use powers she had not been taught. Her first sight of the intoxicating Carr McKenna left her breathless, and her second encounter gave her hope for a future she never thought she had.

A playboy, a second son and a shifter, a man who thought his life would be carefree, Carr McKenna was shocked to discover the woman he'd paid as an escort is a firestarter who is running for her life. He is the leader of all the McKennas around the world and that he has multiple powers. His passion for Margo and the need to defend her might cost him his life as well as hers.

## Sweet Talkin' Sugar
### Book Four in the McKenna Clan Series

Lyonesse McKenna, was dreaming, or was she? From the instant Lyn saw Deacon McClain across a black jack table in a crowed Las Vegas casino the unmistakable attraction sent Lyn's senses flying into overdrive. Her family of shapeshifters believed in soul mates. She'd always been skeptical yet she couldn't help but question the way her heart sped when he looked at her.

When Deacon appeared in Las Vegas he knew his first job was to save Lyn from a Sea Demon, but the next order of business was to convince her he would someday mean more to her than she'd ever expected. But her stubborn nature and unbendable spirit consumed Deacon...and he had to chase away all the demons real and imagined in order to win her heart.

## Sweet Surrender
### Book Five in the McKenna Clan Series

Ripped from her family at the top of Infinity Cliff, Kimi McKenna finds herself thrust somewhere into the future. Dark elements threaten to destroy the earth unless Kimi can work together with the white witch to stop the destruction. Confused by her mate's role in the conspiracy, she refuses to acknowledge the connection. But amidst raging fire and attacks on the people she is coming to hold dear, she allows Maska O'keefe into her heart.

Maska O'keefe has loved the beautiful shapeshifter for years. Unable to save her life years ago, he vows to watch over her as he is given a second chance to convince her that even though he is a witch and not a shifter, they are indeed soul mates. Kimi's divided loyalties between her family and the cause she is now a part of will determine their relationship. Only the part she plays as the messiah can bring this to a conclusion in the final battle.

## Sweet Dreams
### Book Six in the McKenna Clan Series

For Cas Doyle finding the shifter of her dreams was a matter of life or death. She walked into the Red Neck Bar and Grill in Cactus Junction with a hope and a prayer he would be there and she would recognize him. What she needed was for him to take her home and take her virginity. Cas never thought to be a one-night stand. She had no choice.

Guy McKenna knew eventually he'd find his soul mate. He didn't expect the reality to happen this night. When he saw her he knew. She was dressed provocatively, enticing him to an extreme he never felt before. What he didn't know was if he could convince his protective family that Casidhe Doyle was indeed his soul mate.

## Dakota's Bride
### The first book in the Lakota/Pinkerton Series

When Emma St. John received her brother's letter imploring her to escape her stepfather's vengeful scheme and to trust Dakota Barringer with her life, she was willing to chance it. But the handsome, brooding riverboat owner Emma found in Natchez a danger of another kind. For Emma soon found herself surrendering to an unrelenting desire.

Raised by the Sioux when his parents were killed, Dakota had been betrayed once before by a white woman. He wasn't about to trust another, especially one claiming that her stepfather, a powerful U.S. senator, had framed her as a murderess. But he couldn't let Emma's intoxicating effect on him. Now Dakota would risk his very life to protect the innocent beauty who had seduced him with her tender love.

## My Angel
### The second book in the Lakota/Pinkerton Series

A BEAUTY IN BUCKSKINS

When her father decided to send her to a finishing school back East, Angela Chamberlain refused to be confined to stuffy drawing rooms. Instead, the daring spitfire who could shoot like a man and ride like the wind longed for a life of adventure and romance—and she knew exactly who could give it to her. Devil Blackmoor was a hired gun with a dangerous reputation. But Angela was willing to go to the ends of the earth to capture the handsome devil's heart.

A DEVIL IN DISGUISE

He'd come to America looking for excitement, but Devil Blackmoor got more than he bargained for when he encountered a beautiful rebel who answered his kisses with a wild innocence that touched his very soul. Yet standing between them were more obstacles than either ever dreamed. For Devil had strapped on a gun for the wrong man. And that made Angela his enemy. Now he'll have to choose between his duty and the woman he loves more than life.


## The Locket
### The third book in the Lakota/Pinkerton Series

The year is 1894. Seeking revenge for crimes against his family, Misha Petrovich follows a path that leads straight to Ariel Cameron's boarding house in Mist Harbor, Oregon. A family heirloom in Ariel's possession leads Misha to believe she is guilty. The locket has been handed down to the oldest girl in the Petrovich family for generations. Ariel is innocent of wrong doing, but her father is not. Misha is torn by his feelings for Ariel and his need for restitution against her father. Knowing that the relationship between them is fragile, Misha does everything in his power to protect Ariel's father. His efforts are to no avail when her father is shot. Ariel comes to realize Misha's steadfast courage and determination to protect her and her father despite what has happened to his family. Ariel's love and devotion heals Misha's heart.

## *The Talisman*
### The fourth book in the Lakota/Pinkerton Series

Running from a marriage that lasted one night, Dr. Moriah McKeown discovers the land she has settled on is coveted by determined and lawless men. Yet the proud young woman who once vowed never to abandon her home has second thoughts when her adopted children are threatened. Her only recourse is to enlist the aid of a dark, dangerous gun for hire.

Haunted by the past and a betrayal he will never forgive, Ian Civanovich uses his fast gun and his reckless courage to forget the faithlessness of a woman in his past. He will trust no female—nor will he rest until the threat hovering over Moriah McKeown is put to rest.

## *Forever His*
### The fifth book in the Lakota/Pinkerton Series

Struggling to come to terms with the part she played in Jacob St. John's death, Etta Barringer resigns from Pinkerton Agency and seeks peace and solace in a Rocky Mountain Cabin.

Jacob has vowed to discover the reason Etta has betrayed him, sold him out to his enemy and left him for dead.

Isolated in their cabin, they discover their love for each other and learn to trust. But the trust is shattered when Jacob learns she is married to his sworn enemy; the man who left him in the desert to die.

## *Allura's Secret*
### Twelve Dancing Princesses Book One

Allura McClellan is horrified by her father's decision to take out an ad in the Times awarding her to the man strong enough and smart enough to win her hand and uncover her secrets. She's an intelligent young woman who takes great delight in the freedom allotted to her by her father. She's well aware that marriage would effectively curtail the adventures she's shared with her sisters and cousins.

Hunter Gray is nothing like the other men who've arrived to vie for Allura's hand in marriage and everything that goes along with it. However, he is the first to refuse to concede defeat and pursue her despite her attempts to disguise her true appearance. It's her temperament that is of more concern to him than her looks. Hunter has worked all his life with the hope of someday owning his own land. Now that it looks like there's a very real possibility that everything he's ever wanted is within reach nothing is going to deter him – including Miss Allura's disagreeable disposition.

### *Amorica's Wager*
#### Twelve Dancing Princesses Book Two

Amorica Hepburn was sent to London to find a husband. Finding a man was the last item on her agenda. With her two cousins, Amorica wagers she can dissuade her suitor before the others. Despite her efforts she discovers a chemistry that cannot be denied. Suddenly she is the arrogant man's wife, pledged to a marriage neither desire. But swept off to his ancestral home above the Dover cliffs and into his strong embrace, Amorica is soon possessed by a raging passion for the husband she had vowed to despise...

Damian Andrews couldn't afford to trust the emerald-eyed spitfire who happened upon his secret. Amorica's hatred of all men of his kind only inflames the war that rages between them. Still, he can not control the intense desire his stubborn bride inspires, or make her surrender to his will until he has conquered the headstrong beauty on the battlefield of love...

## Ravyn's Marriage of Inconvenience
### Twelve Dancing Princesses Book Three

### A REGAL BEAUTY

When the duchess decides to wed her to a wastrel and a fop, Ravyn Grahm takes matters into her own hands and declares her engagement to another man. Instead of fessing up and telling her great aunt what she has done, she goes through with the pretense. Ariec Lakeland is the bastard son of an earl and has a dangerous reputation. But Ravyn is willing to do most anything to keep the duchess from discovering the lie.

### A DEVIL-MAY-CARE SMUGGLER

He'd bought land in America, looking to put down roots and end his life of adventure, but Ariec Lakeland got more than he bargained for when he encountered a beautiful heiress who made a promise she didn't want to keep. But the promise could not be undone and standing between them were more obstacles than either ever dreamed. Ariec had made plans to spend the rest of his life in America and that was at odds with Ravyn's plan of living in England and running her father's estate. Now, he'll have to choose between his dreams and the woman he loves more than life.

## Christel's Sunrise
### Twelve Dancing Princesses Book Four

### He Made Her An Offer...

Life has thrown Christel McClellan some experiences that could have devastated a less determined woman. Beautiful, self-assured and fiercely independent, she is trying to forget the loss of her stillborn child. But is the child alive?

### She Couldn't Deny...

Life is carefree for Ryder MacLaren who loves to see what is on the other side of the sunrise. Laird of Clan MacLaren, he is wealthy, handsome and happily unencumbered...until stunning Christel McClellan enters his life. When he hears her story, he believes the child she thought dead has been sold to a wealthy buyer.


## *Storm's Passion*
### Twelve Dancing Princesses Book Five

SHE MADE A PROPOSAL...

Life strikes Storm Graham a shattering blow when she learns her father has bartered her to a man she detests. Storm is beautiful, self–assured and fiercely independent, and refuses to be a pawn in her father's schemes, yet she can find no way out of this bargain made in hell. Going on the offensive she asks the wealthiest man on the eastern coast of England to marry her, never believing she might fall in love.

HE TRIED TO REFUSE...

For Hadden Johnston life has provided everything he ever wanted, including a sanctuary for homeless children. He is wealthy, handsome and happily unencumbered...until stunning Storm Graham marches into his life and proposes a marriage of convenience. Yet this type of marriage to a woman who inflames his senses is far from acceptable. If he's going to be tied down, he will move heaven and earth to have this woman warming his bed.


## *Gotta Have Fayth*
### Twelve Dancing Princesses Book Six

A regal beauty with raven hair and piercing blue eyes, Fayth Graham is unwilling to parade herself in front of the wealthy Lords of England during the season. Seeking a means to dissuade any man wishing to wed her, she seeks a way to ruin herself for marriage. When she unexpectedly meets a man with sparkling gray eyes and an infectious grin, she decides this is the man who will keep her from agreeing to obey.

He returned from six months at sea, looking for a few nights of pleasure with a willing lass, but Jarret Kinsley got more than he bargained for when he met a beautiful debutant who responded to his kisses with a wild innocence that touched his heart. Yet the obstacles looming between them might rip them apart. Both had vowed never to marry, so when consequences of their dalliances got in the way, Jarret would have to choose between the life he's always desired and the woman he loves more than life.

## Ella's Pleasure
### Twelve Dancing Princesses Book Seven

### A WHISPER OF PLEASURE
Ella Hepburn was an auburn haired debutant from the harsh Scottish coastline—a wild innocent to be seduced and tamed. A spirited beauty, she captivated Drake Montgomerie's jaded heart—while succumbing to the smoldering desire she felt for her unyielding suitor.

### A WHISPER OF DANGER
In Drake Montgomerie's glittering world of money and privilege, young Ella discovered passion and desire could overcome everything she'd been taught to resist—entangling Drake, the heir apparent, in a lethal coil of aristocratic family intrigue. But grave peril would only nurse the sparks of a love that knew no limits and a magnificent ecstasy that would not be denied.

## Eveleen's Seduction
### Twelve Dancing Princesses Book Eight

### A WHISPER OF SEDUCTION
A brutal attack on Eveleen Hepburn's cherished island off the Scottish coastline leaves her shattered and bewildered. Learning a man she once trusted can kill as easily as he can breathe even though the deed saves her life, creates questions that need answers. An innocent beauty, she enchants Logan Maxwell's cynical heart—giving in to the raging passion she feels for her mysterious suitor.

A WHISPER OF INTRIGUE

In Logan's Maxwell's world of espionage and privilege, young Eveleen discovers truths about herself she never expected, and a need for passion and love can overcome all her fears if she learns to accept certain truths. She finds herself entangled in a lethal battle for land that was once owned by French nobility, taken from them during the revolution and sold to Maxwell. But grave peril would unleash the flames of love that simmers, creating a magical union that cannot be refuted.

## Tavia's Deception
### Twelve Dancing Princesses Book Nine

WHISPERS OF DECEPTION

When her father decides to send her to London for her season, Tavia Hepburn resolves to see the world instead. The raven haired beauty decides to disguise herself as a lad and find employment on a ship bound for Barcelona as a cabin boy. But she never bargains on finding passion and love to a red haired sea captain who rescues her from certain death.

WHISPERS OF MURDER

For James Macmurra, the world is black and white until he meets a young debutante, who turns his world upside down. He's unable to deny Tavia's intoxicating effect on him. In a match tense with obstacles, unwillingness to divulge secrets, and unforeseen peril, irresistible desire and passion grows into undeniable love. James would risk his life to shelter and protect the innocent debutante who seduces him with her sweet love.

## Larena's Fascination
### Twelve Dancing Princesses Book Ten

WHISPERS OF FASCINATION

Fiery, free spirited Larena Graham never wanted to marry a duke.

She is thrilled to be in love with the fourth son of an aristocrat, Gavin Broon. But when it seems Gavin ignores her, she set her sights on politics and bettering human life. Unsuspecting intrigue and a plot against her, she continues her dangerous plans despite Gavin's wishes.

### WHISPERS OF TRUST

Gavin has every intention of properly courting the beautiful Larena until he must leave the city in order to put his affairs in order. Returning to London, he finds the woman he means to make his own is embroiled in political protests that could lead to a prison ship. Larena must learn to trust the handsome Scotsman whose most pressing mission is to protect her and keep her from harm.

## *Tira's Education*
### Twelve Dancing Princesses Book Eleven

### WHISPERS OF EDUCATION

Learning how to build ships is Tira Hepburn's only dream until she meets Jamie Lundin and her world is turned upside down. With her raven black hair and vivid green eyes, she tempts Jamie and pushes him to defy his vows. She never bargains on finding an irrevocable love and a passion to a man who cannot fulfill her dreams despite his burning desire for her.

### WHISPERS OF A BARGAIN

Arrogant and self-assured Jamie is brought up short when Tira captures his heart. All his carefully made plans are put to the test when he decides to teach her the art of ship building if she will spend a week with him alone on his ship. He is unable to deny Tira's intoxicating effect on him. When Tira leaves him behind unwilling to live with him without the benefit of marriage, he races after her. Jamie will risk everything to shelter and protect the innocent debutante who seduces him with her sweet love.

## *Aidan's Love*
### Twelve Dancing Princesses Book Twelve

Whispers of Love

Aidan McLellan has loved since she first set eyes on him as a young girl. Spontaneous, wild and eager to grow up, Aidan haunts his waking thoughts day and night, insinuating herself into his life. With her fiery red hair and sparkling sapphire eyes, she seizes Blade's heart even while he tries to resist the innocent child until she becomes a woman.

Whispers of Courage

Blade has waited what seems a lifetime to claim the woman who captures his heart as a little girl. Claiming his inheritance before his younger brother takes what is rightfully his, Blade must convince Aidan of his sincerity after years of avoidance and wed her before his father dies so he can return home, securing his rightful place. Everything is put to the test when his life as well as Aidan's is threatened by the man who once called him brother.

## *Don't Hustle Letty*
### Good Girls Book One

She's a good girl...

As tempted as Scarlett was, she had too many secrets to let someone enter her world—secrets that would send any reasonable man to the farthest ends of the earth. Bobby was far from reasonable and despite her desperate attempts to hold him at bay, he would not let her past destroy their future. With her escort service, Scarlett used men and their insatiable lust for women to capitalize on the means to survive and prosper. She vowed to never wed, to never put herself in the control of a man.

...nonetheless he has other ideas.

Lord Robert Munroe, with his newly acquired title of marquis goes to Scarlett's for training on how to comport himself. The marquis, better known as Bobby, knows how to pick a pocket as well as get into a bloke's home to steal them blind. What he doesn't know is how to be a gentleman. When he sets his sights on the prim Miss Scarlet, Letty, to his way of thinking, he decides she is the woman he wants to call his wife. He tempts all that she is with sweet words and tender coaxing until she is unable to refuse all he hopes to give her.

## *Only Caro's Baby*
### Good Girls Book Two

The Scheme

Genius botanist with theories of inherited traits, Caroline Kenworth desperately wants a baby. Finding a suitable father won't be easy. Caroline's super-intelligence makes her feel pushed aside, unwanted as a woman. As a bluestocking she is determined to spare her child the suffering that plagues her life. Which means she must find someone very special to father her child. A person very...well...ignorant.

The Target.

Duncan Murray, the Earl of Downsberry, well known for his lack of intelligence as well as his rakish ways with women, seems as if he is the flawless man to fulfill the role. His amazing good looks and Scottish brogue are misleading. Caro learns too late that this debonair earl is a lot smarter than she first thought—in addition he's not about to be used then abandoned by any woman who has schemed to steal his sperm.

The Detonation

A dazzling solitary woman whose desires to learn what it would be like to become a mother... A man who is in control of all he does never allowing anyone to usurp his role will settle for nothing less than surrender... Can lust coupled with physical attraction drive two strong-minded yet vulnerable people to a completely unforeseen love?

### *Only Caro's Baby*
### Good Girls Book Three

She's a good girl...

Born a bastard, Honey McRae is taunted and bullied by her half-brother most of her life. Branded with a tattoo of the Saber and the Rose by the men's association, she is desperate to be free and escapes the country estate where she was held prisoner. Resigned to a passionless life devoid of men, she fights the nightmares that haunt her. Despite her past fears, she accepts the fact she will never be able to give herself wholly to the man she loves. Until that man, bold and breathtaking, decides he will find a means to woo her into his arms.

Nonetheless...

Stolen at birth and sent to live in the bowels of London, Billy–once a pickpocket and thief–discovers he is actually the Duke of St. Aubries. He is determined to win the woman he fell in love with the first time he saw her, the lady with a tattoo on her breast, a woman who has been cruelly used. He disputes her notion that men are only capable of inflicting pain...instead he binds her to his heart with his gentle and patient loving.

### *Betsy Be Good*
### Good Girls Book Four

AN ENGLISH ROSE

Sweet Betsy Darling, the oh-so-prim and innocent tutor for children born of rich aristocrats, is a woman on a mission—she has but a short time to lose her standing as a respectable spinster. Arriving in Glasgow with skirts flying, parasol pointing, and plump mouth issuing demands, she understands only one thing will save her form losing all she holds dear: complete and utter disgrace.

## A BRAW HIGHLANDER

Known throughout the city as a bad boy with more money than he needs, Evan Murray has lost his temper one too many times, and now he's suspended from teaching at the university he loves as well as Halstead & Family the financial firm owned by his family. An apology which he refuses to issue is one of two things that will restore his career. The second is his complete and utter respectability! Now he's been coerced into escorting the bossy, parasol toting Miss Betsy Darling, and she's hell-bent on chasing down a tattoo parlor, dressing in skimpy clothing and worse...lots worse.

## *Twelve Days to Love*

When Archer Steele shows up at Calanthe Durand's failing plantation with an alligator over his shoulder, Cali thinks she's never seen a more handsome man. During the war she had to defend herself and her servants from both union and confederate soldiers. Independent and self-sufficient, she vows to never marry.

But Archer Steele has different ideas. The first time Archer sees Cali in town, he feels an instant attraction. He decides he will do everything and anything to convince the beautiful Miss Durand he is worthy of her love. During the weeks leading up to Christmas, he gives her twelve gifts in hopes she will fall in love with him. Yet they are faced with challenges they must overcome before Cali can commit to a marriage.

## Door to Heaven

Jessica Lawrence is the stepdaughter of a woman born in the twentieth century transported back in time to the year 1868. An acclaimed suffragette, she raises Jessica to believe in the equality of women. Jess Law believes everything she was taught, and when the time is right she becomes a private investigator. Courageous and impetuous, Jess finds danger in her quest to save all women from white slavery. Her passionate mission results in a wedding to Roc Newman, a man she knows can steal her heart...

Roc can't trust the sapphire-eyed spitfire who invades his home in search of secret papers and knocks him flat with her karate moves. Jessica's refusal to obey his wishes serves to inflame the war between them. Still, he cannot control the intense desire his reluctant bride inspires, or make her surrender her independence, until he has conquered the headstrong beauty on the battlefield of love...

## Rebel Heart

HER REBEL SPIRIT DEFIED HIS OUTSIDERS SOUL...She was velvet and silk, eyes the color of a summer storm and amber hair. Victoria DeMontville, because of a promise and a codicil to her father's will, was forced to marry one man to protect her from another. She hated Cameron Savage with a fierce passion. But to hold on to her genetic research and find a cure for the deadly Signe virus, she must pretend to love the enemy at her door, come with weapons of fire to melt her icy heart...

HIS OUTSIDERS TOUCH IGNITED RAGING PASSIONS... He wore a mask, disguised as the Phantom, a true legend come to life. Even as war and debate over new genetic research engulfed them all, he would find his greatest adversary in the beauty who'd branded him an outsider and barbarian, the woman he was born to possess, his soul mate.

## Safari Moon

Solo St. John, a wildlife photographer, is preparing for a trip to Alaska. Suddenly, Solo finds women of all sorts invading his privacy, his home and his office, all cooing nonsense words and blatantly throwing themselves at him. Solo doesn't know why, and he has no idea how to rid himself of the persistent women. He finally decides to beg a favor of his best buddy Nyssa Harrington.

In love with Solo for the past ten years and knowing he doesn't return her feelings Nyssa doesn't want to talk to Solo. She knows if she accepts his phone call, she will not be able to resist the temptation to hope again.

## Straight to Heaven

Running from demons, Alexandra McMurdie stumbles into Forbidden Ground where up is down and elements of nature are contested. Though a strong independent woman in the twenty-first century' she is unprepared for life in the 1800s. Her first site of the formidable James Lawrence makes her heart skip a beat, giving her cause to reconsider her desperate need to find a way home.

Born with a silver spoon, James' life was torn apart during the War Between the States. Moving west he vows to put the life he once knew in the past. When he discovers a half-frozen woman near Gold Hill, his heart begins to thaw. His love for Alexandra and his need to keep her from a man who has pursued her through time might cost him his life as well as hers.

## A Valentine's Anthology

*The Lending Library*-a fantasy by Christie L. Kraemer
Faeries try to fit into the human world when the forest where they make their home is destroyed by a mysterious enemy.

*Chasing Rainbows*-a contemporary romance by Genene Valleau

An eccentric aunt, an inventive uncle, a mother who wears poodle skirts, and a brother who wears pearls provide a hilarious backdrop for the courtship of a young woman who yearns for a "normal" family.

*The Gift*-an historical romance by Christine Young

A man and a woman on opposite sides of the Civil War get a second chance at love after one final battle returns soldiers to their war-torn homes to rebuild their lives.


## *A St. Patrick's Day Tale*
### Christine Young, C. L. Kraemer, Genene Valleau

Tumble through time...

...to Ireland in 1817, when tensions are high between Protestants and Catholics and fae people guide the fate of villagers. A lovely Catholic lass stumbles upon the weakly ritual fisticuffing between Irish lads. She falls into the lap of a handsome young Protestant. Family ties, grudges, and two conniving faeries threaten their budding love. But the faeries outsmart themselves when they hijack a time machine that has mysteriously appeared in their forest and are whisked to...

...Eugene, Oregon in the 20th century, amid a property feud between the local faeries and night elves. The conniving faeries from Olde Ireland try to stir up more mischief. However, a warrior gnome convinces the magic folk to control their own destiny, and forces the intruding faeries to take refuge in the time machine again, spinning their way toward...

...A modern day castle in western Oregon. An eccentric inventor is determined to reclaim his wayward time machine and save his beloved wife from her latest misadventure. If only they can travel safely past the black hole...

## *a May Day Anthology*
Christine Young, C. L. Kraemer, Rosemary Indra, Genene Valleau

Highland Miracle — Christine Young

HURTLED THROUGH TIME, Sean Michael Sterling, landed in the midst of a May Day celebration he didn't understand, assuming the role of Laird Sterling.

ILLIGITAMATE CHILD OF NOBILITY, Reagan Douglas searches for a way out of her half brother's house.

Defying the Odds — C.L. Kraemer

The night elves on the hill aren't happy without their magic. They concoct a plan to punish those who were involved in the act that rendered them almost human. Meanwhile, Uther, the rogue night elf, has returned to woo the Librarian to be his eternal mate.

Love in Bloom — Rosemary Indra

When childhood friends reunite it takes two fairies and a matchmaking daughter to help them admit their true love for each other.

No More Poodle Skirts — Genie Gabriel

After drifting for years in the innocent age of the 1950s, a woman struggles to join today's world by finding a career and a new love, with some help from her zany family.

## *Once Upon a Christmas Moon*
Christine Young, C. L. Kraemer, Genene Valleau

TWELVE DAYS TO LOVE

When Archer Steele shows up at Calanthe Durand's failing plantation with an alligator over his shoulder, Cali thinks she's never seen a more handsome man. During the war she had to defend herself and her servants from both union and confederate soldiers. Independent and self-sufficient, she vows to never marry. But Archer Steele has different ideas. The first time Archer sees Cali in town, he feels an instant attraction. He decides he will do everything and anything to convince the beautiful Miss Durand he is worthy of her love. During the weeks leading up to Christmas, he gives her twelve gifts in hopes she will fall in love with him.

## BOOTS AND BLADES

An ancient evil from the old country has arrived in the high desert of Oregon. Gnome children are vanishing then re-appearing, showing various stages of traumatization. Tiamoon, warrior gnome, will put her skills to use alongside Killian, a handsome warrior, also in need of a cause.

## CHRISTMAS PAWSIBILITIES

With their world destroyed and their space ship malfunctioning, the dogizens of Planet Canid have little choice but to crash land on Earth. They face tortuous experiments at the hands of the Geeks in Green...or they can trust an eccentric inventor and his zany family to deliver the Canine Queen's puppies and help them celebrate new lives.